RAW DEAL

They'd worked months for this bust and it was all going down the toilet.

McCarthy was staked out a couple of cars in front of him, listening in on the Kel bug he'd wired under Tony Vitaliano's dash board. But something was wrong. It was taking too long. Tony sounded nervous. And nervous could make him dead real fast.

Just make the payoff and get it over with, McCarthy whispered, grabbing on to the shotgun nestled between his legs.

Suddenly, he caught some fast action in out of the corner of his rearview mirror. Another man appeared from nowhere, squeezing Tony between him and Bobby Gee. There was a brief struggle. McCarthy could see Tony was reaching for his gun, but another pistol came up at the cop's temple.

"Don't make me use the gun," McCarthy heard Bobby say. "Put your hands where I can see them. . . . Good. We're going to the top man. He wants to see you."

Then there was silence.

The bad guys were snatching Tony, his partner, kidnapping a cop.

The worst day of Bill McCarthy's life had just begun.

VICE COP

BILL McCARTHY AND MIKE MALLOWE

ZEBRA BOOKS
KENSINGTON PUBLISHING CORP.

ZEBRA BOOKS

are published by

Kensington Publishing Corp.
475 Park Avenue South
New York, NY 10016

First Zebra Books Printing: January, 1993

Printed in the United States of America

931474

ACKNOWLEDGMENTS

I've learned many things writing this book: Foremost among these insights is just how important the love of my mother and father were to my survival in the Life—for they gave me the vision of what ought to be.

The importance of having three "rabbis" or "hooks" in my life—mentors—who each happened to have a Jewish surname. They were Chief Kenneth Gussman, Chief Aaron Rosenthal, and Dr. Sam Janus. They were genuine teachers and helpers.

The importance of my two children, Christine and Billy, who gave me great guilt for my recklessness and who ultimately provided my reason for escaping the Life.

And finally, the most important thing I have learned is that my schoolteacher wife, Millie, still has plenty to teach me. Forever and eighteen days I love you. . . .

To Tony Vitaliano and the other police officers who remain on duty—thank you and be safe.

BMc.

AUTHORS' NOTE

All of the incidents and people depicted in this book are real. It is a true story. However, for reasons of both privacy and security, many of the names have been changed. Where appropriate, certain events have been slightly altered for purposes of dramatic continuity. This tinkering is almost entirely chronological and not substantive.

Prologue

NEW YORK CITY, JULY, 1977

"You talk about being scared. This happened during the big blackout. On every street there was looting, anything they could carry. The city was out of control.

"I remember lying on the floor of the police bus that night, going to wherever they were taking us, and staying down because they were shooting out the windows. Snipers all over the Bronx.

"We pulled up at a corner and jumped out. I saw five or six guys go in through the window of a looted store. There was a kind of darkness that night like I've never experienced. No moon and, of course, all the streetlights and building lights were out. Dead black.

"I ran in behind these guys, alone.

"It was an auto parts store. As they scattered, trying to hide, going down into the basement, a couple of them bumped into an oil can display and knocked it over. First I heard the crash; I couldn't see that much. Then, I smelled this lake of oil beginning to spread all over the tile floor. I started slipping in it. Alongside another display aisle, I could make out two black guys crouched down.

"I didn't realize it at that moment, but as I went after them, I hit the spilled oil on the run and slid; I went up into the air and came down on my back. Hard. I was all wet with this stuff, covered with oil and knocked half-dizzy. When I looked up those two guys were standing over me.

"I went for my handcuffs and tried to get up on my feet, but slipped and fell again. They backed off. I could see they weren't sure if I was coming up with the cuffs or with my revolver. They also weren't sure how many of me—how many cops—there were.

"All I could do was cuff them both together and march them down into the basement while I looked around for the rest of them.

"There's four more down there; I'm sure of that. Plus my two prisoners. The only edge I have is that they probably think I'm a whole squad coming down to get them. I *couldn't* be crazy enough to be going down there by myself.

"Finally, I'm down in the basement of that store, with my gun in one hand and my flashlight in the other, holding these six guys up against the wall. *But no other cops are showing up*.

"They're beginning to look at each other with this funny expression on their faces. Like, now they *know*.

"One gun, six guys, all bigger than I am, and this is a flashlight that I've had in the trunk of my car for the last two years. Except for the beam from that flashlight you can't see a damn thing down there.

"I will never forget the absolute fear that I felt at that moment. We just stared each other down for I don't know how many minutes while I tried to figure out what to do—and I could see that they were doing the same thing as I was. To jump me or not to jump me—that was the question. We're just eyeballing each other in the darkness, waiting to see who makes the next move.

"I knew I would never be able to get all of them if they did rush me, but I had my mind made up that I wasn't going to go down by myself, either. I'd take somebody with me.

"And I'm saying to myself: McCarthy, why did you *ever* become a cop?

"And then, just as they begin to move around on me, shuffling, shifting from one leg to the other, looking to get the jump on me, the battery in my flashlight starts to go, flickering, missing. Then all of a sudden, the light goes dead.

"Dead black."

One

The *Life* is right now; it's instant, no past and no future. It's this moment. No other possible existence. In Vice, every player lives in the Life.

MOTHER'S MAXIM

THE MARQUEE

"I can shut my eyes today and I still see the marquee— a marquee like a theater sign, with all the flashes and the little white lights running along the sides. That was the show; that was the Life and I was part of it. I was up there on that marquee.

"I see Vice.

"I see Times Square; I see the race; I see the filth; I see the massage parlors; I see the porno bookstores; I see old men trying to take small boys up to rat-trap rooms on the pedo patrol for quick, anonymous sex.

"I see all the people running—desperate, lonely people running as fast as they can just to stay in the race. In the Life.

"I see the little urchins and the little buzzards perched on shelves all over the place, all over the street. Cut purses just waiting to drop down on you, cut your pocket, steal your money. Cut your throat, take your life. If ever you tripped and fell, they'd strip you naked, steal your shoes, take your wallet and turn your pockets inside out before you knew what hit you.

"I see Forty-second Street, Eighth Avenue, the strip, the Minnesota Strip, Forty-ninth Street, the Lark Hotel; little blond whores and big black pimps.

"I see fast money and champagne ladies and goulash houses—gambling joints. I see blackjack, three-card monte. I see little, old, soft, fat guys—wiseguys—with wads of cash. I see them playing cards and getting laid and staying drunk all night.

"I see good-looking whores, great-looking whores, in apartments on Park Avenue, places where the doormen let you in.

"I see whores who don't make any bones about the fact that every man they see is a dick with a dollar sign. I see white men with money to spend on hard-faced, skinny black whores—hookers whose pupils are so dilated that their eyes, bloodshot eyes, look like they're swimming in semen. White men's semen.

"I see the basket cases, raving for a bed at Bellevue and a warm place to spend the night. I see the junkies with zombie eyes and empty hearts, their arms and legs covered with sores, with scabs, with pus you could push through to feel to their bones.

"I see the bad cops and the good cops; cops like me; tough guys with their shirts open, loud shirts; sharp guys, fast lives, good detectives. The best in New York City, which automatically makes them the best in the world.

"I see the official NYPD forms, the arrest logs, with all the neatly typed entries for crime statistics. There were specialty squads for rape and robbery and homicide, for every thing else. But there was never any single category for the crimes of Vice. There were just too many separate sins in the Life. So the police department called it *other*. Nothing else fit. That was Vice. *Other*.

"I see it all there waiting for you if you were a cop—temptation, corruption, sex, the danger. Every day it would be there. It was like going to the supermarket; walk up one aisle and down the other. Just fill up your basket. Anything you wanted, it was all marked. You knew the cost going in. It could be your career, your marriage, your pride, your soul.

"I see you paying your money and taking your shot and it would stay with you all day—the rush, the excitement, the compulsion, the feeling that you just couldn't get enough of it, enough of the Life. And all you had to do was survive. Come out alive.

"When I close my eyes today, what I see is me, Bill McCarthy, a Vice cop. I was part of it all. I understood the game and I was good at it. I belonged there. In the Life."

Bill McCarthy had disciples and enemies and absolutely nobody in between. He was the kind of cop who liked to take the first bite, the kind of cop who never stopped believing.

That made him dangerous—to the bad guys and to the New York City Police Department. When he retired on July 1, 1987—the day that Bill McCarthy finally gave up the Life—the people who were glad to see him leave could have filled the outfield in Yankee Stadium. Most of those people were relieved; a handful of them still expected McCarthy to come back somehow and get even. He was that kind of cop.

During nearly twenty-one years on the street, mostly in the Life, in Vice, McCarthy learned that there are only two ways to look at the world—as a civilian and as a cop. The cop approaches life as one of the walking wounded, as a casualty of his line of work. He can't help himself.

The mere fact of his survival and endurance make him suspicious, aggressive, and not a little nervous in the company of noncops. It's a form of battle fatigue, only worse, because with cops, the battle is never over. Their private war goes on, and as they grow older, they become a little more desperate with each escalating danger. They can never look forward to the clean resolution that comes with the catharsis of combat. A cop's life is a limbo of blue for all eternity—no black or white, no right or wrong; their conflicts are remorselessly gray.

A long time ago, society gave cops like Bill McCarthy guns and blackjacks and expected them to serve as its bouncers. No long-winded explanations—just keep the riffraff out. Nightstick justice.

Language, even common words, had to take on new layers of meaning for cops. "Death," for example, wasn't some inescapable consequence of the gift of life; for cops, "Death" became a wily, familiar foe, almost a friendly enemy, one who would always be there, waiting, at the beginning of every shift.

For all this they can expect low pay, lower status, and the lowest possible standard of performance from a debased criminal justice system that feeds on the husks of burned-out policemen.

McCarthy never had to shoot anybody, but people have shot at him. He's never stabbed anybody, but he's been stabbed, more than once. He's never planted a bomb, intending to do as much damage to as many people—helpless, anonymous victims—as possible, but later in his career, as the commanding officer of the NYPD Bomb Squad, McCarthy and his men were called on to locate and disarm hundreds of such bombs.

As a rule, he didn't like other cops and never really trusted them. To a large extent, that feeling was mutual. But they all knew "Mother"—part of it as in "that no good mother . . ." and part of it as in "Mother will never let anything bad happen to you." It became McCarthy's code name as well as his trademark.

Either way, he really was like a mother to the men he commanded, which meant that it was his responsibility to get the job done and to make sure that cops with iron balls—decent, honest, incorruptible cops—didn't get killed in the line of duty. Or caught in the merciless gears of the New York City Police Department.

Just mention that name today, "Mother," even years after his retirement, and you are likely to see some grizzled, cynical cop nod his head in immediate recognition, maybe spit or swear before he repeats the name, and then say what they almost always say, their tone a mixture of grudging respect and disbelief: "Mother—that was one crazy son of a bitch."

There is no higher compliment in the NYPD than to be labeled a madman. And Bill McCarthy was just that. Crazy.

As a package, he still makes a lasting impression with his prematurely balding head, a respectable padding of muscles, and a deceptively medium build—five feet ten and 160 pounds when he's in shape and running every day or jabbing at the heavy bag. Which he usually is.

Back in 1974, when he was just twenty-nine, at the height of his undercover roles, and as the brains behind Operation Sinbad, McCarthy appeared to be a perfectly reasonable, good-looking young cop. He deviated from the norm only in that he possessed a rock-solid upper body—developed from years in the ring—and a pair of scarred shoulders that had taken down dozens of tenement doors. But by no means was he a monster. Oddly enough, however, McCarthy always sent people away convinced that he was bigger and taller and stronger than he actually was. Call it presence—something McCarthy possessed in abundance.

There was only one physical attribute that truly set him apart. He had the coldest, deepest-set hazel eyes that any of the cops who worked for him had ever seen. Also, his face never changed expression when he was on the job; not unless he was using it to scare some poor slob.

That's when his face would twist into a gargoyle mask,

15

those deep-freeze eyes of his popping out of his head in a steam bath of rage.

With good reason, most of his men were more afraid of him than of anybody they were likely to run into on the job. Bellowing like King Kong, he was known to pound his fists on his chest just before a fight. He used to bang his head against the wall in the bars that they raided, just to let them know that he was there, or he'd scream, "Hey, I'm gonna taste me some ear."

And they knew that he meant it. Every word. Because he *had* eaten ears before. At least that was part of the McCarthy legend. Apocryphal or not, it didn't really matter. Once, so the story went, McCarthy had bitten a pimp's bodyguard on the nose, ripped his ear half off and then chewed on it. Things like that made an impression. Especially on fellow cops.

He was acutely aware of the fact that, as a cop, his true talent lay in bleeding. McCarthy led by example— head first. As a boss, he was obsessed with the notion that no other cop's blood, real or bureaucratic, should ever be on his hands.

Police commissioners came and went, but cops like McCarthy stayed. And those commissioners, who had thirty-thousand other cops to think about, to promote, to transfer, to discipline, or to crush, if need be, were always aware of Bill McCarthy. He was not a well-kept secret. In his world, in Vice, he had come to be revered, universally, as a madman.

McCarthy *did* have a smart mouth, too, an educated mouth, and in the NYPD of his time there was always the risk of that working against you, because any cop who might be caught reading *The New York Times* in the precinct could be branded a communist or worse.

As a young man, McCarthy went on the job not even sure what the Mafia was, but by the time he left, every major organized crime family in New York had heard of Bill McCarthy. He was the crazy Vice cop who was bad for business; McCarthy cost them money. He cost them plenty.

McCarthy never took a bribe as a cop, not one dollar; but even to this day, long after his many undercover assignments, there are still people in Manhattan who believe that Bill McCarthy was the most diabolically corrupt cop who ever tried to shake them down. He was a good actor, he had to be. He was Mother.

As the head of the Pimp Squad, McCarthy lived with men and women who sold their bodies until every organ wore out. Much of his career in the Life was spent attempting to apprehend compulsive pedophiles who preyed on children—buying them, selling them, raping them, abusing them, victimizing them in every way.

When he began, only the most sophisticated criminals trafficked in drugs, and among that group only the most enterprising dealt in cocaine. But by the time he was finished every five-buck hooker, every pipe-whore who came through the Pimp Squad was hopelessly addicted to crack cocaine.

He watched as the constant dangers in the Life shifted from nightly armed struggle to near-Armageddon.

And Bill McCarthy endured. In the end, he was able to walk away from the Life with his head held high, taking more from it than he gave. It was a good run. Never once did he stop believing.

Bill McCarthy never intended to become a cop, never intended to become Mother, never dreamed of spending the best years of his life in Vice, but that's what happened, and this—told largely in his own words—is his story. It's the tale of an honest cop who lived the Life.

Like every cop, McCarthy began his odyssey as a rookie—as a frightened, well-meaning young recruit who was profoundly unprepared for the calling he was about to take up.

Long before Vice, there were the streets of Harlem and the long, bloody summer of 1966.

Two

*The Harlem that cops know is a butcher shop.
People are just meat. Want a leg of lamb? You got
a leg of lamb. Want a dead body? You got a dead
body.*

MOTHER'S MAXIM

HARLEM, 1966

"First of all, I *never* went to the police academy.

"I was appointed a policeman June 20th, 1966, and
they immediately took us down to a tailor on Canal Street
to be outfitted with two blue summer shirts and get measured for our pants. The shirts had brass buttons. I still
remember that.

"Rookies were supposed to wear khaki or gray—gray
for my class. But I never wore gray. None of us were
ever allowed to be rookies.

"They gave us a gun in a box and sent us up to a
range. We fired fifty rounds. Then they told us to put the
gun back in our holster and don't ever take it out again.

"Two weeks later the pants were ready—blue pants—
and I was in Harlem, in a blue uniform, like a real cop,
in a riot. Summer of 1966. Two weeks later.

"It was incredible. I had never even been to Harlem
in my life. I had heard about it and I knew it was a bad
place. It took me fifteen minutes to drive from Queens.

18

I paid twenty five cents to go over the Triborough Bridge, right up the main drag and get off at 135th Street and all the time I'm saying to myself, Jesus Christ, fifteen minutes and a quarter, and I can go from an Irish Catholic neighborhood where everybody looks out for everybody else, to this. If these people ever find out that they can pay a quarter and go the *other* way, it'll all be over; that'll be it for Queens.

"There was tremendous racial tension that summer. The riots started in Brooklyn as a result of neighborhood brawls between the blacks and the Italians. A retarded kid had been shot and killed by an unknown assailant and both sides decided to take it out on the cops.

"The rioting became so fierce that Mayor John Lindsay went out into the streets to try and mediate things. But they wouldn't listen. He was trapped somewhere, in a store, I think, and when he attempted to leave, they turned his car over and started setting fires. He had to scramble out and hide in an Italian restaurant. The cops couldn't even get in close enough to pull him out of there.

"There's been a lot of stories about what happened next—volumes of revisionist history, but I was there. I saw it.

"Somebody had the bright idea to run over to Joey Gallo's social club and see if he could calm things down enough for Lindsay to be rescued. At least he could talk some sense to the Italians. That was the plan.

"So Crazy Joey Gallo and John Lindsay had a sit-down. And Gallo took care of it for him. Just like two heads of state at a summit. The mob boss and the mayor.

"How Gallo did it, I don't know. But the word went out. Crazy Joe said to cool it. And to back it up, he put so many shooters out on the street that people got the idea. Now, Gallo had an ulterior motive. He was hoping that Lindsay would remember the favor. And who knows? Gallo probably saved John Lindsay's life.

"That became my first civics lesson as a policeman.

What the cops couldn't accomplish, either a full-scale riot or organized crime could.''

McCarthy had a friend, another rookie, whom they called the Shoe. All the Shoe ever wore were big, ugly, ripple-sole shoes. You could hear him coming before you saw him. Today, the Shoe is a captain in the Bronx.

"The Shoe was as strong as an ox. And just as shy. I never saw him go out with a girl. His marriage must have been arranged.

"We were in a skirmish line during the riots, like an old infantry formation, trying to move forward and clear one of the big avenues there. The Shoe is right beside me. All of a sudden, he gets tapped on the shoulder, and goes away with a woman from across the street.

"A little while later the Shoe crawls back to this kind of foxhole that we've set up behind an overturned car. The bastards are shooting at us again. We're pinned down like it's the D-day invasion—right in the middle of New York City. In a foxhole.

"The Shoe is ash-white, his face drained of any color. He looks like a ghost. His real name was Terry. I ask him, 'Terry, where have you been? We could've used you up here. These guys are shooting at us.'

"He stammers, 'I just delivered a baby.'

" 'What?' Now, I know that the Shoe has never even seen a woman naked in his life. Never been to bed with anybody. The Shoe played baseball, that was it. I don't even think he knew where the hell babies came from. He was just like a big kid himself. And here he had to deliver a baby.

" 'A baby.' He said it again. 'I did it. She told me what to do, this lady. It just popped out and I caught it— like I was playing second base.' ''

* * *

The inexperienced cops from Bill McCarthy's rookie class who hit the streets in that summer of 1966 comprised the thinnest of blue lines. On their heads they wore World War II—era army helmets, steel pots, and in their hearts they carried the banners and all the working-class biases of places like Queens and Ozone Park and Bensonhurst.

The rookies were arranged in alphabetical order, by borough. The high command of the NYPD was bunkered in safety behind the paperwork walls of the old Police Headquarters at 240 Centre Street. They looked on as the riots of that summer meandered through some of the most dangerous real estate on earth, becoming one enormous brawl that spread from block to block and house to house.

Almost from the moment he put on the uniform, there was fighting all around McCarthy—behind, in front, on either side.

In one incident, a gentle kid named MacNamara manned the line with McCarthy. Suddenly, a single punch to the face knocked MacNamara down. McCarthy called for a medic—this was combat—but there were no medics. His friend just lay there bleeding. The only response that made any sense to McCarthy was to keep his head down and try and shield himself and MacNamara from the debris and projectiles that people—including women and little kids—were pouring down on the rookie cops from rooftops and windows.

Nobody ever seemed to be in charge; the riots had all the makings of a massacre—a bureaucratic massacre—and none of the top cops wanted to be around to pick up the tab for it. The kid cops with McCarthy were lucky if they could even find a sergeant.

Despite the mass confusion, the incessant sirens and the tireless waves of rioters who kept charging the police lines, McCarthy felt very much alone; more like a spectator than a participant in his own life. He certainly didn't

21

feel like a real cop—a real cop would have known what to do.

Already, he was inventing a defense mechanism against the cycloning action and fear. With calmness and detachment, McCarthy was distancing the person from the uniform, the man from his mission. In the eventful years to come, as a Vice cop, he would use this studied disengagement that he had learned on the streets of Harlem to assess his own performance against the unbending standards he was setting for himself.

As soon as the riots temporarily ran their course—in full retreat most of the time, the cops *didn't* put them down—McCarthy was assigned to the old 3-2 precinct in Harlem, at 135th Street and Eighth Avenue. Radio Motor Car #565, sector 7. He was pulling the 6:00 P.M. to 2:00 A.M. shift with Tuesdays and Wednesdays off.

That might have qualified as the single most dangerous intersection in the entire United States during that smoldering hot spell of 1966. McCarthy would float as one of the extra bodies, dividing his time between the 3-2 in Harlem and the 7-3 or 7-9 in Brooklyn, where he had met Joey Gallo's crew.

His first official "day" at the 3-2 in Harlem was a sweltering Thursday night before the July Fourth weekend. Every cop in New York was expecting the worst.

He arrived for his first-ever roll call along with ten other rookies. There is nothing more fabled in the mind of the public than the ritual of police roll call. That included McCarthy himself. He expected to see what he had seen on television and in the movies—rows of crisply uniformed police officers thoughtfully logging that day's schedule as a caring, wise old sergeant looked on.

"Right in the middle of my first-ever roll call a black lady comes running in, wearing a raincoat, crying, in hysterics; and she goes up to the desk sergeant, scream-

22

ing, 'The motherfucker did it, the motherfucker did it!' She opens her raincoat; she's naked and one of her breasts is cut off.

"She's bleeding, pulling her coat open so the desk sergeant can get a better look; she's cut up like something they just yanked up off the table from surgery—but this isn't surgery, this is where I'm supposed to go to work every day.

"I'm ready to pass out, but the old desk sergeant is bored stiff. He half raises himself up off his chair, and I can see him looking at the tit that's been cut off, kind of comparing it with the one that's still there. He yawns, just points to a bench over on the side and says to her, 'Shut the fuck up and sit the fuck down. We'll get to you.' And that was it.

"Then, one of the other rookies comes back with a guy who went nuts, wacko; tore his clothes off in a taxicab and he's screaming something about he's gonna lose his scholarship. And of course, nobody pays any attention *at all* to him because he isn't bleeding. They don't even bother to tell him to go sit in the corner. He just stands in the middle of the room raving.

"And I'm saying to myself, 'Do I really want to go out those doors?'

"That roll call turned out to set the pattern for all the rest—twenty-one years' worth.

"It was some old guy who hadn't been out from behind his desk in twenty years standing up there and droning on, reading the internal orders—and nobody in the place paying any attention to him—as he tried to tell *you*, who had just been under enemy fire, what the conditions were like out on the street. It was insanity.

"Other roll calls depended on which boss was working. Some of them were frustrated military types and the roll call sergeants had to keep them happy. That kind would actually inspect uniforms. The old guys really laughed at that. They'd make you go up and bend over,

23

turn around and hold up the tails of your coat so they could see if you had a shine on your ass. And guys would always be trying to pass gas while they did it. That was twenty years ago. Now, if I told that to the kids today they would never believe it."

The plan called for one rookie each to be paired with one senior police officer; by breaking up the teams of veteran partners the police would be able to double the number of patrol cars on the street during the peak hours of the summer disturbances. There was only one problem: The older cops didn't want any part of the rookies.

"Seven of the nine rookies who went out before me, at six P.M., were back before six-forty-five P.M. with arrests—for gambling, narcotics, assault.

"The senior cops had all gone out and gotten rid of the rookies as fast as they could by giving them the first collar they saw. Anything to dump them. They didn't want them around while they were out doing their normal corrupt routine; doing their shakedowns, in other words. They couldn't trust us. And they certainly weren't about to split a note with a rookie.

"And this is all on the first night—in my first hour in Harlem. This is my real indoctrination into the NYPD.

"The person I was assigned to ride with happened to be over at a hospital with a psycho. So I was the last rookie to be picked up. I was standing there, waiting, like a little kid at the bus stop. I expected them to tell me to go sit next to the woman with the one tit.

"When I finally did get picked up, my partner's name was Mattie Morgan—Mad-Dog Morgan.

"I'll never forget him. He had a nightstick that looked like the leg of a piano. The thing was sculptured. He talked to it. He was a big, big guy, loud voice, like a wrestler.

"We're not out on patrol ten minutes and as soon as we pass the first liquor store in our sector, we hear gunshots.

"Three guys come running out of the liquor store and the next thing I know, we've got the three of them up against the wall. They're in handcuffs.

"I can't believe it. I'm numb. I still can't get the woman with her tit cut off out of my mind, but I've already seen a shootout and I'm making a felony arrest. Guns drawn.

"Just before we got them, one of the holdup men threw a .45 automatic down the stairs of a tenement. Mad-Dog hated cellars, he was afraid of rats, so he sent me down to get the gun.

"I go down these wooden stairs. They were not solid stairs, just like lattice steps, and there was all kinds of shit down there in the darkness, boxes, junk, old mattresses, there was even standing water in these deep smelly puddles; rats, too, I'm sure. But I'm all gung ho, looking around for the gun.

"Damn, if I don't find a cocked .45 automatic. I was so delighted that I found it, that without even thinking, I pass it up, in the darkness, still cocked, through the stairs steps, to Morgan. I had it by the barrel with the barrel end facing me. If I had knocked it against the step, I would have shot myself.

"We go back to the station house; Morgan's got his chance to get rid of me. So I'm gonna take the collar.

" 'Kid,' he says, 'you got the collar. Good man. You'll probably get a day off for this.'

"Meanwhile, he's gonna kiss off, get back his own partner and go out and do whatever they want to do.

"At the station house there's already nine collars ahead of me, all rookies. Now, these old guys didn't make nine collars in a month. But the captain in the precinct doesn't want to lose the best arrest statistics he's had since he's been there. He comes out of his office and says, 'Uh uh, the rookies ain't takin' no collars. Only senior men.'

"Since we weren't real cops at that point the credit for our arrests would not have gone to his precinct but would have reverted back to the academy. Naturally, this change in their plans really pissed off the senior cops because now they were stuck with all the paperwork. And they were still stuck with us. I think that captain damn near had a mutiny right there.

"That was my first patrol. And I couldn't get over it—fifteen minutes and a quarter; that's all it took to go to Harlem. Four or five people were shot that night, all kinds of armed robberies, people screaming. And this was the *calm* between the fights.''

The old-timers were out to break in the rookies—and break them in fast. Dirty tricks were commonplace. They would send the young cops into a tenement, sometimes to serve a warrant, often just to teach them a lesson. "Come on over here, kid. We need you, kid.'' That's how it always started. The old cops would knock on a tenement door, practically bash it in, pretend that an arrest was about to be made, and then, as soon as the door began to creak open an inch, shove the rookies in front of it and run like hell.

It was frightening for the people inside the apartment, humiliating for the rookies, disastrous for already tense police community relations, but the warped old cops considered it great sport.

"One of these old cops was a thief, a crooked, big, fat slob; he must have weighed about 260 pounds. I gave away about a hundred pounds to him, maybe more. I was skinny then. He convinced all the rookies that he was

26

some kind of hero. He was like the Pied Piper. All the new cops followed him, tried to imitate him.

"One day I found out that he gave a traffic summons for illegal parking to a cop, just to be a prick—that was a huge joke to him. But this particular cop was parked over by a cancer hospital because he had his little kid in there. He was getting chemotherapy. He comes out of the hospital and finds out that his car has been towed away. I happened to be in the precinct when the poor guy came in. As a matter of fact, I lent him the money to pay to get his car out of the impound lot.

"And there's this big slob laughing his ass off, over behind the sergeant's desk, because he had really screwed this man with the sick child. I got him out of there in a hurry because I didn't want him to have to get in a fight, too. And I just waited.

"At the end of the day I went up to the slob in the locker room and said. 'Why'd you give that guy a ticket over at the cancer hospital?' And he lied. He denied that he was the one who did it. But I had seen the summons with his signature on it. I called him a liar to his face.

"We were changing our clothes, ready to go off-duty. But I didn't care. This was worth it. I took off after that animal and I chased him down Twelfth Avenue in my shorts. And I'm proud to say that when I caught up with him I gave him an old-fashioned ass kicking. And we were in the same squad. We worked the same jobs. After that, he would never let himself be in the locker room at the same time that I was there."

The worst precinct in the city at that time was the 7-9, in Bedford Stuyvesant, on Gates Avenue. The police station had been put under siege more than once by the neighborhood, and usually, the only cops who were assigned there were the kind who had made powerful enemies—or the rookies like McCarthy.

* * *

"This one hot, rainy night I was working with a black officer. The guy had muscles. His shirt was pulled tight across his chest and arms like a weight lifter. His head was shaved bald and he had medals that ran up his shoulder and down his back. He had so many medals he looked like a Mexican general.

"I get in the car with him, and the very first thing he says to me is, 'They teaching you any of that civil rights bullshit at the police academy?'

"I said, 'All the time.' What else was I supposed to say?

" 'We got some mighty fine caves over here,' he said.

"I'm thinking—*Caves? What's he talking about?*

"The first thing he does is pull the car off the street so we can go into an after-hours club. There's only one white guy in the bar—me. They pour my partner a shot of whiskey, about six ounces straight, no ice. He polishes that off and then he hands me a glass too. I just held it and looked at it. Then, the girls come up and start to feel his muscles. We're saved by the radio.

"We get a call—'Psycho in the cellar.' That's a crazy person who's in the basement of a tenement. You could get ten calls like that a night.

"We go to this house, down to the basement and there's nobody there. Then he says, 'Ain't this a mighty fine cave, boy? The caves is where the animals live.' Now I know.

"The person who had made this call lived up in a fourth-floor walkup. We go up there, me and this real cop. I'm right behind him.

"We pass a woman in the hallway. She's smiling at me, and she's walking as if she's headed out of the building. About thirty years old, black. I was very concerned about modesty and it was a very narrow hallway, so I pressed myself up against the wall to avoid bumping into her breasts. My face was turned the other way to allow her to pass by and give her the most room.

"The real cop now starts to look back for me and he sees that the woman has a knife at her side. But I don't notice a thing. She's the psycho in the cellar we were supposed to get. She's still smiling, very strangely, and she comes right up to me. I have no idea what's going on.

"All of a sudden, she lunges at me with the knife, and I go down. My partner has already reacted—he jumped on her and caught the sleeve of her blouse, but didn't get her arm fast enough. She sticks me in the side, in the love handle on the left. I never even saw it coming.

"I wasn't hurt very badly; we had to get the cuffs on her before she tried anything else.

"I get one handcuff around her wrist; she's holding the other handcuff in her free hand and she's fighting, and I'm still trying to subdue her without touching her breast.

"My partner is behind her and I'm in front. She kicks me in the balls about three times, and the real cop is actually *letting* her kick me. He wants this to be a lesson.

"We finally get her handcuffed, and my partner goes upstairs to get the complainant, who was this woman's aunt. He leaves me downstairs, he's so disgusted with me. 'Can you take care of her now?' he asks.

"I have her up against the wall, handcuffed, but damn, she keeps coming at me. I'm still too bashful to touch her tits and this just isn't working. I get nailed in the balls again. Hard.

"The real cop can't take any more. He comes flying down from the fourth-floor landing and just jumps on her.

"He bangs her right off the wall. That's it. I honest-to-God thought he put her right into the next apartment— I could see plaster dust; I thought he stuck her through the wall.

"After all that, after we finally got that psycho bitch

under control, we went back to the station house. I could either arrest her or "psycho" her. Just take her to Bellevue. You don't need a supervisor for that. So there's less paperwork involved.

"Now, I'm bleeding a little bit from the stab wound. So the black cop says to me, 'Do you want to go sick? You gotta go see the surgeon. He'll come to your house.'

"I said, 'Whatta you mean, he'll come to my house?'

" 'Yeah, the next day, if you go sick, the sergeant on patrol will make sure you don't go out of the house.'

" 'You mean my mother will find out? I can't let my mother know. She never wanted me to be a cop.'

"He says, 'Sure, the guy will come to your house to make sure you aren't faking.'

"I didn't want to go sick after I heard that. I was afraid that if my mother ever found out that I'd already gotten hurt, that would be the end of my police career. So we psycho-warded the woman with the knife. They all liked me after that because I had just saved them a ton of paperwork—on the arrest and on my going sick.

"The riots taught me that I had to ambush people. I didn't give them a chance. I mugged them. Dance contests go on. Fights don't. Fifteen seconds and the fight's over. I'm not a headhunter. If you know what you're doing, go for the body. If you want to win a street fight, that's how you do it. They never expect that.

"People think that cops know how to fight. They don't. They're scared. Like everybody else. Like I was scared— all the time. You don't learn how to take a punch going to the police academy for twelve weeks.

"After that episode in Harlem my whole approach to the bad guys changed. It became what I call the *rodeo method*. It was like roping a steer. Get him cuffed, get him down, get him under control. Then he can't hurt you and the show's over. As I gained experience, I rarely hit anybody because hitting never got anybody handcuffed."

Three

You are a Cop for life, just like a priest. If somebody had told me then that I would spend the rest of my life as a cop I would have laughed in their face. Or maybe spit in it.

MOTHER'S MAXIM

HELL'S KITCHEN, 1945

Bill McCarthy was born hopelessly Irish and incorrigibly Catholic on March 6, 1945, at Saint Claire's Hospital in Hell's Kitchen, on the West Side. Today, it's an AIDS hospice.

His family lived in Jackson Heights, Queens, in a house on Ninety-second Street. He was the third of five children, with two older, mothering sisters and a younger brother and sister. Their grandmother lived with them. She spoke Gaelic and had gone to the sixth book in Ireland, a remarkable educational achievement for a woman of her generation. She knew a thousand poems; a poem for any occasion.

His father was a supervisor in a foundry—the Neptune Meter Company—in Long Island City. He'd started out as a molder and would spend the next thirty-one years feeling the furnace blast—never less than 135 or 140 degrees.

"The earliest memory I have is jumping off the stoop of our church on a Sunday afternoon and landing on a broken bottle and the glass puncturing my wrist and my blood running all over the place. My father put his hand over my wrist and ran everywhere in the neighborhood, trying to find a doctor's office that was open. And when he finally did get a doctor, he couldn't take his hand off my wrist because my blood had coagulated on him; his hand had frozen solid. I still have the scar—it was just one sixteenth of an inch from hitting the vein you want when you try to commit suicide.

"My father is about five feet six, 165 pounds, a small, brickhard Irishman, but he had a size fourteen ring—he had hands that were like a shoemaker's hands. Hard as sandpaper.

"In the foundry where he worked, you took these sand molds that weighed between 110 and 115 pounds and you poured melted brass or steel to make a utility meter, and he would pick up that form and put it on a conveyor belt. My father would pick up about 150 pounds two or three hundred times a day.

"They used to supply the foundrymen with beer in buckets and salt tablets. If you didn't drink the beer you dropped dead. They would stay in there ten or twelve hours a day. Summer and winter.

"My father was totally responsible. For him, very simply, that meant he worked very hard, brought his check home and gave it to my mother. Entertainment was Lawrence Welk on a Saturday night. Throughout my childhood, we said the family rosary every night at seven o'clock. My father was disciplined. He ate the same lunch for thirty-one years—ham and cheese on day-old Wonder bread, rye, and on Fridays, it was American cheese with mustard.

"He gave up drinking as a sacrifice to God when my

mother was pregnant with my youngest sister, Madeline. They were both supposed to die, the baby was so premature. They didn't and he always said that the only reason was because he made that vow. He never touched liquor again in his life. He believed that he had cut a deal with God and he had to stick to it. It's been thirty-seven years now and he still hasn't had a drink.

"My mother died very young of a blood clot that lodged in her lung. I was there in the hospital with my father; I was a cop then. He turned to me, looked into my eyes and said, 'She's not dead, only asleep, because she's still warm.'

"He had already given up cake for my Uncle Tommy to go on the wagon, and that had worked. He stayed sober for ten years. And he truly believed that he had saved Madeline and my mother once. But this time, God hadn't let him know in time, so there was nothing left that he could give up. My father was a strong-willed man.

"I had to pronounce my mother dead to my father. 'She's not alive, she's not breathing, there's no pulse. Look!'

"Then, he turned to me with these big, awful tears in his eyes and said, 'If He only let me know; what could I have given up?' "

McCarthy had been a ferocious, dedicated schoolyard basketball player. One hectic summer he actually wore out two basketballs traveling all over the city scuffling to get into the best games, like the schoolyard classics at 108th Street in Rockaway where the spectacular Maguire brothers took on all comers. They were do-or-die shootouts.

To play at 108th Street you had to win. If you lost, you didn't get to play the rest of the day because there were twenty teams stacked up behind you waiting for their chance. In that era Rockaway was the best pressure basketball in New York, and McCarthy managed to stay on good teams and play all day long. And he didn't do it on talent, he did it on persistence, on endurance.

Nobody practiced longer or harder. He developed incredible stamina, taught himself to be relentless, especially on in-your-face defense, never letting up. He agitated and annoyed and almost always found some way to beat you.

"After grade school, Blessed Sacrament Grammar School in Jackson Heights, I went to Power Memorial at Sixty-first Street and Tenth Avenue. The Irish Christian Brothers. I was there with Lew Alcindor, with Kareem. I was a little ahead of him.

"I grew up boxing. I boxed every Friday night of my life. I boxed the way most kids play basketball. I can't do it anymore. I'm too old and my timing's shot. But I loved it; couldn't get enough of punching that heavy bag.

"I practiced boxing in a club, had a gym in my basement. My father was a boxer. A man who dated a girl in my building was a professional boxer. I learned how to box. I got into the Joe Louis thing when I was fourteen years old.

"I wrestled for one year when I was in college. I always lifted weights. Then later, in the police department, I sparred nine rounds every week.

"Now, if you're familiar with being hit, you can assess if it's actually a good punch or not. Your response is based more upon the physical reality of the punch as opposed to the social, psychic surprise.

"I might have thought, Oh, he didn't hit that hard. That wasn't a good punch. His technique is terrible. I've made an assessment. I'm not in shock. I had that advantage over every other cop I knew.

"That's why most white people can't take a punch—not even white prizefighters. If they get knocked out, they get knocked out from *shock*, not from the power of the punch. They may never have been hit before, not really hit. Black people get hit all the time. There's a difference.

"As a learning tool, you really cannot overestimate the value of being knocked on your ass.

"I've been knocked out three times, but never on the job. I've also been hit on the head with a pipe. I've been kicked in the head. A guy tried to steal my basketball in the park when I was seventeen years old, and two other guys jumped me and beat me until I was unconscious. I crawled under a car and just lay there.

"I was also stabbed when I was in high school.

"I was on a staircase in a public school during the race riots and I just happened to be in their way—six black girls. They stuck an umbrella right through me, underneath my belt. Just stuck it in me and then they were trying to beat the shit out of me when another guy came down the staircase. I was on my way up to play basketball on the fourth floor. Oh, man, did that hurt!

"I had my jaw broken in college. A sucker punch. I didn't get knocked out. The guy broke the bone that connected the jaw to the skull. It wasn't shattered, just knocked off the hook.

"I was at Saint Francis College in Loretto, Pennsylvania, outside Pittsburgh. There was a seminary there and I was thinking of 'going up the hill,' as they called it. That meant going into the seminary to study for the priesthood. It just so happened that in Loretto the seminary was separate from the rest of the college, way up on top of one of the Allegheny Mountains. That's where the expression came from—to go up the hill. This was before Millie, before the police department.

"It was Ash Wednesday. I came back from 6:00 o'clock mass to the dormitory, and I said, 'Lent, Lent, Lent! No women, no women, no women!' And I took his girlfriend's picture, folded it up politely, and put it in

35

the garbage pail. That was enough to set this guy off. He's a disc jockey in Pittsburgh now—at least he used to be."

Like every first-born male in a traditional Irish Catholic family, McCarthy's soul, as well as his ass, should have belonged to the church. Without so much as a word of consultation with him, his mother had preordained him for the priesthood, for bishop or better.

She promised him that if he did take his vows, she would have her engagement ring melted down so that she could put the diamonds in his first chalice. That way, every time he consecrated the host he could think of her. At the very least, she instilled in her son a very noisy conscience.

" 'Be a good man'—that's what my mother used to whisper in my ear. I was dedicated to being a good person. To saving my immortal soul, to gaining my rightful place in heaven. To her, that was an end in itself. Scrupulosity, that was me. I have never missed communion on Sunday in my life but twice. I had pneumonia, I think. I have never missed mass, never just rolled over in bed on a Sunday morning. I can't. She wouldn't let me—alive or dead. I did become an altar boy and that appeased her somewhat. But I knew that I'd let her down."

When he married the former Milagros Concepcion Rodriguez-Medina on September 17, 1967, McCarthy's life quickly refocused itself. That event, probably more than anything else, made him decide to become a cop. But, as he told himself, he would only stay on as a short-timer; he was just in it for the paycheck.

* * *

"Becoming a cop was, for me at least, the psychological equivalent of going into the Peace Corps. That's how it was in the 1960s.

"It was only years later that I realized a policeman's life was right for me. The combination of energy, enthusiasm, honesty, and violence—I had to find something that could accommodate all those things.

"As I went along in school I was greatly affected by the concept of the 'guardians' in Plato. I believed that I was destined to be a guardian, a protector.

"They needed cops back then. You could walk in there on a Saturday morning without an appointment and take the exam. A friend of mine was going to take the police test and he says to me, 'You wanna take the test?' I figured, why not.

"On a Saturday morning in November 1965, I walked in and took it. I think I got a ninety-seven. And then I forgot all about it.

"About six months later, when I was a sophomore in college, I get a letter from the City of New York. It begins, 'You will be appointed June 20th. . . .'

"*Appointed! Holy Shit*! I didn't know what I'd gotten myself into. But then, I sat down and figured, I *will* need a summer job. I was gonna do push-ups at the police academy, I was gonna get paid for doing push-ups and I was gonna quit in September. It was a goof. I was a jock, I was going to go to boot camp for the summer, work out, build up the pecs.

"I had a part-time job in a bank that summer, and my last week there I see this knock-out girl coming in as a teller-trainee. Her name was Millie. She was Puerto Rican. All of a sudden that didn't make one damn bit of difference.

"I went right up to her and said, 'So, when are we going out for dinner?' But she didn't want any part of me. She was very sophisticated, especially compared to me, and at the time, she was living on her own in Manhattan and was going out with a guy who owned two night-clubs. Millie was a high society person as far as I was concerned. I used to wear Bermuda shorts, torn shirts, and I rode this little motor scooter.

"I got her address from work and I went up to this house and I rang the bell. 'Is Millie here?'

"A woman opened the window on the second floor and screamed something in Spanish, then, 'She not here.' I started to give her a real hard time. I'm the only white guy there. Then, I realize that I have the wrong address. Millie had moved and they never made the change at work. And I see all these Puerto Rican men starting to close in on me. And right there on the spot, I figured out how to apologize in Spanish.

"A couple days later, I found the right place. 'I'm here to have dinner,' I told her, but immediately, I can see that it isn't working.

" 'You have some nerve just coming in here.' She was mad.

" 'Okay. You still have to eat. I'll take you out.'

"She went into the bedroom to change her clothes. I followed her in and sat on the bed. That was the wrong move.

"She became outraged, started screaming. I had stepped over the line. I had violated the law that said a nice girl does not invite strange guys into her bedroom. And believe me, I was strange then.

"But I calmed her down. We did go out to dinner. And we got married. It all happened so quickly. I was all set to make some fast money as a cop, but only temporarily; squeeze every drop I could out of the job, save up, get a handyman's special out in Levittown and start banging out the little rabbits.

"Let me tell you that twenty years ago, to walk into an Irish house in Queens with a Puerto Rican girl and say you're going to drop out of college and become a cop in order to marry her—that was an event.

"And it didn't bother me that everybody in Millie's family were cop-haters. Including Millie. But I was a cop before she tried to talk me out of it, before she even met me. My wife hated the police. She was afraid of them. She grew up on the other side. If a cop came to the door, she wouldn't answer it. Not even today.

"When she was a little girl the cops had come into her neighborhood for some reason, run into her uncle or some relative; there was a fight and the cops killed him right there on the street. Shot him in the head, right in front of the kids. They were the kind of cops I worked with as a rookie.

"I stayed Irish and she stayed Puerto Rican. My marriage was the ultimate melting pot. The kids we produced were cultural by-products. It was like cooking my corned beef with garlic. I'll never forget what happened the day that our daughter Christine was christened. Both of our families had gotten together at the church, for the ceremony, and everything had gone well there. They were perfectly civil to each other.

"Later, during the party I was talking and drinking and feeling pretty good, and decided to check on the baby. Then, all of a sudden, I couldn't see the baby anywhere. Millie was busy, too—but Christine wasn't with her, either.

"I got a little nervous. Was the baby sick? Where was she? So I went looking through the apartment to see who had her. I found her in her crib in one of the bedrooms.

"I'll never forget what I saw. There she was—all in white, like a tiny doll—she was sound asleep. Smiling. It looked like Millie's relatives had raided their local botanica and had put all the stuff on Christine's crib. And there was an old woman in that bedroom; she was standing very close to the crib, chanting. There was a little sack of black cowhide, curled like a monkey's paw. It was hanging around Christine's little pink neck.

"I told Millie later on that she better not expect to see

any of that at the Irish Catholic christenings that my sisters had.

"I guess I didn't marry an Irish girl because that would have been like marrying an echo—one, holy, Catholic, and apostolic.

"There always seemed to me to be something magic about Latin girls. They'd say, 'I wonder what they're giving at the movies?' instead of, 'I wonder what's at the movies?' I thought that was the sexiest thing I'd ever heard.

"Marrying a policeman or becoming involved with a policeman was not the sort of thing for a Puerto Rican person to do. A policeman was the enemy, whether you did anything wrong or not.

"In the summer, on a hot night, when they put on the fire hydrants for the kids to cool off, Millie and her little brother used to go under the water.

"One night they didn't hear the other kids yell 'la hara,' which was the signal that the cops were coming. They got caught and the cops put them—these two little kids—in the back of a police car and just rode around the block. Then they brought them back, showed everybody that they meant business, and turned off the fire hydrant.

"That was the day that Millie learned to hate the cops."

Four

A *Station House* is a cop's ghetto. It's dirty, filthy
green, it's beat-up old lockers and showers that
don't work and toilets with no doors on the stalls or
paper on the rolls. It's home.

MOTHER'S MAXIM

BROWNSVILLE, 1966

A sniper had barricaded himself on an apartment rooftop.
His real target had been a police sergeant who was leading
a riot patrol on the street below. But the sniper's aim was
faulty and he had killed a child instead.

McCarthy was one of the cops in that patrol. He heard
the gunfire, but had no idea where it had come from.
Then he saw a child who was playing on the pavement
across the street suddenly go down, blood geysering from
a huge hole in his small chest.

As he and the other cops started running across the
street to try to help the little boy who had been shot, more
projectiles—rocks, bottles, chunks of concrete—rained
down on them in the murky silence of the humid night.
Suddenly, the men on either side of McCarthy dropped
down to avoid the debris. Pinned down, the patrol had to
sit it out until reinforcements finally pulled them to safety.

* * *

"I remember another big, big, *huge* retarded kid. I was walking down the block and this woman comes up to me and tells me her son won't go into the house; he has to go in for dinner. I check him out and he has to be at least 350 pounds. Just a brute of a kid.

"She's screaming, 'Officer, officer, my son won't come into the house. Will you help me get him into the house?' And I went over to that guy. He could've eaten me, could've swallowed me whole. I talked to him for a while and guess what? I ended up in total agreement with him. If he didn't want to go back into that house that was fine with me. You know why? Because I was the only one there who was about to *make* him go back inside and I didn't really care what he did as long as he didn't eat me. That single incident was a valuable part of my education as a cop—knowing when to make a stand and when to look the other way.

"There are plenty of times when the best, most ethical, most moral decision a cop can make is to look the other way. This was one of those times. The situation did not call for me trying to fight this big kid. For what? For his mother to feel like she was still his boss? That whole neighborhood was just waiting for me to use a stick or a jack on that kid, waiting for some excuse to hate me. I refused to give it to them."

Later that summer, McCarthy was an extra man again. The police were so short of bodies that they were assigning rookies to work with other rookies. None of them had a clue as to what they were supposed to be doing.

It was here that McCarthy really came to appreciate the infantry aspect of police work. Even patrol cars were scarce; in those days they used to let the rookies off at a certain corner and return eight hours later to pick them up again—provided, of course, that they had survived their tour.

* * *

"Cops who become too dependent on their guns act that way because they have never learned how to be *alone* on the street.

"Now, when a guy comes into the job, he instantly gets a partner, he gets training. He never works alone. He never has to learn how to talk to people. He can spend his entire tour talking to his partner, never talking to a citizen, and when they do have to talk to citizens, they don't know how. They're rude, crude, and abrupt.

"In 1966, you only got back to the station house alive if you knew how to be a diplomat. You had to be Henry Kissinger. It was all ingenuity and resourcefulness. You had to cajole, and encourage, and get them to cooperate with you if you were alone. There were no radios, phones, not that many police cars.

"It was very lonely if you didn't talk to the people.

"When I started a late tour alone, if I saw a bum on the street, that bum did the late tour with me. I wouldn't let him go. If a drunk or wino walked by me, I made him stay with me. I'd talk with a wino the whole night. I'd stand in a doorway with that guy, I'd even get him cigarettes, I'd buy him coffee, and I'd talk to him—ask him what's the story, where's he from, why is he here and I'd just get to know him and that would make the night pass by.

" 'You're under arrest. Your job is to keep me company.' That was my line on the late shift.

"People on the street are much younger than they appear. People who look sixty years old could be twenty-nine. Incredible people, bright people, very accomplished people, who, all of a sudden, had the plug come out of the wall and they fall apart.

"Most of the policeman I knew, in Vice especially, did not respect themselves or other people. I made a

43

promise to myself in the very beginning that I would never let that happen to me.''

Regardless of their good intentions, however, it was almost impossible for rookies like McCarthy not to surrender to the hardening cynicism of the job. His own turn came when he and his partner, another rookie, were out on patrol when they spotted a blazing fire erupting from the upper stories of a tenement. ''About three blocks ahead of us I looked up and saw this smoke pouring out of a building. Now, being the track star, I tell the other guy, 'Go find a fire alarm and pull the box.'

''I sprint the three blocks and there are about forty or fifty black people across the street; as I get there, I scream, 'Is there anybody in the building?' The crowd starts saying, 'Two old ladies on the third floor; two old ladies on the third floor. Two old ladies on the third floor.' They're chanting.

''So I go into the building. The place is in flames; thick, thick smoke, it was like breathing dirt. And I get up to the second-floor landing and part of the wall collapsed, the floor collapsed. It was black and filthy, and I was choking and I can still hear them chanting: 'Two old ladies on the third floor, two old ladies on the third floor.' And I was embarrassed. I was afraid to come out without the two old ladies.

''There was an exposed waste pipe on the wall, so I tried to shimmy up the waste pipe, thinking I'm going to get their attention by banging my nightstick on the wall. I took a couple more deep gasps of breath and started banging. But then, I must have blacked out because I fell off the waste pipe, hit my head on the landing, and somehow, I ended up down on the first floor. The floorboards must have given way and I just dropped like a rock.

"When I came to, a couple firemen were pulling me out into the street; I was vomiting, choking, and heaving. My uniform was smoldering.

"I remember being taken to the hospital and there were all these people with green outfits on, green masks, and they were putting this oxygen thing on my face. I'm coughing, I couldn't stop coughing; I couldn't breathe. Then, this person in a surgical gown—I don't know if it was a man or woman—was coming at me with this needle that looked about four feet long; they were coming right at my face with this needle. I thought, Jesus Christ, it's gonna go right through the bed. But they stuck it through my mask instead of through me. I was still hacking my lungs out, saying, 'Jesus Christ, thank God they didn't put that in me.'

"Several hours later, I'm still hacking and the sergeant on patrol walks into my hospital room and asks, 'Are you going sick, kid?'

" 'Should I go sick?'

"He says, 'Listen, that's up to you. Do you wanta go sick or not?'

"I said, 'Is the guy still gonna come to my house?'

" 'Yeah,' he answers.

" 'Never mind,' I told him. My mother couldn't find out about this, either.

" 'Fine,' he says, and takes me back to the station house. My uniform smells of smoke. They're practically dragging me up the steps, but there's no way I can go sick. Everybody's glad again—no paperwork for them.

"There was an old Irish lieutenant on the desk wearing these thick, Coke-bottle glasses. He doesn't even look up. I'm coughing my lungs out.

" 'What the hell is the matter with you?' he asks. 'Do you think you're a fucking fireman?' And still, he hasn't even looked at me.

"I almost started to cry. I'm saying to myself—here I

45

run three blocks, I go into the building to try and save two old ladies, I fall, black out, maybe almost get killed and what do I get? This jerk is giving me a hard time.

"So now I go in the back room and my partner's there. I haven't seen him since the fire, since I sent him to yank the call box. I say, 'Jesus Christ, what are we supposed to do? We're cops, aren't we supposed to go in after people in a burning building?'

"He just looks at me in this funny way, like he knows something he's not supposed to know and says, 'They're angry with you because nobody has lived in that building for the last six months. The crowd lied to us. We fell for it. They just wanted to get us killed. The old guys told me they do it all the time around here, any time a white cop's involved.' And then he looked at the floor like his heart was about to break and walked away from me.''

Five

There are two *Penal Laws*, two books; a big one and a little one. The normal civilian wants you to deal with him by the little book, but for the rest of the world they want you to smack it in the head with the big book.

MOTHER'S MAXIM

MANHATTAN

"When I finally got out of Harlem, I had a chance to make the first arrest that really taught me how the justice system worked.

"I was on Madison Avenue in Manhattan and I heard a woman scream. I saw a guy jump out of a Volkswagen, knock her down and steal her purse. I was a rookie and I was with two old-timers. I was yelling at them when I saw the guy jump back in the car. I wanted to chase the guy, but they didn't want to be bothered. 'What's the hurry, kid?'

"They said, 'Are you gonna take the collar?' In other words they didn't want to make an arrest or have to go to court. 'Are you gonna take the collar, kid? You want it or don't you?'

"I said, 'Yeah, I'll take the collar.'

"So the car went up a couple more blocks: Madison Avenue is northbound and they turned down to go east on some street off of Madison; they crossed Park, made

47

a right turn, now going southbound on Lexington. Then we get stuck in traffic on the eastbound side.

"I jumped out of the car on Park Avenue and ran east to Lexington. When I turned onto Lexington Avenue, there was the Volkswagen, almost angle-parked in a bus stop with the engine running and the doors open. But the car was empty. There I am, empty car, doors open and there's nobody around.

"I happened to look into a shoe store, and there was a guy with combat boots on, sitting on the shoe stand, like he was going to get a shoe shine, except his chest was heaving. So I ran in and grabbed him and dragged him out of the store, tore him off the seat. I just knew it was the right guy. I never saw him, but some guy with combat boots on isn't getting a shine. He was a beat-up guy with an army jacket on. A young guy in his twenties.

"As I was dragging him outside, there was another man coming out of a candy store and he just had this surprised look on his face, so I grabbed him, too.

"Then I dragged them both back and finally, the radio patrol car came—the two old-timers had been chasing them sort of casually—I threw them into the car and we went back to the lady. She said they were the guys, all right.

"Now, in the car there were eleven pocketbooks. The car was stolen. There were eleven different pocketbooks from eleven different street robberies, in addition to the twelfth pocketbook of this lady.

"So when I went to court, I had thirteen complainants—the owner of the car and the owners of the twelve pocketbooks. All of the complainants, by the third court appearance, were pissed at me because all they wanted were their pocketbooks and the car back, all of which were evidence; but I was the hump who wouldn't give them back their pocketbooks.

"The two thieves were very different. The rich kid had a private attorney; the poor kid had a public defender.

They were going to make a plea bargain. The rich kid was going to get a suspended sentence; his mother was in publishing. And the poor kid—his father was a nonunion plumber or something—he was going to have to do time. That was my first taste of 'justice.' And that was also the first time I really learned what the public thinks of the police.

"The public wants to be safe. They want to be able to go to the store without getting mugged and when they go back home they want to find their television still in their living room. And they don't ever want to see your face, otherwise. Don't interfere with them. Don't give them a traffic ticket. Don't get in their way because you are the hired help.''

In February 1967, over nine months after the riots, they finally sent McCarthy's class to the police academy on Twentieth Street in Manhattan, on the East Side, between Second and Third Avenues.

At that time the course of instruction was supposed to last four months, with one major test scheduled following each month. Fail one test and you were automatically washed out. At least that's what the curriculum called for. With McCarthy's class, however—already wounded, bloodied street cops—some exceptions had to be made.

"I only took two tests, spent a grand total of two weeks there and graduated. They needed us back on the street again.

"By then, after the riots, in the summer of 1966, after some of the action we had seen, a few of our guys already had medals and most of us looked like we had *ninety-mission hats*. That's one of the odd quirks in the NYPD— at least it was then. You could tell what kind of a cop a man was by the way he wore his uniform hat. With rookies and deskmen the hard visor would be shiny and the peak stiff; the more time you spent on the street, the more battered the hat became. The really *bad* guys—and by then we were the baddest of the bad, or at least we thought we were—would take the stiffening out of the round part of the hat, smash down the peak and fold it up and wear the hat with the sides pegged back like the old World War II flying aces, hence the name: a mission hat. Like you had flown ninety missions or something and lived to tell about it. Now, a cop had to *earn* the right to wear a mission hat. You could not fake that. The other cops would *know*.

"Each individual cop runs the police department. I learned that early. The political clique at the top do what they want to do. They issue orders like crazy. But it's up to each individual cop how much actual service he's willing to give to people.

"Up until I left the academy for good, I had never been anywhere except an 'A' house. There's 'A,' 'B,' and 'C' houses. A 'C' house is very quiet. Maybe somewhere in Queens, no real crimes. A 'B' is a little busier, not much. An 'A' house is the highest enforcement activity, the most undesirable, as far as safety. And all of my precincts were 'A' houses during the riots—the 3-2, the 7-3, the 7-9. There's very little difference anymore. They're all bad. If you want to get a preferred assignment later on, as part of your career path, you can accelerate the movement if you have had your dance card punched at an 'A' house.

"I assumed that when my probation was up I was just going to be assigned permanently to the 3-2 precinct, an 'A' house, because I already had a seat in a radio car there. I was like a regular. But technically, as a rookie, my permanent 'command' was still the police academy. My paycheck used to go to the police academy.

"At the end of my probation period, on our graduation

day, in fact, in March 1967, I was sent downtown to pick up my own paycheck. Every two weeks they used to let one guy go down and pick up the paychecks for everybody. But for some reason, it was different this time. And we were suspicious.

"As soon as you stepped off the elevator at headquarters, they had people there directing you: If you speak Italian or Spanish, go over to this table. If you have a chauffeur's license or if you drive a truck, you go over to that table.

"I had a chauffeur's license to drive commercially. I used to drive a cab. And I used to drive a truck on the beach. I worked at the Surf Club in Rockaway; I used to drive a truck to pick up the garbage on the beach.

"So now I go back and two weeks later, the orders come out and I get assigned to the SOD—the Special Operations Division—Traffic, 'B.' They didn't even have their own tow truck squad then, but they wanted to start one with fifty-six rookies. We had to use old sanitation department wreckers.

"The next thing I know I'm pulling traffic duty in downtown Manhattan and handing out summonses. Two months later, they start this tow squad and I was given one of the trucks. They never asked me—you're here, that's it. Drive.

"Traffic had been manned by dump jobs from all over the city. They didn't ask them. They forced them there. Like old-timers who were from shit-holes—shit-holes are places where you would do anything to get out but you were dumped there by commanders. Now, you had fifty-six guys with eighteen, twenty years on the job—retreads, wrung-overs, dropouts, rejects, and then, all at once, you assign them there together with fifty-six rookies.

"I got lucky. I'm only there a few months when they would occasionally take me off the tow truck and give me

51

an assignment driving for one of the bosses. Eventually, I became the steady chauffeur for one particular sergeant— who is now my son's godfather.

"I chauffeured him around in a patrol car. A sergeant in those days was a big deal. They could even issue search warrants. They could do whatever they wanted to you and there was nothing you could do about it. There was no bill of rights for cops, no union lawyers or grievance committees.

"I discovered that this sergeant loved to get involved. He would actually make arrests, go in on other guys' busts if he could be of help; he acted like a leader. That was my very first experience with a boss who wasn't afraid to act like a real cop. He was the sergeant of all the sergeants that were up there. He'd roll on anything. The more problematic, the better. Racing along sidewalks, upstairs, fights, lock 'em up. This was an old-time, smash-'em-in-the-head-and-lock-'em-up sergeant. I loved it.

"There was no penalty for him to do all that because that man could type 120 words a minute. He could take a blank piece of paper and put it in the typewriter and type a finished report like a machine gun—all black, Underwood, perfect copy, first time out. Anything you wanted. That's the penalty of being involved. Paperwork. It has to be on paper."

The captain running the Traffic detail then was Kenneth Gussman. McCarthy had attracted his attention from the very beginning. Eventually, Gussman became McCarthy's "hook," his "rabbi," and was ultimately responsible for getting him into Vice. Anyone who intended to go places in the NYPD needed just such a hook to pull him along and yank him out of tight places. In their first meeting, however, Gussman didn't know what to make of this hip-shooting kid from Queens.

* * *

"I called Gussman a crook. That could have been a big mistake. I was in Traffic, Gussman's chauffeur, another tit-job. He gave me a dollar and told me to go buy him cigarettes.

" 'I don't buy cigarettes for anybody. Get it yourself.'

"He said, 'What?'

" 'No, get your own. I don't buy nobody cancer.'

"Later that night, I was eating a sandwich in the police station and he said, 'You're a pretty spunky kid. You don't talk to a police captain like that.'

"I just told him, not trying to be cocky at all, 'I don't buy anybody cancer. That's not my job description.' Then, we got talking. He tells me he used to work in the Sixth Division—that's the plainclothes division in Harlem.

"I said, 'Oh, you're a crook then.'

"Gussman just looked at me.

" 'Listen, if you were in the Sixth Division, in plain-clothes, you were on the pad, because if you weren't on the pad they would have written a book about you and I wouldn't have had to be introduced to you when I met you. You would be a folk hero.' Gussman spent the rest of that night trying to convince me that he wasn't corrupt. Finally, he tells me that he's going to keep his eye on me. We never talked about it again."

One day something *did* happen while McCarthy was serving what he viewed as his purgatory in the tow squad.

There was an incident at the exit gate of the impound lot near the Lincoln Tunnel. The people whose cars had been towed could show up at the impound lot, pay their fine and reclaim their autos. Provided, of course, there was anything left of their cars.

The night McCarthy made his bones in the tow squad,

one of those unhappy, irate customers had attempted to run the barricade at the gate without paying. In the process he ran down a cop and nearly killed him.

"This is a hit-and-run, right in front of me. I take off. In pursuit. This is at Fifty-sixth Street and Twelfth Avenue. The guy goes across Fifty-sixth Street, down to Ninth Avenue, makes a right turn on Ninth, starts traveling south, and I start chasing him in the tow truck. I was going about sixty miles an hour in this old piece-of-shit tow truck. I was winding out the gears—it's not exactly an emergency vehicle.

"He turns down Forty-first Street, and I thought he was going through the Lincoln Tunnel. I go around the corner and start racing, but suddenly, I don't see the car anymore. And I stop.

"Behind me there's three parked cars; I back up and he's the third car. The guy had turned the corner and pulled over on me. So I jump out of the car, I get my gun out, and I go up to the car and the guy had the window open, and the next thing I know, I'm dragging him out of the car through the window. He's resisting all the way.

"There was a sanitation man who was sweeping the street there in front of this real skel bar; nobody in there except vagrants and lowlifes. He has one of those little carts with the garbage pail in it.

"Now, I get this guy out of the window and I'm trying to handcuff him on top of the hood of the car, and he's resisting. The gun is no good to me. I can't use it and I'm afraid he'll get it off me and use it on me.

"But, I know this sanitation man is there. I say, 'Here, take this.' And hand him my gun.

"This is a cop-hater's bar. You go down the stairs. It's like in the cellar of this building. We'd had all sorts of problems there before.

"All these people start filing out of the bar—they're winos, street people, buzzards, lowlifes. They really are skeletons. Scumbags, street urchins; they're white, black; their teeth are rotted. And they're watching the fight and they're rooting for the other guy. Meanwhile, I think this whole thing is a setup because when I pulled this guy out the window, he's a black guy and I swear to God he looked like Sammy Davis, Jr. Just like him. And I start to look around for a camera.

"But I'm wrestling around. I glimpse out of the side of my eye that this sanitation man wants to drop dead. He wants to get out of there. The crowd is screaming at him; he's staring at the gun. The gun is pointed at me. They want him to shoot me. And I know I have made a terrible error.

"Finally, I get the guy handcuffed and I get the gun back, and the crowd is still screaming and yelling, and I get out of there as fast as I can. I throw the Sammy Davis, Jr. guy into the truck, take him into the station house and the cop who got run down isn't hurt too badly, so I let him take the collar.

"I stayed in tow service till I made sergeant. I was there for over three years. I started sergeants school the first week of January 1972, right after the Knapp Commission hearings on channel thirteen; Serpico, that whole thing.

"We were the first group from the academy to be selected under the Knapp guidelines. We were what they wanted the police to become."

Six

Loyalty in the police department means you're willing to lie for someone else. Loyalty to me meant that I would always be the way I promised to be for another person. I would never be an ambush. Any person I worked with, I had to tell them right away that I wasn't on any pad. They had to know from me that if I caught them stealing, *I* would be the one to lock up their ass.

MOTHER'S MAXIM

THE KNAPP COMMISSION, 1970

An honest cop, a short, swarthy, intense detective named Frank Serpico—whom Bill McCarthy knew of from the old 7th Division, plainclothes, in the Bronx, but never a cop he worked beside—caused the formation of the Knapp Commission in late 1970.

By then, McCarthy was beginning his fifth year as a policeman; to the old-timers, to cops with twenty-five or thirty years, that meant he was still a rookie.

Serpico's disclosures about corruption ended his own police career prematurely and nearly cost him his life. As a graphic, eye-opening instructional tool for America, however, the value of the moody detective's shocking testimony could hardly be overestimated.

Serpico compelled people to accept the existence of systematic corruption in precisely the same way that Joe Valachi had convinced skeptics, a generation earlier, that the Mafia was an embedded fact of life in the United States.

The pervasiveness of rotten police apples inside the NYPD had never seriously been doubted. Before Knapp, there were the Kefauver Committee hearings in 1951, the Seabury investigations thirty years before that, and the original inquest into NYPD wrongdoing, the Lexow Committee, which began investigating in 1894. As a direct fallout of Knapp, there were follow-up probes in New York and in every other big city in America in the ensuing years.

However, police apologists, clinging to the moldy mythology of cops and cop-groupies, insisted that the thieves were individual perpetrators and that corruption was not system-wide. Insiders knew that such a benign scenario had never been the case. Cops were either "grass eaters" who passively accepted whatever cash fell their way, or "meat eaters" who actively put the bite on any hand they saw. Either way, a slack system tolerated them.

"Back when I broke in in Harlem and Brooklyn, during the riots, one of my first partners was picking up money, with me in the car, and I never even knew it. Had no idea. He was as corrupt a cop as I ever met. He was taking bookmakers' money, gamblers' money, pimps' money, right in front of me. And I just thought he had good community relations with the black people. I was that naive. That's when I first saw how the pad worked.

"Everyone would shake his hand and lean in the car and talk to him. Of course, they were giving him money and I never knew it. I thought they just wanted to see him, they'd come over to the car to say hello. I thought that was wonderful. And he loved to have me in his car because he didn't have to split it. It was a great deal for him.

"This guy had been on the job twenty-odd years. That's what I couldn't understand. I used to say, 'With all the seniority you've got, you can go anywhere. Why don't you ask for Queens or someplace?' And he'd say, 'Oh, no. You'll love it here. You'll see.'

"There wasn't even a decent place to eat in that precinct, but these cops refused to transfer. They were pulling down too much on the pad. To them, it was beautiful.

"I used to pay six dollars for a hamburger—22 West 135th Street. It was the Black Muslim restaurant. They hated me, but I said, 'I got money, I'll pay.' I used to go and sit in their restaurant and I was the only cop eating decent food. Everybody else was eating fried pork and chits. And it only cost a quarter. A lousy quarter. But that wasn't what they charged a cop.

"When I had two years on the job I went up against a plainclothes cop who had sixteen. Very cool, streetwise, always wore suits. He was another crook. He was making money. We were in a regular patrol car over on the East Side. He was driving and I was the recorder, as they say.

"He said to me, 'Hey, kid, go get me a sandwich.'

"Now, what he was saying was, go into that store over there and get me a sandwich—for free. But I wouldn't do it.

"I got out of the car on Lexington Avenue, at about Sixty-fourth Street, walked around to the driver's side, opened the door and yelled at him to get out of the car.

"He started to give me a hard time and I dropped my gun belt right in the middle of the street. I said, 'Now if you want to get back in this car, you have to get past me to do it.'

"He couldn't railroad me because he knew that I would tell what he wanted me to do. I would have gone on the six o'clock news with it.

"The outcome of that incident was: one, that I drove that car back to the station house *alone*. I left him standing there, on Lexington Avenue. And two: I got the point across that I had no time for peer pressure and all that police-code-of-silence bull. As far as I was concerned, a crook was a crook. I'd lock up a cop just as soon as the next guy.''

Frank Serpico and others, like Sergeant David Durk, his confidant and contact with the world above ground during his long undercover entombment, effectively killed the myth of the honest police aristocracies. Any cop, of any rank, was open to a payoff, under any circumstances. That was the shameful reality of police life as the Serpicos, the David Durks, and later, the Bill McCarthys, discovered it.

Many small bands of bright, capable cops—frequently the best cops—had, in effect, become the most feared and efficient shakedown crews in a city already conspicuous for graft.

The cops raised the protocol of extortion from art to science. "Pads," or bribe schemes, existed everywhere, on every level, in every borough. Almost any cop in any part of New York could collect an extra thousand dollars a month or more, simply by looking the other way.

Building contractors who were used to paying off Mafia soldiers and associates to ensure labor peace claimed that payoffs to the police amounted to another mob tax on top of their standing illicit obligations, and told the Knapp Commission that bribes to the NYPD increased the cost of the average construction project in New York by as much as 5 percent. The Mafia itself could not pretend to be doing much better than that.

That two-year investigation, pushed rapidly by the reform mayor, John Lindsay, changed the New York City Police Department forever. Its methodical, precinct-by-precinct exposure of massive, structural corruption demonstrated the alarming vulnerability of a police force that had become impervious to outside inquiry and as clannish and hierarchical as the Ottoman Empire. Before Knapp, cops took other cops seriously. Period. Civilians didn't count. There was no unbolting of the heavy doors masking that closed blue society of incomparably dangerous, devious men, gifted men capable of breath-taking artifice.

When political expediency forced the Knapp Commission's final report to be made public in 1972—probably well before the commission's true work had been finished—there was evidence to suggest that half a million dollars a year were being pocketed by rogue cops. Nearly all of that money originated with the five traditional organized crime families of New York and eventually worked its way down to the cop on the street, through successive layers of hangers-on, go-betweens, and bagmen.

Usually, the money went to protect highly profitable prostitution or narcotics operations. Sometimes, the cops acted as mercenaries for the vice lords who were paying them. When they assumed these roles, the cops would be called on to arrest rival racketeers or merely serve as muscle whenever and wherever they might be needed.

"You didn't have to do anything overtly illegal to get put on a pad. All you had to do was go out and bang the balls off of whomever the hierarchy identified. Go knock over Harry's gambling operation. You were just doing your job, as far as you cared. That didn't mean that Harry's joint wasn't worthy of being knocked over, either. Because all the gamblers were bad, all the bars ran whores and drugs.

"The only line that most cops would have drawn was between the honest guys who just made their observations of illegal activity and took it from there—and you could *always* find something illegal—or the dishonest cops who flaked people, who planted phony evidence like dope or numbers slips. You could come up with all the evidence you needed—legitimately—even though the investigation itself might be part of some larger shakedown scheme that a captain or lieutenant had ordered.

"Now, why did the higher-ups identify that particular place—Harry's joint, for example—for you to go out and knock over in the first place? Why—because they were being bribed to do it. By *whom* was always the big question. More than likely, it would be some organized crime guy who wanted to hurt his competition. But the competition was breaking the law anyway, so even though it might have been selective enforcement, even good cops didn't have a big problem with it.

"A shakedown was known as making a guy good. If you made him good, you made him pay you off, either to stay in business or for services rendered."

The extent of the institutional corruption was so vast and so unsettling, even to reformers like Patrick V. Murphy, the enlightened New York City police commissioner, that the attitude of most cops was to turn sullenly inward, in a state of genuine shock, and brand the investigation a witch-hunt that violated even the most basic civil rights of the targeted cops. And, a strong case could be made that the snowballing investigation did, in fact, degenerate into exactly that. Regardless of the way in which a suddenly vengeful criminal justice system decided to retaliate against allegedly crooked cops, however, the existence of the corruption itself could not be debated. Certainly not by people like Bill McCarthy.

Though painfully embarrassed, Murphy's office cooperated, and even launched an aggressive purge of its own, as did a succession of different district attorney's offices.

However, even the lowest-level players on the street could have saved the prosecutors' time and energy.

They knew the cops; they knew the rules. Any arrest, no matter how bad, could be squared for the right price.

Manhattan dope dealers had long favored a two-thirds/one-third arrangement. If caught and busted, two-thirds went to the cops on the take and one-third was retained for sale. Any out-of-pocket loss would merely be passed on to the eager junkies in the jacked-up price of the dope. That was capitalism. Everybody stayed happy—including the cops.

Both the public and the press were unprepared for the Knapp findings. The degree of organization that fueled the bribe-taking was stunning. Even hardened prosecutors were amazed by the casualness with which cops, routinely, picked up payoffs *every* time they went out on patrol. In fact, it became apparent that many cops went out on patrol for the express purpose of collecting payoffs and for no other reason. McCarthy had witnessed all that as early as his rookie summer in Harlem.

McCarthy would eventually work with David Durk in the Organized Crime Control Bureau. There, they attempted to shanghai the best detectives from each other; men they could trust. Their job, in part, was to do battle with the corrupt, old-boy NYPD system.

Another central figure in the Serpico saga was a sympathetic inspector, Paul Delise, known as Saint Paul because he was a straight cop who would have nothing to do with the pads.

Saint Paul became the first superior officer to publicly back Serpico's resolute efforts to expose the pad system in Manhattan as he had done in the Bronx. In fact, when Delise realized that no other cops would serve as Serpico's partner, preferring to freeze him out, Delise told him not to worry; they would jump all the rules, all the traditions, all the department protocol against an officer of inspector rank (a full two steps above a captain) serving with a mere plainclothesman—and Delise became his partner.

Already fifty, long out of foot-pursuit shape and a deskbound administrator for many years, Delise still hit the street with Serpico, chasing the bad guys, taking down the felony arrests and, in the process, so risking his own life as a matter of principle and professional pride that Serpico would later confide that he was sometimes more worried about Saint Paul than about the investigations.

McCarthy already knew how infected and influenced the police department could be by graft, but as part of that untouchable Saint Paul crowd, he also witnessed the metamorphosis that principled cops could bring about.

As long as a kid like McCarthy could avoid being blinded by the light, by all the glamor, by all those blinking, constantly running marquees that he saw whenever he closed his eyes, he might have a chance to make it.

That was a wide-open, never-to-be-duplicated era of giants in the NYPD, controversial supercops like Serpico, like Eddie Egan, who would be immortalized as Popeye Doyle in *The French Connection*.

Some of those people would end up working with McCarthy or for him; gung-ho, nitty-gritty, investigative types. Detectives who went out and made their cases—classic lone wolves.

In reality, however, a detective needs constant direction. He's told what to do, when to do it, and how; he may, in certain cases, be very tenacious and stay on a case longer than most people would give him credit for. He might even be lucky enough to break the case, but without exception, he has to have a lot of organization behind him. That was where they intended the Bill McCarthys to come in.

The detectives could start the balls rolling, but they could only roll so far. The organization refused to allow its prima donnas just to run off in all kinds of directions. It had been burned too many times before.

The tough street guys were essentially lower-level investigators and somebody had to control them in every unit, set the tone. That was what had been lacking, those honest, enlightened field commanders who could actually *lead* their best investigators and establish an intensity level of both integrity and performance.

With McCarthy, you were never at a loss for direction. He would become the most recognizable prototype of the post-Knapp cop in the NYPD, swept along by the momentum of the reform, responsible for the probity of his team and, eventually, in command of the most sensitive beat in New York—Vice.

"There were so many innocent things that were all part of the corruption syndrome—like food that you could eat for free, coffee and buns and the newspapers. All the drivers on the newspaper trucks had sample copies that they carried around to give out to the police. They were marked "bad" because they had a little red dye on them. The *News,* the *Mirror,* the *Post*, they all delivered papers to the police. The milkman delivered milk to the police. The bread man delivered bread to the police. And there was nothing hidden about it. It was acceptable. It was not corruption.

"But, in addition to that, the cops were all down with the gamblers. All the corruption was systemized and the only thing that I was ever told by my uncle—who was a cop—was that 'you're not gonna be a detective; you're not gonna go into plainclothes; you're gonna be a boss. Study. You're not gonna be no detective, because being a detective is how you learn to steal as a cop.'

"It's a boss's job. That's what my uncle was trying to tell me. Why? Because you could tell other cops what to do and get paid for it. That's heaven for a cop. And even if you are corrupt, you get a bigger cut as a boss. That is a sacred tradition in the NYPD.

"In those days whatever a cop's quota was, his pad, his dirty money—a cop's share was a thousand dollars and a sergeant's share was a share and a half, fifteen hundred; a lieutenant got two shares, that's two thousand, a captain got three shares, three thousand, and so on all the way up. That's how it was. It was a boss's job. You made more money and had less risk.

"Naturally, as soon as I made sergeant, in March 1972, and much to my uncle's regret, they promoted me to plainclothes. There was no hotter spot in the entire NYPD.

"After Knapp, they wanted brand-new, clean, sanitized, threatened sergeants on probation. They took thirty-five of us out of a class of one hundred. We were supposed to be the cream of the crop because we were the youngest cops in the history of the department to pass the test for sergeant. We were told that we had the highest IQs; we were the best-educated group ever and, presumably, we hadn't been around long enough to have become *too* corrupted. That was our major attraction.

"Seniority was normally forty percent of what it took to get promoted to sergeant. Twelve years to make sergeant was average. I did it in five. I can thank the Knapp Commission for that. Now, with all the outside politics involved in the police department, they make sergeants in about twelve minutes—and they're all kids. Back then, though, it was a much bigger deal than it is today.

"As part of the indoctrination they threatened the shit out of you: You're going to jail if you take a dime. That was the message. They were trying to make an individual commander's ass pucker with a concept called accountability. They created internal checks to test people. These were all recommendations of the Knapp Commission to prevent corruption in the future.

"They were imposing additional responsibility on new sergeants like myself so that if anybody on our teams did anything wrong, we were going to go to jail with them.

"They were going to try to impose all these controls and make a sergeant the man in charge. From that point on, a cop couldn't make a collar without a sergeant being present and being responsible. That meant making sure that no money changed hands. Before that, they just had to make the quota any way they could: five misdemeanors and two felonies a month.

"I arrived in the most provocative, interesting place in the whole world. At precisely the right time. In Vice."

Seven

The *Sergeant* had all the real power on the street.

MOTHER'S MAXIM

PUBLIC MORALS, VICE, 1972

One day in late March 1972, just before graduation, as McCarthy was leaving the academy to head downtown, he found Captain Kenneth Gussman waiting outside the classroom for him—the very same officer whom he had once accused of being corrupt.

The visit was unofficial, Gussman assured him, but important. McCarthy had no idea what was coming.

In sergeants school he had earned high enough marks in the leadership area to make several commanders around the city aware of him, and his hard-nosed proclivities. McCarthy just assumed that Gussman was among them. They didn't have any particularly close relationship, just a mutual respect.

Many other sets of interested fingerprints had also been left on McCarthy's file. He had recently earned his bachelor's degree from John Jay College, at night. It was a culmination of the degree work that he had interrupted to marry Millie and join the police department several years before. Not only that, but McCarthy had also launched his pursuit of a master's degree. Not many other people in the entire police department could make the same claim. Gussman was aware of all this because he had been doing his homework.

He knew, for example, that McCarthy's preference then was Narcotics, where plenty of smart cops were looking to get their career tickets punched. But Gussman also realized that McCarthy would have little say in the matter of his next job. Still, Gussman decided to meet McCarthy that day more as a recruiter than as a superior officer.

As the two cops walked outside together, the captain bought McCarthy a hot dog and soda for lunch—no cigarettes, this time. Then, as they strolled under a pleasant ocher sky, Gussman steered them away from the academy grounds on the East Side at Twentieth Street. As they walked, Gussman explained that what he had to tell McCarthy was best said out in the open, away from both listening devices and eavesdroppers.

Gussman then laid out his problem: While McCarthy had been working his way up and out of Traffic, and into sergeants school, Gussman had been attempting to do the same thing for himself. And he had succeeded. His new assignment was as the commanding officer of the new Public Morals Division, Vice, in the recently christened Organized Crime Control Bureau. This newest wing of the enormous NYPD infrastructure was the bureaucratic response to the anticorruption recommendations of the just-completed Knapp Commission.

No one could claim to truly understand the rune stones of the New York Police Department. You could spend a lifetime trying to interpret them and still miss a central passage. Duplicity was a commonplace.

The OCCB was a controlled experiment in widespread reform. Both McCarthy and Gussman, based on their own experiences, had reservations about how realistic or practical this new approach could be, but it did present a rare opportunity for police work without interference. McCarthy was intrigued.

"This was an institutional reaction against the time when the plainclothes cops, the detectives, had been renegades. They were running around doing whatever they wanted. All anybody had cared about prior to Knapp was making things good for the pad, taking in enough bribe money to go around.

"Right after the Knapp Commission when you had to be honest, when they demanded that cops be scrupulous, that was like the promised land for me, with my altar-boy religiosity. I could hear my mother whispering in my ear again."

Even though the OCCB had been set up for the express purpose of hothouse-nurturing the new, supposedly corruption-free sergeants as role models for their men, the traditional NYPD hierarchy was imposed on top of that. And that's what had Kenneth Gussman worried enough to seek out Bill McCarthy. But, from the outset, the chain of command and the mechanism for ensuring ethical behavior among the cops seemed murky.

There was, for example, a lieutenant over every sergeant, and captains or inspectors over those lieutenants. An almost uncountable number of those senior officers still belonged to the bad old world of pads and payoffs. They regarded the Knapp Commission and its new disciples as mere obstacles, as the enemy. They had every intention to keep on doing all the illegal graft-taking that they had been doing.

Within the new Organized Crime Control Bureau there were to be almost autonomous, competitive subdivisions—Narcotics; Public Morals, where Gussman had been sent; Field Control (which was really Internal Affairs, cops who spied on other cops); and the Administrative Division, meaning intelligence and wiretaps.

This made little sense from a management point of view (forget the potential for civil rights violations; the cops were still reeling from Supreme Court decisions like the rulings about issuing *Miranda* warnings at the time of an arrest), but managers weren't running the show; cops were running it and they happened to be panicked, frightened cops at that.

Within this maze of bureaus and divisions, the most volatile area was the Pimp Squad, one of the traditional mother lodes of police payoffs and shakedowns. It had always been the ideal place for even sharp cops to get jammed up.

Captain Gussman needed someone running the Pimp Squad whom he could trust—really trust. He needed a hardhead like Bill McCarthy, a man who was simply too proud, too stubborn, too sanctimoniously bent on doing the right thing even to consider taking a note. And that's exactly what he told the new sergeant.

Gussman believed in him, in his honesty. That long, argumentative night they had spent together years before—arguing over corruption and a damn pack of cigarettes—had convinced him. McCarthy was the only guy the captain wanted.

After he had offered the job to McCarthy, Gussman fell silent. Their walk had taken them all the way to midtown, a distance of several miles. While McCarthy thought it over, Gussman sat on a park bench and lit up a cigarette. The moment he caught McCarthy looking at him disapprovingly as he puffed away, the captain immediately tossed the burning stub into the bushes.

McCarthy smiled in approval. Then he thought some more about what Gussman was offering him: the chance to run a clean squad.

There would be unprecedented risks in this arrangement. For one thing, Gussman was a Jew and the NYPD was one of the most thoroughly anti-Semitic organizations on earth. As soon as the other cops in Public Morals realized why Gussman had selected him to run the Pimp Squad, there would be suspicion, jealousy, even accusations that McCarthy was no better than another Serpico.

But then he remembered something that Millie had once confided to him. When she was a little girl, and years later, as a grown woman partying in Spanish Harlem's notorious after-hours clubs, she had witnessed too many police payoffs. It always went the same way: The cops would walk in, slap a few people around, maybe grab a bar-girl's ass and expect to be taken care of. Being taken care of could mean anything from a blow-job in the back room to free drinks, and invariably, money would change hands. Then they would walk out, to utter silence. And the more recklessly they abused their power, the more deeply her people hated them.

Even before they were married, Millie had put it to Bill in the one way that she knew he would understand. "I could never sleep with a man," she had told him, "who is spoken about the way the cops are spoken about after they leave from picking up their payoff money." And then she had fixed him with those same flashing dark eyes that he had first fallen in love with back at the bank.

McCarthy never forgot her warning. It was the one and only discussion that he and Millie ever had about cops taking bribes. But it was enough.

McCarthy glanced over at the bench and saw that Gussman was reaching for another smoke. The captain wanted an answer. He deserved one.

"How do I know that *I* can count on *you*, if I get in a jam?" McCarthy asked him.

Gussman struck his match. "I didn't send you out for cigarettes this time, did I?" Gussman answered.

McCarthy understood. Gussman was grinning at him.

"You just got your new Pimp Squad boss," McCarthy told him.

"I knew I had him all along."

Then, the two men shook hands on it.

McCarthy was first sent to the OCCB's Administrative Unit. That lasted a little less than two months. It was a desk assignment, learning how to read and write intelligence assessments, developing skill with wiretaps. Gussman decided that would be a good way to condition McCarthy for his new responsibilities.

The same day that he left that brief assignment to transfer into Vice, into the Pimp Squad, an older, embittered inspector, familiar with the lures and the prevailing climate of prosecuting cops, but totally unaware of the understanding that had been hammered out between Gussman and McCarthy, looked Sergeant McCarthy right in the eye and predicted warily, "Just wait, in three months you'll be back here—in handcuffs."

McCarthy walked out the door without saying goodbye.

Eight

Cops are recognizable. That's the essence of their profession. You can have no real home life as a cop. You can't even eat your lunch. Somebody in the restaurant is gonna say, "Look at the cop; he uses salt." And they all spend their day seeing if you pay for your food. Somebody's always gonna say, "Watch, the cop won't pay for his food." And even if you do pay for your food the person will say, "Yeah, but he didn't *have* to pay."

MOTHER'S MAXIM

CENTRE STREET, PERMANENT CADRE

From March 1972 until December of 1976, McCarthy served in Public Morals as a sergeant.

He began in a cold, gray, government-issue office building at 137 Centre Street. When McCarthy worked days, he would have to go in and unlock the door, turn off an alarm connected to the central communication system and bring the place to life. Public Morals was on the third floor, Narcotics was up on the eighth—that's where McCarthy first met Bob Leuci, later to be afforded the Hollywood treatment as the *Prince of the City*. The Organized Crime Control Bureau, Administrative Division, was on the seventh. The School Patrol and assorted other city agencies like the License Bureau and Parking Violations were scattered throughout the rest of the place.

McCarthy's Pimp Squad was the only team in the city of New York that worked Vice from ten o'clock at night until six o'clock the next morning. That was the night life, the players' time—the most dangerous dark hours when corruption-prone cops had limitless opportunities to make money. The Pimp Squad had the run of the city—loose women, fast cash, and cocaine. He might as well have been the police commissioner.

The organizational chart called for one sergeant, like McCarthy, to tightly monitor a six-man team: one detective sergeant with six hand-picked helpers, some of whom were "white shield" plainsclothes investigators, and some of whom were full-fledged gold shield detectives.

McCarthy would have been known in the old days as a "five-borough man"; his jurisdiction included Manhattan, Queens, Brooklyn, Staten Island, and the Bronx. After Knapp, "five-borough man" was changed to "permanent cadre" in the headquarters division of a city-wide unit. But it still meant the same thing, and in the NYPD, it meant power under either designation.

Historically, as far as corruption was concerned, it also meant that McCarthy was in the best spot in the world to make the most money, dirty money, because he had the entire city to rob. He knew everything that was going on and his authority, even as a sergeant, superseded any local commander because he was Vice, permanent cadre.

"I'm told that in 1961, a sergeant where I worked—it wouldn't have been in the Organized Crime Control Bureau then, because that didn't exist yet; it would have been called the Police Commissioner's Confidential Investigating Unit or the Public Morals Administrative Division, but basically the same jurisdiction—would have gotten envelopes full of bribe money, money from the pad, shoved into his locker right through the vent. That's how wide-open it was. A sergeant could have expected about nine thousand dollars a month—a share and a half. A cop would have gotten six thousand; a lieutenant, twelve thousand—that's two shares. Most of the money would come from the gamblers.''

During his first five years as a cop, McCarthy thought that any day he was going to quit. That had been the hidden agenda in virtually all of his career moves. As soon as he completed his college degree, he would be gone. But everything changed. Both his promotion to sergeant and his degree came more quickly than he ever thought they would. And then something else happened.

Millie got pregnant. She had told him while he was still on the sergeant's list. Suddenly, he needed money—real money. Not just for himself anymore; not just for the two of them. With the sergeant's raise he would be making more money than he could reasonable expect to make on the outside. From that moment on, the NYPD had him.

Once he settled into the strange routine of Vice, following the timely intervention by Gussman, McCarthy found himself getting *back* to the office to begin his paperwork at five o'clock in the morning. In the years to come, every aspect of his life would be literally turned inside out, even sleeping and eating.

McCarthy had never been a night person. Vice, however, gave him no choice in the matter. When most ordinary people were plowing into afternoon traffic, beginning the long commute home to the suburbs after a difficult day, McCarthy would become accustomed to just starting his shift as a creature of Manhattan's dark night. As a Vice cop. That underworld became his home and he learned to love it there—perhaps too much.

McCarthy, always a family man, lived in those distant suburbs too, with one wife, two beautiful kids, and a dopey dog. He didn't actually have a white picket fence, but he did have the mortgage that went with it.

Sometimes, McCarthy used to wish that he were going

home with the commuters, going home to Millie and their children, to their good life in Sloatsburg. The two of them were still the kind of lovers who had to be touching each other before either one of them could fall asleep, her smooth thigh warm and soft against his.

Once, in the middle of Manhattan, at the corner of Thirty-third Street and Eighth Avenue, he stole up behind Millie and dropped to his knees, in uniform, and began kissing her, progressively working his way up her legs, feet to ankles to knees, as a gathering crowd watched and as Millie, mortified, tried to keep from slinking down a vent grating.

In another way, however, McCarthy sometimes felt as cut off from Millie, from Sloatsburg, as it was possible for a man to be. Vice had done that to him as it had to countless cops before him.

Putting it all in perspective like that made him realize that his house in Sloatsburg—and even Millie—was actually the part of him that was growing fainter by the hour; it was like some old wedding portrait that had been left in the sun too long, and he could see himself fading from the picture. That was scary. He hated to admit it, but there were times—the bad times, mostly—when there was just too much competition from his other Life: the street Life, the whores and the pimps and all the bubbling, percolating plots in the Life.

The pace wasn't exactly killing him, but it was changing him. Before very long, he was eating little and sleeping less; no more than three hours at a time. Exhausted or not, some internal body mechanism snapped him awake by one o'clock every day—then he would run to burn away the tiredness, to kill the lonely afternoons. Ten miles every day. Weights for half an hour in the gym; three hundred turns on the incline board; five hundred hand pushups; then the parallel bars. Boxing next. Punch the heavy bag for half an hour and then more running on an outside track—two and a half miles from his house to the track, five miles around, back home again, all in under two and one half hours.

After spending all night making collars, taking in prisoners for booking, maybe breaking into a house or nightspot to execute a search warrant, then writing up the incidents, he would then have to quickly shut himself down and prepare for the inevitable crash, for the long drive home.

If they told him to stay until six, to brief the day team that was just coming on, they really meant that he should hang around until seven or eight.

This continual yo-yoing of bodies and schedules and emotions and marriages exacted the sort of toll that often resulted in divorce, burnout, even suicide and drug addiction. McCarthy saw what it could do to the men he worked with. He tried not to face what it could be doing to him.

Once he finally did arrive home, after working all night, it might be nine-thirty or ten o'clock before he was ready to settle in. The house would be empty, Millie would be off somewhere, working, leading the normal life dictated by the natural progression of light and dark, of mothering and child-rearing.

Inevitably, McCarthy found himself withdrawing further from that natural order of things. Vice had its own rules, its own dislocated sense of time and place, of values and motives, even of day and night.

Working in the Life came to demand his full attention. In practically all ways, McCarthy's family was the loser. Although they understood what was happening to him, even though they could see the pressure that he was under, appreciate the danger, they sometimes found it hard to bring themselves to forgive him.

MILLIE:
"In Sloatsburg we lived in a yellow house on Sheridan Avenue. I loved that house. I started my family there, brought my babies home to that house.

"It only cost thirty thousand dollars, but that was the limit of what we could afford. We would spend the next sixteen years there, make it through some good times and bad.

"Bill missed out on a lot of things and it just used to hurt me so to see it happening. Like things with the kids. Meetings, obligations, social functions with the neighbors and stuff like that. All the little problems the kids had getting along. He didn't have time for any of those. They weren't important. Only his cases seemed important. We felt shut out of his life at times.

"If something came up, I had to stop him dead in his tracks. I couldn't just let it go, and let it go. I would say, 'We have to talk. Just sit down and we'll talk or you're not getting out of this house.' I had to stop him or he would just go to the job and let it go.

"Then, when he would come home and play daddy to Christine, our daughter, or to Billy, our son, I would be resentful because I had been doing so much on my own. Usually by the time I felt that way, it had built up and up and I couldn't take any more. Then he would stop. But I always had to make him aware of it. He couldn't see that for himself. He would have to see my anger. I would have to do something to get his attention. But always, instead of acting out my resentment, I've told Bill about it. We've been able to talk. Most cops and their wives never talk.

"When I would grab him and say, 'Try to be home a little more,' it was basically for himself, as well as the children. I knew there were things he was missing out on that he wanted to be there for, but he would lose all track of the time.

"And the children. There were times, especially as they got older, when they seemed to have conflicting feelings about their father. They wouldn't pay that much attention to whether he was around or not. And I couldn't stand to see that because it hurt Bill so much. And that hurt me.

"So, it reached the point where we had a big fight one day. The kids, my daughter especially, still bring this up every once in a while. We don't have fights like that often and this one was a biggie. A screaming and yelling fight and slamming doors. I finally went into the shower because I had to go out; he left the house too and he slammed the door so hard, the house shook.

"He got in the car and he told me he didn't know where he was going to go. But he got right back out and went into the basement while I was in the shower. Then I went down and we talked.

"I really wouldn't like my son to become a cop. No way. Because now the job is even more dangerous than it was. And if my daughter, Christine, said that she wanted to marry a cop, I would have to sit her down and make her *really* understand what I went through, what she would be giving up.

"I used to have this recurring nightmare—that I kept missing an airplane. We were all supposed to be going on a trip somewhere, in this fantasy. Every night I would dream that Bill and the kids would get on the airplane in time, but I always missed it. And as it was taking off down the runway, I was yelling at the people in the airport to stop the plane—*stop it*! But they never did and I'd never make it."

Nine

A *Dangerous Man* is one you can't predict. A man with a gun, that's not danger, that's everyday.

MOTHER'S MAXIM

THE TEAM, THE PIMP SQUAD

One of the main jobs of the Pimp Squad in the early 1970s was policing after-hours clubs and Times Square. That was how McCarthy broke in. It was the beginning of the upward crawl of commercial sex and pornography from its oozing underground black market to the economic big leagues when, eventually, even the hardest-core sexually explicit loop would become readily available in your friendly neighborhood suburban video store.

The six-man Pimp Team that McCarthy took over had a hard time accepting him at first. He was only twenty-seven when he started, loud and opinionated, and they were mostly older and wiser and even more cynical. The only thing they knew for certain about McCarthy, at first, was that he used to drive a tow truck. They were ready to gobble him up.

The two most experienced members of the team were John Gorman, a quiet, thoughtful cop who read hardcover books and who happened to have a brilliant career ahead of him in the police department, and Tony Vitaliano. Although both were barely into their thirties then, they were already highly regarded in Vice.

Through transfers and manpower problems, the makeup of the teams in Public Morals was constantly shifting. Half the time, the sergeants, who actually ran things, just kept swapping problem children back and forth.

Tony Vitaliano—Tony-the-V was the Pimp Team's best undercover man. He looked more like one of the bad guys than the bad guys did—silk suit, thin shoes, a tiny gold horn around his neck. And a gun.

Normally his voice rasped as though he'd just swallowed a whole mouthful of East River sediment—sand, gravel, and bald tires. The way Tony barked he could have been hiding polyps the size of walnuts in his voice box.

Tony Vitaliano understood the Life by instinct. He had been born to it—right parents, right neighborhood, right relatives back in Sicily. He was just a tough cop from the South Bronx—and all that you could ever hope for in an Italian gangster, East Harlem, through and through. McCarthy always told the backups who didn't know Tony how to recognize him: "The guy who looks the baddest, that's the cop." Tony couldn't drink worth a damn—two drinks and Tony was loaded, they'd have to carry him out—and that was a liability, an undercover who kept getting falling-down drunk, but in Tony's case, he was worth it.

After a job, he would come back to the roach-trap office at 137 Centre Street, just a short walk from the Tombs, and type a whole report without a mistake. Amazing. And he'd do it with a throbbing scotch headache.

JOHN GORMAN:

"McCarthy seemed to be personally offended by what he saw in Vice, in the Life. It gave him the extra impetus, and being a supervisor, he could then translate that down to the group of men who worked for him and they would, in turn, reflect his personality and his method of operation, and that's pretty standard in the police department. If you have someone who is apathetic and thinks things are okay as they are, you'll find his men will reflect that attitude, too. Under McCarthy, our team went out and turned up excellent cases. We did a real hard charge on things that other people thought were less than important: like the abuse of child prostitutes in the Times Square area. *No one* was working that then, except McCarthy's guys. The rest of the police department was very cold about it, almost matter-of-fact. So the kids were being exploited, so what? A whores's a whore, regardless of the age. So where's the crime?

"Not McCarthy. *That* issue, commercial pedophilia, became his crusade, and, in turn, our crusade too.

"He was a damn good cop, a damn good man. He pushed it because of his own personal convictions, because it really outraged him, while a lot of other people would just sweep it under the rug and not want to see it. The feeling then was that it was just one of those so-called victimless crimes, but McCarthy raised the consciousness of the entire NYPD. And he received very little credit for it."

John Scarpa—Short, pudgy, not at all imposing; he couldn't do a sit-up. Seemed more like an insurance man than a cop. He already had the hollow look of burnout. But McCarthy had run into Scarpa a few times before, at the police academy, and he liked him. On the surface he might have appeared to be an underachiever, but McCarthy suspected that Scarpa could do anything he had to do. His strength was in his even, unflappable calm.

As soon as Scarpa realized how straight the new sergeant was he began to call McCarthy "Zondarel," which meant "saint" or "savior" in Scarpa's Italian dialect. The nickname began as a put-down; it didn't stay that way.

Harold Schiffer—Known universally as a "Jew who could fight." He was a competent, impatient investigator, one of the top 10 percent in Brooklyn South Public Morals. He was also an army veteran and a Zionist, practically a Judeo-phile. Schiffer was given to somber suits and trench coats; he exuded the brazen confidence of an old-time private eye. The minute Schiffer walked into a room he could transform it into a set for some *film noir*.

After the army, Schiffer had traveled to Israel where he volunteered for one of the forwardmost *kibbutzim* in Palestinian territory. His first week there, he later told people, he saw more action than during his entire U.S. Army tour.

Schiffer was from a neighborhood known as Pig's Town in Brooklyn; a hundred years before they used to slaughter pigs in his backyard. But nobody joked about it to his face.

He had been brought up in a very Orthodox home, with a grandmother who spoke only Yiddish and parents who were deaf. He went to school while he was in the police department and McCarthy used to help him with his homework.

Schiffer had never seen anyone as driven as McCarthy. He was always giving someone on the team what Schiffer liked to call his Sermon on the Mount. But that was just McCarthy's way, Mother's way. He was the best cop Schiffer had ever seen, the craziest cop in New York when it came to right and wrong.

At a black pimp bar on Second Avenue, the team once jumped a car that looked out of place; two white men, both known gamblers. The car was stolen and there were drugs inside.

While they were booking the prisoners one of the men from the car—a fresh hood with mob connections—happened to notice the name of the arresting officer, "Schiffer."

"What kind of name is Schiffer?" the gambler demanded. "You're a fucking Jew, aren't you? You're a Jew? I know why you're doing this. I probably stole your lunch money in the schoolyard. You mocky."

Schiffer, normally a pro, lost it that time. He blew up; the other cops had to drag him out of the station. He had taken his gun belt off and was ready to take the prisoner outside and fight him, one on one.

But no one was allowed to brutalize prisoners on McCarthy's team—whether they deserved it or not. It took some doing, but they finally calmed Harold down. But no one could ever forget the rage in his eyes.

About two months later, the gambler who had taunted Schiffer was shot to death, assassination-style, as he walked out of a restaurant called Separate Tables. The murder was never solved.

Schiffer, of course, had absolutely nothing to do with the hit, but the team always joked about it darkly; no one ever wanted to see Harold that mad again.

Mike Sullivan—Had a face and manner that made people think of Mugsy Maginnis from the old *Our Gang* comedies. A central casting New York detective. Small, ruddy-faced, hot-tempered and with a potbelly and bent nose that looked as though it had been broken at birth, Sullivan was known as *"Camarón"* in the Puerto Rican bars. That was the Hispanic slang for "shrimp"; all the Irish cops had soft pink skin that looked like a shrimp's.

Sullivan had been a high school math teacher before becoming a cop and that had made him immediately suspect in the anti-intellectual NYPD. But McCarthy liked him because Sullivan could take a punch. He turned out to be the back-down-from-nobody alley fighter that the team needed.

McCarthy had inherited both Schiffer and Sullivan from the Porno Team in Public Morals. That was a parallel unit within Vice that had a considerably higher profile within the department.

Schiffer had also come in under Captain Gussman, the man who had handpicked McCarthy for the Pimp job. Since both Gussman and Schiffer were smart, straight Jewish cops, and because the NYPD had traditionally been a virtual extension of the Archdiocese of New York, Schiffer had taken a bad rap, early on, from his Irish and Italian Catholic brother officers who frequently hated Jews as a reflexive carryover of their own upbringing. Schiffer was suspect as the captain's mole, or "field associate"—the term for departmental spies right after Knapp.

Following a run-in with his supervisor on Mulberry Street, in Little Italy, after a botched mob surveillance, Schiffer had been forthwith exiled to McCarthy's Pimp Squad with this admonition from his previous commander: "The Jew bastard captain tried to put a fucking Jew on my team—now he's your problem, McCarthy."

Tough Mike Sullivan had been the victim of a similar clash with a boss. Sullivan had refused to back down. That was it for him. Both turned out to be two of the best detectives McCarthy could have asked for.

"When I walked into the Squad, the lieutenant there was a drunk. He used to drink with another guy on my team, Billy Webster. They'd pay for the booze on Webster's expense account—three hundred dollars a month as the chief intelligence gatherer for the team, which was a fortune in those days—and they always went to the same joint on Forty-seventh Street. It was all a scam. The only intelligence they gathered was from each other.

"Webster was a pretty bad guy from the Middle-West; I guess now you'd call him a white supremacist. He wore cowboy boots, carried a gun that looked like a cannon, and had dedicated himself to saving the NYPD from the Jews.

"Those two hooked up with another cop who had come on about the same time I did—and he was just as bad. Everything was a conspiracy with him. He imagined that somebody was always trying to stop him from doing the big case or preventing him from making the big arrest. The other two idiots convinced him that it had to be the Jews. So they automatically hated Schiffer and Gussman and they hated me more because I was in on it with the Jews. And, believe it or not, these weren't bad cops. They were very capable. But from day one, they did not want me there.

"Cops love to intimidate each other and these guys were prime examples of that. But it never worked with me.

"I had five fights with other cops and three were with bosses. Every one of them was a coward, a bully who was getting by because no one ever tested him. They got by on rank.

"There was one cop who used to cock his gun and chase a Jewish rookie I worked with around the locker room, for no other reason than the fact that he happened to be a Jew. That made me sick, it made me angry.

"I told this asshole to stop doing that and leave the Jewish kid alone. But he kept on doing it. So I grabbed his hand with the cocked gun, and I stuck the barrel in my mouth and I said, 'I'm gonna get you locked up for murder, you asshole.' That was such a shock that he backed down right away.

"I could see that my new assignment in Vice meant working with that kind of cop again. I had to take a stand right from the beginning.

"After my first month, Webster's expense account went from three-sixty down to forty-eight dollars. So he begins badmouthing me. I was no good; I would never work out; I was too educated; I didn't know how to talk to people, street people; I was a Jew-lover like Gussman. And they threatened to keep all the informants away from me.

"But that didn't scare me because I knew they were liars and drunks on top of that. And I knew their confidential informants were all a smoke screen for the boozing."

One night when he was in the Centre Street office by himself, shortly after McCarthy had started with the Pimp Team, one of those informants called in.

Immediately, he realized that he would have to win her confidence and put her at ease—all on the telephone, stranger to stranger.

She said she was a prostitute and so was her sister. He must have kept the line open for two hours, squeezing out every droplet of intelligence that he could gather, cajoling them, sweet-talking them, getting the message across that he wasn't a cop on the dark side.

What McCarthy didn't realize at the time was that Chief Paul Delise, Saint Paul, Frank Serpico's old comrade, had *also* been secretly listening in—trying to see what the new sergeant was made of. It was just one among the many games that were being played after Knapp.

As soon as McCarthy ended his conversation with the whore and finally started to put the phone down, another voice mysteriously came on the line—Delise's voice—and he said to McCarthy, "Sergeant, I want to speak to you after you have finished."

Delise had locked himself in the Public Morals office, in a room that they all thought was empty, and had remained in there from six o'clock in the evening until McCarthy had showed up at eight-thirty. He had been sitting in there in the dark, waiting for the Pimp Squad to come in, then he would begin eavesdropping, monitoring their phone calls searching for one honest cop.

Later, Delise, who was a very powerful presence at that juncture, said that he had been really impressed with the way McCarthy had handled the informant.

Then, like a spook, Delise simply left, disappeared into the night. No further explanations, no hint of his real purpose for being there.

For two weeks after that, everywhere McCarthy went he was convinced that Saint Paul was still following him.

Ten

The only way to survive in the police department is
to be anonymous, because if they can point you out
for some reason, then they can attack you. Cops
operate out of fear and jeopardy. In the police
department, *Power* is based on rank, not
intelligence.

MOTHER'S MAXIM

Two weeks into the Pimp Squad, the lieutenant who hated
him encountered McCarthy on a Friday night and told
him to go out with John Scarpa and "have a quiet night."
He was the untested sergeant and Scarpa was another
cop the lieutenant didn't like or consider a heavy hitter.
Already, McCarthy was being frozen out and he knew it.

"We were like the lowlifes of his team—McCarthy and
Scarpa. In police talk, 'Have a quiet night' means 'Don't
do nothing.' So, okay, I'm not gonna do anything. But
now, they have me mad.

"I knew that Vice had been after this one particular
pedophile for something like a year. But they hadn't done
anything with him. At the time, he was probably the
biggest—by that I mean the most active, the most visible—pedo in New York. His street name was Peter Big
and he *was* big, huge, maybe six feet five and three
hundred pounds. Thick glasses. If you wanted to make a

cartoon of the typical pedo, the dirty old slobbering monster, this was your boy. But Peter Big had managed to get his cases wired every time the police had even come close. He was a Manhattan millionaire and appeared to be a legitimate businessman who ran his family's import/export company.

"It was time for me to try to make my bones with these cops if I was ever going to be able to get them to work for me.

"I take Scarpa with me and we go over to the old French Hospital on Thirtieth Street, between Eighth and Ninth Avenues. Peter Big was in the building right next to it. Very sedate, with gray granite and dark awnings and a wrought-iron railing outside. The place was still pre-war Manhattan.

"We observe all these kids trafficking into this apartment house. I see which bell they're ringing—sixth floor. The apartment is in the name of a Chinese doctor, but it's really Peter Big's place. This Chinese quack is a Dr. Feelgood for the Upper East Side beautiful people. He was like their private narcotics connection. Pills and all sorts of other prescription drugs. This was just a sample of the intelligence they had on these people, but guess what? No arrests had been made.

"Whenever this Dr. Feelgood makes a house call, somebody usually sends a limo or a private jet to pick him up. Peter Big had managed to nose his way into this circle because quite a few of the notables in it had the same sexual preferences as Mr. Big. So he actually pimped for them, too.

"The way it worked was, if you wanted him to import some rare silk for you, antiques, something like that, he could handle it. But, if you wanted a matched set of ten-year-olds, boys, who could speak no English, that was possible too. Feelgood made the introductions and cleaned up the messes.

90

"For whatever reason, the feds had ignored his activities despite the fact that much of it was interstate and offshore and should have, therefore, fallen within their jurisdiction. But that was an old story with them. The word was that somebody as high up as Washington, D.C., was a link in Peter Big's daisy chain, but we never knew for sure. That could have been nothing more than loose cop talk, but somebody had certainly enabled this pedo to live a charmed life.

"Collectively, the cops in Vice had developed a personal grudge against this pervert. He embarrassed them and kept reminding them that, as cops, minus any real political juice, they could only enforce the law up to a point.

"That night, during our surveillance, six kids come out together and they get in a car. John Scarpa turns around and says to me, 'Mr. Big is open for business.'

"I waited for the car to turn around the corner, then I said to Scarpa, 'Let's jump the car.' He looks at me like I just said, 'Let's set ourselves on fire.'

"With these cops, in that squad, where no one was ever around to take charge, this was revolutionary. Scarpa really gets excited; he's ready to charge. All of a sudden, he's out with a sergeant who wants to act like a cop, too. I don't care who he is, a cop gets revved up by that.

"We hit the siren, put the light out on top and cut in front of the kids in the car on Eighth Avenue.

"I jumped out and started lining people up against the car. Scarpa thinks he's in heaven. This is the real thing; we're acting like real cops.

"The car turned out to be hot—thank God, because I had no reason whatsoever to pull it over—and we lock up the six kids. Ordinarily, that would have been the end of it.

"But we take them all to the station house and start to question them. All six admitted that Peter Big had done blow-jobs on them. The oldest kid was thirteen. They're all between nine and thirteen. Now, I have the witnesses and the crime. Peter Big is going down.

"We go right back to the French Hospital neighborhood, just in time to see another kid going in. He takes the elevator. Scarpa stays downstairs and covers the exits while I run up the stairs and I hit the sixth floor just as the kid's getting off the elevator.

"I hid in the stairwell and waited. As soon as Peter Big opened the door to let the kid in, I was right behind them.

"The apartment looked like an Oriental bordello. There were these soft red lights in lamps with gold fringe. Expensive antiques everywhere.

"Peter Big sort of cowered, then just sat down on a divan and glared at me. He had on a long dressing gown and silk pajamas. Big, fat, soft hands, like velvet. He had the softest hands I ever touched. He didn't protest, just sort of simmered. But the expression on his face said it all: Let's just get this out of the way so I can get back to business. He would come downtown with me, make his phone call and get the pinch blown out.

"There were two more kids in there, in his bedroom. One was half naked and the other one had part of his shirt off, like he was getting comfortable. Just little kids, but ghost-eyed little kids. They took it all in stride, too. Neither one even made eye contact with me. When I first went in, I actually think they figured I was there for some action too. Just another customer. That's how casual it all was.

"Peter Big had his satin pillows all fluffed up at the head of his bed, the spread was turned down; the night table had a single candle burning on it and there were these little porcelain jars, just exquisite, with creams and lubricants in them. The whole room smelled so sweet I almost vomited.

"I locked him up, took him downtown. Then, I got a

search warrant and came back to the apartment. We looked around and came up with 295 pills and a gun. Now, it's turning out to be a nice pinch. The pills could tie in the doctor, too. That could lead us to the rest of the pedo ring.

"I had separated the six original kids and questioned them; each kid described the sexual act that had occurred individually with Big. I would be able to prove that each one had been sexually abused because I could describe with such specificness the sexual act: Peter Big blowing the kid, taking the semen, spitting it into the kid's belly button, then licking it around on his stomach to make it look like a glazed donut. That was his thing. Later, we found out that he would use a razor to carve the kids' thighs with X's and other marks. He was a sadist and was actually much more dangerous than we thought. The gun, for example, came as a complete shock.

"Peter Big had been collared before and was very slick. He had never allowed one kid to witness him having sex with another kid; that way no corroborating witness could testify against him. Plus, he knew the cops would lay off.

"This time, however, I got him good.

"The next morning, I check in with the stolen car, nine sex collars, all corroborated, a gun, and 295 pills. And Peter Big was the guy they had been working on and allegedly couldn't get. I guessed going in that I had just absolutely ruined somebody's day.

"The lieutenant gets me aside and lays into me. He was so mad he couldn't even get his breath. All he kept yelling was, 'Do you realize what you've done? Do you know how this is going to look?'

"What I didn't find out until years later was just how badly I had humiliated him. There I was, supposed to be this young whippersnapper, supposedly the youngest sergeant in the police department at the time; I knew nothing about plainclothes, and I had already been tagged as some kind of Honest John freak, a Knapp Commission guy all the way, who didn't belong *anywhere* in New York, and especially not in Vice. Yet me and Scarpa— the two lowlifes—had taken out this guy and had shown up the hotshot detectives.

"From that night on, the other Vice cops thought I might be worth listening to."

But McCarthy soon realized that there were no final victories in Vice.

The night after he arrested Peter Big, he drove past the old French Hospital again. It was just past midnight. The pedophile had already been released on bail. McCarthy watched as Peter Big, who appeared to be just getting home for the night, came hurrying out of the building's underground garage. The pedo's zipper was open and his pants looked disheveled. McCarthy knew instantly that he had been someplace else with some other kid.

In the police department of McCarthy's early days as a Pimp Squad sergeant, a boss was not supposed to get involved in the action. That was why his direct involvement in the Peter Big case proved to be so eye-opening. Making arrests meant going to court, and if he was in court, then he couldn't be back at Vice directing the team. And every single team was decidedly sergeant-driven.

If one of the team members made a good collar and then had to go to court, though, that still left five men plus the sergeant. Nothing made McCarthy rebel more than this fuzzy concept since it denied any boss a meaningful leadership role. But that was the antiquated system that had evolved. Few bosses questioned it because it allowed them to avoid most of the danger, much of the work, and it always provided a scapegoat—the detective—for collars that went bad. But McCarthy just couldn't accept it. Almost immediately, and certainly following the Peter Big case, he developed a reputation as a sergeant who *would* get involved, no matter what.

Peter Big did allow McCarthy to make his bones, not just with the cops, but with the people on the street, too. One of the first vice operators to really check him out was an old madam known as Miss Cindy. She had *heard* what this new cop was made of, but she still had to *see* for herself.

At that time, "Miss Cindy" was believed to be the proprietress of the largest whorehouse in New York. She was Italian and connected. All five mob Families had used her girls. She paid off no one, surviving instead solely on the considerable strength of the services her young ladies rendered. No one, including Sydney Biddle Barrows, the Mayflower Madam who would later set herself up as direct competition for Miss Cindy, had developed a more impressive clientele.

McCarthy was introduced to her on the corner of Sixth Avenue and Fifty-seventh Street in midtown; she was cautious and afraid of wiretaps. That first meeting with her had to be open-air.

McCarthy pulled up in an unmarked car, parked, but didn't get out.

The old woman, dressed like any one of a hundred other New York dowagers out for a late afternoon stroll, approached McCarthy cautiously. She stared at him, appraising him as though he were one of her new girls. As she leaned against the door of his car and started talking to him, he felt himself tighten uneasily. McCarthy had to listen hard, there was traffic and street noises and no possible way to record anything that she was telling him. But that wasn't really his intention today; today he was courting her, like a kid standing inspection by his first date's mother.

Neither was what the other expected. McCarthy was surprised by how elderly she appeared, how frail, how thoroughly used up. Whoremongering was a brutal business, he couldn't understand how an old girl like this could survive. But she had—which meant that he still had a lot to learn.

For her part, Miss Cindy was more than a little put off. She'd heard stories and, frankly, this young sergeant didn't look as intimidating as she thought he would. Or should.

"The key person in any of these vice operations was the manager or madam. They functioned as the foreman. If a girl could only do fifteen or twenty guys a day before she broke down completely, the madam would try to push her into doing twenty-five. It was just piecework to them. What's another five johns? Another five dicks?

"I wanted to get her working for me because I knew she had broken in half of the most expensive hookers in the city. At that point, Vice was involved with the murder case of one of the guys targeted by the Knapp Commission. I had been ordered to try and find one particular prostitute whom this guy had arrested ten years earlier and who might have valuable information.

"I went from one madam to another until I was finally referred to Miss Cindy."

Still evaluating McCarthy, Miss Cindy told him about a girl who worked for her. The girl had run into some bad trouble with a pimp, Karate Jim; he'd beaten her up, put her in the hospital, ruined her looks and her earning power.

At no point did the old lady show the slightest compassion for the injured hooker. This was a business disagreement and a valuable piece of her property had just been practically destroyed. One of her busiest whorehouses was known as the Factory. The name fit, too.

Now, what was the new kid from the Pimp Squad going to do about her suddenly damaged goods? Her hands on her hips, her face twisted into a rouged question mark, Miss Cindy waited for an answer.

McCarthy felt all of his instincts pulling him back to the elimination basketball games at the Maguires' school-yard in Rockaway. Miss Cindy had winged a ball straight for *his* face, and now she was watching for him to flinch. Miss Cindy didn't give a damn about the law, about judges or the courts. All she was interested in was swift, certain street justice. Would McCarthy be man enough to handle that?

"I told her to tell the girl to get in touch with me as soon as she was able. I was going to lock up Karate Jim the minute I laid eyes on him.

" 'No,' she says, 'he's bad.'

"I knew I had to send out a message right here.

"You tell him I want to meet him. He's supposed to be a karate expert. Well, so am I. And I want him. I want him bad.

"I actually happened to be taking karate lessons at that time. I knew I wasn't any good at it, but I could talk my way out of anything.

"Then, I jumped out of the car—she thought I was going after her—and I did a vicious side-kick right there on Fifty-seventh Street in the middle of traffic, really snapped out a kick.

"I said to her, 'You tell him that's what I'm gonna do to him.' I couldn't sense if she was impressed or not. But I wasn't about to vacillate; she had to know—and then had to spread the word—that I was prepared to carry through with exactly what I said I would do.

"Two hours later, I go down to a pimp bar where I

think I might find this Karate Jim. And I have to admit, I'm a little shaky myself. I figured it would be a fight, but, win or lose, at least I could get it over with.

"I go into the place, it's already smoking. The word had gotten out that this crazy sergeant from the Pimp Squad was out to get Karate Jim—*this psycho is a trained killer*, that's what they were saying already.

"At least I had one question answered. I guess I did impress Miss Cindy.

"In the bar now they're coming up to me: 'I understand you're looking for Jim; he ain't here, we heard he left town; Jim don't want to die, man.' All this stuff.

"I figure I'm nuts not to roll with it. I say, 'Yeah, you tell Jim I'm gonna kick his pimp ass. No pimp is safe touching a woman in New York. That's my job. Every working girl out there is *mine* now. This is my turf now. Anybody beats on another whore, I beat on him. Jim *insulted* me.'

"I'm coming on with all this macho act. And believe me, it *was* an act. Nobody's even challenging me; why not?

"So what happens? The guy actually *does* leave town. I find that out the very next day. And remember, I have never so much as *seen* this Karate Jim.

"Then, a week later, the story gets even bigger. They got me having *killed* this Karate Jim; that's why he's not around anymore. I'm bad. And what had I actually done? I had jumped out on Fifty-seventh Street in front of some old madam and kicked at the air. That was it. But that was also enough.

"I learned a valuable lesson. You have to convince them that you are crazier than they are. That's how you get away with it. Then, you just wait for the results to come in.

"The Karate Jim thing took off. Even with the cops. They were no different from the people in the pimp bar. Somebody repeated a story and they believed it. Then the cops would pass it on with *their* embellishment.

"A little while after that I actually did have to go and serve a subpoena on this black guy who owned a karate studio. Obviously, he *was* the real thing.

"It's nighttime and I go in; the whole studio is just lit with candles. Creepy.

"I look around. Don't see anything, don't hear anything. Then, all of a sudden, they start to drop out of the ceiling on me. And these guys *were* karate experts. They jumped all around me in the candlelight. They all must have been perched up on the rafters like cats on shelves.

"They really came at me. All this kung fu stuff. I'm just swinging back, like in a barroom brawl. This is one of the worst fights I've ever seen and I'm in the middle of it.

"At my karate school, as an exercise, they used to turn out all the lights and beat you with a bamboo stick. That was a normal part of the training. But it was just in school.

"This was the first time I ever had to try it for real. So I just started kicking back and screaming out all the words I knew in Japanese from class. I had to make them think I knew a lot more about this than they did.

"And it worked. *Again*. Another bluff. They backed down and I finally got them under control. I even served the papers. If only they knew.

"I go back to the station and the story's like a miniseries by now: *Did you hear what McCarthy did this time? He took out a whole karate school.*

"After that, when I'd have trouble in a bar, and a guy would want to fight me, I'd get this crazy look on my face and start to scream and punch myself, I'd slam myself right in the head: YOU WANNA FIGHT ME? YOU WANT TO? COME ON, COME ON! LET'S GO!

"And he wouldn't want to fight anymore. That's theater. But I really did punch myself. 'I'm ready. I'm willing to go. No problem. I'm ready.' Then, I'd calm down and say, 'Hey, I feel like somebody just punched me.'

"I wanted to get to the point where I could just turn on the switch. And I worked at it. I'm a guy who *practiced* going nuts. I became deliberate as hell about it.

"In the meantime, I'm winning over Miss Cindy. I found out that she thought she was getting arrested. Now, you would have thought this old girl was somebody's grandmother. Her apartment was full of plants. She'd just walk around in there in these very expensive dressing gowns, watering her plants all day. But in the back of her head, she's worried about doing hard time. A woman in her seventies, at least.

"All the time I'm still trying to get her to put me in touch with the prostitute from ten years ago who figured in the murder investigation.

"The next time I see her, Miss Cindy is in a restaurant on Fourteenth Street, on the East Side, Irving Place. She's eating truffles. And hyperventilating. Something really had her agitated.

"Now she was a true organized crime madam, as opposed to a phony who only claimed to be protected by somebody high up. The wiseguys loved her stable. It seemed like nobody of any consequence could get laid in New York unless Miss Cindy had a piece of the action. That went right from the political big shots all the way down to a social club in Brooklyn.

"She was sharp, too. For a long, long time she had never even taken a collar.

"At that time there were only three Chinese cops in the police department. She knew them all by sight. Now, she also happened to have one of her houses that catered to Asian clients exclusively, mostly Chinese. Because she knew the three Asian cops they could never get near the place. So it was practically impossible to bust her for that house.

"She wanted another favor. She had a partner with whom she had had a falling out. The partner managed the Chinese house. But the partner was sloppy; she would allow Caucasians to come in when she was on the door. That was her beef. The partner wasn't careful enough. Sooner or later, she was afraid that the partner would allow a Caucasian cop to come in and that would be it.

"I was supposed to go in as a customer and arrest the partner for running a house of prostitution. Take her out of the picture. Sort of a preemptive strike. In return, I would get what I wanted from Miss Cindy. She never attempted to bribe me; it was strictly on the basis of exchanging information.

"I got that cleared with Vice, went in with a couple guys and made the pinch. It was quite a scene. All these Chinese guys were running around half-dressed, diving under beds, crying, and the girls were naked, pulling the covers up over themselves; everybody's yelling in Chinese. And over in the corner there's a television on; I think it was a kung fu movie.

"It didn't take long for Miss Cindy to deliver. She came up with the prostitute we wanted from ten years back and Homicide was able to question her about the murder of a plainclothes cop who had figured prominently in the investigations undertaken by the Knapp Commission. That hooker turned out to be one of our most reliable sources. You just can't have too many people from the Life who are willing to talk to you."

Miss Cindy became one of McCarthy's best introductions into the glamorous side of vice, the "high-priced spreads," as they called the expensive hookers. One of the most useful things that he picked up from her, and from her Chinese connections, was a sense of just how specialized the whorehouses could be. The variations— in terms of sexual services offered or the kinds of women employed or the ethnic groups and tastes that were catered to—led to just the sort of intelligence that he was hoping to find.

Eleven

The average *Prostitute*, if you were to strip her naked, is bruised, abused, her plumbing leaks, and her underwear is stained. It would be like screwing a jar of pus. And you shouldn't screw what you wouldn't kiss.

MOTHER'S MAXIM

On a good night, the Pimp team would hit four or five pimp bars and "visit" three or four after-hours clubs.

Often, they doubled as warrant-servers for the Porno Squad, working the day shift, crashing peep shows, live sex emporiums, and adult bookstores. They would count on three collars at each spot—the two guys working the floor and the one guy "on the stick," at the door.

Following the pimps took McCarthy's men to the kinds of bars, the after-hours clubs, where you could still buy a drink past four in the morning. The clubs were open everywhere—midtown, Chinatown, Little Italy, wherever there was sex or gambling.

In appearance, they could be anything from plush to pedestrian, from dignified old supper rooms to degenerate dives. No one, including the Vice cops, could ever spot the after-hours clubs from the outside. The owners went out of their way to make sure that every building facade or location retained that run-down New York look. However, once you were inside, you usually had to go up in an elevator, or down into the basement or through a front operation into the back room. There was always some kind of improvised fortification, like a steel door, and frequently, a Pete-sent-me porthole.

One of McCarthy's search warrants was aimed at locating a pimp who was a suspect in a murder case. The team had to execute the warrant at a dingy club on Spring Street.

It was a deserted, industrial neighborhood where the manufacturing had left decades before; mostly tall, vacant loft buildings and ancient loading docks pimpled by bunches of half tires where the trailer-trucks backed up to the freight entrances. There was a slaughterhouse nearby. In the daytime, from two blocks away, you could see the blood running scarlet along the pavements, puddling in the curbs, smeared on the workers' long white coats, caked on anything you could touch.

The after-hours pimp bar was on the second floor above a dive that was open to the public. The whole block was owned by a businessman who rented almost exclusively to the mob.

The entrance to the upstairs after-hours club was protected by double steel doors. The setup was practically a prototype of how to run an illegal gin mill.

A vestibule fortress resembled the bailey of a medieval castle—as soon as you took down one iron-grated gate, another, with the two steel doors, confronted you. The defenses were designed to trap raiders, cops, between the two gates. But McCarthy and his men had to get inside.

''They called the doorman the 'manager,' but he was just an ape. All muscle, mean as hell. Sometimes, you could just bluff these big, dumb guys. But not this one. He was blocking our path. Since I was still in the early process of making points with the troops, I had to take the lead. Normally, I went in as the 'sledgeman,' the guy who swung the heavy hammer. But with steel doors like this place had, all the sledge would do is bounce off, right back in your face.

"We had to come on like *The Untouchables*. I got through the first gate, squeezed in, pried it apart. My men are right behind me, but if you can picture this, they're all still on the *other* side. They can touch me through the grating, but they can't help me.

"I'm in there, between the two gates, just me and this monster—and he's bearing down on me, swinging a baseball bat, a real Louisville Slugger.

"I made a move to dive for his stomach and tackle him, but he made a better move, swerved, slammed me into the second steel gate; I was pinned.

"All at once I see him cock his bat over his shoulder like he's into his home-run swing. My head is the ball. My cops are behind me, trying to push through. But it just isn't working. And they're begging me to let them shoot this ape, crying like little kids. They all have their guns out; I'm the supervisor. I have to tell them to shoot.

"I go down into a crouch and use one arm to shield my head. Just as he swings, the bat kind of slides off my arm, just misses the elbow. If he'd planted himself a little better, he'd have crippled me.

"As he's coming out of his swing, I hooked his legs with my feet and kicked like hell. He fell down and I landed on top of him. The amazing part is, I'm still clutching the warrant. I took that piece of paper and shoved it right down his throat.

"Then, my cops come in."

While they were rolling around on the floor, the warrant was torn and became covered with blood. But the blood *wasn't* McCarthy's. He'd won—and no one had been shot. That became one more important moment in his long struggle to win his team's respect.

Through raid after raid, case after case, McCarthy was getting a riveting indoctrination into the Life. As he interrogated the johns and the other assorted repeat customers in the Vice underground, the consumers in the Life, he confiscated an impressive collection of both government and corporate IDs, credentials that had been issued by some of the Fortune 500 companies, places like Gulf + Western, Time Inc., most of the leading investment banks and brokerage houses on Wall Street, just about all of the big law firms.

At first, he thought that the Life appealed mainly to highrolling associates of organized crime, but those wanna-be gangsters were just one faction, an important one but a small one, especially compared to the men and women in the Life who carried cards from all the right clubs and all the most expensive addresses.

The johns McCarthy arrested came from every imaginable profession: lawyers, teachers, judges, businessmen, rabbis, priests, even an occasional bishop. He traced one prominent pedophile to the main offices of the Archdiocese of New York. No one was immune from the compulsion of commercial, dangerous, and degraded sex.

The Life was reemerging after having been driven underground for better than a decade. The city itself was in a rebirth, reestablishing its place as the capital of the world. Real estate, commerce, political undercurrents, even crime were all on the upswing.

Nightlife in Manhattan was just coming back then, in the early 1970s. Joe Namath and the big sports celebrities probably started the rejuvenation of New York's club scene with places like Bachelors III—at least as far as the Vice cops were concerned.

The people in the Life pass through; clubs and bars change their names and their particular franchises, the details and the circumstances and the lewd minutiae of Vice have to be redefined for every generation, but the appetite itself, the craving and the inclination, remains a constant.

"When you run with that pack every night, begin at midnight, wear out by four or five o'clock, you burn out fast, become jaded. That trendy little club on the East Side that you couldn't wait to get to after work gets old fast. So you start looking for someplace new. Maybe a little wilder, a little cruder, a little more on the edge.

"Maybe just getting laid isn't god enough anymore. That's too tame. So you decide to go out and *pay* for it, make it a cash deal so that the girl becomes your property for those few minutes. She has to do anything you tell her to do. She's a woman who's different from anybody you've known before. Sex with her is the most risky, most exciting thing you've ever dreamed of. She's a whore. A hooker. A piece of meat that you went out and bought on the street. You can't get that back home. Not that edge.

"And, if you work in town, in Manhattan, that edge is no further away than the friendly neighborhood hooker on Seventh Avenue. The more wasted you become, the better she looks. And she might take you to a pimp bar that serves complimentary cocaine instead of matchbooks.

"It's exactly the same principle as drugs. You figure that your last high will never be as good as your next high. So you keep upping the ante. And you get drawn in, sucked in, a little further and further. It's gradual. But it's also cumulative, addictive. Maybe you don't even notice it. Then, bang, you've crossed the line without even realizing it.

"You're hooked: You can't make it through the day without some kind of fix—sex or cocaine or for people like me, like cops, danger.

"Believe me, I understand that kind of compulsive personality because I happen to be one.

"Plus, there is that intoxicating element of real danger. The pimps carry guns and knives; the whores are sexy-tough, little hustlers; and there are so many other kinds of characters around. In the Life you rub shoulders—and other body parts—with the kind of people you only ever see in the movies. Especially the women. That's what keeps drawing people to vice, people who should know better.

"I've seen a guy go into a porno store, look at a movie—a white male in his thirties, in a three-hundred-dollar suit, wearing a London Fog—right across from City Hall Park in the middle of New York. Then he comes out, drops his attaché case and starts masturbating right in public, jerking off, not even in a booth.

"I used to go into those places, the porno stores, with a search warrant, and the customer would be inside a peep show booth pleading, 'Please, officer, please, officer, just wait another minute, I'm not finished yet.' He'd be jerking off in there. 'Please, please let me finish.' Even his getting arrested had to wait."

No one was allowed to belittle a hooker around McCarthy. The days of the Pimp Team treating the hookers as disrespectfully as the pimps themselves ended. Plenty of old-time Vice cops didn't appreciate this approach, but McCarthy wasn't running for office. He sought results and was convinced that his methodology would succeed.

Eventually, as his own educational pursuits progressed, he even came up with the idea of developing personality inventories to test the women his men arrested. That began as an academic experiment, field research for McCarthy's master's thesis, but it soon became still another innovative intelligence-gathering tool.

"I became very comfortable in Vice. It's like being a good fly fisherman. I knew where to go in the pond to catch the biggest fish and I knew *how* to catch them. It became a matter of knowing how to troll the line.

"And all this information that I was getting, I was trying to make sense of it, use it, formulate it, allow it to determine my moves and my team's moves three, four weeks in advance. That was the only way to beat the people on the street, in the Life. Forget about outhustling them; they were and are and probably always will be the masters. All you could do was try to outplan them.

"As far as being in the Life went, if it happened in New York, the whores knew about it and if they knew about it, I could find it out.

"One thing I found out all about was sexual deviance. I understand it. I can predict it. I had this academic interest in psychology at the same time I was working in Vice. It was amazing how one pursuit fed into the other.

"I handed out my personality inventories to every whore I could find. Here I was, supposed to be a Pimp cop, but I was actually more interested in them as people—badly abused people. Cops being cops, they thought I was the craziest psycho in the world. And maybe I was. That kind of reputation was useful, too. I would do crazy things because I enjoyed that identity.

"I used to dance in all the black bars that we hit. When they had music on, I'd sing. The black guys would all be dancing too and I'd say, 'You call that dancing?' Then I'd show them my stuff. The pimps couldn't believe that a white guy could dance like I did, like a maniac. But I learned all those steps back at Power Memorial on the West Side. The whores would watch me and say, 'Man, you must fuck good.' And I'd just get this little smile on my face and nod my head really slowly. Any cop who says that Vice isn't one of the funniest, bawdiest, loosest places in the world to be, along with being one of the most depressing, of course, is full of it. Every night was a party.

"Then we would move in for a captive audience, literally. Within minutes we usually had every person in the place up against the bar railing with shotguns pointed at them. That was how we always took down a tough spot— scatterguns. And it was all a bluff. Only once in my entire police career was I anywhere near a shotgun that went off, and that turned out to be a big mistake.

"But the guys in the bars, of course, never knew any of that. They didn't know what to make of me."

Neither did most of the other policemen in Manhattan Vice. The one thing they were sure of was that McCarthy was the most uncoplike cop any of them had ever seen. He approached his job as a vocation; there was a decidedly priestly zeal—as well as rigidity—in his efforts to clean up vice in Manhattan and in his curiosity to discern how it had gotten so dirty in the first place. Telling "McCarthy stories," "Mother stories," became an insider's passion among the Vice detectives. Respect for his methods, which seemed odd at first, especially in the intellectually moribund NYPD, was painfully slow in coming. But it did come. After his first year in Vice, there were very few cops working that beat in New York who hadn't heard of "Mother."

"To make a collar we had to witness a sex act or sexual performance, or we had to be solicited for sex. And the rule was that we couldn't get naked or actually have sex with the girls. If you did, then it was all over. That was what always separated the real johns from the cops. But nobody who ever worked for me got in any trouble. If you ever touched a girl on me, even once, you were gone. I was Mother and I had to back it up every time.

"It took a cast-iron stomach to sit through some of those sex club acts. One of the more famous 'performers' used to be able get up on the stage, bend over, and stick a hot dog up her ass. Then she'd blow, shoot it out, and hit a guy in the third row.

"I used to have to send undercovers in there because all the hookers knew me. I used to coach the new cops: 'Don't sit in the last row. Don't sit in the last row.' They were all so afraid to sit in the last row, because she used to blow the guys in the last row. She'd come down off the stage and say, 'I'm gonna get all those gay little boys in the back.' There was no place to escape. That woman happens to be an upstanding Jesus freak today.

"As a cop, you were there to watch the performance, but in addition to watching the performance, you know that a prostitute's gonna come up and say 'I'll give you a blow-job for fifty dollars.'

"You're gonna lock her up for prostitution. You can say to the bartender, 'Look, is there some place I can get laid?' He says to you, 'Yeah, there's a girl back there.' That's the way it works. The cop is undercover from the outset. He can end up arresting the girl and the bartender. That's an easy collar.

"Our job was to get the evidence and get it safely and be able later to make accurate police reports and, if it ever got into court, testify. That was a lot of paperwork. We wasted hours and hours preparing cases that would proceed two steps beyond us and then get blown out, fixed. But it was all part of the game.

"The cops have a saying that the job is not on the level. That it's a game and you just play along. But the job can be on any level that you want it to be on. And, if it's only a game, then nobody should ever get hurt. Tell that to a dead cop."

110

The typical Times Square area whorehouse of the early 1970s was located in a dreary storefront, masquerading as a "massage parlor" or "dating service" or "escort bureau" or even a topless bar. Sometimes, there might be a peep show or X-rated theater or "adult bookstore" located on the ground floor. Without exception, though, real sex would be available upstairs or "in the back."

The interior of the storefront might consist of a sitting room—a few folding chairs with a table and Polaroid shots of the "hostesses." Behind that were the "session rooms"—dirty, bare-walled cubicles, equipped with little slabs of plywood, covered by foam rubber or paper or, in the more expensive places, sheets. And there would always be a plastic waste paper basket, filled with rolled-up pieces of tissue—with used condoms in the tissues. The women who accepted money for sex in these cubicles almost always had three things in common: They were young, battered-looking, and silent. That was the low end of sex-for-pay.

"The whores might be waiting out in the sitting rooms, lined up against the walls like kids at a dance. You'd come in and see them smoking or watching television or picking from some greasy bag of french fries. You walked in there and picked one out.

"Don't ask me what the attraction was. Maybe she looked like somebody you used to know, or you liked her tits or she happened to smile back at you. I've seen thousands of them, busted them, interviewed them, allowed them to cry on my shoulder; I even made some of them fill out surveys for my college papers if I happened to be doing something on prostitution. And I dearly love sex—but I never ran into a single one of them that even made me hard. Ninety percent or more of the attraction has to be inside your own head. Up close they are just sad, pathetic, exploited human beings.

"After you paid this old bitch, the madam, then you could rap with one of the girls for a few minutes and then, just about as fast as you could get your pants down, you'd be allowed to screw her for maybe nine minutes. Any longer and they'd ask you to pay for two sessions.

"Later, there were fancier places like Plato's Retreat, but that was one of a kind. By then, it was like a tourist shrine. The real whores didn't even work there. Another variation were the bathhouses. You might see a fountain and some running water in there, but it was still the same thing—cheap, hollow, depressing sex.

"There was one bar we used to hit that was a real hangout for Wall Street types. I don't think any of the johns in there had an income under a hundred thousand dollars, back when that was serious money. It was called the Wild West, over on Thirty-fifth Street. They liked to tell the customers they would 'give them a little heat.'

"As soon as you sat down at one of the tables, a girl would walk over and sort of straddle your lap. Then, while she's sitting on your lap, after a few minutes, you would get this warm rush on your thigh—'heat,' urine; that was their act. Water sports. The girl would piss all over you. That joint used to pack them in, believe me. The johns who didn't want to be pissed on knew enough not to sit down, because as soon as you did, you were asking for it.

"There was another whorehouse called The Episode, where each girl would do eighty tricks a day. After a week, you looked like you had ridden a horse from here to California. They were bowlegged. The better whores, however, all had some kind of a gimmick.

"The madams taught them—the trick is to get a guy so excited about anticipating sex that when you touch him, he goes off right away, explodes. That only took them thirty seconds. It meant less actual, physical exertion to the transaction. That's more efficient for them. Or, you try to do only oral sex. Less wear and tear.

"As the price goes up, the conditions change somewhat. A high-priced call girl is attractive, has some sense of society, can make a few sentences of conversation before the client pants like a dog and, most importantly, she can charge triple the price. But eventually, when her innocence and attractiveness start to diminish, she'll have to increase her sexual activity to make the same amount of money and that will accelerate her physical disintegration. Ultimately, even the whores who started out charging five-hundred dollars a night will arrive in the herd of the streetwalkers—those ambulating jars of pus.

"In Vice you learn that the definition of a whore is a person who takes green paper from white men and then gives them permission to spit on her—or him—with semen. That's what a prostitute is: a receptacle for white men's semen. Most johns are white, middle-aged men in business attire. It isn't always white men, of course, but most of the time they're white. And about half the time or more, the prostitutes aren't. The johns come from that class of buttoned-down suburban office workers. Sex is an irretractable compulsion with them. They are misinformed and naive, ignorant of the danger, of the jeopardy. But, believe it or not, AIDS hasn't even slowed it down that much.

"There are many different kinds of prostitutes, but regardless of how glamorous they appear to be, no matter how much they charge, no body is made to take that kind of work. You can't get laid twenty, thirty, thirty-five times a day. You just can't stand up to it.

"Every whore I ever arrested powdered her nose. You get rid of prostitutes by getting rid of cocaine. If there was no cocaine, you'd have no pimps. If you had no pimps, you'd have no whores. The cycle feeds on itself. This is basic: A woman or a man sells his or her body to get the money to afford the coke. That might sound facile, but it happens to be true.

"You deal with all sorts of drug addicts in Vice. Without a doubt, the saddest ones are the prostitutes. They're all losers. They end up trying to sell bodies that are covered with filthy scabs, blown-out junkies with sunken veins. I've seen people scratch their scabs and almost bore open holes into their arms.

"You pick up their tongue and underneath it will be lacerated with canker sores. They inject the dope under their tongues to try to clean up their arms when they have to go to their probation officer.

"In the gay bars—which were worse, more wide-open, more likely to feature sexual performances that involved most of the audience—you rarely had the stereotypical old hag madam. That's where they called them managers. Always men.

"The Beloved Disciple was a converted church in Lower Manhattan. You passed through the confessional booth, gave the password and proceeded down a flight of stairs—like descending into Hades. That passageway opened onto the dance floor of an after-hours club.

"At night, even outside, people walked around almost naked. They would wear cowboy's chaps and leather hats, but nothing else. Their asses and dicks were hanging out.

"In another place where we were trying to serve a warrant, I went in alone, undercover, in leather, and had my cops dressed up with electric suits and whips. But they never let them in.

"Gray leather was chic. If I wore that jacket, I could go anywhere. The club is packed. The only spot available at the bar is in front of the flap door that the bartender uses. I take up my position, intending to let the raiding party in later.

"Urine was the fetish here, too. Like a gay version of the Wild West club. The only way you could avoid getting urine in your drink was to order a can of beer. The guy next to me paid thirty-five dollars for a 'sports bourbon,' which is bourbon and urine, and he kept complaining that it was diluted. Too much bourbon.

"I'm sipping my beer. One of the other customers comes up and grabs me by my balls. He says, 'I'm bashful.'

" 'If you're bashful, I don't want to meet your brother.'

"Then, he spits in my ear and bites me on my ear lobe and rubs his hands all over my chest and says, 'Ooooh! I just got back from Caracas. I'm a steward with Pan Am. All these men. They're exhausting me.' He's rubbing his hands all over my chest. He now has my shirt out of my pants.

"I tell the guy, 'Listen, I'm waiting for my boyfriend and I really don't want him to make a scene. He's very jealous. I would love to meet you. Is it possible that I could meet you some other time? But if I'm seen with you now, there's gonna be a scene.'

"I stayed there for two hours by myself. I would say that I had my balls squeezed about eight times, guys trying to kiss me, spit on my neck, but I was able to psyche myself up to handle it. Most cops couldn't.

"They were all dropping down and blowing each other, but that wasn't the collar I was looking to make. So I left. Just another shift in Manhattan Vice.

"Before I left I had to use the bathroom. I knew that was going to be a mistake. But I had to go.

"I try to use the urinal and there's a guy sitting on it. I guess I stared. He says, 'What's the matter with you?' He wanted me to piss on him. There's a guy defecating in the toilet and another guy is standing over him, while the guy who is blowing him is getting screwed in the ass and there's three guys outside masturbating, watching.

"I left the bathroom in a big hurry.

"The majority of them were white; ninety-five percent had unbelievably muscular bodies. Big truck drivers, football players, S-and-M people. And a lot of them were ex-convicts because there's so much homosexuality in the prisons. They just get to like it. To them—and some of the ex-cons told me this—it was good sex without all the bullshit conversation you had to go through with a woman trying to get laid. They'll tell you that women are a pain in the ass. You gotta date them, feed them, and hope.

"I couldn't get over the anonymity of it. They don't even say hello or goodbye. They don't introduce themselves. A guy will blow you and you won't even get his name.

"All the bathrooms had glory holes. You could stick your dick through the wall and another guy on the other side would blow you. There's a hole in the wall of every toilet.

"The next week we arrive and we don't get in. So the next time we go in with a warrant. We get in then. But no dope or booze. The place has been sanitized.

"I take the manager in the back room and he says to me, very sweetly, 'Sergeant, you got your warrant signed on October 24, at 6:24 P.M. hours. Right? We knew all about it.'

"My warrant reads: October 24, 18:24 hours. It's the same date and time.

"You have ten days to execute that warrant from the minute that the judge signs it. Which meant that the manager or someone had access to the sealed court records. That's a very serious breach of police security.

"I tell him that I will pay him ten thousand dollars if he tells me who gave up the warrant. Who was the corrupt person who gave up the info about the warrant?

" 'Sergeant, you're making a big mistake if you think it's only one person.'

"He was right about that. We traced it down and there was a state senator, a district attorney, and a court officer involved. All of them were homosexuals who knew people connected to that club. I found that out unofficially. Couldn't make a single arrest.

"The Anvil kept a string of llamas downstairs; you could make it with the llama. They still do that.

"The main floor show was 'the master.' He was a giant black guy, I think he was an ex-pro football player, and all he wore was this big, metal-studded harness that looked like a heavyweight fighter's championship belt. The master started out by climbing a pole that was in the middle of the dance floor.

"He'd crack his penis against the studded belt until he had an orgasm. He did that every hour on the hour. Then, he'd look around the dance floor, select some lucky patron and put Crisco all over the guy's ass. Then the master would stick his hand up the guy's ass all the way to his elbow, and end it by picking the guy up with one arm, walking him around the room, banging his head against the ceiling.

"Same show every night. People would line up, sticking money in the master's face, begging him to pick them.

"One night when we were there the master pulled his arm out of the guy's butt and his rectum prolapsed. It came right out on the master's arm. I thought I was witnessing a murder. But he survived. A week later that guy was back in the club, looking for the master."

Conventional cop wisdom still maintained that whores and their pimps were essentially free-lance operators. It denigrated both the job of the Pimp Squad and the value of any intelligence to be gathered there. McCarthy's team finally exploded those myths along with several others. Naturally, the people with vested interests in maintaining the old way of thinking, including corrupt cops and the pimps who paid them off, became furious with McCarthy; but they had to get in line.

The mob Families were also wondering what was happening as one after another of their most lucrative houses gave way to one of McCarthy's sledges.

Both inside and outside the department, questions were beginning to be asked. The underworld had been paying out top dollar, for years, to generations of cops who doubled and tripled their legitimate incomes by making sure that the sex clubs were left alone or "protected." But for some reason, the Vice team headed by McCarthy hadn't gotten the message.

Twelve

A *Corrupt Cop* is the most definable person in the whole world. The people in the Life know exactly what to expect from a corrupt cop. He has a standing invitation. Everybody wants to know him.

MOTHER'S MAXIM

On night around eight o'clock, just before McCarthy was getting ready to unlock the door at 137 Centre Street and report upstairs to Vice, he heard someone calling his name from the quiet darkness of a doorway near the side of the building.

He knew that the municipal offices would be practically deserted by that time of night, and the sidewalk behind him was nearly empty too. His gun was jammed into the small of his back, between the waistband of his dungarees and shirt; there was a lightweight jacket over that.

Before even acknowledging the voice, before looking in the direction from which it had come, McCarthy moved his arm and hand around under the jacket to get a grip on the handle of his .38 detective special. His team had been busting pimps nonstop the past few months, serving a record number of warrants, slowing down Vice business all over Manhattan and, in general, earning an unforgiving reputation in the Life. Sure as hell, he reasoned, somebody was here either to offer him a payoff or try to take him out for good. Either way it would be a problem. McCarthy was only in suspense about one thing—would it turn out to be another cop or a bad guy?

Then, the voice piped up again: "Sergeant McCarthy; Sergeant William McCarthy." He said it a little louder this time; there was traffic on the street and the noise from it was beginning to build.

Staring into the blackness, he waited. This was the nervous time. Suddenly, he was very scared.

"Captain Gussman wants me to talk to you." Then the voice reeled off both McCarthy's badge number and his confidential police ID number, a series of random digits meant for internal security use only.

He now knew that the voice had to belong to another policeman or to someone with access to the most sensitive files at One Police Plaza. So it appeared that another cop was approaching him after all. They had given him six months since the date of his appointment to Vice; now it would be time for McCarthy to take a stand or get on the pad. He was sure that the "reach" was about to be made.

"I want to see both hands first," McCarthy called back, as he carefully took his gun out from under the jacket.

Two large, pinkish hands appeared, slowly coming out of the shadows cast by the overhead street lights.

"That's fine, right there," McCarthy said. "Now, just hold them up. Come forward one step."

As the Vice cop moved in, he saw that the nails on each hand—big, fleshy masculine hands—were neatly manicured and buffed. Whoever it was, it didn't look as though he'd done any serious work in a very long time.

Just before beginning to frisk him, McCarthy pulled the man out into the uncertain light. He was tall, he had at least a head on McCarthy. Their eyes locked on one another. In that instant, McCarthy jumped back a full step. Focusing on the face before him—a disconcertingly familiar face—McCarthy couldn't conceal his surprise.

It was an inspector whom he had known fairly well over the years. Not a friend, by any means, but an officer whose savvy and cunning he had come to hold in high regard.

McCarthy hadn't seen him recently, however. He'd been transferred to work out of the first deputy commissioner's office in the Puzzle Palace. In fact, no one really knew what he had been up to, although departmental gossip linked him with some secret offshoot of internal affairs. This guy was from the wrong side of Foley Square, as far as McCarthy was concerned.

The inspector smiled like a hungry man who was just about to tuck the napkin into his shirt. Then he indicated that they both should remain away from the light, on the side of the building. McCarthy immediately complied.

"Captain Gussman sends his regards," the inspector began. Then he stopped, looked quizzically at McCarthy and continued. "He also said for me to tell you that no one would be sending you out for any cigarettes." The inspector waited for some reaction from McCarthy, but the Vice cop refused to give anything away. "He assured me that you would know what they meant."

"Gussman was right, I do," McCarthy answered in an unusually clipped tone. "What's with the cloak and dagger stuff?"

At least he knew that this whole thing somehow had Gussman's seal of approval, and he did trust Kenny Gussman. That was a relief.

The inspector, a craggy Irish bull elephant with a white crew cut and rippling rolls of loose skin that cascaded down a sloping forehead, brought his face down level with McCarthy's.

"Best not to give any of the big ears a chance to overhear what I'm about to tell you," he said. "You've been making people take notice of you, lad." There was animation, but no detectable emotion in his voice.

"Is that good or bad?" McCarthy asked.

"Ah, it's all in one's point of view, isn't it?"

They were both silent for a moment. Then, the older man added, "I'm sure you're aware of the fact that your fan club has been very active."

"Does that leave me dead or alive?"

"That's your choice," the inspector said.

McCarthy didn't understand, not at first. His face became a little more questioning than he intended it to be.

"Let me simplify it for you." The inspector was reading him quite accurately. McCarthy had to give him that.

"There's still a Sergeant's Club, bigger than ever, which you are no doubt familiar with, and they would love to see you join. And so would we. But . . ." he paused like a vaudevillian making certain that his timing was impeccable, "but, you haven't exactly been out soliciting an invitation. Or have you? No bullshit now, lad."

It was as though the inspector spoke in code. Old school, very old school. McCarthy respected that, knew where he was coming from. The "Sergeant's Club" referred to one of the pads, or bribery schemes, that the Knapp Commission had been struggling so singlemindedly to destroy. The reform crusade had not worked, not entirely. The New York City Police Department had been corrupt for hundreds of years; Knapp had been in business for slightly less than three.

McCarthy wasn't a member of any Sergeant's Club; he never had been. Abhorring corrupt cops as he did, he had distanced himself from a large segment of the department. Working in an area as potentially lucrative as Vice had only served to make his refusal to partake in any of the payoffs that much more notable.

"If you talked to Gussman, then you already know I'm not on a pad," McCarthy said. "And *that's* no bullshit. So why should the first deputy commissioner have any questions about my motives?"

"He's a cautious man," the inspector answered.

"We've seen hard-chargers like you before. Some of them turned out to be charging so hard just to increase their price. But you're right. Gussman vouched for you. Among others."

"Why come to me?"

"Target of opportunity, my lad," he replied, sliding the phrase off his tongue like a reptile shedding its skin. "You can either keep on doing what you're doing, which is fine with us, of course, or you can make yourself infinitely more useful. Which also happens to be the considered opinion of Saint Paul. He stood up for you too."

So Paul Delise, Serpico's mentor, was also in on it. McCarthy thought back to the night Saint Paul had tapped his own telephone, monitoring all of his conversations. How many other nights had he been listening?

"We need you inside," the inspector said directly, "as deep undercover as you can get."

"How?" McCarthy was already known as Mother. He had a reputation and he lived up to it. "People know who I am, how I operate. I haven't exactly been quiet about it. And I doubt that they would buy a flip-flop at this point."

"I wouldn't be so sure about that," the inspector said. "Things change; a man like you can begin developing more refined tastes, new friends. That all costs money."

"You want me to get lost in the Life?"

"Do it gradually, but not too gradually. Go as far and as fast as you can. Make it look good, but plausible. Hit the bars, the after-hours clubs, chase the whores. Do all the things that a sergeant faced with those temptations might normally do." The inspector cleared his throat for effect. "Then, begin to let people on the street get the idea that you're prepared to listen to reason. Square a few beefs for certain people, get them owing you favors—the right kind of favors. Let them know that you intend to collect. If I know them, they'll just think that you played out the string as an honest cop for as long as you could and finally decided to do what a thousand other guys have done: cash in and go for the fast money. Why should you be any different?''

''And after the 'gradual,' what then?''

The inspector was obviously ready for this, the script had already been written. ''Then, if it ever comes to that, you will have a very convenient blowup with your good friend and superior officer, Kenneth Gussman, who, God bless him, will begin to very publicly suspect that you are on the take. He will accuse you in front of a carefully selected group of witnesses of our choosing. At that point, you punch Gussman in the mouth and begin acting like you're guilty as sin.

''Unless I miss my guess, the suitors will start crooning at your window. You'll be irresistible. A disgruntled Vice cop, with a hard-on against all of his old friends. The bent-noses should fall right in line.''

McCarthy just listened. The whole point of the proposal that was being thrown at him amounted to: Let's put cops in handcuffs. The game they were playing would eventually involve the highest level of intrigue that NYPD had ever known. Counterespionage within the department. Intrigue on top of intrigue. And they wanted him to become a major player in it.

The inspector continued. ''We yank you out of Vice, under a very dark cloud, and assign you to a patrol district, still as a sergeant. Use your head, under those conditions how long do you think it would take for someone to invite you to join the club?''

''Probably until about the second shift,'' McCarthy said, smiling.

''Precisely. My orders to approach you come directly from the first deputy commissioner. It's up to you. Think it over. But don't *talk* it over. Except with your wife. If she's against it, a woman can make your life a living hell. I know.'' He looked like he did.

McCarthy's head was spinning like the little ball on a roulette wheel.

The old man handed him a small piece of paper, folded once. "Call this number by twelve noon tomorrow," he said. "All you have to do is tell us one word, 'yes' or 'no'; we'll take it from there. If it's 'no,' you won't be hearing from us again. Sleep on it, lad." And then he left. No handshake, no parting words.

McCarthy couldn't concentrate at all that night. He kept weighing the pros and cons. They were asking him to assume what amounted to a new identity. While it might be worth it as a career move, the toll on his family would be tremendous. He already knew what Millie thought about cops who took money. Her admonition that she would never sleep with a man who was talked about the way those cops were talked about in her old neighborhood had become the touchstone of their marriage. He knew that, in the end, she would never stand in his way. He would be able to get her to agree to it, if he decided to go forward with the undercover role. But would it be worth it?

And how would he deal with the likely eventuality that his new role would almost certainly result in some of his fellow officers being locked up? If it came to that, McCarthy had always believed that he would know how to deal with it, with the scorn and the accusations that he was a traitor to the badge. But would he?

On the way home the next morning, he almost missed the exit for Sloatsburg. By then it was daylight and he was facing a searing sun. It was an exit that he had always turned onto by reflex, by automatic pilot, thousands of times before. Not this time, though. Was that a forewarning of what his life would be like?

After the night's events, after the adrenaline had finally shut down, after the race was over for a day, he would finally have to face Millie. And tell her.

He was always preoccupied, always trying to plan two steps ahead, more focused on who he was supposed to be in his investigations than on who he really was. Now, if he accepted their proposition, it would only get worse.

As far as the consequences were concerned, McCarthy knew practically nothing about the dangers, both physical and emotional, that long-term undercovers faced, because at that point, in the early 1970s, the NYPD had no experience at all in running such operations. Frank Serpico had been a one-in-a-million aberration, a dedicated idealist who had brought the department and the city along on his personal mission, kicking and screaming all the way.

McCarthy knew that he was no Serpico. He didn't want to be one.

His wife was still in bed when he finally got home. She was almost awake. He started talking, carefully explaining what had happened, reconstructing the cryptic conversation between him and the inspector.

By the time he was finished, Millie was wide awake, her head still in the center of the pillow, her dark, thick hair spread out on either side like the most luxuriant fan that he had ever seen. She had remained quiet, breathing steadily, her chest rising and falling under a thin sheet. Whenever she concentrated like this, her eyes appeared not even to blink. Millie's tense motionlessness alone spoke to him.

The last part of it that he brought up was the children, Christine and little Billy. Somewhere down the line, they might be faced with a kid in the schoolyard who taunted them about their father—either that he was a bad cop or a snitch.

"I don't know if any kid can handle that," he said without turning to look at her.

"You can't do it," she said finally, firmly. "Nothing's worth that."

McCarthy raised himself to an elbow and faced her. "If you aren't going to be there on this, then I don't want it either."

Time passed. Too much time. "Yes you do," she answered. "You want it more than you ever wanted anything. It's in your voice. This is what you dreamed about. This would mean really being a cop." She practically pounced on him; he thought she was going to hit him. "Don't lie to me, Bill. Or to yourself."

He wanted to just let it go now. The inspector was right.

Then it was Millie's turn. "This is the way that it's going to be," she said. "I will have to push our baby's carriage around the block, and have people look at me, and point at me and the baby after we leave, wave their fingers, and say what they say about policemen who take money. And I will never be able to tell them that it was all an act. The women will stop talking when I come near them; they'll just get that look. Because, deep down, they want me to know that *they* know. Nothing else will ever make them feel so good.

"That's what you're asking me to do."

Then, he kissed her and asked, "Will you be there with me? I have to know now."

She reached over, took his hand, kissed it, then, ever so gently, she took his face in her hands and touched her lips to his.

He immediately pulled the sheet off, got out of bed, sat next to the night table and picked up the telephone receiver. Then he carefully unfolded the piece of paper that the inspector had given him.

Millie sighed, rolled away from him and placed the pillow over her head. But the pillow could not drown out the sound of her husband's voice.

"Yes." That was all Bill McCarthy said. Then, he placed the receiver back on its cradle, walked away from the bed, away from Millie, and left their bedroom.

Thirteen

A *Prison* isn't a place as much as sounds and feelings—cold, clanging. When they close that gate behind you, it locks in place. Send a cop to prison, regardless of the crime or length of time, and it's always the death sentence.

MOTHER'S MAXIM

On the surface, very little changed at first for McCarthy after he agreed to assume his undercover role for the first deputy commissioner.

Suspicion and wariness had become the new guiding principles of the NYPD after Knapp. What started out as a healthy sort of paranoia, inspired by the movement to reform, quickly collapsed into a form of psychosis.

"If the gambling module phone rang, and if a guy on the Pimp Team happened to answer that phone, the captain would yell. Nobody knew what anyone else was doing. Nobody was supposed to know because you had to worry about people selling out what you were investigating.

"The department spent an inordinate amount of time then devising what they called integrity tests. These tests involved cops following other cops, attempting to catch them in compromising situations. They were like spot checks against corruption, but almost immediately, that got out of control. Half the cases we worked on then weren't really cases at all, but elaborate integrity tests. And you never knew if *you* were the real target or somebody else.

"The police department always wanted you to do something wrong. The other guys you worked with always wanted you to do something—not really wrong—just a little wrong, so that then, they could do wrong too, and know that you were in no position to turn them in.

"There wasn't even a reasonable standard of integrity. It was a gross standard of integrity. The standard of integrity that I required for myself was a schizophrenic, psychotic standard. But it made me free to target whomever I wanted.

"In the 'integrity test' that the NYPD was constantly experimenting with, they actually staged an event, like a bribe, and then monitored it to see if you would behave in an appropriate manner.

"Once, I was called to assign two people to go to a certain bar at twelve o'clock on a particular day to see if there was any prostitution action going on in there, a very famous bar in Manhattan.

"I asked the captain who gave me the order whom he wanted the integrity test on.

" 'What are you talking about?' he said.

" 'Isn't this an integrity test?' I was furious, because now I was sure it had become an integrity test on *me*.

"He denied it again. 'It's just a bar on the East Side and I wanted to see if there's any prostitution action going on.'

" 'Listen,' I told him, 'since you're not willing to take me into your confidence, then I have no obligation to you. I'm gonna go out there, assign two people and tell them it's an integrity test, and then on Wednesday everybody gets stars on their report cards.'

"Finally, the captain said, 'Now, wait a second. . . .'

"What had happened was that the Internal Affairs Division had called him and directed him to do an integrity test on two people—to assign them as they are normally assigned, through the sergeant.

"Then he admitted it. 'How do you know it's an integrity test?'

"I said, 'Because in my whole life, nobody ever told me to send two men three days from now anywhere.' They'd normally tell you to send the guy right away.

" 'All right, it's an integrity test,' he said weakly, 'Give me two names.'

"I gave him my two best men.

" 'Why would you do a test on your two best men?' he asked.

" 'Why? Because they're the only two I'd ever trust. The rest of them I *don't* trust, already. You only test the ones you trust.'

"He just looked at me like I had explained the mystery of the universe to him.

"I was sure that a bribe attempt would be made on the cops at the bar by a spook from Internal Affairs.

"I decided to play along—except, I made it my business to drop by the bar myself, unannounced, just to make sure that my people weren't going to be set up. I had one man outside as a backup.

"I go in, sit off to the side and wait to see what happens. My detectives were already in there. They didn't see me.

"At the bar there are a few people, tough guys, winos, businessmen, a typical New York crowd. There's also this hooker I happen to know, Maria—a gorgeous Italian woman, about thirty-five years old, who once upon a time had been the queen of the Manhattan wiseguys. She had suffered some tough breaks over the years, but in that faint bar light, she still looked good. I hadn't seen her in a long, long time.

"She jumps up from the bar as soon as she sees me and runs into the kitchen. Next thing I know, the pimp who owns the place tells me that Maria has to see me right away in the back. He sounds excited, points toward the kitchen.

"I go in and there's this Maria, in the corner, crying, bawling her eyes out. I was sort of surprised she even remembered me.

"All of a sudden, she raises her head, gives me one of those looks, and grabs me, hugs me, almost knocks me down. Then she reaches around and pulls her shirt off. No bra, no anything. Just two of the biggest breasts I ever saw. She hugged me some more. Smashes her tits right against my chest.

"I couldn't just act like, 'Oh, get away from me, you're a whore.' So, I put my arms around her, tried to calm her down.

"Now I *really* think it's a setup. All the pimps who had been paying off the cops were mad as hell at me. I figured this was their way of getting rid of me.

"They were going to take a picture of me with her, naked, give it to my enemies in the police department and get me transferred, or fired or arrested; get a morals charge on me.

"By that point, I was looking around for the cameras. It's either blackmail or an integrity test. I go down, regardless. But, if it's a test, where the hell are the Internal Affairs cops?

"Maria starts telling me her story. As she does, she spins around and shows me this stab wound on her back, an ugly scar. That was why she had taken her shirt off.

" 'The guy who did this to me is sitting out there at the bar,' she says. 'I know he's gonna do it again. He'll kill me, you have to help me.'

"Now I'm confused. Is this a test or the real thing?

"I check the bar. My two cops are in the booth, and now there's a very obvious plant from Internal Affairs with them. He's beating their ears, attempting to bribe them.

"I'm not concerned about those two. I know my detectives aren't going to go for it. They'll report it to me and that will be the end of it.

"But what about Maria? 'Stay put,' I warn her.

"As soon as my cops leave, I take the guy at the bar and spread him, search him, the whole cop routine. I take a bowie knife off him and call for a wagon. As soon as it comes, I send him on his way.

"Then, I go back to see if Maria is okay. But she's gone.

"Was it attempted blackmail or an integrity test? To this day, I'm still not sure. But that was the NYPD in the witch-hunt days.

"Looking back on it, the approach that was made to me that night on Centre Street could very well have been an integrity test too. I didn't even consider that then. I was too much in love with the idea of going undercover.

"All this integrity testing was something in addition to the real cases, the legitimate police work, like running wiretaps and taking out pimps and dealing with all the leads that called for further investigation as a result of what was intercepted on the wiretaps.

"You could never be sure of all the influences at work, real or imagined. You never knew, for example, which powerful person, inside or outside of the department, you might inadvertently be scaring by listening to the taps. You never knew how badly you could be hurt by the things you were finding out.

"And you didn't know all the devious ways that you were being obstructed, administratively, at the top levels of command in the police department, by the decisions that were made about 'go' or 'no go' on a certain case.

"That intrigue and interference even worked its way down to whether you could obtain a certain warrant or not. I used to cringe sometimes when I requested a warrant because I never could be sure who might not want that warrant served. Nor did I know the lengths to which they would go to stop me.

"We had a new police commissioner, Patrick Murphy. He was John Lindsay's man and we figured him for an egghead, an academic. The only weapon he ever used in his whole life was a typewriter. But his mandate was clear. He was there to force the whole hierarchy of the police department, practically an entire generation of commanders, the guys who had come up right after World War Two, to either get out or be demoted.

"That's what it was really all about. A purge. That was Lindsay's answer to corruption. Murphy was his hammer.

"Practically the whole Thirteenth Division, for instance, which was a Brooklyn unit, was locked up. There were cops in handcuffs all over the city."

Bob Leuci, whom most people came to know as the Prince of the City, typified the kind of cop who ran afoul of the integrity tests in the early 1970s. He was one of the best case-breakers in the SIU, the Special Investigating Unit of the Narcotics Division.

Targets included the men and women who were the pioneers in such dope connections as the Colombian and the East Asian. The French Connection to Marseilles had already become a celebrated case. They took over from there.

Pad money and temptation were all around the celebrity cops in the vaunted SIU. Some of them succumbed. Bob Leuci had his own problems at that point, his own dark corners. With ruthless efficiency, the prosecutors attempting to prove the existence of systematic corruption in the SIU used Leuci to make cases against lawyers, bail-bondsmen, organized crime figures, and, ultimately, against his own partners.

133

* * *

"By the start of 1973, I was working for the division commander, in the tower of power, One Police Plaza, on the twelfth floor, Central Investigation Section. *Permanent cadre,* the supersleuths, the cops' cops. Years later, I would return to command the Vice headquarter unit.

"What you actually did there was surveillance on members of your own division or special jobs for the commissioner.

"They still had me out in the field, of course, attempting to attract attention. I was literally waiting for the first nibble, the first good payoff reach.

"Bob Leuci, in the SIU, was down on the eleventh floor. We had a parallel existence. I was doing in Vice what he was doing in Narcotics. Trying to make the biggest cases we could.

"SIU had always been a bunch of renegades—the sort of undisciplined, free-lance detectives who had never been answerable to anybody. I was one of the new sergeants who had been put in place to try to control cops like that.

"Leuci was never a guy I trusted, not like a David Durk or a Saint Paul. He convinced the world that he was an honest cop who had committed one indiscretion, had experienced guilt pangs about it, and had then gone to the government to make a deal to square things. I was always skeptical. But, then again, at least I was being consistent. I rarely got along with other cops. To me, Leuci was a meat eater like the rest of them and he sold out his partners.

"I always had very mixed feelings about what Leuci had done. What made it worse was that, technically, I was about to go into the same business as Leuci. I kept agonizing over whether I had made the right decision. The idea of working undercover against pimps or anybody else who tried to bribe cops was great. But if another

134

cop somehow got caught up in all that, and I had to work on him too, well, that gave me no satisfaction at all.

"The most obscene part about the whole *Prince of the City* saga was that in the end, the prosecutors decided to give some captain, instead of some ordinary cop, the deal to cooperate—to become a state's witness, based on Leuci's testimony. It looked to me like the brass were taking care of their own once again.

"I call them the Legion of the Melting Shields. They consist of the top cops at One Police Plaza who, when they experience any degree of political pressure, for any reason, fold. Their tin badges start to leak down their legs. Instead of using the leather shield cases to carry their badges that the rest of us have, the exclusive members of the Legion need asbestos cases.

"I just hoped that, as I got in deeper and deeper with my new role as an undercover, that no one from their Legion would ever be in a position to decide my fate.

"Nobody really believed that the city wanted to do anything to clean up the corruption. They had been forced into it, publicly dragged through the streets. Experienced, mature people at headquarters never trusted Lindsay or Murphy or their motives. It was a time, however, when a cop could actually do an honest job and no one would dare try to stop him."

The changes that were seismically ripping apart the NYPD were no less alarming to another interested group—the Five Families.

Every time Carlo Gambino consulted his Richter scale he saw another twelve register. Big Paul Castellano was the underboss. John Gotti was still biding his time, attempting to develop the personal loyalties and the power base that would one day allow him to make his move.

All Five Families shared the same concern. They needed corrupt cops to remain in business. The prospect of real reform was threatening. The last thing they could tolerate was the police suddenly changing the rules in the Life.

However, many of the very people in power—in law enforcement—whom they used to call would no longer answer their phones.

There was only one solution. The Families would have to begin finding and recruiting some new cops, some new people who were willing to listen to reason. All they had to do was find them and pay them. Enough.

Fourteen

As soon as people suspect that a cop is *Taking Money*, people will line up to hit on him like a bakery, like people taking numbers after the twelve-fifteen mass on Sunday.

MOTHER'S MAXIM

For close to a year, McCarthy led a double life. In one incarnation he was racing around all night as the Pimp Squad boss, directing his two-man Vice teams. He tried never to ride with the same detective twice. Not only was he trying to avoid favoritism, but he was also testing them, constantly evaluating their work habits and honesty. They hit the streets of Manhattan in Cadillacs, Thunderbirds, Continentals, Buick 225s—all flash cars, sharp cars known as "seize cars" because most of them had been confiscated from the pimps. Even this was innovative for its time. It redefined the definition of "unmarked car."

In his other life, McCarthy was attempting to subtly let it be known that he might, indeed, be open for the "reach."

"All the time, I was planting seeds in people, dropping them in conversations about things I wanted to do and about how much money I would need to do them.

137

"My own life-style changed, too. I guess I became the *Super Fly* version of a cop—drinking scotch and running around all night. And feeling guilty as hell about it when I would go home to Millie. It was the biggest con job I ever pulled—all working from my base in the Pimp Squad. I conned most of the cops and all the bad guys into believing that I had begun to turn into the kind of cop who becomes so immersed in the Life that he can no longer keep his balance, no longer distance himself from it."

Living out his bluff, McCarthy began to socialize with the kind of rogue policemen he had once taken pains to avoid. It was one thing to spend all day chasing the bad guys; it was something entirely different to spend all night carousing in their bars and clubs, attempting to score with their women and reveling in the kind of borderline behavior that usually landed normal people in handcuffs, sitting in the back of a paddy wagon.

The handful of cops who did know about McCarthy's new role came to see in him still another dimension—that of the diabolically clever undercover operative. His playacting was uncanny.

"No one ever challenged me. No one had the guts to challenge me. If I told people in the Life, through my actions, that I was corrupt, then I had to be corrupt. That went for the other cops, too. They had no trouble accepting that. Figuring out the motives behind the actions of honest cops gave them far more trouble."

Throughout this period, the team was still dealing with pimps and prostitutes on a regular basis, discovering anew that the things they had learned at the academy and the guidelines in the NYPD *Patrol Guide* would never apply in the Life.

Every after-hours bar in New York "paid." That was the expression. The cash either had to go to some Mafia Family or its associates or to the cops—or frequently, to both. Every vice enterprise had to "belong" to somebody, the hookers as well as the real waste. That was the only way to guarantee protection. Money made it happen every time. Forget about the sex or the dope or the gambling—they were just the commodities.

"A 'goulash house' was a place that would have drinks and gambling and women. That was the old Mafia term for the after-hours clubs. Some of those places were elaborate as casinos. Very heavy people inside. All made guys. Wiseguys. Capos and up. And gorgeous whores in low-cut dresses wearing the fanciest jewelry that money could buy.

"If you have wiseguys, you are automatically going to have good times and good-looking women. That's the sweetest part of the Life. Take the typical wiseguy's girlfriend, for instance.

"She's a broad who can give you a blow-job while she's still chewing gum. To them, that's a true Italian princess. She could go under a table and give head while you eat spaghetti. A bimbo. "She's got big tits; has to have great tits. That's a job description. Her name's Maria. She's wearing tight pants. And she's got all this teased hair that if you touched it, it would stick to your hand. She's just another whore, but a whore with a Madonna complex. And she likes to be around power. That's how these girls get off. They're into subservience. They pamper their man because he gives them all these favors—he's their god. Whores with a contract."

Eventually, McCarthy got his men all thinking the same way with each prostitute or pimp or john they arrested: Every time you rolled somebody's finger for a print, you enjoyed the opportunity of a lifetime. That print could tell you whether there's a warrant outstanding, a detainer, or even a traffic ticket. Some of the biggest cases were solved through breaks that came about in just that way. McCarthy's unit was developing valuable intelligence from the ground up. From the pavement on Seventh Avenue.

"Every night you had to be out there. In the middle of it. Living it. Gathering intelligence, collecting IOUs, proving yourself, over and over. You had to be out in the Life. We were the Pimp Squad, the pimp police. They knew us, we knew them.

"They would all talk to me because they thought I already knew everything they were telling me. When we would go through the big, thick books that contained mug shots, it was like we were going through a family album, just reminiscing. That's how close I got to it.

"The pimps and the girls in the Life were never 'informing' on anyone, because they didn't think they were telling me anything I hadn't guessed. Plenty of times one of them would approach me because they thought they might learn something from me. They were all afraid of each other, suspicious, worried. They were all threatened by each other, convinced that every one of their friends was working undercover for the cops. And we did everything we could to foster that belief.

"I was also locking up pimps. If a whore took a beating and wanted to sign papers on 'her man,' I would have her make a tape-recorded phone call to the pimp, tell him, 'Honey, I'm gonna give you all my money; I loves you and I wanta come back.' If he would agree to it that would be incriminating, and that was excellent evidence. That's how you did it—playing them off against each other.

"The notion that pimps are *real* men—and that's what a prostitute would say—just means that the pimp can't be pussy-whipped. Every other guy she meets pays for her pussy; that's her only source of income, of power over the johns. But the pimp doesn't *have* to pay. Therefore, she really has no hold over him. Ergo, the pimp must be some kind of superman.

"That sounds simplistic, but most of the women I met in the Life were looking for very uncomplicated answers. What they never understood was that many of the pimps are asexual. The reason they can refuse the woman is not because they have so much sexual facility or the will-power not to perform; it's just lack of libido.

"I would go out every night trying to jump pimps. We used to stop them, haul them out of their pimp-mobiles, bang them up against the door or spread-eagle them over the hood, and demand some ID. We would never accept their driver's license as identification. We had to see their social security card. The reason for that was we could then take that SS number and find out if the guy had filed income taxes or not. You cannot, in the United States of America, find out if a person has filed taxes unless you have his social security number. That was how we finally got some of them.

"Following the pimps took us to the after-hours clubs.

"An after-hours club is where you go to blow your coke. And dance, be seen, flaunt your gold chain and your fancy woman.

"That's the high society of the Life. Being able to show up at and spend your money in one of these pimp clubs or after-hours bars was what you worked for.

"This was the night life—but the underground night life, the secret Vice clubs. It might not even start until three in the morning, four. The pimps would come in with their bottom lady, their top earner, and treat her to booze and coke as a reward. She would carry his coke and his gun for him, in return, and take the collar, if the cops happened to come in. He wouldn't be holding anything. Two hours later, he'd spring her from the lockup.

"There was no point to making all that money from sex for pay if you couldn't spend it. These aren't the kind of people who are going to go to Dun & Bradstreet for investment advice; they aren't sophisticated enough to start investing in offshore banks. That came much later with the Colombian cartels.

"Then you would see people jet-streaming on coke. Flying. You will never see anybody doing coke sitting down, not for long anyway. They're all speeding around, jumping, dancing.

"In one part of the room, a guy will be hitting on a girl; over on the other side, a pimp might be trying to 'cap' a whore, or recruit her for his stable; talking sugar-shit to her. Just constant activity. Not connected, but not entirely unassociated, either.

"The most notorious pimps, the flashiest ones, were known as the 'gentlemen of leisure,' the Super Flies. For all their garishness, they did seem to have a little more style, finesse, then.

"You would see them wearing gold coke spoons, dia-mond-studded, around their necks. Everybody, men and women, had at least one extremely long fingernail, for scooping up the powder. I've seen them throw down hundred-dollar bills and be able to squeeze the corners so they would pop open when they snorted.

"The people who ran the after-hours clubs were always in the legitimate bars, trying to invite and encourage people to come to their clubs later and spend money.

"But these were people who were already in the Life. How would you do it? Tell them you got a new cassette player? Come on. No, you'd have to tell them that you had good coke. And, as a matter of fact, the manager might be bringing in samples of coke right there, just like a Fuller Brush salesman, trying to sell his stock.

"Square people think that prostitution means a woman who spends her life on her back with her legs spread. But that's just what they do during their working hours. That's not the Life.

"Cocaine is the Life. It's crack if you're only clearing fifteen dollars for a blow-job. As you can afford to, you trade up. Conditions change; there will always be a different drug of choice. Next it will probably be ice—that's a derivative of methamphetamine. In those days, though, it was coke. The people who did it figured they were okay; it wasn't like they were taking heroin. Heroin was what they called *real dope*. Coke had star-status. It was celebrity dope. They were doing a thousand dollars a night up their noses. That was the reason they lived, the whole point of their lives.

"The clubs were dominated by the black pimps. But not owned by them, never owned by them. Ownership was strictly organized crime.

"I was in plenty of those places and I actually saw salad bowls full of cocaine, maybe a hundred thousand dollars worth of coke sitting out in a bowl on the table, like you would put out a bowl of potato chips on a coffee table for a party. A kilo out on the table.

"Anybody in the club was invited over to take a dip. Half the time, in the beginning, it was so brazen, so accepted that if you went to those places you had to do coke, that they didn't even care if you were a cop—you were still welcome to a friendly snort.

"Even if a cop went out *not* intending to get into trouble, he couldn't always help it.

"From the dealer's side, the major contractors for the big loads were all Italian or Chinese. The Colombians were just getting into it. Asians are taking over the actual importation now, but then, on the street level, the Five Families were the only game in town. All the dealers used coke then, from the little guy to the big guy—from a scratched arm to a five-hundred-dollar suit.

"There were so many things going on simultaneously at so many different levels. Nothing happened by itself. Besides pretending to be corrupt, and attempting to attract attention that way, I still had to do my normal Vice routine, like busting places for gambling or pedos. If you wanted to, if they allowed you to, you could have gone out into Manhattan every night, cast your Vice net, and reeled in some pervert like Peter Big. This was New York. It was all out there.

"However, there was never a time in Vice when you were not touched by political considerations.

"For example, you would suddenly be called away from all the organized crime or pimp intelligence that your team might be working on to respond to somebody's personal request.

"That always seemed to happen with pedos. A report would land on your desk that the gay child of some prominent person may have gotten himself in big trouble by dropping his load where he shouldn't have, or by trying to buy pussy or dope from the wrong people.

"These kids would walk on the wild side, over and over, and never expect to have to pay for it. But the Life has a way of evening things out. Invariably, some kid from an Ivy League school would spend the night with some male prostitute or transvestite, get fucked in more ways than one, and now he's in the hospital, bleeding from the ass, and his father or mother or the family priest wants revenge.

"They make a phone call to the right person. Pressure is applied. It could be political or religious or low-level blackmail or something as innocent as just wanting to do somebody you may see at the next cocktail party a favor.

"The cops—*always* the Vice squad, which means my

144

guys—are called in. We don't even get the whole story until later. But we're the soldiers. We have to go out and mug somebody. That's how the system works. That's why there is so much delay, why things take so long to get to court. The police can never operate freely in an ideal world, they are constantly being menaced by some mysterious authority figure who is biased to make sure that an investigation comes out one way or the other.

"And those were simply the typical working conditions of Vice.

"At the same time, I'm doing this Jekyll and Hyde undercover routine, waiting for some fruitful contact to be made. And, it seems to be happening. Slowly. I'm beginning to hear whispers about all these people on Park Avenue who want to bribe me to lay off their whorehouses. Cops from all over Manhattan were coming up to me, envious as hell, telling me about all the money I could make, wishing to hell they were me.

"Talk about balls in the air."

Fifteen

The *Feds* are not cops. They only make arrests by
appointment and that appointment is the result of
some meeting where there were yellow legal pads
and Cross pens and magistrates and attorneys and
everybody felt very safe. They are fancy restaurant
cops. They do nothing summarily, and if you don't
do anything summarily, like jumping out of a car
and grabbing a guy who's raping a woman, then
you aren't a real cop.

MOTHER'S MAXIM

Some of those balls that McCarthy was attempting to
juggle were represented by the contacts he was making
on the street. By that time, he was concentrating his
efforts on the Upper East Side, the traditional power
neighborhood in New York. There, vice was a refined,
variegated experience. Pleasure, especially the illicit
kind, seemed to hold a unique appeal for people who, to
McCarthy's way of thinking, should have known better.
He would never be able to place himself inside the head
of the dissipate.

There was one case in particular that had always intrigued—and infuriated—him. It had begun as a Vice
job. Then, the FBI had stepped in, citing jurisdictional
prerogative. The animosities and competition among the
different levels of law enforcement had ruined more than
one investigation. When it came to brokering these turf
wars, the cops usually lost.

* * *

"The heir to one of the oldest family fortunes in New York had allegedly been kidnapped by two people from Ireland. The trail was cold. An arrest had been made, too. Kidnapping seemed like a pretty mundane job for the feds. Except for one thing. The case had all sorts of holes in it. And the cops knew all about it.

"This was a very celebrated Upper East Side family. The FBI had recovered the young heir under mysterious circumstances. But they refused to provide us with any details. My beef was that it had been a Vice job all along and I had always wanted in. But, no go.

"The kidnap victim was homosexual, a well-known pedophile. He eventually married and fathered a child and became a socialite. But on the street, in the Life, the real players knew how kinky his tastes were and how deep his pockets were.

"We never believed the kidnapping story, we always thought that he had been the victim of an extortion plot. That was where the two Irishmen fitted in. But there was never anything we could hold the heir on. We couldn't *prove* that he had made a false police report. The feds didn't even want to consider it.

"I knew about a very vicious gang that only shook down pedos. As marks, they liked to prey on rich guys, or out-of-towners who used credit cards. That was the gang's MO.

"William McKinney, who had been a police impersonator for over thirty years, was the leader of this gang. You run into them in law enforcement. They are people who pretend to be police officers in order to force innocent or not-so-innocent victims to pay them bribes to avoid being arrested. It's rare for one of them to stay in business very long. You hear about them pretty quickly. But this McKinney was a real exception to that rule. He'd made a profession out of it—and a damn good living, too. His particular scam was to make false arrests on sex charges, then offer to let the mark buy his way out.

147

"He had been arrested thirty-five times and had to be the most exceptional police impersonator I ever met. He would only pick marks who didn't have soled shoes. They had to be wearing new shoes, expensive shoes. That was a quirk he had. I think he believed that it would lead him to a better class of victims.

"After one of his accomplices would set up the victim, McKinney used to break into the hotel room—during the sex act, if he could time it right—and make his 'arrest.'

"McKinney actually had the balls to bring the victims down to the Manhattan district attorney's office while everybody was out at lunch, usually between one P.M. and two P.M.

"He'd take them into one of the interviewing rooms, pretending to be a detective, and extort money from them right there in the Manhattan district attorney's office.

"A variation would be for McKinney to pick up his 'prisoner' from another member of the gang and then take him to a real police station to be booked. That was brazen.

"McKinney parked outside the station, left the mark in the back of the car. He would pick a police station that had a low windowsill so the occupants of the car could see him go up to the desk, speak to the sergeant there—while he would really be asking for directions—and come back out. The real cops had no idea they were being used too.

"He'd get the desk sergeant to write the directions down—it all seemed innocent enough—then he'd go back out to the car and show the slip of paper to the victim.

"McKinney told them that the paper, which he never let them read, of course, was a 'booking slip.' As far as the victim was concerned, McKinney had to be the real thing. He'd just come out of a police station with a piece of paper in his hand. At that point, they would go somewhere else and, after cajoling and crying and coaxing,

148

McKinney would allow the victim to bribe him out of the arrest.

"He became such a convincing impersonator that McKinney could go into any station house in New York, walk behind the desk, sign the blotter, call himself 'Inspector McKinney,' and there probably would not be a cop in the place who would challenge him. He knew the system, and the jargon down so well that he could even pull it off on cops. A cop would not believe that McKinney wasn't a boss. He even looked the part—white hair, heavyset, a real Irish bulldog.

"McKinney forged his own search warrants, his own arrest warrants. He typed them up on stolen police department forms. He could write or talk in any legal terms; he had all the blank affidavits and could manufacture his own court documents. He could come to your door with a piece of paper signed by a judge; you'd look at it and swear it was authentic.

"During the course of their operations this gang had also extorted money from an United States Army general, who eventually committed suicide. But not before he paid fifty thousand dollars.

"Every Vice cop in New York knew about William McKinney. He was another Peter Big, another huge embarrassment.

"In an unrelated case we chanced to lock up a skinny, fourteen-year-old blond hustler—a chicken; the pedos are the chicken hawks. He flipped and began to cooperate.

"This kid tells me that his lover is a pedophile king named 'John Wayne' and that he had been used as the pedo bait in some famous kidnapping case, which was really a shakedown, after all.

"As soon as he told us that, I knew that he had to be talking about the same case that had been bugging Vice for years.

"This kid's name was Larry Waters. He was mad at

McKinney over a beating he had taken from him, so it was get-even time.

"There are certain bars in New York where people who want to buy children for the purpose of sexual exploitation go. It's an underground network.

"Larry Waters would wait to be picked up at a place on the East Side. This was the same bar that the 'kidnap' victim had frequented years back. A typical meat rack. The male whores just lounged around waiting until a pedo came in and started feeling them up. When one of them hit on Waters they thought they were just getting a date; they didn't realize they were getting McKinney, too.

"To try and trap McKinney, we took a room in a hotel in midtown and planted a detective there who was supposed to be a rich pedo. The plan was for Larry Waters to single him out to McKinney as a potential mark.

"But I didn't have much faith in Waters. So I secretly introduced into the plot a 'disgruntled' Irish policeman who had been laid off by the city. They only worked with other Irishmen. Another quirk.

"There actually had been layoffs at that time in New York, so it was a solid cover. I had this cop befriend Larry Waters, who believed he was really a laid-off cop who wanted to do a little hooking or pimping on the side. Waters bought the story because so many cops really do moonlight that way. And get away with it.

"Waters introduced this undercover guy to McKinney and he was invited to join the gang. They loved the idea of having a real cop to work with. So now, I have somebody on the inside. And I've had Waters from the beginning. I was double-banging Waters. He figured he was double-crossing *me* and McKinney. That's how these people were. They couldn't walk across Fifth Avenue unless they lied about it.

"Larry Waters then returns to the extortion gang and says, 'I got a date with an out-of-towner who's got a lot of money. We're supposed to meet at the Holiday Inn on Fifty-seventh Street.' This out-of-towner is actually another one of my men.

"The plan was for Waters to come into the suite and within fifteen minutes he would go to bed with the guy. Then, immediately, McKinney would break into the room and 'arrest' the pedophile.

"If the mark resisted or didn't offer to buy his way out, there would be violence. They would always beat up the mark a little bit. Just to seem like real cops.

"At the appointed hour, we are in two adjoining rooms, waiting for McKinney to show. We had the room wired like it was in stereo. There was even a videotape camera going. I brought in a tech guy to hide it in the bathroom and do all the recording. He's in there with his headset on. This was going down like a documentary. I was so careful.

"The connecting door had been taken off the hinges so that we could pop it and surprise them.

"My undercover cop is set. If he feels that he is in danger, and he wants us to come into the room, for any reason—it didn't matter if we had the case made or we didn't have the case—his only obligation is to give us the *code word* and drop to the floor, preferably behind the bed. I didn't want to have to worry about shooting him. The code word was *slick*.

"Nine o'clock, Waters comes into the room. Right on time.

"In the adjoining room, there's me, a Vice detective, Pete Madison, and our captain, Larry Hepburn. Hepburn wanted in on this one, too. As time went by, Captain Hepburn would become a major influence in my career; back then, though, we were still feeling each other out.

"Pete Madison is positioned on a chair, facing the adjoining doors. Our door is already open, so it's just their door that we have to go through. I'm ready to go.

151

"We sat there in silence. Waiting. Madison is carrying a double-barrel shotgun, breathing heavy. He's my artillery.

"As far as we're concerned, this is a go.

"At some point within the next fifteen minutes, they're going to break into the room. My cop is in there in his underwear; we're wearing bulletproof vests; this is it.

"Almost as soon as Larry Waters arrives in the room, he drops his pants, jumps up on the bed, and pretends to start screwing my detective to make it look good for McKinney and his gang.

"By this time, we're all breathing pretty heavy. I can actually hear my watch going *tick, tick, tick*.

"Madison is really turned up. He puts two rifle rounds in the shotgun, clicks and the barrel back into the stock and closes up the thing.

"I look over at Hepburn to see what he's doing, he's behind me on the edge of the bed. I can hear *him* breathing, too. This is wraparound tension.

"And all of a sudden the shotgun goes BA-BA-BA-BOOM! I hit the floor and Hepburn jumps up from the bed like he's on a trampoline and Pete Madison has been knocked over backward; he's somersaulted over his chair from the recoil of the cannon he's just shot off.

"That BOOM was the loudest thing I ever heard in my life. Not just a gunshot, but an explosion. I was right next to Madison. The gunpowder clogged my nostrils. If it were helium, it would have lifted me off the bed.

"It looked like Hiroshima—the cloud of gunpowder rose right up; it was only a seven-foot ceiling and it spread out like a mushroom cloud.

"I look over and there's a hole in the door as big as a basketball. The tech guy comes running out and rips his earphones off.

"It was only at that point, after all that delayed, benumbed reaction, that I realized that *we* had fired the shotgun. Madison had discharged it by accident. That was one of the single scariest things that ever happened to me as a cop. That thing was like an elephant gun. We couldn't have done any more damage with a rocket-launcher.

"I open the door to the room where Waters and the detective were. But I don't see anybody. I'm sure that we've killed Waters and the undercover man and maybe the people in the next room, too.

"The slug had exited the room and had traveled out across the hall through the front door of the room we were in. It took out shrapnel from the first door and drove it through the second door. One solid deep-bore slug. A cannonball. That's what we used. No birdshot. Our big guns fired solid projectiles. It was devastating.

"Never, ever again would I allow anyone to even touch a shotgun, except me. Had we fired that gun inside, against the interior wall, it would have taken everybody out in the next six rooms.

"It wasn't until then that I see Larry Waters' head coming up real slowly next to the bed. My cop is *under* the bed. He isn't taking any chances. Miraculously, neither one was hit.

"Now I have to check next door. See if we killed anybody. I run downstairs, get the key off the manager. I threaten the manager that if he comes upstairs, I'll arrest him, I'll throw him in Rikers for the rest of his life. We had never warned him that we were cops in the first place. Understandably, the guy was going nuts.

"The people downstairs in the lobby heard it; they felt it. The manager is convinced that we're a gang of terrorists. He absolutely does not believe that we could be cops, not the way I'm acting.

"Thank God, the room next door was unoccupied. Because the rifle was pointed down, it hit the floor, tore up the carpet, and ran along the floor of that room. It shredded the carpet, hit and ricocheted off three walls and the slug was lying in the middle of the floor.

"Now, McKinney still hasn't come yet. But he *better* show up because I now have to write up a report proving that at least I arrested *somebody*, because we have accidentally discharged a shotgun in a hotel suite in midtown Manhattan. That will take explaining.

"I tell Waters, 'Get back to McKinney and bring him here at eleven o'clock. Tell him your mark got cold feet and you had to talk him into it again. But tell him he *has* to show because your man has been flashing big bucks.'

"In the meantime, I go back to the station to start the report. You have to notify about ten thousand people that this happened. The duty captain interviewed me. He swore I had to be drunk. He smelled my breath. He wanted to come back to the hotel with me. I ranted and raved. I'm telling the captain in charge, 'You can't go over to the hotel and fuck up my case.' In the end, he decides not to. He doesn't want to get his name mixed up with this.

"I used my gun a lot, but I never liked guns. Experiences like that one helped confirm my aversion to firearms. I never shot anybody. It was just a very effective prop. I was always afraid of guns. I wasn't afraid to wrestle with people, but I was always afraid they were going to get my gun and shoot me with it.

"I have a saying—good guys carry them in their holsters, bad guys carry them in their hands. If you gotta go for it, it's too late. Any cop who has to go for his gun is asking to die.

"I never went anywhere without my gun. I had two—a service revolver, a Smith and Wesson .38; and a snub-nose .38—that was my off-duty gun. I still have the guns, but I haven't looked at them since I left the job. They're hidden in my house.

"Some cops are patent leather police. They're the guys who touch their holster and get a hard-on. They're into leather. They have matching belts, buckles, and holsters and speed loaders and quick-draw and dry fire. Most of them are maniacs. Probably they shouldn't even be armed.

"After what happened in the Holiday Inn, I wasn't sure that *we* should be armed.

"I go back to the hotel. I only have about a half hour. I vacuum the rug. I vacuum the hallway floor and I get two red napkins and stuff them in the holes in the door. I had to hope that the bad guys didn't notice the holes in the door.

"Eleven o'clock comes. Bingo. Waters shows up, goes into the room, my detective is in his underwear, his fly is open; he's standing there scratching his crotch.

"In walks McKinney and a second guy, a masher. The next thing you know, we hear the night table go over; they hit my detective, knock him over the bed, slap him around till he's bleeding; then the lamp goes, all this furniture is crashing. He was a tough kid. Before it all started we had gone over the potential peril and he had said to me, 'Mother, if I have to take a beating, I can handle it.'

"Then, as we're listening, they negotiate a price, tell him how much it's gonna cost him to get out of this arrest. Then he says, as loud as he could, without screaming, 'Okay, *slick.*'

"That's our signal. We break down the door.

"The big guy with McKinney says, 'Fuck him, let's kill him. It's a setup.' And he goes for a gun. Madison and the undercover kid jump McKinney.

"I drop my shoulder, I hit the big guy. I just kept my shoulder down and drove him into the bathroom and banged him against the sink, cracked his back. But he keeps on coming—he's about six-six, 260 pounds. He runs right over me, charges out of the bathroom.

"He took me down hard. I didn't see it coming. But I still have him by his leg and he drags me out into the hallway, stomping on my shoulder and my neck.

"I finally get to my feet and who comes in to help me

but Captain Hepburn. We'd forgotten all about him and left him back in the other room. Hepburn starts punching in this narrow, dim hotel hallway. That's great, except that he's punching the hell out of the back of my neck trying to reach around and get to the other guy.

"After I take a mauling, we finally get him handcuffed. And he starts screaming, 'Don't handcuff me, don't handcuff me, I'm psychotic. I can't be handcuffed.'

"The tape is still running. Everybody's doing the right thing. Then Captain Hepburn says something like Clint Eastwood would say, trying to sound tough, like, 'I'll knock your lights out.' The only thing I had to defend at the trial on that whole proceeding was, 'Who was that voice on the tape threatening to beat the guy up after he was handcuffed?' Hepburn had watched too many movies.

"The next day, coincidence of coincidence, we find out that the big guy who practically tore my head off, the muscle for McKinney, just happened to be a fed himself—a special agent for ATF—Alcohol, Tobacco and Firearms. He moonlighted as a legbreaker for McKinney.

"That was just one of the reasons why I never liked working with the feds."

Sixteen

Manhattan Vice **is doors with little windows. And knocks on those doors and people peeking out and letting you in. It's lookouts and bouncers and whores. And booze. And cocaine. It's like a costume ball. Except everybody is Count Dracula.**

MOTHER'S MAXIM

The night that Sinbad first began—December 3, 1973—Bill McCarthy was parked in a rubbish-strewn alley, on the east side of Third Avenue, midtown, peeing into a Clorox bottle. He was on a surveillance. So much for the storied glamor of detective work, of Manhattan Vice.

He was sharing his space that evening with two mangy dogs, several cats, a family of long-tailed rats, and several winos and vent-men who appeared to be in various stages of semiconsciousness.

From time to time, McCarthy would twist into a squat and very carefully aim a stream of pee into the wide-mouthed opening of the Clorox bottle, which he'd looted from Millie's laundry, then he'd toss out the contents through the side window of the car. He tried hard not to spill any on his hands.

Stationed there like a movie cop, with black binoculars taped to a black dashboard, he was spying, watching a bar from a prone position on the cold floor of his brown,

1972 Matador station wagon, a car that he was convinced no self-respecting thief would ever try to boost.

He had to use his own car on this surveillance—he was squashed underneath the dashboard—because all the regular Vice cars were up on blocks. New York was just then taking its first hit of bankruptcy. That turned-out-pockets high would become addictive. The cops, being on the front lines of municipal indigence, felt it first. Of course.

McCarthy had been planted inside the Matador for a total of eleven hours; his back hurt, his neck ached, his torso was twisted. Thermoses of bad coffee had already turned both his stomach lining and his kidneys into screaming casualties.

He was headed into the twelfth hour—real darkness now—and still no sign of the drug buy that was supposed to be going down. More than anything else he wanted to get his hands on the junkie informer who had set this whole thing up and make him die a painfully slow death.

The joint he was watching, Adam's Rib, was one of the suspected pimp bars that his team had targeted as a likely payoff spot for cops on the take. Making cases like that was the lifeblood of Vice.

In an unrelated piece of what, at the time, seemed to be good luck, an informant had also snitched to them about this big drug buy that was supposed to take place that very night at the club. McCarthy's Vice team would work it from their end, initially, then turn it over to Narcotics if the tip was good. A double-bang case like that always looked good in the old personnel jacket.

But eleven hours was a long time to wait. For anything.

McCarthy figured he'd make it an even twelve. He'd just hit the Clorox bottle again, so he knew his bladder would be good for a while. Then he'd bag it and head home to Sloatsburg.

These plans were taking shape in his mind as he stuck his head up from the floor and happened to see a white

158

male, alone, move in close and disappear behind his station wagon.

This could be the beginning of the buy.

Suddenly, McCarthy was back at the top of his game. He listened and looked and waited: the three most important things that any detective must do.

Apparently, they didn't even realize that he was in the car. He was ecstatic. Even New York grows quiet eventually, and this was one of those moments. The windows were rolled down despite the cold, and he thought he could hear himself and the guy outside breathing. It was that still.

The man who had disappeared behind the Matador walked briskly; he was skinny, puny almost, his spongy white skin set off by a dark turtleneck sweater. Topping it all was a balding head and a meticulously trimmed beard, the kind you had to check in the mirror half a dozen times a day to make sure that not a single stray hair had curled out of place. Actually, he looked sort of normal except for the nervous way he kept checking over his shoulder. McCarthy didn't recognize him. But so what? Half of New York was into buying either dope or sex. Join the club. He didn't particularly care whom he locked up.

A minute or two later, a huge black man, big enough to be a draft choice of the Giants or Jets, with rippling, body-by-Nautilus muscles, his flesh glistening in the moonlit night, came trotting along, leading two dogs on one leash, Great Danes. The dogs literally had their noses in the air and pranced like the kind of nasty, pampered mutts who were used to microwaved bones.

McCarthy had no idea what to expect next nor could he guess who was about to buy what from whom.

But, from behind his car, he could hear the sound of a belt buckle being opened, then the distinct unzipping of zippers. In his mind's eye, he could visualize pants coming down and being dropped. His experienced ears even picked up the muffled sound of skin scraping on the ground. Then he heard the telltale moans of sex.

What the hell was going on?

Fascinated, McCarthy still kept himself carefully concealed, but snaked his way over the car interior, to the cargo area in the back, to see just what was going on.

At that moment, one of the dogs started howling. And she wasn't baying at the moon.

Both men were crouched behind his car, still unaware he was inside, using it to balance themselves, while they had sex with the dogs, screwing them doggie-style, from behind, as the animals weaved from side to side on those long, unsteady legs. All four of them—two dogs and two humans, as near as McCarthy could tell—kept rhythmically pumping out brief, urgent balloons of condensed breath in the gnawing cold. The pulsing regularity of sex was made starkly visible.

Then the two men dropped the leash and the black guy and the white guy started humping each other; the big black guy bent the little white man over at the waist and quickly took charge, lifting and positioning him like a doll. In the space of about ten minutes, they changed positions and variations about five times. By then, the rear of the Matador was vibrating so much that McCarthy actually started bouncing around inside.

As soon as they were finished, the big black man put himself back in his pants, zipped his zipper, and marched away again, still leading the two enormous, now whimpering dogs. Next, McCarthy watched as the little white guy made his exit, passing his car a second time; he had his handkerchief up to his face and he was wiping white splashes of semen off his perfectly trimmed beard.

Throughout the entire strange tableau, not a single word had been exchanged between the two men. It had been eerily anonymous sex; the only sounds that had been made came from the dogs or from the zippers and buckles.

McCarthy's first instinct had been to jump out and arrest them. But that still would have left him wondering which crime, exactly, had been committed, unless you counted cruelty to animals. And he wasn't about to get the dogs to sign papers on either one of them. It just wasn't worth it. The drug deal might still be going down somewhere. At least he could hope.

It wasn't by accident that those two had found each other. Their whole point was the chance of being discovered. Compulsive behavior. McCarthy had seen it before. That was the most electric aspect of the whole thing— that risk of being found out. There were equal elements of amusement and disgust in his reaction. Vice was getting to him, all right; was it ever. He didn't need a police counselor to tell him that.

Before the twelfth hour had become the thirteenth, McCarthy straightened up in the Matador and called it off.

As he drove home he kept thinking about the typical— at least for Vice—New York street scene that had just unfolded. Bestiality off-Broadway. God, did he love New York. The only thing he wanted to do was take a hot shower and stay in there forever. He didn't even plan to wake Millie.

One week later, following his orders, Harold Schiffer and John Scarpa, two of McCarthy's best cops, were parked outside a different after-hours club on East Fourteenth Street, hoping to witness the same alleged drug buy that he had had under surveillance, or better yet, the same corrupt behavior by cops that had brought Vice to the land of the pimp bars in the first place.

At a few minutes before 2:00 A.M. they watched as a car pulled into the intersection at Second Avenue. It was a pimp-mobile. No mistaking that. Long and loud and tacky. There was even a layer of cheap fur on the swept-

161

back roof where the padded vinyl had originally been installed. Lincoln Continental. So fine.

Within seconds, the door opened, the pimp emerged, a massive black Super Fly in a purple felony hat, wearing a long fur coat and two stunning women on each arm.

McCarthy had passed on the description of the two men who had humped the dogs behind his car, hoping that one of them still might somehow be involved in the narcotics traffic in the neighborhood. There was no question that the black pimp matched the description of the dog-walker.

As the two cops watched, the pimp began to sniff at the damp night air just the way his two Great Danes had a week before. Then, walking like a circus act, arms in arms, unsteady, reeling, they all began moving together. The women showed plenty of nylon ass and stretched garter belts under their short skirts; they were carrying enough cleavage to hide a crate of melons. Then the five of them turned the corner at Fourteenth Street.

This was the night Life. In all its lewd, almost theatrical glory.

Schiffer, dressed like Sam Spade, saw them knock on the door of the club, gain entrance, and appear to head upstairs.

It looked interesting enough to be enticing. He was a nosy cop to begin with and it had been a slow night. Schiffer's natural restlessness and curiosity had already won out.

"Let's check it out," he said to Scarpa, a cautious, thoughtful Italian from Queens who had probably never once lost his lunch money at school.

Scarpa followed his nature and was skeptical: "They ain't gonna let us in there."

Schiffer listened, as he always did, but he refused to hear.

"You don't know if they will or they won't till you

162

ring the frigging bell and the door opens and the guy looks at us."

Scarpa still thought he was crazy. And maybe he was. There had to be some reason why he got along so well with McCarthy.

"Nobody's gonna even know why we're up there," Schiffer told him, as he opened the door and climbed out. "Don't worry about it, Johnny."

The two cops quickly crossed the street and soon were right behind the pimp and his swishing stable. Schiffer knocked and the door opened, just a crack.

From the darkness inside, two small, watery rodent eyes stared out at the tall, sinister-looking detective. These were the moments that Harold Schiffer lived for. Not *being* a cop as much as *playing* a cop.

Immediately, he could see that the doorman was an old, wrinkled Jewish guy that he knew from somewhere. What Schiffer couldn't discern from the man's make-them-work-for-it non-reaction was whether he knew him from being a *cop* or from the synagogue or the garment district or who-knew-where. With Schiffer, perhaps the leading Zionist in the NYPD, it could have been anyplace in New York.

"So, how're you doing?" he said to the old man. "I know you from somewhere, don't I?"

The doorman took a second long look and said something in Yiddish that Schiffer missed. Then, without saying another word or hesitating, he opened the door wide enough to let the two men in.

Escorting them, he found seats for both detectives at the upstairs bar. It wasn't much of a bar. Just six or seven stools and a bartop that needed wiping.

Schiffer glanced over at one of the large, seedy booths in the rear of the club and caught a snapshot image of the pimp they'd seen outside fondling one of the girls who had been on his arm. He had his hand inside the front of her dress, cupping a large nipple and breast.

163

The place looked "dirty" as only experienced cops could assess. Several of the biggest pimps in New York were there—Schiffer and Scarpa both recognized them—along with some of the highest-priced whores in Manhattan. They were all off-duty now. This was their downtime and there wasn't enough money in the whole world to get laid just now. Everybody needed a break.

There was cocaine everywhere; the city's black and white underworlds were mixing freely. Women were lazily dancing with other women and the pimps were quietly talking shop. At practically every booth, heads kept tilting back in the abrupt, spastic jerk that always followed a hit. Coke was still daring then, new; it was the Super Fly high.

Schiffer also saw another face he recognized—Barry Stein, a pretentious hustler and a very ambitious hood. Stein affected a businessman's clothes and mannerisms, but underneath the thousand-dollar suits Schiffer imagined a character composed of pus and larval droppings.

Stein noticed them, gave both cops a quick once-over, but made no move beyond that. If he smelled the musty scent of the NYPD on their baggy suits, he did a good job of not showing it.

This club—which seemed to be Stein's, the way he walked around giving orders to the barmaids—was almost unknown to the rest of Vice, outside of McCarthy's own team. And they weren't even sure what it was. But that mystery was clearing up now—it was an R-and-R retreat, sort of like an old-fashioned opium den, safely removed from the combat zone on Seventh Avenue or Times Square. Here, you took a toot and let down your hair. Everybody's batteries came out for a recharge.

A place like this could prove to be too valuable to bust prematurely. They had a perfect excuse to make a move, to pull out the handcuffs because of the coke, but they were there, they hoped, to gather intelligence, to try to stay mildly undercover in order to build up to bigger and better things. Narcotics could always make the pinch for the odd kilo later on. That wasn't necessarily doing it by the book, but that was the way good Vice cops always operated.

Schiffer and Scarpa both ordered drinks. They realized in that wordless sense of knowing that passes between two police partners that they had stumbled onto something very big here—but they had no way of knowing how big.

Schiffer had to diplomatically turn down a complimentary round from the old cocker doorman who was now beginning to act friendly, mostly in Yiddish. That made Schiffer sure that he *didn't* know him from being a cop. The detective checked his watch. Almost 3:30 A.M., approaching last call. And the place was still going strong.

To prove a liquor code violation the bartender would have to actually accept U.S. currency in exchange for a drink. They were witnessing that. Plus the cocaine. Within their first five minutes there, they had gathered more than enough for a warrant. Without ever realizing it, Schiffer and Scarpa had launched Sinbad. The day would come, later, when Bill McCarthy was ready to kiss them for it.

But all that was long before they snatched Tony Vitaliano.

Just before they were ready to leave, one of the whores—a good-looking girl with straight black hair and no underwear as far as they could see—asked Schiffer to dance. Just before she'd made her move, Barry Stein had stopped by her booth and whispered something to her.

Once she had Schiffer on his feet, on the floor, with his arms around her shoulders and her arms encircling his ass, she began what amounted to an informal frisk, beginning with her knee planted firmly and provocatively between his legs. Then, to keep his hands safely occupied, she lowered them to her breasts.

As they moved, very slowly, languidly almost, she

began rubbing him up and down, from his ankle to his thigh. She was feeling around for a gun.

He could have told her he wasn't wearing one. He wasn't that stupid. But she had clearly been given orders to find out for herself. Very deftly, very quickly, she continued to pat down the small of his back, both armpits, and finally his groin—where she discovered a monumental erection, but no .38 detective special, no weapon.

As soon as the song ended, she kissed him and excused herself, heading for the ladies' room. Barry Stein immediately got up and followed her.

That's when Schiffer and Scarpa decided to exit too.

Out on the street, Scarpa asked, "What was that all about? The whore?"

"Just checking," he said. "I imagine Stein asked her to see if I was a cop, if I was holding a piece."

"You weren't. Neither was I."

Schiffer smiled wickedly. "Which means that now, he just isn't sure. Are we or aren't we? And if we are, what the fuck were we doing there tonight if we didn't lock anybody up?"

Seventeen

A good *Boss* in the police department will tell you
what he wants you to do and if it turns out bad, he
will remember that he told you to do it.
A boss who will never hurt you is a boss who
doesn't make decisions. A boss who is a real
gentleman will take care of you when you get
drunk. Because he's a gentleman. But, when you
want him to be your advocate, to go to bat for you,
to bang on the table for you, he won't be there,
because he's too much of a gentleman. If it doesn't
work out, you're all alone.

MOTHER'S MAXIM

McCarthy was poking skeptically at a tuna and American
cheese on whole wheat, nursing a warm Pepsi and just
finishing up an article about the Knicks in the *Daily News*,
when Schiffer and Scarpa stopped by his desk to tell him
what had happened with Barry Stein and the pimp bar on
Fourteenth Street. By then, a gray, snowy dawn was
breaking over the silver obelisks of the New York skyline.
The rest of the world was stumbling to a sleepy breakfast,
but McCarthy and the Pimp Team in Vice were only just
beginning to wind down from the night before.

He listened as he always did, took a small bite, smelled
the too-fishy-tasting lump of a sandwich as it stared back
at him from the nest of its thick deli wrapping paper, and
decided to stick with the Pepsi. The one thing he knew
for certain was that his stomach would never recover
from being a cop.

"When the broad felt you up," he said to Schiffer,

"did she happen to whisper anything in your ear about what pleasures fifty bucks would buy?"

Schiffer smiled uneasily. "Sorry, boss," he answered. "No solicitation."

"So what do we have?"

"Liquor code violations coming out the kazoo . . ." Schiffer said.

"Which are bullshit, at best . . ." McCarthy interjected.

"And people taking cocaine like they were drinking coffee."

"Which *isn't* bullshit," he cut in this time.

"So?" the detective asked him.

"So . . . I think we go for a warrant. But I don't send in you two guys again because we may be able to use you on this later. If we're really lucky, Stein still isn't completely sure that you're cops."

"I like that," Scarpa said, opening his mouth for the first time.

"So do I," McCarthy answered. "I'll go in with Vitaliano. We make a move tomorrow night."

"You go for the coke, right?" Scarpa asked.

"Wrong," McCarthy replied, surprising both of his men. "All we go for is the illegal liquor sales. We go for the bullshit pinch. Then, we see what happens." He looked up from his desk, grinned, and took one last, desperate bite at the tuna and cheese.

Schiffer and Scarpa immediately understood.

What McCarthy didn't have to explain was that he was hoping—gambling, actually—that in the process of serving the warrant, which was technically a glorified misdemeanor, a nothing case, somebody at the bar would panic and begin waving money in his face, or in Vitaliano's, to try and make things square.

That would be a Vice case; the kind that he was looking for. He'd been angling for months to get someone in the Life, preferably a pimp with connections, to hit him with

168

a payoff deal. That could start a plan in motion that McCarthy had been hatching for months. It was to be the genesis of Sinbad.

The three of them nodded to one another and started to head home. "By the way," McCarthy called after them, "did anybody screw any dogs?"

Early on, McCarthy had realized that he had to let his team know what kind of boss they could expect him to be. That was why he could count on cops like Harold Schiffer and John Scarpa. The very first thing he had done was impress upon them the fact that he was not a gentleman—at least not in the traditional NYPD understanding of that term. He did not tolerate drunks; he refused to cover for anybody.

If they still wanted to work for him, that was fine—but it had to be on McCarthy's terms. Back when he was an ordinary street cop he saw that partners were people you had to make deals with fast. They could be either good or bad. But you had to agree. You had to be of the same mind. Honest *or* dishonest.

That was most important. And for McCarthy they had better be honest. He didn't care if his partner was a big guy or a little guy, a coward or a brave cop, or if he smelled. He just never wanted to have to worry about him being dishonest; he would have nothing to do with that.

When he became a sergeant and took over the Pimp Team in Public Morals, he went to great pains to get that same message across. The rest, he hoped, would take care of itself.

Frustration for any cop was knowing what to do, but not being able to do it. Allowed to do it. Vice was like going through a dark, dangerous forest to get to the good part, to get to the significant arrests. He had to guide them, had to show them how to keep trying to push the rock up the mountain, never stopping for a second, because that's when it would roll back over you. If you wanted it to happen in Vice, you had to *make* it happen.

The police department didn't want to see all of its cops become frustrated, because that meant that there would be too many guys walking around out there with guns. Frustrated, well-armed guys. And that could become very costly, very fast.

They tried to avoid that by allowing the system to subtly teach its cops, even its potentially good cops, to survive by doing nothing. Absolutely nothing. Do fucking nothing—that was the message of government to its law enforcers. Do only what they made you do. Slide by. But there was a fallacy in that. Just about every cop McCarthy had ever met had, at one point or another, joined the police department precisely because he wanted to *do* something. Maybe he only wanted to be corrupt—but damn, he wanted to go out and make even that happen. You could never take that away from cops and expect them not to rebel in their own devious ways.

McCarthy saw his role in Vice as being that of an expediter for his team. He had already formed some very definite opinions on what separated good bosses from bad. If pounding his fist on the desk in a superior officer's office was what it took to make his men respect him— going in and pounding it for them either because they couldn't do it for themselves or because they were afraid to—then he had made his mind up to follow that course. He had never worked for a boss like that, but he had always wanted to. That became his vision, his dream. And even in a place like the Pimp Team in Vice, you had to have a dream.

He much preferred becoming a partner, rather then a boss, to the detectives under him. He saw it as his responsibility as well as an opportunity to show them exactly how he wanted the job done. The team was at its best when he infused it with his holy sense of mission—

if that made the chief of detectives a devil, so be it. As long as it allowed McCarthy to emerge as the simulacrum of the mythic leader his Vice cops had been looking for he was willing to ride with it.

The reaction of his team to this approach, to a boss who actually wanted them to be better cops and take chances and run risks, was profound. To McCarthy with his tough brand of idealism this only seemed natural, the way things were supposed to be. But to the cops who worked for him, it had been a revelation. No one had ever come in before and said all this and then tried to make good on it.

In the beginning, it had been tough getting them all to think as a single unit. He started to have his "team" meetings outside the office, away from the big bosses. He picked a place in Chinatown. There was blunt symbolism in that too. Chinatown, with its Tongs (organized crime gangs imported from Mainland China, centuries-old, tribal) and whores and elaborate secret gambling casinos, was the proverbial belly of the beast. Vice cops had to be really hardass honest guys to hang out there and *not* become corrupted. Chinatown to the NYPD was like the ancient seat of all Vice temptation. To McCarthy's mind that made the setting perfect.

They would spend a great deal of time there together, feeling each other out, getting to trust one another, developing the esprit de corps that every unit in the police department wished it had. And since they were in the neighborhood anyway, they also developed more new, valuable intelligence on gambling and prostitution in Chinatown—as much by accident as by design—than all the Pimp Teams before them.

It didn't take them long to determine that most gambling was multilevel in Chinatown, with games like Mah-Jongg upstairs and the secret casinos downstairs—*three* sub-basements down, in some cases, below the noodle factories and fortune cookie bakeries.

171

Fetching, honey-skinned whores with watery almond eyes—downcast eyes—were delivered on order, like complimentary drinks to a crap table in Las Vegas. Once a girl had become too Americanized, too fluent in English, or simply too burned out and broken down—literally too loose and stretched—from the constant demands of marathon sex, she would be rotated back to Hong Kong or the mainland, back to a peasant brothel where the less demanding local customers didn't consist of high rollers who might drop a hundred grand in one night of looking at snake eyes.

Few of the women lasted past their twentieth birthdays; many started at fourteen or fifteen. By eighteen they had usually become the debauched senior citizens of the Chinatown whore trade. A handful might then drift into massage parlor work, which was relatively safe, if a bit like being held captive all day. Others who remained were recruited for the thriving escort services—pussy delivered to your door. That was dangerous as hell, because you never knew who or what would be waiting behind that door. In fact, McCarthy had never met an escort girl—and he knew dozens—who had not, at one time or another, been raped, assaulted, kidnapped for a few hours, or subjected to some combination of all three.

The one thing that the foreign whores would never do was work the streets. Maybe back home, but never in New York. Here, they were as much prized for their passivity and willingness to hang around all night doing absolutely nothing, waiting until a customer happened to remember them, to look up from his card game, as they were for their skills in bed—skills which distinguished many of them as the finest hookers in Manhattan. By contrast, American women were expected to be more aggressive, ready-to-please, sexual initiators who weren't afraid to whisper "Suck you off?" in the ear of a total stranger. Or even scream it through his car window.

Each political faction among the Chinese also had its

own gambling parlors. The Communists had the most elaborate setup. They used a place near Catherine Street called the House of the Gold Doors. Except the doors weren't actually gold, only *painted* gold. Underneath they were solid steel. That was the sort of information that would come in very handy to the next cop who tried to take the place with a sledgehammer. And McCarthy himself was frequently the team's sledgeman.

All the while, the Pimp Team was becoming that cohesive unit that McCarthy had aimed for.

About a week after Schiffer and Scarpa had made their observations, the Pimp Team received the go-ahead to serve the warrant on Barry Stein's bar. But there was an added complication. There was a new captain in charge of Vice then—Larry Hepburn. He wanted to see a pimp bar because he'd never been near one in his life and he decided that since he was now the boss of Public Morals, visiting a pimp bar might be a good idea. He saw it as a field trip, as a class trip almost. By then, his reputation as "Flash Gordon"—because of his space cadet tendencies—was already sacred writ in the NYPD.

Hepburn was an odd duck, a ruddy-faced, redheaded eccentric, a sort of absent-minded professor, tweedy and frequently lost in a pungent cloud of pipe or cigar smoke, who had only recently been handed Vice. His predecessor, another prize, had been unable to reconcile his strict New York Catholic upbringing with all the pornography he had to confiscate and look at and with all the half-dressed whores he had to interrogate. On the surface, Hepburn was an improvement, but as far as McCarthy was concerned, he still seemed ill suited to command Vice. Hepburn was a guy who went through life perpetually amazed by what he found. That almost innocent sense of credulity could get a cop sent to jail in the corruption cauldron that was Vice.

The midlevel bosses like McCarthy, who served directly under Hepburn, were struck by his intelligence and honesty—in fact, he had been chosen for the sensitive job precisely because he was straight, and because nontainted bosses were hard to come by in the paranoid era that followed the revelations of the Knapp Commission.

McCarthy groaned when he found out that Hepburn had selected his team for the show-and-tell. But he wasn't surprised. The new captain might have seemed like an eccentric, but he was nobody's fool. Hepburn was a genuine police buff who recognized and admired superior performance, and that was exactly what McCarthy's team had been consistently turning in.

They were scheduled to serve the warrant on the Fourteenth Street bar at approximately 5:00 A.M.—well past the legal closing time. The team had assembled at midnight, reviewed their work for that tour, and then hit the street.

McCarthy and Tony Vitaliano took Captain Hepburn with them and began barhopping. They planned to end up at Barry Stein's place.

Hepburn was excited, like a kid almost. At one point during the evening, when he had disappeared to use the men's room, McCarthy turned to Vitaliano and said, "Can you believe Flash?" Then he began mimicking the captain. "It's like, 'Oh, wow, we're going to the zoo to see the zebras. Take me to see the elephants. Then I wanna see the chimpanzees, and the orangutans. Oh, boy, look at the orangutans. Oh, look at the brown one! Look at all the pimps!' "

"The guy's a buff," Vitaliano said. "The department's full of them. He's a good guy. What do we care? For once we have a quiet night."

Both cops knew that working under "buffs," as they called them, was the story of the NYPD. Commanders, usually, they were highly entertained by the job, almost like groupies. Most had never really been called upon to do anything more than look good, have "command presence," which actually meant they had to look good in a uniform, especially at funerals for slain cops or while marching in parades or turning out for other functions at the Building at One Police Plaza.

Hepburn had come from that environment, that background, and the cops in Vice were watching him skeptically. He would more than make up for his buff status during the crunch time of Sinbad, but that night, in the very beginning, no one could guess that Hepburn would turn out to be a member of the smallest minority in New York—a boss, an officer whom the real cops looked up to.

Everything seemed to be a surprise to Larry Hepburn, including even hunger. Once, he had showed up for an undercover job on a bicycle because his car wouldn't start so he rode to work on his kid's bike instead. The Flash stories were endless.

In every bar they hit that night, Tony Vitaliano could have passed for a blood relative of the Columbo Family. As long as people didn't know him as a cop, they would be convinced that he was a hood. He looked the part. McCarthy and Hepburn stayed in the background while Vitaliano went into his act. He was supposed to be playing the part of a small-time hood out on the town. He milked the role like a farmer with both hands on an udder.

In the kinds of places they were visiting, you always walked in, looked around, and then went right down to the end of the bar and stood there with your back against the wall—but not *too* close, you didn't want to bring home any roaches—and then you watched the front door and the bathroom door. That's where the action would develop: sex and drug deals through the bathroom door— if you saw someone down on her knees, you knew she wasn't making a novena—and stickup guys with guns in their hands through the front door. Just as long as you had those three things covered in the Life—sex, drugs, and guns—you had it all.

Places like that were being robbed all the time, any time, and McCarthy wanted to be situated with no blind sides and only one door that he had to watch. You never, ever sat down. In fact, that was the first instruction he had given to Hepburn that night. Never relax; not here, not in this kind of place. You just never knew who might come walking in, or what sort of piece he might be holding. Any way you could, you tried to take the high ground in a pimp bar.

They spent the first few hours in the first few places checking out the local talent, recognizing some tough guys—a pimp bar was like their clubhouse—and waiting to see if anything happened to fall their way.

By the time they hit the third place, Hepburn was still in a trance and the other two cops were growing impatient. Vitaliano had turned sullen and McCarthy was looking to start a fight. Boxing was like a tonic for him; he didn't much care whether he won or lost, the workout would relax him.

They were in a bar now where the girls were indiscriminately working the crowd, trying to separate the pimps, who wouldn't think of paying, from the johns, who couldn't reach for their wallets fast enough.

There was a tier of blue-padded booths, like overstuffed furniture, just above the crowded floor level, set off by a handsome wrought-iron railing. This was where the girls were making their money—women with vacant looks and preoccupied expressions—giving customers rough hand-jobs under the tables, behind the long, oversized tablecloths that covered the small, round cocktail tables. It was right out in the open, not ten feet from the couples dancing on the floor, urgent sex in the middle of a crowded bar. Classic whoring.

McCarthy timed them. The captain was oblivious until

it was pointed out to him. Five minutes, no more. Five minutes of a girl sort of leaning into her john, their shoulders touching, not really in intimacy, just in closeness, as her hands would then quickly disappear into the guy's lap. A minute or two later her wrist and arm would begin pumping furiously between the john's thighs, working him steadily in that knowing, pistonlike rhythm, while she never left her seat in the booth. A few of them used their free hands to sip drinks.

It was as regimented as close-order drills. Exactly five minutes later, or less, one john after another would suddenly bolt back red-faced, squirm around in a little spasm, and jerk his head and upper body as he climaxed, shooting off into one of the small napkins that the whores had thoughtfully provided. Linen napkins. The same linen that would then be circulated back, maybe laundered, maybe not, to be used as napkins when you sat down to dinner.

There were variations from place to place, but it was the typical industry of the bust-out bar. Occasionally, a girl would actually drop under the table for a blow-job, but that was rare. The whores hated that. It was too much work. After seven or eight guys, you were nearly out of commission; your knees would hurt, your tongue would swell up and you'd have trouble swallowing and your jaw would ache so much you could barely open your mouth. Plus, the johns were constantly bucking back and pulling out too fast and coming on your face or hair or clothes. Then you had to add in extra costs for ruined makeup, dry-cleaning bills, and so forth. Blow-jobs were just too damn much overhead. At least that was how one of the women in the Life had explained her reasoning to McCarthy. He never forgot that.

He had heard all these complaints and more from many of the women his team arrested. Essentially, they were business-women, depending more on volume than anything else, and, even with the cops, they enjoyed shop-

177

talk. For them, sex had to be fast, anonymous, relatively safe, and above all, cost-effective. Put all those criteria together, and you couldn't beat a friendly hand-job. You could work all night that way, john after john, and never have to worry about anything more serious than a sore hand and stiff shoulder. As long as the bar was supplying the tablecovers and the johns, it was a snap. That might not have seemed especially romantic, but the johns were in no position to complain. Not every whore had it that much to her liking; many of them really had to put out, on their backs, but no human body was ever intended to take that kind of abuse night after night. They usually didn't last very long. A year or two or even three, at the most. Then, either the Life or the drugs killed them. Once their looks and bodies went they had to rely on volume alone and that was invariably the quick beginning of a very rapid end. It was cocaine in the beginning, crack later on, as the trade and the traffic on the streets changed. McCarthy had buried his share.

They had been watching many different versions of this activity all night, wherever they went. Hepburn was getting an education. But the time was racing by and they would soon be due at Stein's bar on Fourteenth Street.

McCarthy was pointing that out to them when, to his absolute amazement and momentary panic, who happened to walk into the bar they were getting ready to leave but Barry Stein himself. It was as if he had leaped right out of McCarthy's thoughts. He'd been a Vice cop for a long time, but nothing that spooky had ever happened before.

The three of them froze. McCarthy knew Stein from mug shots, but the two of them had never met. Larry Hepburn was a total outsider. However, as Stein quickly took in the crowd and the people leaning against the bar, his eyes immediately settled on Tony Vitaliano and stayed there.

McCarthy instantly reviewed everything he knew about the pimp. He'd just gotten out of Attica prison, done fifteen years; he had to be in his mid-fifties by now; pretty big guy before he went upstate. He had been in on a swindle involving airline tickets and he was the one who got caught. That part could have been a setup; Stein taking a hard fall for somebody bigger. His bar on Fourteenth Street, a bar that he had suddenly started to call his own only a few short months out of Attica, with no visible income, could very well have been his reward for services rendered, for doing somebody else's time in the joint.

The most interesting thing about Barry Stein was his old girlfriend. She was a madam with better mob connections than practically any other woman in New York, at least any other woman McCarthy was aware of.

The word on the street was that the girlfriend had given him up to the cops so she would be free to screw around with one of the premier wiseguys. Stein had had no alternative but to accept that deal uncomplainingly—if he wanted to stay alive, that is.

But she had done more than spread her legs for another hood. She had robbed him, too. And that was a far more serious offense. Years later, long after Sinbad, McCarthy would discover that Stein had also been hatching a plan to have his old girlfriend framed by the police so that he could get five minutes alone in her apartment, just five uninterrupted minutes, with no chance of her or her new boyfriend coming in on him. That would have been his payback for the way she gave him up. It turned out that she had stuffed every venetian blind in the place with his money, in that fat hollow bases at the bottom of the windowsills. Almost a hundred thousand dollars of his stash was missing and that was where he figured it had to be hidden.

The only thing they knew that night, though, was that Barry Stein had somehow gotten the jump on them.

Then, as if on cue, Stein began to make his way through the crowd, toward the cops. He was one brazen son of a bitch.

Hepburn had no way of picking it up, but McCarthy, pretending to cough into his scotch and water—he'd been downing scotch all night and struggling not to give in to the buzz he was developing—asked Tony, in a hoarse whisper, "You two acquainted?"

All Tony had time to do, before Stein was on top of him, was nod a hasty yes.

McCarthy still couldn't believe the timing on it all. But the only thing he could do was lay back and make small talk with one of the better-looking whores as Barry Stein grabbed Tony the V for a huddle down at the other end of the bar.

Stein was sweating. After the briefest sort of preliminaries, he offered to buy Tony a drink and said, "I think there were two guys in my place last week and I think they were cops. I maybe have a problem." Then he described, accurately and in detail, Harold Schiffer and John Scarpa.

Vitaliano listened, said nothing beyond the obligatory grunts and waited for Stein to make a play. He noticed that the pimp's hands were actually shaking. He was sniffing badly, too, as though he had the worst head cold of his life. Coke, Vitaliano thought, as Stein's small hands involuntarily sought out his nostrils every few seconds.

The cop still let the long silence that had suddenly developed between them do his talking.

"So, look, Tony," the pimp finally said, "it would be worth your while."

That was all. Not another syllable. But that was enough.

Tony said, "Wait, I'll have to talk to my boss." Then,

180

he momentarily left Stein and walked over to McCarthy. "We're in," he said. "This guy wants to reach."

The sergeant smiled. Just a little. They couldn't risk giving it away now. They just looked at each other. They knew.

Reach meant pay, payoff, bribe, cough up whatever it would take to make the problem go away.

McCarthy and Vitaliano acted as though they were conferring for Stein's benefit. But they had rehearsed all this long before.

Then they left Captain Hepburn at the bar, still looking around wide-eyed as though he were on a tour, and the two cops walked outside with Barry Stein.

They talked some more in the cold and wind of Manhattan. Stein skimmed over the surface of the frozen ground as if he were tap-dancing on a bed of nails. Some part of his anatomy, it appeared, always had to be in motion. McCarthy, who had never seen anyone as nervous as Stein, blew into his hands to keep warm. The remaining effects of the scotch were completely gone now—temperature close to zero had taken care of that. Tony was utterly into his role now and was rapidly taking over the conversation. Suddenly, the three of them fell silent as a bus and a car exchanged blasts of their horns.

Stein repeated it again. "Listen, I think I got a problem."

After more fencing he explained that a few nights before two guys who looked like cops had been at his place, for no apparent reason, scoping out the talent and preparing, he was afraid, to either close him down or shake him down. He never mentioned the presence of the drugs. Finally, referring to Scarpa and Schiffer, Stein said, "I could tell, them guys will be back to cause me problems."

McCarthy, as Tony's boss, appeared to agree reluctantly. "Okay, this could be a pain in the ass for me, but we'll look into it."

Now the two cops had done their part. But not as far as the law was concerned. Even though they had just entered into a conspiracy with a convicted felon for the purpose of obstructing justice in exchange for a bribe, they would need more. A lot more. They would need tapes and a log of contacts and the kind of irrefutable evidence that a smart lawyer would be unable to turn into mush in front of a jury. McCarthy was only too familiar with the routine. They hadn't really, technically, said more than ten words about anything in particular. And they had no idea what kind of information or intelligence they could squeeze out of Stein. All that would have to come later. Much later. But this was a start. A great start.

Wrapping his light jacket tighter across his shoulders, the pimp told McCarthy, "Maybe there's something we can work out where I take care of you . . . ."

The cops listened some more. This was what they were waiting for. Stein was incriminating himself more every time he opened his mouth.

"What did you have in mind?" McCarthy asked.

Stein refused to become any more specific than that. "It can be arranged" was all he would commit himself to.

That would have to be good enough. McCarthy then made an excuse to go back into the bar.

He found Hepburn and told him that they would have to leave immediately. Something had come up. At that point, in that bar, he was afraid to tell him any more.

"No way," Hepburn said. "This is fun here. All these pimps. All these whores. Where we going now? Why do we have to leave?"

McCarthy became more insistent.

"Why?" Hepburn pressed him. "Why can't we do the warrant tonight? I need to know. Why not? Tell me."

"I can't go into all that in a fucking bar," McCarthy said. He was getting hot himself, trying to act cool and nonchalant in front of the pimp.

182

Just then, Stein and Vitaliano walked back in from the cold. McCarthy saw them. Stein was beginning to look at McCarthy and Hepburn like he was now regretting what he had just done. That was the last thing the Vice cop wanted. The whole situation was crazy. Stein had no idea that McCarthy was there with a warrant in his pocket, a warrant that could close Stein down. But now, of course, they had to forget the bullshit liquor violation and really set him up good for attempted bribery and whatever else they could get. If it went right it could turn into an old con man's sting. And there could be no more deserving a mark than sleazy Barry Stein.

Finally, McCarthy half-screamed at Hepburn. "No talking here, Captain, we *gotta* leave now."

"I didn't finish my drink."

Hepburn was the most dense man McCarthy had ever seen.

"Captain, I said we *gotta* get out and if I have to I will hit you over the head and carry you out of here. Something very big is going down right now. Something I can fill you in on later. You see that guy with Vitaliano?" He pointed to Stein.

Hepburn nodded.

"He's about five seconds from realizing that we are setting him up for the worst fall of his life. I can see it in his eyes. He's about to change his mind. He's the kind of a guy who changes his mind with a gun. *Capisce?*"

Hepburn frowned like he was a little kid being forced to leave somebody's birthday party. "But I told my wife I'm gonna serve a warrant tonight. They'll all be waiting for the details tomorrow."

McCarthy started to physically lift him up from the barstool. At that point, the captain came along peacefully.

The guy definitely wanted to bribe them. That much had been established, they quickly explained to Larry

183

Hepburn outside. But they would need permission to go on what was known as a "control pad," which was the same thing as setting up a sting. A real pad would have been the real thing—bribery. And the old NYPD had been notorious for the number of cops on pads. The okay for an undercover operation like this would have to come down from Internal Affairs.

Anybody could serve a warrant. But if they could go along with Barry Stein for a while, if they could get the narcotics connection in the club, locate the big supplier, see who *his* connection was, then that, as McCarthy pointed out to Hepburn, "could be a fucking marvelous collar."

Right there on the corner they had what amounted to a team meeting and decided to go ahead with it. Hepburn promised to take care of Internal Affairs.

A few minutes later, McCarthy found Stein in the bar. He'd just come out of the bathroom and his nose looked as though he'd been able to make a score while the cops had been outside. His nervousness had been replaced by an even more annoying overconfidence.

"We got a deal," McCarthy told him. "I just squared it with my man outside."

Stein looked at the Vice cop as though he had just ordered him up from the menu and now he was having second thoughts. "You just bought the deal," the pimp said. "But remember one thing. I just bought *you*."

McCarthy suddenly felt like one of his whores. He also had to fight hard against an overwhelming urge to take the warrant out of his pocket and shove it down Barry Stein's throat. But that would have been too easy. He had far better plans for this chump.

Ignoring the insult, McCarthy continued. "What are we talking about on my end?"

"I want Fourteenth Street left alone. That's a hundred

184

a week. I may need other places left alone. I may need some places hit. I'll let you know."

"A hundred each, right?" McCarthy haggled. This part was especially humiliating, bargaining with this piece of shit. But as long as he was pretending to be a corrupt cop, he had to act like one.

"Each," Stein finally said. "You guys are *worse* than whores."

They didn't bother to shake on it. That was a good thing, too. McCarthy would have broken his arm.

The night had almost ended. And what a helluva night it had been. From where he stood on that windy corner outside this foul pimp bar McCarthy wanted to believe that he could see all the way to Sinbad's conclusion. But that, of course, would have been fooling himself. Still, he could see enough of the future to know that something unforgettable was about to take place, something bigger and probably more dangerous than anything he had ever faced before.

McCarthy looked down toward the slow buildup of traffic on the East Side. The morning didn't get much of a chance to wake up and blink the sleepiness away in New York.

First there were a few sets of headlights, just two pinpoints moving purposefully along the black, silent streets. Then a whole school of them. It was going to be one of those bitterly cold December days in the city that began with a blue tint leaking through the clouds, just before the dawn sky exploded in deep reds and yellows as the sun broke through. The whole thing was almost too pretty to be part of the Vice world. But it was. Even in Vice.

Just then, Tony Vitaliano and Larry Hepburn came out to see if Stein was gone.

"It's okay," he told Tony. "The sleaze left. We're all in on it for a C-note a week."

The two cops laughed. Their acting had been more than convincing. Captain Hepburn looked just a little nervous. This was new to him; he hadn't been a street cop for a very long time.

"Do you know what we just did?" McCarthy said. "We just made that little creep's whole day. As soon as we went in with him, his status in the Life went way the hell up. Now he has a police contact. He's going to go around and tell people all over Manhattan that he has two Vice cops in his pocket."

Tony was beaming. "It's that great," he said; the incongruity of that statement bounced right off him.

"We're bought and paid for now," McCarthy confirmed, thoroughly pleased with their night's work.

Then, as if to punctuate the amazing events of the last couple hours, Tony the V cleared his throat and hawked up a mouthful of spit which he deposited on the exact spot on the pavement where Barry Stein had stood.

"Hey," McCarthy pretended to rebuke him. "Let's show a little respect for our new partner."

"Respect this," Tony answered, suddenly grabbing at his crotch.

This time, even Flash Gordon broke up.

Operation Sinbad had begun.

Eighteen

Some of the most honorable people I ever met were
Crooks.

MOTHER'S MAXIM

Following that initial encounter, McCarthy and Vitaliano
began to meet with Stein on Second Avenue and Fourteenth Street once a week. Stein would walk up to them
on the corner and hand them an envelope with hundred-
dollar bills inside. In the beginning, few words were
exchanged. That cash, as well as all subsequent money
accepted by McCarthy or his men as part of Sinbad, was
then turned in to the Public Morals Unit, Headquarters
Division, One Police Plaza.

The money was never late; the count was never short.
This went on for three months, from December 1973
until February 1974. McCarthy had decided—and had
convinced his bosses—that the best way for him to establish his identity as a cop who could be "reached" was to
convince people that his Pimp Team was in the bag as
well. Few corrupt cops could accomplish much for the
people paying them as loners anyway. Having a whole
team or squad on the pad, however, was not only cost-
effective, but was also the traditional way of trickling

down payoffs in the NYPD, from commander to individual cop. In this case, from Sergeant McCarthy to Vitaliano, and thence to the others.

In the beginning their meetings took place out in the open, always close to passing traffic. This was clearly a precaution on Stein's part against electronic eavesdropping. Later, after they had become more comfortable in each other's presence, they would meet inside the after-hours club. By then, the two cops had become relaxed in their unaccustomed roles and Barry Stein had evidenced such quick trust in McCarthy that he quietly started dropping hints about other possible money-making opportunities into their casual conversation.

The two cops always tried to be together. There were two good reasons for that. First, for mutual protection. Second, one of them would always be in a position to serve as a witness. Someday, they hoped, all of what they were getting would end up in court. The prosecution would need at least one unimpeachable witness.

Another point to consider was the protocol of the underworld. Having Tony along gave McCarthy added weight as a significant contact. The mob mentality demanded that a valet, a coat-holder to the mighty, be present. That was Tony's mission—to act as a straight man. Eventually that playacting would change, as it so often did in undercover operations, and Tony would become the focus of the game.

There were different roles for different people; within a single case as complex as Sinbad, the cops knew that they could be called upon to assume multiple, simultaneous identities, from good cop to bad cop to hood. The trick was in keeping them all separate and in remembering which role went with which phase of the clandestine game.

At every turn, it seemed, Stein or his friends were planning some illegal deal that could bring the police down on them. As long as he was willing to act as a participant, no matter how passive, McCarthy could expect a cut. That was the deal that was tacitly being offered to him.

People like Barry Stein worked full-time at the science of corrupting. A week never went by that didn't include some mention of hot merchandise that was for sale, or some vice racket that needed police protection. McCarthy didn't even have to act that interested. All he had to do was listen.

In most of their conversations, the availability of narcotics came up. It was the coin of the realm in vice, the hard currency of the street. Stein's reasoning was consistent: Since the cops confiscated so much cocaine during raids and arrests, and since their intelligence on the activities of various pushers was the most thorough in New York, it only made sense to turn to "bad" cops like McCarthy as the most reliable sources of drugs.

Stein approached him about it three times. He needed all the cocaine he could get his hands on. McCarthy kept putting him off, arguing that it was all too risky, but he also let him know that he was weakening. That stretched the string out a little further. McCarthy never said that he *couldn't* get it for him. He just acted reluctant.

Once, when they were sitting in the club about three o'clock one afternoon, with the girls just starting to come in, getting ready for the customers that night, Stein leaned over to McCarthy and said, "How do you feel about a stickup?"

"I don't have any feelings," he told him. "That's too dumb to discuss."

The pimp grinned at him as if to say that McCarthy would understand it all after he had finished explaining it. "It's not dangerous if the people we stick up can't complain," Stein said. "That's the beauty of it."

He wanted McCarthy to begin helping him rob drug dealers. He had it worked out that whenever they were together with a group of people—and if that group included one of the dealers he had in mind—he would identify him for the cop by putting his arm around the pusher's shoulders. McCarthy was to take it from there.

Together, they drove to several heavy narcotics spots in Manhattan and the Bronx. They used Stein's car; the pimp drove and McCarthy acted as the muscle for him. He didn't always make it clear that McCarthy was a cop who happened to be in his pocket, but he did make it clear that the tough Irishman was not to be antagonized. Stein knew just where and with whom to apply his ominous threat of intimidation.

Every place they stopped, there would be one or two people whom Stein would put his arm around. They were the ones who held the heavy weight, the big kilo loads. Most of the names and faces were new to McCarthy. It was valuable intelligence.

At that point he didn't know how much of it was current with the Narcotics Squad, but at least he would be able to point a finger at some people about whom the police had previously only had suspicions.

Stein urged McCarthy to use the Pimp Team like a stickup crew and just follow these dealers, learn their patterns. Then confront them and threaten to lock them up, unless they came across with a payoff. He was also very anxious for McCarthy to steal their narcotics so that Stein could resell them.

McCarthy's split would be half. He could distribute his share to the rest of the squad any way he saw fit. Relative to the going rate on the street, that was a handsome offer. Stein genuinely seemed to like the cop and wanted to get even closer to him. McCarthy had given him the idea that he had a great head for business.

Tempting as that plan was from an intelligence point of view, since it would eventually take the police to many of the top dealers in Manhattan, McCarthy still couldn't agree to it. It wasn't NYPD policy. The people he was reporting to, at the first deputy commissioner level, refused even to consider it.

Technically no one, not even an undercover cop, could stick people up—thereby committing a felony—and then give the proceeds, drugs and cash, to someone else, to Barry Stein.

That was where McCarthy had to draw the line. There were imaginative ways to get around it. For example, McCarthy could have introduced other undercover cops to Stein for him to resell the drugs. But there wasn't enough of a budget for that, nor did the people running the show have that sort of risk-taking vision.

This was taking place in 1973-74 and the police were, literally, making up the undercover manual as they went along.

During the course of all this Stein had only one stipulation: He would only finger dealers for McCarthy to rob, providing that he could guarantee they wouldn't be arrested.

That was his curious kind of morality. It was perfectly ethical, from his point of view, to steal from them, extort them, beat them up; that was part of the cost of doing business in the Life. But Stein would never be party to getting anybody locked up. McCarthy had to swear to this.

Stein maintained his honor. He wouldn't actually cooperate with the *police*, but he saw nothing wrong in cooperating with a corrupt policeman.

For his part, McCarthy had a separate agenda. He had to keep reminding Stein that he wanted to make friends, line up easy payoffs, turn over some fast money. He couldn't take a chance on robbing people.

For a little while, that held the pimp off. But McCarthy also knew that it would start up again. It was only a matter of time.

McCarthy sensed that people like Stein were motivated

by common sense. There were certain things that one bad guy would never do for another bad guy. Like take a stupid risk. Eventually, every cop who ever worked undercover came to understand this. The average bad guy knew when and how to say no. Otherwise, he had no one's respect.

In the end, McCarthy and Vitaliano just had to be convincing actors. Offers of sex were even more trouble-some than schemes to make money. It was common prac-tice to *insist* that a cop on the take have sex with one of the girls—just to test his credibility. Barry Stein offered one of hookers to McCarthy after a few meetings.

Faced with that sort of temptation, with that kind of clearcut opportunity to prove oneself to the target of the investigation, most cops will succumb and thereby jeop-ardize the whole case and other people's lives, or they might fall apart and actually admit that they are under-cover. It's never the bad *guys* who find you out, it's the women.

McCarthy handled it in the only way he could. He screamed at Stein, "Go to hell! You think *I* need *you* to get laid? Take your slut and get out of here. Who do you think you are? Do I need you to pimp for me? You think I'm gonna get laid when you want me to get laid? I'm no performing dog."

Stein backed off. The woman was sent on her way. Actually, the decision was easy for McCarthy. Any kind of sex play was an impossibility. He was wearing a wire throughout this period and the device was concealed around his testicles.

During the course of their meetings that winter, Stein introduced McCarthy to a man named Freddy Kane, who claimed to be a part owner of the club on Fourteenth Street, where the Vice cops were supposed to be provid-ing protection.

Suddenly, there was a second player in the game.

Kane, about six feet two, a very dark-skinned black

man with a thin build and a hoarse, three-pack-a-day voice, always showed up in sunglasses. McCarthy knew that he was an East Side pimp with an uncommonly fancy stable of hookers. However, his main source of illegal income was gambling. He used marked cards and could play poker all night long.

Kane seemed promising. One of his partners was William Smith, Philadelphia Smith. Smith, a huge, brutally violent pimp, would become player number three. He treated everyone, especially his women, with a sadistic cruelty that bordered on the psychotic. The turnover in his stable was constant; every week he sent a different hooker to the emergency room.

Smith also lived out the stereotype of the Super Fly, sporting capes and what the Vice cops referred to as "felony hats"—wide-brimmed, garish fedoras in the early 1970s (probably baseball caps worn backward today).

Philadelphia Smith was never without a knife or a gun. Or a Bible. Before sitting down with anyone, including McCarthy, who met him one night in Stein's club, Smith had a habit of laying either the gun, a German Luger, or the knife, a big bowie knife with a blade that was fat enough to slice through a ham, on the table in front of him. Then he'd put the Bible next to the weapons.

At that first meeting, Philadelphia Smith came right to the point. He was in the market for police intelligence. Could he deal?

After a long pause, the Vice cop answered, "Can you pay?"

Smith glared at him, reached into his pocket and pulled out what McCarthy guessed was about five thousand dollars in cash. He fanned it out on the table. Barry Stein was practically drooling.

"What that look like?" Philadelphia Smith growled.

"It looks like we're in business," McCarthy said. "What do you need?"

Smith had recently been out partying in Las Vegas, where his car had been riddled with bullets. He had barely escaped. He was scared. The attack had been unprovoked, as far as he knew, and the person or persons behind it remained a mystery. Smith was afraid that it would happen again, on his home turf, in New York. He didn't believe that they—whoever "they" might be—would miss again.

McCarthy had heard nothing about any of this, nor did he have any guess as to why it had happened. Smith, though, was convinced that the cops *had* to know. The cops knew everything, he said.

McCarthy felt like saying, "I only wish . . ." but he just listened.

The big pimp wanted to see the police intelligence file on the incident. McCarthy, for his part, was pretty positive that no such file existed. At least not in New York. He could check with the Nevada cops. That was a longshot too.

McCarthy took it as a challenge. He hated Smith and was already warming to the chance to scam him.

He questioned the pimp about what had happened, carefully extracting information and details that he didn't even realize he was furnishing to the cop.

A few days later, based entirely on what Smith had inadvertently told him, plus a few guesses supported by inventive and uncheckable fabrications, McCarthy wrote a phony report on official NYPD intelligence forms. Vitaliano typed it up. Flawlessly. The two cops improvised as they went along, embellishing, hinting darkly at the presence of "West Coast mob interests" in Las Vegas and concluding with the admonition: "The intended victim, William Smith, appears to be a marked man." By the time they were finished, they were laughing so hard, they could barely look at each other.

The "report" traced the attack to a fictitious pimp in Las Vegas who, being aware of Philadelphia Smith's formidable reputation, decided to launch a preemptive strike against him before he had a chance to move into that wide-open town. The report named no sources whom Smith could call on his own and served the higher purpose of flattering Smith's enormous ego.

A week later, McCarthy delivered the report to Smith. He allowed Barry Stein to see the file, but made sure he had no opportunity to read it. Stein wasn't that stupid.

McCarthy, Stein, and Philadelphia Smith all sat down around a large round table in a back room of the club. McCarthy waited.

After spending about twenty minutes with the report, his face buried in the text, tiny wire-rimmed reading glasses propped on the bridge of his nose, Smith looked up, slowly removed the glasses and said to McCarthy, "They worried about me, right?" He sounded very satisfied with himself.

"Scared enough to try to kill you."

Smith's mind was already on the next order of business. "Now, I got to know who set me up, man." Then he reached for the bowie knife. And the Bible. "An eye for an eye, brother. I am in need of a name."

McCarthy didn't have a clue. He couldn't take a chance on fingering anybody, either, because Smith might attempt to kill that person. Right here and now he could look very good or very bad.

"You set yourself up," the cop said, as Smith turned suddenly skeptical. "Anything that goes down in New York gets pony-expressed out there. People been calling you *the* man here. Some big ears heard that."

Smith thought that over. "I *do* have a reputation," he said.

"There you go." McCarthy felt his stomach sliding back down from his windpipe.

"You done real good," the pimp finally said.

He opened the Bible and folded the intelligence report inside. Neatly.

"I hope you pay real good," McCarthy said.

"There best be more where this came from." Smith handed an envelope to the cop.

McCarthy counted out five thousand dollars. Then he checked the envelope and nodded to the pimp.

That improbable incident marked him as a crooked cop who could deliver anything for the right price. It cinched his credibility and his place on Stein's pad.

At no point in his entire police career had Bill McCarthy ever felt more a part of, more a player in, the Life than at that very moment.

"It was fun, so much fun. It was like being the head puppeteer. You were pulling people's strings, watching their hands move, their legs jerk around, and the bastards were so dumb they thought they were doing it all by themselves.

"We kept on moving, kept going, convinced that, sooner or later, the head-bangers like Philadelphia Smith and the sleazeballs like Barry Stein would give us somebody really significant.

"And we were going from guy to guy, from Smith to another bagman for Freddy Kane, and then another and another. We were moving right up the line. And I'm doing absolutely nothing, really. Just taking envelopes of money from people and building my reputation as the biggest whore on the NYPD.

"I can tell you that, personally, my dealings with these pimps were doing nothing to enhance my standing among the cops I worked with who *were* straight and who *didn't* know what was going on. It got to the point where I would walk into a room, all conversation would stop and they would walk out one by one. The only cops who were friendly to me were the ones *I* used to do that to.

"By the end of February, I meet Bobby Brody. *This* was the kind of guy I had been looking for. In the pecking order, he was several steps above Barry Stein; actually, he was what Stein hoped to become someday.

"First, he's a white guy, the first one since Stein. These people are not equal opportunity employers. Color does make a big difference. I have now moved up a notch. I'm not dealing with the street hustlers now.

"We figured Brody owned about six bars in Manhattan. All hidden interests. He was known as a major corrupter. He'd been paying off cops for twenty-five years that we knew of, but he had never taken a collar.

"Brody was in his fifties, Jewish, a knock-around kind of guy, very good-looking, charming, tough, but far from being a thug. He carried himself like a gentleman. Respectable-looking, good suits, never any foul language; if he showed up someplace, even the hookers disappeared.

"He worked out of a bar that he owned on Lexington Avenue, in midtown Manhattan, called Tattler's. In the old days, a cop was not allowed in that bar. Only bosses. The bosses would show up in there regularly to pick up their payoffs. Visit with Brody, have a drink or two. All very civilized.

"Tattler's had whores in it. Brody just pretended they weren't there. The man was very old school. And they had to be the cleanest-looking hookers you ever saw. You could have taken your mother to that bar. Hell, half the old cops in there taking payoffs were white-haired Knights of Columbus or Holy Name Society men.

"Tattler's was diagonally across the street from another place, The Vogue. Now, The Vogue was a *serious* organized crime bar. Brody was a regular in there, too.

"I told Brody I wanted to make a move, 'across the street.' On The Vogue, be introduced over there and start making my own connections. He knew what I meant. But he told me, 'Billy, you're big, but you're not big enough to go over there. Slow down.'

"He advised me that, as a sergeant, I didn't have

enough weight to go into The Vogue and try and shake them down or work with the characters in there. They dealt at a level way over my head. But Brody didn't want to insult me or turn me off, either. He was as diplomatic about it as he could be.

"Brody's son had died right before I met him and he was deeply depressed over that. I found out that he had sealed his son's room in their house and wouldn't let any of his things be touched. There was this horrible emptiness in his life. It was there all the time, the way he looked right through you.

"To help fill that void, he sort of adopted me. He would never tell me how his son died; that was too private. I surmised it had to do with drugs, but I never brought it up. That was like an open sore.

"He became my coach in the ways of corruption. That was what he knew best, and he wanted to pass it on. I learned more from him than from anybody. But he would never give me any names. I guess because I really wasn't his son, he had to keep that distance between us.

"That was frustrating, the way he could separate business from emotions. He did confide in me that it was actually him, and not Barry Stein, who owned the after-hours club on Fourteenth Street where it had all started. Stein was just the front man, with no real power.

"He let me know that to prove to me how much he was coming to trust me. He also took over the direct payments to me; it had been his money all along. I came right after the gas and electric bills. None of them ever missed a payment. They were the most conscientious people I ever saw.

"At that point, maybe four months into my new undercover role, I was simultaneously being paid by four different people—to provide protection. I suspected that it was all Brody's money. He was quite an organizer. I was beginning to feel like Mr. Fix-It.

"In terms of my police identity, of course, I was still

functioning as the head of the Pimp Squad. The difference was now I was behaving like a corrupted cop.

"All the whores knew me, all the pimps, all the bigger fish like Brody. Everybody knew me. All they ever wanted to know was whether they had a problem. I was their insurance policy. That's how they treated me. I would tip them off about anything coming up and square it for them. That was my job.

"After a few more months with Brody, he tells me that he needs cocaine. I recognized this as the exact same pitch that I had been getting from Stein, back at the beginning. That way I knew that it had been coming from Brody all along.

"In a way, it was crushing. I knew how much he had loved his son, how much basic decency there was in him. Yet, here he was, ready to forget all about his son, all about everything if he could only score the right coke connection. That made me realize that it was all just a business decision with these guys—and you could not hold your own in the Life, you could not stay in business, without cocaine.

"As an undercover, regardless of how deeply you've gone in, you have to maintain your perspective. You can't get sucked in by the romance, by the good times or the camaraderie—or even the genuine friendships in the Life. Not when you also realize that your value is strictly measured by your usefulness. In this case, by my access to cocaine. I was, in effect, worth my weight in white powder to a man who had been coming to look upon me as a son. That was shattering. But I used it too. I stepped back from that relationship and let it motivate me to perform my job as a cop.

"Maybe, in a strange way, it saved me. Who knows? I was getting to like Bobby Brody an awful lot. I was getting to the point where I *did* want to protect him. I stopped that in its tracks. I focused on what I had to accomplish.

"Brody came at me three times about getting him cocaine. To him, I was a caught cop. He was paying me. He had a problem. His source had dried up. Now, all of a sudden, I had a problem too. And he was paying me to fix it.

"Legally, I wanted tape-recorded conversations of his repeated, independent requests for drugs. I would need the tapes to prove that I hadn't entrapped him or supplied him after only one request. By the third request, I was wearing a wire at every meeting with him. He was making my case for me.

"Actually, there wasn't much coke around at that particular time and what was around wasn't any good. It had been stepped on, or diluted, cut too many times. The customers were complaining. Brody was losing business at his clubs and bars. He couldn't compete in the Life. He was afraid that he might be driven right out of business. It was that serious.

"Now, what I dreamed up was this: There was a pedophile up in the Bronx who was my informant. I knew he used drugs. I decided to pay him a visit.

"I threatened to arrest him if he didn't one, give up his supplier to me and two, tell me the next time he was getting a delivery. I told him that I could take him in at will on a pedo rap. Not exactly true, but close enough.

"By the time I left, I had what I needed. His connection was a pusher in the Bronx, a guy I had run into back when I was hanging out with Barry Stein. The next delivery was a week away. I convinced the pedo that I was going up to the Bronx to rob this supplier and steal his dope.

"I had my cover story. If Brody ever checked, he would turn up the pedo who would explain to him that I was scoring coke by stealing it from his supplier.

"On March 28th, 1974, I finally 'sold' Bobby Brody four ounces of cocaine. It actually came from the police drug pile, from the evidence locker. My bosses okayed

200

it, because they knew that neither Bobby nor the narcotics would ever leave my sight. Not for a moment.

"The special prosecutor in New York then was Maurice Nadjari. He had come in because of the Knapp commission. What I was doing had to be approved at the highest levels and that was Nadjari's office.

"During my first year undercover, I would wear a hidden microphone and tape recorder approximately 250 times. The case number for that wire was #N-72-73. I will never forget it.

"Nadjari's men had secured two adjoining rooms at the Statler Hilton Hotel, at Thirty-third Street and Seventh Avenue. I was in one room with Vitaliano, waiting for Brody; Nadjari's people were in the adjoining suite.

"We were sitting there, red-eyed, with a half-empty bottle of scotch between us, when Brody walked in. It was all for show.

"The cocaine was in a briefcase—in a neat, square package. Brody whistled when he looked at it; all he said was 'Jesus Christ!' He thought I was hell on wheels.

"I told Brody that I had knocked over some dealer to get it. He looked at me in a way that he never had before. At that moment I knew in my heart that he had already checked; he'd had somebody either follow me up to the pedo's apartment or chase the guy down. Either way, what I was telling him wasn't news. He couldn't hide it. He really *didn't* trust me.

"Then, Brody made a small slit in one of the plastic packages, dipped his little finger in and licked it.

"Brody's tongue swelled up. He said, 'Holy Shit, my mouth! God, what *is* this?' Then, he drank the whole eight ounces of scotch, there on the table. Drained the bottle.

"He turned to me and said, 'Oh, Billy, we're gonna make a lot of money together. We can step on this five times. I can't wait to take this to my chemist. It's unbelievable.'

"I wondered what it must have been like being his son for real. I got the chills.

"Meanwhile, the whole transaction is being recorded. We have a spiked mike and a video—he's on camera. The operation was clinical it ran so cleanly.

"Brody shook hands with me and left the room.

"The minute he stepped outside, special investigators from Nadjari's office pounced on him in the hallway and grabbed the cocaine.

"To make it look really good, they brought him back into our hotel room and began slapping me and Tony around.

"I resisted arrest. Hard. First, they reddened my face; then knocked the wind out of me. Handcuffed me. It was a real collar. I *forced* them to do it that way by acting like a belligerent ass. It was the only way. I made sure that Brody saw me getting knocked around.

"They dragged me out separately from him and Tony. We drove to Nadjari's office, to the fifty-sixth floor of the World Trade Center.

"Brody was brought in a different car. We were placed in separate rooms. The interrogation took hours—under a naked light bulb, just like in the movies.

"After we thought that we had held out long enough to make it look good, Tony and I agreed to cut a deal. We'd flip; work off our case by giving them Brody.

"The beauty of it was that the Nadjari people who were with us then, questioning us, really *didn't* know it was an act. That's how tight our security was.

"We did it as another means of establishing our identities—mine and Tony's—as corrupt cops. We even had some of Nadjari's people fooled. Our cover was still tight.

"Brody bought it all. How could he not have?

"After we were released, I remember being on Eighth Avenue and Thirty-third Street. It's about two o'clock in the morning, and I was crying and telling Brody I was

202

gonna commit suicide because my career was over and I had gotten him arrested.

" 'Billy, you don't have to do that,' he said, trying to calm me down. 'Don't do that. We can make this right. I got other people I can reach out to. You'll see.'

"He really meant it. When I mentioned suicide, that scared him. *That* told me what must have happened to his boy. No wonder he refused to talk about it.

"Finally, I agreed not to kill myself.

"What you have to understand is that this was a triumph. Maybe bittersweet in a way, but still a victory. Here was Brody, a guy who has been in the Life for twenty-five years, a certified badass, and he had never even been arrested. Now, we had him on a felony. And he didn't even realize that I had done it to him—he was too concerned about losing another son. What a goddamn troubling night that was.

"It was Bang Double Bang. We were pulling off the perfect sting. And I felt like a louse. But, in an awful way, it felt good.

"When I drove back home to Sloatsburg that night, back to Millie and my real world, it suddenly hit me. Here I was living out the adventure of my life. Playing cops and robbers big time.

"Where had it all come from? How had I ever gotten to this amazing event in my life?"

Nineteen

A Mob Guy **could be anything from a fat, roly-poly
Italian papa who eats too much spaghetti to a
smooth businessperson, very con-Ti-nental, the
tanned, Mediterranean type. But all of them spend
their entire lives belching, eating, and taking
Maalox.**

MOTHER'S MAXIM

McCarthy was standing in a wig shop on Park Avenue
South, fingering a long, curly blond scalp. He held it up,
allowed the rays of sunlight that streamed in through a
window behind him to frame the fake tresses and then,
very carefully, he tried it on.

Tony Vitaliano, impatient, was waiting with him.
"Beautiful, Bill," he said. "You look great in drag. I
could take a shot at you myself. You do it on the first
date?"

McCarthy ignored him, then checked out his reflection
in the mirror. Full-face, profile, left, right. He smiled as
he brushed a stray curl away from his temple.

"You're too weird, Bill," the short, dark cop said.
"Too fucking weird."

McCarthy removed the hairpiece and put it back on its
display rack. He was already eyeing something red and
frizzy.

Just then, the man who had been keeping them waiting
opened his office door and appeared. He didn't greet

them but motioned for both men to follow him. As they watched, a man named Albert Gold seated himself behind an ornate, antique desk that seemed long enough to be part of the interstate highway system. His eyes were narrow-set, horizontal, and flat. One eyebrow, the left, arched as though Gold's face had little control over it.

The desk faced Park Avenue. Clearly, this massive boulder of furniture was his buffer as well as his talisman. After taking up his defensive position behind it, Albert Gold finally suggested that his visitors be seated.

It looked as though it would be a long meeting.

Bill McCarthy tried hard to look relaxed.

Gold was thick around the middle, soft in a way not normally associated with the people the two Vice cops usually dealt with. He seemed very anxious to impress upon both of them just how busy a man he was. Gold could say "Hello," and act as though he were granting an audience.

As far as McCarthy was concerned, however, he was just another pimp, albeit an influential one. They sized him up to be a total jerk—but a jerk with some very intriguing connections.

Like most of the men who ran the after-hours clubs and supplied the pimps with cocaine, Gold was an ex-con. His legitimate business was one of the largest whole-sale importers of wigs in the United States. He claimed that his products consisted of "90 percent human hair"; the origin of the other 10 percent was left up in the air.

Gold also possessed an IQ over 170 as measured by the New York State Department of Corrections as part of his presentencing catalog. He was a bright, competitive, compulsive gambler. As a whoremaster—one of his lucrative moonlighting sidelines—Gold's reputation was as fastidious as Bobby Brody's. He had never been known to lay a hand on any of the girls. That, apparently, couldn't give him a rush to equal the erotic surge he felt every time he caressed a pair of dice. That's when he would start sweating, loosen his collar, experience an instant elevation in blood pressure, and summon over the nearest casino waitress for a transfusion of a double scotch. In a very matter-of-fact manner, Albert Gold was a total gambling degenerate. His wig business and his whorehouses, in particular, financed his gambling. There was room for very little else in his life.

As a long-time student of his adversaries in Vice, McCarthy had spent considerable time schooling himself in the finer points of Albert Gold. Among pimps, even part-timers several steps removed from the street, Gold was regarded as "serious people." That meant his women serviced clients with unmistakable Mafia ties, among others. Fringe lawyers and businessmen were also plentiful; in fact, just about any OC associate with social-climbing tendencies within the organization tried to get his ticket punched at one of Gold's brothels. They were known as a place where important contacts could be made. As a result, ambitious, dangerous men showed up at his places as regularly as green flies in August.

Gold's was definitely the sort of company that McCarthy wanted to be keeping. Almost alone among the pimps, he could take the investigation to places where no amount of honest police work had ever made a dent before.

One of the brothels supposedly under McCarthy's "protection" at that time was located at at 211 East Fifty-first Street. A pimp with visions of grandeur—Marty Roth—had two connected flats, 2E and 2F, in a luxury apartment building in midtown Manhattan. After renovations, the owners had been able to squeeze seven small bedrooms in there. There was also a living room for meeting, chatting with, and selecting the women, two bathrooms and a tiny kitchen. Five out of the seven bedrooms were usually occupied around the clock. The customers weren't quite up to Sydney Biddle Barrows's standards, but they weren't Times Square, either. It was a kind of middle-management place, catering to rich salesmen, up-and-coming hoods, and prosperous-looking executives from just about every professional field. The women who worked there were just a notch or two below "prime," as Barry Stein would say.

Stein had brokered McCarthy's entering into this arrangement. This confirmed the cop's suspicions that the pimp had been going around, first bragging about, and then selling or "renting" his police contacts—primarily McCarthy.

The Knapp Commission had dried up many of the pads. Crooked cops were almost in a seller's market. Stein was just cashing in—acting just like an agent, getting his 10 or 15 percent, or whatever, based on McCarthy's availability.

"Roth was a young guy, twenty-eight years old maybe, not even thirty yet. An entrepreneur. Smartass. A little kid who thought he was too slick to be a wiseguy type. He was gonna make money at anything he tried, you could see that. Deep down, however, he was electrified by the whores. And by the coke. Already he'd become lost in the Life.

"Marty Roth had a secret weapon. He just happened to be Albert Gold's favorite nephew.

"Exactly one week after Stein introduced me to Roth, and after I agreed to see what I could do about keeping Vice away from the house on Fifty-first Street, Roth called me over to the brothel one night and said, How would you like to meet my Uncle Al?

"I practically came in my pants."

" 'How do I know you're not wearing a tape recorder? How do I know you're not wired?'

"That was the first thing that Al Gold said to us in his wig shop. Not even how-do-you-do.

"I started to take my shirt off. I decided to get rough with him. I was on my feet, pacing in front of his big desk.

" 'What am I here for? Hey, your fucking nephew asked me to come by. I don't invite myself places. I didn't ask to come here. This is bullshit.'

"And I keep taking off my clothes. Tony the V looks at me like I've lost my mind. I just keep stripping—down to my underwear.

"All of a sudden, Gold begins to act very apologetic. He wants to get down to business now, having thoroughly insulted me. But I'm not exactly dressed for it.

" 'You want me to keep going?' I ask him, and I actually begin to step out of my drawers. 'You feel like coming over here and checking my balls for that wire you're so worried about?'

"I really think I embarrassed him. He put his hands up, like he was backing off. I'm still not satisfied, though. So I say to him, 'If you waste my time here today, then you are going to have a bigger problem than you and your nephew think you have.'

" 'I'm ready to deal,' " he said almost sheepishly.

"That's when I sat down and started pulling on my pants.

"It turns out this is another setup like Stein and Brody. The kid, Marty Roth, doesn't own a brick, not the house on Fifty-first Street, not any house of prostitution in New York. All the money, all the juice comes from Gold.

"Through the course of the conversation, we make arrangements to protect his prostitution activities at Fifty-first Street. I set up a payment schedule—fifteen percent of the gross for the first two weeks and twenty percent thereafter.

"That was a big bite; we were really coming on like strongarm cops. We had just muscled in and had, in

208

effect, become part owners of a top-of-the-line Manhattan whorehouse. This now would give us access to the girls, too. All I could think about was all the intelligence we would pick up.

"When you buy into a whorehouse, even through a payoff like ours, you are buying human bodies. That is an accepted business practice in the Life. It is the true meaning of white slavery. Any hour of the day or night, if you want to get laid, a whore is there—a dozen whores are there at your disposal. You have the power over them to come in and sample them like a buffet. That's what we had just been offered. If there is any form of human bondage more perverse than that, I haven't run across it.

"By the time we had finished haggling and he had finally agreed to our terms, we were all pretty tired, wrung out.

"But Gold had one more bomb to drop.

" 'There's another house,' he said. 'And I got a problem there. If this other house isn't part of the protection you can provide, then the deal is off. Take it or leave it.'

"I looked over at Tony and he looked back at me. We had no idea about a *second* brothel. We thought we had already worked our way right to the top. He's already giving up the best whorehouse in Manhattan. What more could there be?

" 'You better tell us about it,' I said, not knowing what to expect.

"The problem brothel was hidden in a townhouse on Thirty-first Street. In Murray Hill. That's a very old, once-elegant New York neighborhood. The location seemed, at first, to be a little out of Gold's league.

"Gold, Roth, and a couple other guys were in on the townhouse. The place made a fortune. But they *did* have a problem. That was no exaggeration.

"Their townhouse had been visited by three unknown males who represented Gennaro (Big Jerry) Moretti. Moretti is mob—real mob. He wanted to buy Gold's share of the townhouse. That meant Moretti's crew wanted in. Moretti was with Paul Vario at that time and Vario, of course, was only about one step removed from the Genovese Family. In other words, the Genoveses are moving in.

"Al Gold also had outstanding gambling debts which he owed to Julie Nardi, a 'made guy,' who was big in pornography. Nardi is with the Gambinos, but he's with Moretti, too, at least on the gambling end. So that's double trouble. Nardi can call on the Genoveses or the Gambinos.

"Nardi saw the Murray Hill townhouse as a natural extension of his porno business. Hell, he was ready to move secret cameras right in and maybe begin blackmailing a few of the customers.

"So, as a way of repaying his giant gambling debts, and keeping his legs from being broken, Julie Nardi also tells Gold that he will just take a piece—a big piece—of the townhouse.

"Moretti doesn't know what Nardi is up to. This middles Al Gold, who will be blamed by both of them for selling out to the other guy. Gold really has no place to go on this.

"But wait, there was even *more*.

"Guido Maranzo, another player, had also loaned money to Gold for his gambling. Maranzo wanted to become his 'business associate' too.

"Now there's *three* of them in on it. Each one is a good fellow, a made guy.

"Maranzo, rather than just robbing Gold, moving in on him and maybe scaring away the johns in the process, offered to introduce gambling activities at the townhouse. That way, at least Gold would be able to keep his dignity and pretend that he still ran the place. The townhouse was Gold's best asset and Maranzo did not want to devalue it in any way.

"Maranzo and Jerry Moretti happened to be from warring factions in the same mob—factions who now found themselves fighting for control of the same brothel.

"I said to Gold, 'No wonder you need protection.'

"All he wanted to know was, 'Can you handle it?'

"Can I handle a combination of *three* made guys representing the two largest Mafia families in the world, the Gambinos and the Genoveses, and all fighting over the same whorehouse? Could I do that?

" 'No problem,' I said to Al Gold.

"He looked relieved. I certainly wasn't.

" 'I knew you could do it,' he told me. 'Bobby Brody said you could pull off anything.'

"Before we left, I could not resist yanking this guy's chain one more time.

"Tony was wearing pimp shoes, with a big, thick heel. Just when Gold believed that I would keep my clothes on, that I was all calmed down over my being insulted about him accusing us of being wired, I reached down and pulled off Tony's shoe.

"Then I threw it up on this handsome desk and said, 'You asshole. The wire was in the shoe all along.'

"I can see that Gold doesn't know how to take this. He desperately wants to believe that I'm joking with him. But he doesn't know me and Tony. He can't be sure. What if we *are* honest undercover cops instead of corrupt fixers?

"He grabbed the shoe and started twisting the heel, but he could not take it apart. He looked up and gave us this nervous, sick laugh. Right? It has to be a joke? Right? He's really sweating.

"I took the shoe back and handed it to Tony. 'Gotcha, Al,' I said. Then we left.

"Actually, I *had* been recording every word of that hour-long conversation. I had the wire where I always kept it—wrapped around my testicles. I had bluffed him when I stripped down to my underwear. Gold never knew. He never would."

As far as McCarthy knew Bobby Brody had never said a word to anybody about getting caught with the cocaine. That was supposed to be their little secret. Hustlers like Brody were forever getting in trouble and running scams behind each other's backs. The way the cop had left it with him, it seemed as though McCarthy was in bigger trouble, anyway. That had been the whole point of the crazy talk about suicide.

To resolve the issue of the cocaine possession, to fix it, to blow out the arrest, McCarthy suggested that they concentrate on getting to a deputy inspector whom he already suspected of being on the take.

Brody liked that; it was the way he always approached problems.

"We were supposed to work on this inspector. Brody wanted me back on the good side of the NYPD. He didn't need a guy who was *too* notorious. What good would he be?

"It so happened that around this time there *was* an inspector who was suspected of protecting another after-hours club at Avenue A and Seventh Street. Other places, too; all black pimp bars. Corrupter bars, as we called them. I passed that information on to my bosses; I assumed they would give it to Nadjari's office.

"But, in the middle of my case, this deputy inspector apparently gets tipped off and has himself suddenly transferred to another borough, out of harm's way. The special prosecutor is left holding the bag. So am I. Our case against him isn't ready yet. Now, it never will be.

"That wasn't part of *my* setup with Brody.

"So now, I know that the cops are playing their own games. We have a leak. Maybe it's in Nadjari's office, maybe it's in the first deputy commissioner's office. I never would find out.

"It really scared me. A lot. This could get me or one of my guys killed. I'm just beginning to appreciate how high up the corruption goes, what total disregard there is for the safety of undercovers.

"We just left it hanging with Brody. There was no resolution in sight."

Twenty

**The *Mafia* is organized crime, but it's not as well
organized as people would like you to believe.**

MOTHER'S MAXIM

From the outside, the townhouse on East Thirty-first
Street, Murray Hill, looked like any one of a hundred
similarly sedate, dignified buildings in the immediate
neighborhood. The pavement in front of the slightly sag-
ging steps that rose to an impressive door and vestibule
was wide and well walked.

Comparable houses were already commanding pre-
mium prices in New York. Give the area another decade
of creeping gentrification and the value of the property
would eventually soar into the million-dollar category.

No one in the local real estate community had even
noticed when Al Gold, the big wig importer, and a couple
of his friends purchased the townhouse. It was a sound
investment and, under the correct circumstances, could
even double as a tax shelter.

Everyone, it appeared, was trying to own a piece of
midtown Manhattan. Why should the Gold group be any
different? They would never lose any money on the place

and could always turn around and rent out part of it as office space to a medical group or small law firm or any kind of business that would benefit from being where the action was in the mid-1970s.

Transforming the townhouse into a splendid, multi-floored brothel, complete with a library, drawing room, fireplaces, spacious bedrooms for trysting and authentic Victorian appointments, had been relatively simple. Rehabbing old buildings was all the rage in Murray Hill anyway, so performing extensive renovations to a valuable investment property was not going to attract unwanted attention.

The main risk was in the presence, twenty-four hours a day, seven days a week, of rotating shifts of well-dressed, stylishly groomed, drop-dead-gorgeous women.

It got so that you could not pass the townhouse, either on foot or in a car, and *not* see a head-turner. Men out walking their dogs in the neighborhood used to linger there, coaxing their pet to get friendly with one of the trees in front of the townhouse. Delivery men caught on just as quickly. They used to double-park their vans or trucks out front, stall their engines, pretend to be searching for addresses—all because they knew that every few minutes (the wait was never longer than that) one of the sexiest women they were likely to see all day, all week, would either come sauntering out of or into the townhouse.

It became common knowledge in the neighborhood that the townhouse was, indeed, some sort of magnificent brothel. Vivid as the images were that fed people's fantasies about the place, the reality of what was going on inside still exceeded those expectations. The women who worked in the brothel were in the business of giving pleasure, no matter how erotic or fantastic a form it might take. Hookers dressed in French maids' uniforms were on call in one suite, bouncing in apron, garters, and very little else; more sophisticated companions in tennis whites, perhaps, complete with tiny, revealing skirts or snug stewardess uniforms, were available on another level of the townhouse. If one of the customers preferred a girl-next-door type, she was available; rubber fetishes were satisfied; so, too, the desire to be dominated, handcuffed to the bedposts, whatever. It was all for sale. Given the constraints of reason, cost, and safety, every variety of female plaything from imitation high school cheerleader to milkmaid, blond and big-breasted and carrying a pail, was on call.

Al Gold was a merchant who understood the peculiar needs of the high-end market. He provided the services and the customers paid. The girls started at $150 a session. Fees of $1,000 a night were not unheard of.

No one approached the door uninvited. Ever. People regarded the establishment as they would a private club. If you belonged there, you knew it and *they* knew it and lengthy introductions were hardly necessary.

There was always a very palpable sense that the townhouse was off-limits to all but a select few. Maybe it was shyness; maybe fear. A natural inclination to avoid confrontation kept normal people away.

There was no doorman, no bouncer; no outward threat. But there didn't have to be. The townhouse, tempting as it was, mysterious, alluring, also bespoke danger. The very first time that he saw the townhouse, Bill McCarthy got the same feeling. This was a menacing, perilous place.

"That May, 1974, Guido Maranzo moved in with gambling and card games, baccarat, poker, dice. And, of course, Maranzo had partners. It was like the mob had come in to pick apart a carcass. For a month everything ran smoothly. I passed the word upstairs and Vice never even looked at the place. Al Gold took that to mean that

216

he was being protected by me. He had no idea that there was nothing to protect him from.

"Then they had a bad falling-out over who was in control of the game. They were really making money at that point.

"In June they shut down all gambling. There were simply too many arguments. That was Maranzo's solution—close it up. Wait for things to calm down.

"Gold became worried then. These were real mob guys. They shot people. He was in over his head and he had no idea what to do about it. A couple weeks later, Maranzo started the gambling up again. Gold conceded that Maranzo was the boss. No argument.

"We decided to go for an application for an eavesdropping warrant at the townhouse. That request brought in the New York Rackets Bureau and the district attorney's office.

"By now, the investigation had really grown. We had officially named it 'Sinbad,' for 'sin' because of the whoring, and 'bad' because every person involved with this was bad news. Even the feds were trying to horn in—you had us, the special prosecutor, the DA, and the rest of the police department. We weren't aware of it at the time, but the CIA, Immigration, the DEA, and all kinds of people in the U.S. Justice Department were beginning to check in too.

"Everybody on our side wanted a piece of it, not just Nadjari. In the process, a good bit of my cover was blown. It became almost impossible, within the New York law enforcement community, to keep my activities secret any longer. As far as we knew, the bad guys were still buying it, but, in what seemed like overnight, every cop in the city became clued in that Mother was actually on the side of the angels after all.

"That would forever alter any future undercover role that I might be able to play, but at that point the only task I could concentrate on was the one in front of me.

217

"Every time Al Gold had a conversation with me, I taped him. I was in almost daily contact, at least by telephone.

"The next thing Gold told me was that a loan shark, Pete (Buttons) Bicardi, had come on strong. He was supplying the regulars with money for the big baccarat games.

"I realized I would have to go for a bug on the loan shark, too. Bicardi, the shylock, was being protected or 'spoken for' by Guido Maranzo.

"Bicardi was an imposing, kinky-haired, 250-pound leg-breaker from Brooklyn. He had successfully secured the loan-shark franchise at the townhouse from his bitter rival, Big Jerry Moretti. Moretti's clout was derived from his association with one of the biggest mob bosses in New York at that time, Aniello Dellacroce. Moretti had also originally sent those three strongarm guys to see Al Gold about buying a piece of the brothel.

"Besides Bicardi, there was another hood at the townhouse—he was actually Bicardi's driver—who, we already knew, had been smuggling illegal aliens in through Canada. The illegals were all from Sicily. They were mobsters-in-training, hit men.

"Bicardi and his driver apparently remembered the old Murder, Incorporated gang and its activities and figured they could make big money with this rent-a-hit-man scheme. The American Mafiosi loved the idea because it gave them another layer of insulation against ever getting caught. Also, the Sicilians were much more dependable than Americans—they didn't do drugs, didn't try to hold the New York Families up for too much money, and you never, ever had to worry about them cooperating with the cops.

"We checked employment records as soon as we got names of the illegals and every single one of them worked in pizza parlors along the East Coast. They were being stashed in the pizza joints as a cover until they were

218

needed. Bicardi was their man—one of their sponsors. He was also willing to lend them money and they loved to gamble.

"And here we were getting limited access to them their first or second month on American soil. In *our* whorehouse, the one we're supposed to be protecting."

Bicardi turned the first floor into a clandestine casino. There were felt-covered card tables; roulette wheels and several enclosures for craps. The baccarat tables were always the most crowded. Next, to protect their growing investment, the Brooklyn hoods set about fortifying the townhouse. A cache of guns was moved in and put at the disposal of their Sicilian allies. Additionally, workmen came in and barred every window from the inside. Bicardi conducted his loan shark business from the secluded third-floor bedroom that had been turned into a library—the room where the wiretap would have to be planted.

The Vice cops were also able to establish that much of Bicardi's money was laundered through an apparently legal water-ice business in Brooklyn. Optimistic plans called for the Murray Hill hangout to eventually turn over between twenty-five and fifty thousand dollars a week through prostitution, gambling, and loan-sharking activities.

Al Gold was content to share the profits with his new partners, but Gold himself was sometimes terrified by the rough trade that began moving in. He was running into difficulties keeping girls, too. Some of the new customers were slapping the women around.

Through August of 1974, McCarthy and Vitaliano, working with the special prosecutor's office, were able to develop the most valuable information to date on the new Sicilian Mafia, as well as on the routine mob business that took place at the townhouse.

"At first, Tony and I did not realize what we had here. In hindsight, fifteen years later, we now know that it was the very beginning of the infiltration of the Sicilian Mafia into America.

"Give them a few years and these punks would become a very distinct *second* Mafia, and would come to operate the biggest international drug connection in the world, a hundred times bigger than the French Connection, but back then, who could have guessed that?

"Some of those first Sicilians that we identified in the Murray Hill townhouse turned out to belong to the mob that went on trial for the international Pizza Connection case in New York in 1986–1987.

"We had hit the mother lode. And we didn't even know it. But that's always the way it works in undercover investigations. You're dropping lines in the water, never suspecting what you might pull in.

"The Sicilians would come into the brothel on Thirty-first Street and take over the whole place. They'd come in with their own cigarette vendors, their own cooks, their own food; they came lock, stock, and barrel. Set up a miniature nightclub within the townhouse.

"I used to say to myself—just let these pigs keep eating, because they'll kill themselves. They'll blow up. All they did was eat, eat, eat. The sex had to wait. Getting laid was way back in second place. They even ate before they gambled. You wanted a good way to get killed, all you had to do was interfere with these guys during their meals. We picked up every disgusting sound on the eaves-dropping wires. Every belch, every fart. Then, before they went home, they would eat again.

"The girls all had to be out of the place by midnight because that was when the serious gambling began and they didn't want any distractions. Broads were bad luck.

"There was one guy who spoke decent English. His

name was Oscar. One night he lost two hundred thousand dollars. I'm listening to this on the other end, dying. This game is bigger than Atlantic City. Oscar doesn't even lose his cool, he's down two hundred G's and he just tells them, very casually, 'I'll have a guy come by in the morning.' That meant that his messenger would have the money. They knew he was good for it.

"The problem I had was that everybody in the place spoke Sicilian. They were all young people, not old people, mostly in their thirties.

"Young American-born hoods don't speak Sicilian. They may know a few words, but they aren't fluent. Of the Five Families in New York, some are more traditionally connected to Italy than others, and those that are connected are dominated by the people who can actually speak Italian. But that's unusual for anybody under the age of sixty or seventy. At least it was until we stumbled on this gang.

"The Sicilians, the real Mafiosi, are very different from American mobsters. They're more traditional, tied to the old country. Worse when it comes to violence and lack of respect for the police, better in areas like gangster skills and loyalty to the clan. And they bring with them this very worldly view that absolutely *anything goes* in the pursuit of cash—that could be murder, drugs, killing innocent bystanders, cutting deals with terrorists or hostile foreign governments. Bad stuff. The thing about them that really hits you is how profoundly un-American they are. As horrible as our OC guys might be, at least we are all working from the same frame of reference. We might be on opposite sides of the street, but we share the same history, the same social values. Not these Sicilians. They come in here, bound by blood, with absolutely no morality beyond greed.

"The American Mafia were like a Boy's Club compared to the Sicilians. Even in the simplest matters. If they were to do their normal rituals, for example, all the tacky *Godfather* stuff, most of which they actually got from the movie, anyway—life does imitate art in the criminal set—they'd have to use index cards, or a Tele-PrompTer, because somebody would need to tell them what they should do or say next. The Sicilians were spontaneously evil; our hoods had to learn it. That was the difference.

"It became very clear that just bugging my conversations with Al Gold was no longer enough. I would have to intercept the Sicilians, too. That was the next order of business."

Twenty-one

One Police Plaza, the Puzzle Palace, is like
whatever's behind the curtain in *The Wizard of Oz*.
It's where you have to be if you're a cop.

MOTHER'S MAXIM

"I was practically ready to pack up one night and go
home when the telephone rang. It was Al Gold and he
wanted to sell me machine guns. I thought we were set
on the whorehouse scam and he hits me with this. Machine guns. *That* even I could not resist.

"I learned that Al and his creepy nephew Marty Roth
were sitting in Al's wig shop, talking about me, as a
matter of fact, about all the business they could count on
now that Vice was protecting them, when a fairly potent
mob guy we both knew, a burglar, but a made guy,
walked in off Park Avenue and dropped a gun on Al's
desk. The gun had a silencer screwed on the barrel. He
said to Al, 'Find me a buyer.'

"Immediately, he thought of Mother.

"He told the burglar to come back the next day. He
kept the gun himself. Figured it might come in handy,
with the silencer, especially.

"The burglar walks in the next day carrying this big
box, like he just bought something at Sears. Gold paid

223

him for the first gun and asked him if he had anything else to sell.

" 'Yeah,' the burglar answers, 'but it's serious stuff. I gotta go heavy on this. Gotta try and make it a one-time thing.'

"Now, Gold figured he must really be into a deal. He looks at the box. 'So, show me,' Al says, and points to the box.

"The burglar kneels down, takes all this tape and rope off the carton and takes out this gorgeous hunk of U.S. Army ordnance. A combat machine gun. Not a MAC-10 or an Uzi, nothing small like that. *This* is a fucking machine gun. It looks like World War Two in the wig shop. The burglar has been walking around all day in Manhattan with the machine gun, deciding which fence to offer it to.

"Gold explains all this and says to me, 'My man here has connections upstate. He's selling crystal meth to some kids who are in the National Guard. The kids, however, are punks and can't pay. The burglar comes up with a compromise. He'll take it out in trade—back up a truck to the armory when they're walking guard duty there and take away as much stuff as he can load. The machine gun is just a sample.

"Al has the thought that since I'm a cop I must know all sorts of right-wing nuts and gun collectors. I can fence for Al as a subcontractor. That's the deal. A fifty-fifty split. Whatever we can't move, he'll just unload on the Westies—the crazy Irish hit men from the West Side. Those bastards, he says, will buy anything that shoots because whatever *they* don't need, they just send over to their relatives in the Irish Republican Army in Belfast, Northern Ireland. He has this all figured out. From his wig shop to the IRA. Gold, whatever you want to say about him, thought big.

"I told him I would see what I could do.

"Of course, I have to clear all this at One Police Plaza.

But how tough a sell can it be? We're about to buy one or more machine guns from a Mafia made man.

"Wrong, again.

"I go in and tell the inspector that Al Gold called me about the machine gun. I want permission to send over one of my men to make the buy.

" 'Permission denied.' The jerk says to tell Gold to call it off. 'Give the gun back.' He doesn't want to get involved in anything this big. 'It could blow up in our faces,' he says, clearing his throat.

"Like nothing has ever blown up in *my* face before. I've damn near made a career of it. This guy isn't a cop, he's a professional ass-coverer.

" 'BUY THE DAMN GUN,' I shouted back at him.

"This is an inspector in the NYPD and he's too scared to make a decision. I yelled some more. 'You can't tell Gold to give the gun back. How can you give it back to a made guy? We can't let it stay on the street!'

"I just stormed out of his office, slammed the door, figured I had just as much juice as he did—*they* had come to *me* about all this undercover stuff—and just went ahead with it.

"If I had sent over a German shepherd from the police kennel to buy the machine gun, the mob guy would have sold it to the German shepherd, just as long as the dog was introduced by Al. That's how tight I was with these people at that point.

"Instead of the dog I sent over the same young detective, Doug West, whom I had used to trap William McKinney and the ATF agent at the Holiday Inn. This was the cop who had been set up as Larry Waters's mark, his pedo john.

"I set up the buy on a yacht moored at the Twentieth Street pier; Customs had seized it and we were using it like a clubhouse for undercover operations. I hid in a trailer at the foot of the pier and prepared to record the transaction. I was just expecting a one-time deal. By then, Al Gold had stepped out of it. That was understandable. He had been asked to broker the deal—which he had done. Now, whatever degree of risk existed would be on my end and the burglar's end.

"At that first meeting, Doug West, representing me, purchased three machine guns—two thousand dollars a piece. The burglar and his man brought them to us, wrapped in Christmas paper like presents. Our money had to be stuffed inside Christmas cards.

"Before they shook hands on it, Doug West asked the burglar if he had anything he hadn't shown to Gold.

"The burglar hemmed and hawed and explained that there might be something else, but no more guns. The kids in the National Guard were too scared.

" 'I might be in the market,' Doug told him. 'It all depends on the quality of what you got to offer.'

"The burglar got this weird look on his face and said, 'Oh, I got quality. Don't worry about that.'

"At our next meeting Doug had to go through the Christmas paper routine again. This time, the package he's opening is smaller and much lighter. It *can't* be any kind of weapon.

"It was a violin. One of the six known Stradivarius violins in existence, the burglar swore. This mob guy wasn't just a burglar, he was a *master* burglar. His crew had stolen it from an art gallery somewhere.

"This was another curve they'd thrown at us. We had to get the violin authenticated, but could we risk bringing in an art expert and introducing him into our small undercover circle? *That* had to be a Puzzle Palace decision. Strangely enough, they okayed it without a whimper.

"In the meantime, Doug had set a price—two hundred thousand dollars.

"We had no intention of paying all that out. At the next meeting, we would grab the burglar and the violin, if it turned out to be real.

"Al Gold, of course, had no idea that Doug was a cop.

So I was on pretty safe ground. I couldn't necessarily help it if Doug turned out to be undercover, could I? According to the story I had been spinning, that would have put me in as much jeopardy as Gold. That was the same kind of a gamble that I had taken—and won—back with Bobby Brody. I decided it was worth the risk. Besides, I can't emphasize enough that once you are known to be on the street, in the Life, you are expected to be in some kind of trouble just about all the time. That would most certainly apply to a cop like me—who was supposed to be on the take.

"All we had to do was wait for the art expert to come in and verify that the violin really was a Stradivarius. The Puzzle Palace had supposedly checked him out. He worked as a professional art courier, picking up, transporting, and providing security for priceless paintings or statues or jewels, or whatever. One day he'd make a stop in New York, the next night he would surface in London. We assumed that he knew his violins.

"During one of Doug's sit-downs with the burglar, in a very seedy restaurant near the pier, they begin making plans for this art expert to come in on the deal—Doug alibied that he was the big money man and wanted to inspect the Stradivarius personally.

"After a few minutes I hear them talking about Doug's watch. I was in an adjoining booth, drinking a beer and sipping pea soup. Those two were going on and on. And the burglar is saying, 'Thirty-five, thirty-five, thirty-five.'

"It was about four o'clock in the morning, and I could barely stay awake. But they're having this animated discussion.

"Later, I asked Doug, 'What was all that bullshit about your watch? What did he mean. "thirty-five"?'

"Doug, a very handsome, low-key, dedicated cop, gave me one of those looks that told me he was uncomfortable talking about this. I didn't care, though. These were burglars who wouldn't have thought twice about killing a guard or a watchman. They were as brutal as they came. And I figured I had a right to know what the hell my guy was discussing with them. I really liked Doug, but hadn't spent time in a foxhole with him. If I even *suspected* him of double-dealing me, however innocently, his ass was gone, possibly all the way to Attica. When you're running an operation like this, you cannot afford not to get to know people on the job.

" 'My watch costs thirty-five hundred dollars,' he said reluctantly. 'It's a Rolex, a *real* Rolex. The guy knew and he was complimenting me on it. I think he's going to ask me to score him one.'

"I let it rest for the moment. I just wanted to wait until I was positive nobody would overhear us.

"That night, right in the middle of all this other stuff that was happening, we had to back up another Vice team that was inside a bar on Forty-third Street, a place called Raffles. It was another one of those pervert bars where they'd stoop down and piss on the ice for mixed drinks.

"We were outside, hiding in my station wagon, hoping that we wouldn't have to go inside and get in a shootout. I figured this was private enough.

"I was concerned because I really didn't know Doug that well. But I had heard about him. Everybody in the department raved about his cars and clothes and apartment. They were envious.

"I had a nice house too, and pretty decent clothes. I could relate to that up to a point. But Doug was way beyond my league.

"I'm saying to myself, he must have cheap rent or something to afford all that. I like the kid and I don't want to believe he's taking money. But cops don't have thirty-five-hundred-dollar watches. Not even corrupt ones.

"We're out there talking and I'm asking him questions. He tells me where he lives—a place on Central Park with a uniformed doorman out front. The only time I've ever been in places like that I'm serving a warrant on a mob guy or going in with a police dog who sniffs out bombs. It is not a typical cop hangout.

"Here I am a sergeant and he's a detective. I couldn't even pay his goddamn rent. Now I'm really worried about this kid.

"So, I say, 'Doug, I don't mean to insult you but I got a problem with you. There's no way you can pay that rent on your salary. I'm sorry, but I can't work another minute with you unless I have the answer. Because if you're on a pad I have to run your ass out of Vice. And I'm not going to go behind your back. I'm going right up in front of your face. You gotta explain to me how you can afford that on a cop's salary.'

"He says, 'I thought you knew, Mother.'

" 'Knew what?'

" 'Other income.'

" 'Other income? What the hell is that?'

"Then he told me. It turned out that his wife was the heiress to one of the biggest oil delivery companies in New York. That Christmas she bought him a Gucci shield case for his badge to match his Gucci gun belt. He showed it to me.

"That was what I loved about being a Vice cop in New York. Where else could you partner with a cop like Doug West—a kid who was worth about ten thousand times more than the mayor?

"Here was a guy who could afford to do anything in the whole world and the only thing he cared about was Vice.

"At that moment, I could see a lot of me in Doug. Not the money part, of course, but the personality type. There was this latent part of him that kept drawing him back to the Life. I'll never know if I went into Vice already harboring that secret need or if Vice turned me into this junkie who had to keep coming back to the street, back to the Life to get his danger fix. Either way, the compulsion had taken over the biggest part of me. Maybe that was why I could always spot obsessive behavior in other people. It was like looking into a mirror.

"Doug West was the perfect detective to use on that case. We had pretended that he was an eccentric collector—art and weapons. The fact that Doug happened to be a very wealthy guy who knew his way around the world of privilege was one of the main reasons he had pulled it off so convincingly.

"But that's common in the NYPD, too. Some of the most talented, gifted people on the face of the earth aspire to no higher calling than to become New York City policemen and thus fulfill their fantasies. That was Doug. That was me.

"I worried about the last meeting. I was afraid for Doug. So much could have gone wrong. The violin could have even been a fake. But it wasn't. That arrest went down—right there on the Twentieth Street pier—like some case study you would diagram on the chalkboard at the academy. We left the pier congratulating ourselves.

"Police work is never like that, though. The perverse streak in the universe that refuses to allow you to come away clean was working overtime.

"Exactly two days after we confiscated the Stradivarius, we locked up the burglar and his helpers and sent the art courier on his way, back to London, I think. His body turned up over there with a bullethole behind the right ear. He'd been executed. Professionally.

"That stopped us in our tracks, let me tell you. My control people freaked out—so did Al Gold, for different reasons, of course. We had no way of knowing whether or not our case had led directly to the courier's murder. That was an easy assumption to make, but not necessarily the correct one. He may have died during the course of a robbery, or he may have been mixed up in something that none of us even knew about. I refused to believe that our burglar and his friends had the contacts to get a guy

230

whacked halfway around the world, but I may have been rationalizing. I'll never know.

"Gold reacted just the way a confirmed career criminal always sees things. He was afraid that I had been trapped in the sting and that I was going to go to jail and that I would make a deal for myself and give him up. For weeks after that, he was afraid to call me. Prior to that, I had been hearing from him two, three times a day.

"The one possibility that he never suspected was that I really was honest and that I was the motive force directing the whole operation. He made the same mistake as Bobby Brody. They just could not comprehend a cop being straight if there was no tangible profit in it. That was one edge that I had that I would never lose. They had spent their lives 'reaching' dirty cops and their way of sizing up any situation was inflexible.

"The Puzzle Palace wanted to shut me down, pull me out. Sinbad would be put on hold. Forever.

"I managed to talk them out of that by persuading them that the only thing I really had left to do was to place the bugs in the Murray Hill townhouse. In the end, I guess they weighed the risks and decided that what we were learning about the Sicilian Mafia was worth running out the string a little further.

"I was all for it. But that Stradivarius caper and the tragic way that it ended would haunt me for the rest of my life. The homicide of the art courier remains open to this day. That was one we could never solve."

Twenty-two

If you have good people a *Surveillance* can be like a symphony. It's poetry. It's ballet. It's your pump pumping, your strum strumming. I looked forward to it, especially if the guy we were after moved and if he was good.

MOTHER'S MAXIM

"I installed the bug on the Sicilians in the townhouse myself.

"I had always met with Gold somewhere else, so the staff at the brothel had no idea what I looked like. I was a true silent partner. I just picked a time when I knew Gold wouldn't be around.

"Gus Garen, from NYPD Intelligence, went with me. He was a wire man; probably the best wire man who ever lived. We pretended to be from the phone company.

"First, we had to distort the phone line. That's easy to do from the outside. Then you just wait for them to call up the phone company to complain about the service. You intercept their call, and a few minutes later respond, pretending to be the repairman. Gus even came up with a genuine truck from the phone company.

"When you get a court order for a wire, it has to be for a particular crime and for a particular person. There are a number of technical problems that enter into a bug— like when can you turn it on? You can only turn it on when the subject of the wire is physically in the place. The rules are really tight. And you can only open the wire on a conversation to which he is a party. If you record other voices, they must be talking about the same criminal enterprise, or it's no good. If they decide to discuss a different crime, then you have to get the court order amended.

"One of the most difficult things is to be able to identify the various voices when you can't see who they belong to.

"I had two plants—a photo plant, a cop outside, across the street from the townhouse; and a wiretap plant, electronic.

"When the target voice, or person, first entered the house, I had to have a guy follow him as he got out of his car, write down the license plate number, and take his picture as he goes to the door. We recorded his voice as he was greeted inside.

"With the plate number I could find out who the car was registered to, match it up with a picture, and match that with a voice overlay. That's how we gave all the players, the Sicilians, names and numbers. Tedious work. No shortcuts.

"To get the original 'voice exemplar' of Pete Bicardi—so we could match it up later—I had his car stopped in Brooklyn by an ordinary traffic cop who was wearing a wire. And guess what simpleminded Bicardi tried to do? He bribed the cop who stopped him; handed him forty dollars. We got it all on tape. That's another pinch.

"By some crazy coincidence, the day we went in to plant the bug just happened to be the same day they settled the longest telephone company strike in history.

"While I was installing the device, one of the Brooklyn wise-guys walks over to us with the newspaper.

"He's standing right over us; we're on the floor. 'Hey, I hear you got a raise today,' he says. 'How much an hour do you make now? You just got a fucking raise, did you know that?'

"I didn't know a thing. But Gus knew. He used to work for the phone company, so he kept up on it.

"Gus begins, 'A Tech 3 gets $11.22 an hour; a Tech 2 gets . . .' and he rattles it off. Thank God, we passed the test and the hood walked away. That was close.

"Finally, we installed that ultrasensitive carbon mike on the thick wainscoting that ran along the wall right over the spot where Bicardi sat. We couldn't do it in the casino on the first floor because that was too noisy and we couldn't put the bug in any of the bedrooms because all you ever picked up in there was a whore panting, 'Give it to me, baby, give it to me.'

"There was a room on the third floor, however, that had been enlarged and converted into a library. *That* was for the serious discussions. So the bug went in there. All this required blueprints and mechanical drawings beforehand. Then, we had to trick the contractor who had made the alterations into telling us what we wanted to know, without alerting him that we were cops. Nobody who bugged the Russians ever went to more trouble.

"Getting the bug in place was only half the battle. Since these people all spoke Sicilian we had to man the listening devices at our end with cops—called interceptors—who were, number one, fluent in the language and, number two, whom we could trust not to tip off the people in the brothel.

"I got thirty names of cops who were fluent in Italian. That's how we started.

"I went back and ran checks on all of them. All the way back to Italy. Who were their relatives? Could anybody be connected?

"Once I decided to even call one of them in for an interview and lay out the task at hand, I would have already given up the investigation. Consequently, I had to be supercautious.

234

"This was all that my enemies in the department had been waiting for. I'm a hotshot in Vice, I'm Mother, I have my own case going. They wanted to see me take a fall in the worst way.

"I told each prospective interceptor: 'I gotta find out two things. Are you honest and do you speak Italian? But I'm gonna give you your out right now. If you don't wanna work here—and I'm gonna explain to you why you might not want to work here—you tell me that you don't think you speak Italian good enough. I won't know if you do or you don't. But you can walk away now and it won't prejudice your record.

" 'Now, I'm gonna tell you why you don't want to work here. If you're a crook, you don't want to work here, because if I find out, I'm gonna stick my gun up your ass and I'm going to fire it six times. And when I'm done, I'm gonna drag you out in the street and run over you with my car, and then I'm gonna piss on your guts and make your children eat 'em. That's if I find out that you're on the take and you're trying to give me up.'

"That first day I interviewed eighteen people and eighteen people told me they didn't think they spoke Italian good enough.

"I went back the next day, interviewed another twenty. Just five could speak Sicilian. I picked one out of the five. He lived in New York, but he *really* lives in Italy. His mother and father didn't speak English; his wife spoke mostly Sicilian. When he went home, he was really going back to Italy.

"This cop also happened to live within one block of Pete Bicardi's house right around the corner from the subject of the investigation. You think anybody in his right mind would have picked him? I took him. I trusted him.

"He spoke every dialect. He could write it, he could read it. The other four guys I settled on understood Sicilian because their grandmothers spoke Sicilian. They were

235

American-Italians. But they didn't compare to this guy. He *lived* Sicilian, Sicilian, Sicilian. When he took his wife to bed at night he felt like he was getting laid back in Italy. Told me that himself.

"The first night Harold Wilson, the assistant DA, came in and went over all the legal, technical stuff—when you could or could not listen in on the wire.

"This was supposed to be a top secret operation. We rented space in a normal Park Avenue office building from a normal landlord. There was no possibility of sending in the troops—all the usual techie people who show up with step-vans and trailers and transformers on wheels. That would have looked like we were invading the neighborhood.

"To make the bug functional on our end, across the street from the brothel, we had to run out over a thousand feet of telephone wire from the carbon mike in the townhouse to the listening post on Park Avenue.

"The only way we could get the line into the plant was to drop it down from the roof, which had an eight-foot overhang, then into the listening post window on the tenth floor where our rented office was located.

"I had to stand out on the tenth-floor ledge and stretch—try and reach the telephone line which was being blown away from the building by the wind. The ledge was no more than twelve inches and I'm afraid of heights.

"Today, with all the improvements that have been made, they could just set up one cop with a tape recorder and a directional mike and stash him ten blocks away. Not back then.

"I'm there that first night with lawyers and people standing around in three-piece suits. They even had trouble opening the window that I was going to have to go out.

"The suits are looking at me. This is my case, this is my wire, that whorehouse across the street is my whorehouse. Out the window I go.

236

"I sent a man up on the roof to feed a line down to me. It wouldn't reach. All I'm worried about is that some decent citizen down there is going to call the police because he sees me up on the ledge and this other person on the roof and he decides that we are trying to break into the building. That's how you get killed by friendly fire in the police department. I've seen it happen too many times.

"I take two steps and freeze. I'm pressed so hard against the wall that I'm cutting off my oxygen, almost blacking out. The guy on the roof is no help—he's upside down trying to reach the wire down, seeing that I'm in trouble.

"It's my worst fear made real. The wind is pulling at me; I can see the ground, hear the car horns, and my damn feet are just *nailed* there.

"The guy up top is screaming, 'Sarge, Sarge, you can do it, don't fall.'

"I just will my arm to work and I start to reach up for the wire, which loosens my grip and I start to feel myself going, falling. And I am scared.

"At that moment, for the first time in my life, I believe I had a vision. I was inching along the ledge, getting closer to the line hanging over the roof and I come right across a window. I looked in that window and I saw my mother. She had died five years ago and I had taken the loss harder than you would expect. The woman had been my friend, my confidante, my mentor.

"She's in that window—her face gauzy, but smiling—and she says to me, 'Billy don't make an ass of yourself. Grab that wire and get back inside.' Which is exactly what I would have expected her to say.

"That was Step One. We hooked the line up to the tape-recorder.

"Step Two was turning my cops into an intelligence-gathering team. Their first night there, my five interceptors walked in all dressed up for an Italian wedding.

They never did anything like this before and I was stupid enough that I never told them *not* to look like cops.

"They were so tuned up. This was superspy stuff to them. Talk about motivated kids. They knew they had to stay in there all night because this game goes on all night. But that was fine. I was so proud I really started to *feel* like their Mother.

"The first thing I had to do was 'untrain' them from the academy bullshit. I told them relax; act like this is just a civilian job in a your own neighborhood. Don't let them know you're cops. After that, I went into what are pertinent and nonpertinent conversations. Every moment had to be evaluated.

"The next night, here they come. One guy's got Italian coffee. Another guy's got Italian sausage. Another guy's got lasagna. Another guy comes with ricotta cheese. You could smell the place when you got off the elevator.

"Once those five guys were together, one thing became very apparent to me. I could have saved myself the trouble of all those interviews. The five guys I ended up selecting all had pinkie rings. Honest to God. All the real Sicilians wear pinkie rings—cops or no cops.

"At that time, in this case, I'm working for an asshole deputy inspector who refused to put two interceptor guys in the room together because he wanted to save on paying overtime. And this is just the biggest case in New York. This is the invasion of the American underworld by the Sicilian Mafia.

"But he won't sign the papers.

"I wanted two guys on each shift who didn't know each other. Each would think the other was from Internal Affairs, checking up on him, and he would be afraid to lie to us. I couldn't adequately supervise them—I don't speak the language. So how do I know if my own cops are being straight about what the Sicilians are saying?

"I told all this to the deputy inspector. Besides that, you needed two people, because the bathroom was down the hall. If one guy has to leave a to take a piss, what're you going to do?

"The inspector comes back at me. 'See if you can get a Porta-Potti.'

"I said, 'I will do better than that. I will get fucking cat litter. My cops can stand in the box and do their business.'

"That was the NYPD mentality. It hasn't changed.

"Once we were installed in our secret office, listening, it was not without its own drama. Or comedy.

"One day I'm out on the street across from the whorehouse, taking down license numbers, and one of my guys comes out and says, 'Sarge, Sarge, you have to come up here right away. There's a guy up here on the tape who just admitted in Sicilian that he killed a guy today and he's about to leave. He's taking an Amtrak train to Washington. He's wearing two guns.'

"My first reaction was to ID him and watch him, but not arrest him, because we can't blow the bug.

"My boss says, 'You can't do that. He's a murderer. Another case will have to be opened.' By now, I'm almost rooting for him to get away with murder. I can't handle any more complications.

"The next day I bring the tape to work. My best interceptor was there. He hadn't been working the night before when all this went down. I say to him, 'Listen to this tape; who did they kill yesterday?'

"He listened about five times, played it over and over, talked to some other interceptor in Italian and all of a sudden they both start laughing.

" 'I understand how they thought he could have killed somebody,' my cop tells me. 'But he didn't kill anybody.'

" 'What? He had two guns. He's leaving on Amtrak.'

"The interceptor explained: 'What he had in the *afternoon*, not on *Amtrak*, was a toothache and the dentist took them out. On the tape he said, "The dentist took them out.' But he took out *teeth*, not *people*. There was one syllable difference in the dialect. What he said, literally, was, "I had a pain. He took them out." Not two guns, two teeth.'

"I almost locked up a Sicilian for tooth decay."

Twenty-three

God meant man to sleep at night and you pray for the night to be busy. *The Late Shift* is the toughest thing in police work.

MOTHER'S MAXIM

The Westies were an Irish gang who free-lanced murder for the Italian Mafia. For generations they had occupied the West Side of New York, near Columbus Circle, a couple blocks down from the Hudson River.

By the time that Al Gold had suggested selling the Westies black-market machine guns, they already had thirteen unsolved homicides against them. The Organized Crime Task Force, Detective Bureau, came to Vice for help. They wanted to set up a phony storefront on the West Side in the hope that the gang would approach it for the purposes of extortion.

With McCarthy already insinuated into the Murray Hill brothel, he seemed like the ideal choice to get the clandestine plot off the ground.

The plan called for the Vice team to record everything that happened in the store on film, and maybe, if the cops were lucky, really lucky some of the Westies might boast about the murders they had committed while the covert camera was running. Most shakedown men made just those sorts of boasts to scare people into paying. The scheme was a longshot, but McCarthy's team was game.

"There was an inordinate amount of concern because the Westies were so erratic and so violent. How do you protect the undercovers who would be in the store?

"The location was a one-window, one-door variety store, with a counter across the front and a huge back room. Looked just like the mob joint on Mulberry Street. Actually, that store *was* the original headquarters of the Westies. That's why we took it over. Add insult to injury. It was like their clubhouse.

"I knew the Westies. This was Hell's Kitchen, my old neighborhood. These guys would shoot you over a stickball game.

"Four people to work in the store at all times—safety in numbers. And there would always be two 'maintenance men' behind the Dutch door in the back of the store, allegedly working on illegal slot machines that we had set up in there for the express purpose of attracting the attention of the Westies. They would *have* to check out contraband slots in their own backyard.

"Based on past experience, though, I wanted to put more than swinging Dutch doors between my undercovers and the Westies.

"Ballistics was just developing bullet-proof vests for female cops then, trying to get the rigid inserts to conform to breasts. Kevlar had just been discovered as a lightweight alternative to the old-fashioned lead shields. That gave me an idea.

"I went to the firing range and checked out four hunks of Kevlar. Then I went to a tailor on Canal Street and paid him to sew the Kevlar into down-filled vests. Now, the police custom-order vests that way, but that was the first operation that I knew of, ever, where a guy could be wearing a sleeveless vest and have it bullet-proofed and nobody knew it.

"We also built a steel-reinforced counter in front of the existing one. We armor-plated the Dutch doors, too. They were so heavy you couldn't use them, the guys had to climb over them.

"At night I had to sneak in the plates of one-half-inch-thick steel and try not to alert the people living near the store who were friendly with the Westies. The amount of work involved was staggering—finding cops who were carpenters to build it, cops we could trust; changing the walls to install the hidden cameras, microwave transmitters beaming to one of our men across the street; we even took over a room at John Jay College, which is close by, to use as a field command.

"When and if the Westies ever attacked in strength, if the deal went bad—as it easily could—it would be a war.

"The only thing the undercovers would have to do was drop down behind the steel-reinforced counter in the front. The guys in the back room could then open up with a shotgun barrage. That way, they wouldn't have to worry about killing the cops in the front with friendly fire.

"I also remembered what had happened when that shotgun had gone off by accident in the hotel. No question about it—we were getting ready for the Gunfight at the O.K. Corral. The Westies could not be expected to just lay down their guns, they were the kind of wild Irishmen who would take blood for blood.

"Once we had rebuilt the store into a bunker, we put out the word all through the West Side that we were open for business—slots, gambling, any kind of action from fencing stolen goods to hijacking. All the stuff the Westies themselves did.

"We kept the same code word for trouble—*slick*—just for sentimental reasons.

"One week went by, two; we waited. Sooner or later,

the Westies would have to show. We were working their side of the avenue in a brazen way. I have to admit that it was beginning to bother me a little that they were staying away, but I couldn't believe that they were on to us.

"One day I'm having trouble with one of the cameras. I call in a tech guy to come and look at it. While the tech guy is in the store, trying to fix it, we find out that they had unintentionally hooked it up wrong when they first put the electronic gear in. Now, the whole undercover operation was transmitting over commercial television, on one of the local UHF frequencies that were available all over the West Side.

They could see everything we were doing in the store. We were prime time—a continuing soap opera. People across the street could watch us while we talked about what we were going to do to the Westies. It was a disaster.

"Now I know why the Westies haven't bothered us. They were probably too busy laughing their asses off. If my undercover operation is on television, I have to shut it down. I jump all over the tech guy who's fixing the camera; he's actually shaking.

"Then, at that very moment, in walks the Department of Finance. They bust us for nonpayment of taxes and begin locking us up. They also grab the tech guy who is carrying his real police ID. Everybody else had a phony ID.

"Finance thinks they've caught a corrupt cop who's working with the Westies—that's who they thought *we* were—and they called a fucking press conference within the hour.

"After all my work, months and months of lugging the steel in, getting the vests, going to the garment center, all the conniving, and then a bunch of accountants from Finance close us down.

"I had to get to the bottom of it. I figured the fix had to be in at the Puzzle Palace. Somebody must have taken a payoff from the real Westies to put us out of business.

"But, as it turned out, it wasn't anything that conspiratorial. What had happened was that the little store next door ratted us out because we had been selling cigarettes cheaper than they were. They called in Finance to get rid of the competition.

"And guess where I got the cigarettes to sell in the first place? From the Department of Finance, up in their warehouse. They had been seized in previous raids as untaxed contraband.

"After that, they *really* started to joke with me about my always refusing to buy cigarettes for people.

"At home, Millie was understandably nervous about the kinds of dangerous, unorthodox assignments I was getting. But I was bullheaded, as usual, and this was what I definitely wanted.

"They started to move me around after that. Sinbad was still in the works; we were intercepting intelligence every week from the Sicilians at Murray Hill and Al Gold had a different scam every week. Our fear was that depending on how much the Westies might have figured out, they could possibly put two and two together and tip off Al Gold about me.

"I wasn't worried, though. I just couldn't see the Westies helping Gold out of the goodness of their hearts. The psychos didn't have hearts.

"The theory was to keep me on the move—but always in touch with Gold and the Murray Hill crew. Don't forget, I was supposed to be available to them night and day, to perform favors and to keep the honest cops away."

There were always more balls, more juggling.

A detective from the 6-2 precinct, Detective Unit, Brooklyn, who had formerly worked in Vice and who knew McCarthy by his reputation in Public Morals, approached him with a worthwhile lead.

The detective had been interviewing an Italian immigrant who was involved with a fraudulent check-writing scheme. This Brooklyn cop figured that immigrant would be a prime candidate to flip and begin working as an informant for Public Morals because he had been a loanshark victim. That was how he had gotten started writing bad checks.

McCarthy drove out to Brooklyn and interviewed him. He spoke with an almost gelatinous Italian accent; his English was on a par with the Sicilian dialects that McCarthy had been hearing in the tapes at Murray Hill.

He had been arrested for bad checks and he also owed money to nine different loan sharks. The man had no place to go except the police. When McCarthy offered him a deal, he quickly accepted.

"This poor little Italian was in sad shape. They were all looking to break his legs. He wasn't tough or even particularly polished, just an ordinary person who had gotten in over his head. I had to know if he would be willing to wear a wire. If so, we would make some loan payments for him. He said yes.

"Now, you cannot just give a guy money and send him out to start making payments. The bad guys will say, 'Where is this guy getting the money?' So before he could start making payments, he had to show some kind of legitimate income, a business, a way of making money.

"He had owned a landscaping company. The business had been very successful, but he had lost it all at the track. He loved the ponies.

"I had a detective working for me, Salvatore Montali, born in Italy, raised in Italy, spoke Italian. He was like one of my Sicilian interceptors.

"I made Sal the money man for a phony construction company. The immigrant had two friends. Both were smart, hard workers. One guy was a bricklayer. The other was a carpenter. They only spoke Italian.

"At first, these two partners didn't know anything about the immigrant's involvement with us, and Sal Montali was simply introduced as one of his American cousins. No questions asked. The partners probably figured Sal was mobbed up.

"They started doing construction jobs all over Brooklyn—refacing houses, putting up brick walls, building additions onto houses. This allowed him to start making minimum payments to the different loan sharks and we recorded the conversations.

"In the course of that we start looking at seventeen different OC people. Every one was a 'made man.' Pure Mafia again. And the best part is, half of these people are steady customers at Al Gold's fancy whorehouses. I'm having trouble believing how all this is coming together, how huge Sinbad has become.

"And the business is thriving. Sal becomes the president of the company. Back in Public Morals we're actually making a *profit* off the undercover operation.

"Sal negotiated loans for capos, all in Italian. The mob began to seek him out as this mysterious financial genius. They never thought he was a cop.

"One of the loan sharks our informant had to meet was Frankie Zuffo. He was ugly, mean, bad. He had hands that looked like my thighs. If he slapped you in the face, he could tear your head off.

"When our immigrant informant went back to these people to tell them, 'Listen, I can start paying you fifty dollars a week,' they didn't want fifty dollars a week. They wanted a lot more.

"When he went to meet this Zuffo, I was in the car, backing him up. I took my gun out of my holster and had it between my legs; that's where I always kept it. He was scared and so was I.

"Zuffo tells him he's gonna kill him—fifty dollars a

week isn't enough. Our informant stares him down and says, pointing to his shoulder, his head, his leg, 'Listen, you could shoot me here, or here, or here, but if you shoot me, you don't get no money. If you want it, you get fifty dollars. Take it or leave it.'

"That little guy had guts. I'll never forget him. I don't think I would have barked at Zuffo that way.

"Ultimately, we arrested the whole bunch. Took out some of the biggest loan sharks in Brooklyn. But not until after Sinbad."

In one very significant way Operation Sinbad was unique. At no point during that case—which took approximately two years to reach its final, violent conclusion—were the people running the Murray Hill brothel approached by shakedown artists in the employ of New York City. Normally, the authentic criminals had to get in line behind any number of municipal workers, representing a staggering variety of offices and agencies, who ran booming extortion enterprises of their own on the side. Anything could be "fixed," from a license that was out of order to code violations that would be winked at for the right price.

These shakedown schemes that actually originated in City Hall or in one of its satellite offices were a source of real anxiety for undercover operatives like Bill McCarthy. There was no telling how badly an investigation could be jeopardized by avaricious city employees.

"We opened a yogurt shop in Brooklyn, on Bath Avenue, Bensonhurst; this was heavy organized crime country. It was another lend-lease deal. The Brooklyn district attorney needed a couple extra undercovers. He specified a Greek and an Italian. Then he said that he also wouldn't turn down a Jewish officer.

"Now, to understand why the Brooklyn DA was so specific about whom he needed, you must appreciate the way Organized Crime guys think. To them, *all* Italians must either be unpredictable Sicilians who behave erratically or dumb U.S.-born muscle guys. They pigeonhole you. A Greek could legitimately operate a store; the Jew is pegged as the moneyman. These people aren't into ethnic sensitivities. They will settle for the stereotype every time.

"I assign the Brooklyn DA the people he needs from Manhattan Vice. They'll be new faces. Everything should go well.

"The yogurt shop was to run along the lines of the store we built to attract the Westies. Slot machines and gambling in the back room. That makes you a much better victim—there's no way you can run to the police and complain, you already have too much to hide.

"The DA wasn't as much concerned with luring the Brooklyn mob into a shakedown—although he would have taken that in a minute—as he was with waiting there until the undercovers were approached by a neighborhood loan shark he was after, Frankie Torrio, Frankie One Eye or Frank-the-Patch, so named for obvious reasons. He'd lost the eye in a knife fight at the age of fourteen.

"Once we managed to get Frank-the-Patch, the loan shark, on tape offering to do business with us, then the DA would have probable cause to plant a bug in his social club, or headquarters. Conveniently, the social club was only a few blocks down from the place we chose for the yogurt shop.

"I wasn't all that impressed with their plan, but I provided the assistance they requested.

"To make absolutely sure that we would get the Patch to notice us, we rented the store from a realtor who was a known OC agent. He handled no clean properties.

"The day we are moving in, the real estate guy comes by and begins snooping around. Two of my guys are pushing these big old slot machines up a ramp in the back, the machines are covered by a tarp like a painter's drop cloth. I give them the signal to accidently-on-purpose let the tarp fall off. Make it look good.

"Naturally, the real estate man sees this. He gets me by myself. 'You can't do this,' he says.'You can't bring those slots in here.'

"I give him a look. 'Why, because it's illegal? Don't worry, we'll never get caught and you won't get in any trouble.'

" 'Who cares about that shit?' he answers. 'I'm telling you that you can't use *those* machines because they ain't *my* machines. This is my store, so you have to use my machines. And I take a piece.'

"This is the realtor, on the first day. Like I said, Bath Avenue was real OC country.

"I make a deal with him not to move any more of my slots in. If he gets some for me, I'll use them in the back room. On his terms. I haggled a little. He left satisfied.

"We officially open for business on a Monday. I still can't believe that the real estate guy has a sideline in slot machines. That morning, in walks a guy from the Department of Sanitation. We don't even have any trash yet. We haven't had our first customer yet.

"The very first thing out of his mouth is, 'You don't need to use commercial. I'll have a truck come by first thing every Saturday morning. Just pay the driver.'

"What's he talking about? He's telling me that there will be no need for me to hire a commercial cartage company to take away my trash because, even though it is illegal for the City of New York to do it, he will have a city truck there to pick up my trash. I pay the driver under the table. Another payoff.

"That same afternoon, on the first day, a different truck pulls up. It's a delivery van, not a trash truck. But we haven't ordered anything.

"The driver comes in and says, 'Where do I put the slots?'

"It's like he's making the most routine delivery. The real estate man had sent him.

"On the second day in business a man in a utility company uniform walks in. 'Once a month, I can turn back the meters. Electrical and gas.' *Then* he introduces himself. He was from Con Ed. This illegal service will cost me fifty dollars a month. A bargain.

"Wednesday rolls around. I swear this is true. Three of the ugliest guys I have ever seen in my entire police career walk through the front door. One takes up a position on the door, the other second one comes behind the counter. The spokesman stands in front of me.

" 'Who are you with?' Just like that.

"That question is the classic mob introduction. It takes the place of 'How do you do?'

"Then, before I even have a chance to answer, he says, 'My name is Angelo. From now on, you're with me. That will cost you five hundred dollars a week. Anybody bothers you just say you are with me and I am with Carmine-by-the-Bay.'

"He was referring to a major league Gambino Family capo—Carmine is from the Sheepshead Bay area. And if you were under Carmine's protection in Bensonhurst, you were in very good shape.

"But this is all wrong now. Carmine-by-the-Bay is the *wrong* mob guy. We already have a loan-shark indictment ready to drop on Carmine. This would be like sticking two hooks in the same mouth.

"Besides, the Brooklyn DA does not have a hard-on against the Gambinos in this instance, but rather against the Bonanos He'll do the Gambinos next week. Frank-the-Patch is Bonano. That's who we have to bug.

"But now, with Carmine-by-the-Bay in the picture, we cannot even approach Frank-the-Patch about getting a loan from him. We can't, in other words, go to the corner, to our neighborhood wiseguys, because Carmine has staked his claim.

"The case is now over. The wrong mob guy is shaking us down. However, we have money and, manpower tied up in the yogurt shop and if we pull out too fast that will blow our identities.

"Before he left, Angelo also told us that we would have to begin using Carmine's yogurt exclusively. Now, it wasn't actually *Carmine's* yogurt. It was a big-ticket, brand-name yogurt, but somehow he had moved in on the local distributor. So Carmine-by-the-Bay had a bigger interest in sales volume than the manufacturer did.

"He explained that as part of the protection we were buying from him, we had to use Bonano slot machines in the back room. We better get rid of our slots and the real estate guy's slots. Then, Angelo and his two giant friends left.

"Thursday Angelo calls the store and gives me the name of a person in the Consumer Affairs office at City Hall whose job it is to enforce city code regulations that apply to stores like ours. 'He's good people,' Angelo said. 'You call him if there's a problem with the city. This is a service that we are providing to you free of charge.'

"That was Carmine's reach in City Hall.

"By the time Friday came around, I was ready to call it a week. But the city still wasn't finished.

"Two cops come in and try to sell my undercover people a hot gun. It had been stolen from a National Guard Armory. For all I know, it could have been a gun from the same shipment that Al Gold's burglar had scored. At least this wasn't a machine gun, though. But I can tell you we made it a point to take care of those two cops.

"I left that Friday. We were no closer to Frankie-the-

Patch than when we had started. I had to get back to Sinbad.

"Other agencies wanted in, however. So I had to leave some of my people there with the Brooklyn cops. Every time a different law enforcement agency monitors—or joins in on—a case like that, a new log number is assigned to that phase of the investigation. By the time we shut down the yogurt shop there were enough different log numbers to build a log cabin."

The Murray Hill brothel, the primary site of the Sinbad activities, had apparently been allowed to function free of these petty extortions. Not that many people knew about Murray Hill, and the ones that did were intimidated by it.

As far as Al Gold was concerned, though, the reason why Murray Hill had remained unmolested for so long was a cagey Vice cop named Bill McCarthy.

However, in a sudden, brutal turnabout, that profitable status quo would be forever altered.

The very first person Gold contacted about it was McCarthy, his personal pad cop.

Twenty-four

In the Life, when an *Insurance Man* comes collecting, you can either buy his policy or buy the farm. Or, you can fight back and make him sorry he ever came. Payback is a bitch.

MOTHER'S MAXIM

AUGUST 1974
THE MURRAY HILL TOWNHOUSE

Albert Gold sounded frantic. As McCarthy listened, his voice took on an unaccustomed shrillness, a tone that was close to a whine. Normally, there was a calculating flatness in Gold's tone. His emotions, especially as they concerned business, were as cold as an amphibian's.

McCarthy had taken the call at his desk in One Police Plaza late on a Friday afternoon. As soon as he picked up the receiver, the tape began rolling.

There had been trouble at the brothel on Fifty-first Street, the big adjoining apartments.

The whorehouse had been knocked over by a Brooklyn crew whom no one seemed to know anything about. Barely able to stammer out the words, Gold recounted to McCarthy that three of the gang members had come into the house on a Wednesday, acting like paying customers, although he had sensed immediately that they seemed more interested in how much cash was going through the house than in how compliant the girls appeared to be.

Nervous, Gold had opened his desk drawer, reached inside and taken out a revolver. He laid it across his lap, just in case. But that night nothing happened. The men simply went to bed with some of the girls, paid up and left. No hassles.

Two days later, on a sweltering Friday evening, the same three men returned.

This time they didn't bother pretending to be johns. Instead, they began batting the hookers around, slamming them on the floor, throwing punches. They beat one woman so savagely that they broke seven of her ribs.

They chased away the other customers—but made sure not to harm them—and told the madam who was running it for Al Gold that her "man" would have to begin paying them "insurance" to avoid a repeat performance. They would be back every week, every night, if necessary. Then, on the way out, they left a telephone number in Brooklyn for the "man" to call. It was a classic shakedown. At that moment, Gold explained to McCarthy, his greatest fear was that these extortionists would discover that he was also the major shareholder in the far more profitable Murray Hill townhouse. If they ever got in there, then he would have to face their extortion as well as the anger of the Maranzo Bicardi faction, not to mention the wrath of the Sicilians. Providing security at the whorehouses was Al Gold's job. He knew that Bicardi would hold him to it. So would the Sicilians.

Gold had a desperate message for McCarthy, "You're on my payroll. Start to earn your money."

The Vice cops spent the weekend attempting to find out who had visited Fifty-first Street and why.

"I talked it over with Tony and the rest of the team and we decided that the best course was for us to meet with this gang and represent ourselves as the real owners of the club—claim that Al Gold was just our front man. Then, we would begin making extortion payments just to see where they went.

"As far as we knew there was no immediate way for this shakedown mob to find out that we were cops. Should they discover our identity at any point in the future, we would just pull out as fast as we could. Take the whole crew out if we had to. It was dangerous, but we didn't want to lose our foothold in Murray Hill, either. Besides, it had to look like we were really putting out for Al Gold.

"Actually, we had been hearing unsubstantiated rumors about these stickup men for some time. It was like the rumble of distant drums in the jungle. We knew that a team of cowboys, renegades, were out there, totally out of control, shaking down every Vice joint in Manhattan. At first, we saw this as another opportunity. These shakedown guys *had* to be connected to somebody. We would just run it down. Add to our intelligence. I had the notion that there might be a movement afoot to take over midtown. I could see one of the Mafia Families secretly using these commandos against the others.

"As it happened, that was not the case. However, we were also wrong to think that this gang was just an aberration. They *were* more than extremely dangerous, wild-assed punks who had come riding into Manhattan like Frank and Jesse James. The Five Families did turn out to know about them, but the gang was considered so unpredictable and so gun-happy that nobody was prepared to take them on. Only about once every ten years or so do you see a group like that. Even in New York.''

McCarthy's immediate concern was preserving the integrity of Operation Sinbad from interference by these cowboys.

Since Tony Vitaliano could so easily pass for an Italian

hood, he was selected to meet with the extortionists as the lead undercover. McCarthy would be the control officer, the primary backup, as well as the overall sergeant/supervisor.

There would be intense pressure on both of them, especially McCarthy. If anything went wrong, it would be his responsibility. His reputation as Mother would face its most severe test. However, in Vitaliano, he believed that he had the most gifted undercover in New York.

"Tony was a complete detective. Probably the greatest characteristic of a detective is how he ties his tie. That was part of the religion of being a detective. The old-time detective would walk around with his tie open, just hanging over his shirt. That meant he was working full-bore. And that was how Tony dressed. If he had to go out for an interview, the tie would be tied with just the first loop over, but never in a Windsor knot. Windsors were only for a wake or a wedding. Or to testify in court.

"The difference between an ordinary detective and a *good* detective is that the good one can get people to say things, give him information such that after he leaves, they think to themselves, I shouldn't have told him that. And a good detective can do it with finesse. That was Vitaliano.

"All we could do was try and pretend that the danger didn't exist. Deep down, we knew better. But this was the biggest case in anybody's career, the biggest undercover case *ever* in New York, as far as we knew. We used to go all day and all night on nerves and exhilaration. You never saw a group of people who were so into being cops.

"Tony called the phone number that had been left for Al Gold. He sounded calm; I was listening in on an extension.

"Tony grew up with these people. He knew how to

talk to them. Right away, they went for it. He agreed to meet with them. It would be three hundred dollars a week. To start.

"This immediately told us that the gang had no idea about Murray Hill, because if they did, they would have asked for much more.

"For the first meeting, we were supposed to go down to Brooklyn, over to a pizza parlor on St. John's Place between Utica and Schenectady avenues. Ask for 'Joe.' That's a mostly black neighborhood now except for the guys who would be there waiting for us. Apparently, they also worked with some black strong-arm men because that corner they picked was black mob all the way. Either they were connected or they were running the risk of poaching. We figured they had to be connected to the black underworld, too. That was almost unheard of then.

"We realized that we would have to go in cold—at least this first time. No backups. Too much of a chance. However, this was a crew that had beaten women unmercifully all over Manhattan; they were killers, too, we guessed. It wouldn't be like storming into Al Gold's wig shop and pulling my pants down and acting bad.

"This was playing for keeps.

"The first time you meet people like this, you must be prepared that they might beat the shit out of you; they're bound to rough you up and threaten you. We went in with our eyes open.

"I was supposed to be Tony's driver. That was my cover. We just reversed our usual roles. Now, I was the schlepp. He wore the wire; the transmitter was in the car. I never expected to have to open my mouth.

"The location where you first meet bad guys is very crucial. It has to be checked. You can find out who was arrested at that spot in the past. They are all creatures of habit.

"We reviewed all we could about past police actions along this part of Utica Avenue. We could not get a make

258

on a single white hood and Al Gold had assured us that these were white guys.

"We were both so hyper that neither one of us got any sleep at all the night before that first meeting. On the way we barely even talked to each other. Tony was like a great thespian concentrating on his role. I was just scared.

"I let him out of the car and he went into the pizza place alone. I hated just abandoning him like that. But I could hear what was going on, of course, because I had the receiver in the car.

"Two countermen were waiting for him. No customers. Just empty tables. 'Either of you guys named Joe?' he asked.

"Nothing for a few minutes. Just an old-fashioned staredown. Finally, one of them wipes his hands on his apron and says, 'Joe ain't in. Try the pool hall across the avenue.'

"Outside, Tony crossed the street, saw the pool hall and went in. One flight up. Any time you're a cop you really hate to see that. It takes you right away from the nearest help. I was the 'help.'

"It's harder to stay outside than to go in. You don't have the same control. In a situation like that, I believed that I could anticipate what they were going to do, and that I could give the right answer before they thought up the next question. But here it was all on Tony.

"Even if it went bad, I was still the boss; I was always responsible. My cop was always off the hook—unless they decided to kill him. That was the risk an undercover took.

"The pool room was nearly empty too. Just one bare light over the table. Three or four hoods backs to the wall, picked Tony up at the door and eyeballed him crossing the floor.

"There was only one guy playing. Black silk shirt, blue jeans. A really hard face. He's concentrating on a shot, nine ball, side pocket.

"Tony says, 'Is somebody named Joe here?'

"The player punches the cue at the white ball, muffs it badly and then looks up, lifts the cue stick off the tabletop and stares at Tony.

"Then he walks over and says, 'I'm Bobby Gee and you just made me miss my fucking shot.'

"Tony begins to give him some explanation, but this Bobby Gee cuts right through it. 'I got these friends,' he says, 'they did the job on your place and they asked me to act as their intermediary. I have nothing to do with this, understand. They want you to buy an insurance policy. You got a nice business there. No reason to see anything happen to it. These friends of mine are just businessmen like you.'

"And that's how it started.

"At that meeting, much to my surprise, they didn't rough Tony up a bit, because they were more concerned with finding out whom he was with. Up to that point, they were following strict Mafia protocol.

"If I go in there, I can look like a hardass guy, but I could only be a victim or a cop. I'm Irish and I look Irish. He goes in there, they have to be nice to him because he's Italian. They don't know if he's with somebody who's protecting him. They don't know if the place they just hit is already connected with a Family.

"If Tony had really been with somebody, they would have had to just back off. Walk away from it with an apology.

"From that initial conversation, we picked up our first important piece of intelligence on these people. They mentioned Tony Spots. He was a connected guy. They had to be working under his license. He had a journeyman's license in the mob, not like a senior mechanic's. He was a middle-level soldier. Possibly, if he had any, Tony's connections could have outranked his.

"But Tony swore that he had no connections and that

he was willing to pay. That was just what they wanted to hear.

"I'm listening outside. I hear Bobby Gee say, 'We're gonna provide you with service. We're gonna protect you.'

"What they don't tell Tony is: We'll protect you from us.

"They go on: 'We're gonna help you. We're gonna be your business consultants; you don't want to operate without us. If you have any problems, you come to us. We'll take care of your problems. Maybe there are some other things we could do together. Maybe we're gonna have some other places and you can help us work there.'

"They even offered to do murders: 'If you're having a beef with somebody, we'll take them out. No problem.'

"After about twenty minutes of this, and after he hands over the money, Tony leaves.

"The lookouts from the pizza parlor are looking me over outside, but they can put up with the fact that he brought one guy with him. That's natural. If Tony was important enough to own a whorehouse, he should be important enough to have a driver like me. Their defenses were down. The second Tony walked outside and put his ass in the car, we got the hell out of Brooklyn.''

Twenty-five

New York has everything. It's got more that's good
and more that's bad than any other place in the
whole world. It's fast, it's irreverent; it's got
tremendous volume, tremendous violence,
congestion, hustlers; all kinds of moves, all kinds of
speeds.

MOTHER'S MAXIM

"We began to take surveillance photographs all over
Manhattan; we became very interested in this group. Followed them. During the next couple of weeks, they hit a
few other places and continued to brutalize people. It
came to a point, very quickly, where we had a real dilemma.

"I warned Tony to be *very* careful. These punks had
already done hard time; they wouldn't hesitate to shoot.
The crew had a history of violence that went all the way
back to Crazy Joey Gallo and even more sinister current
connections that linked it to an associate of the Columbo
Family. They were for real.

"They all looked like wiseguys. Four of them were
brothers—the Gagliano brothers. All about five-ten, five-
nine, average build, between 160 pounds and 180
pounds.

"They needed shaves, had to be cleaned up like street-
dogs, gamey dogs. There was something uncivilized
about them—like each one had too many hormones, too

262

much animal inside them. They hadn't quite stepped over that evolutionary boundary that made them human. They were always on the verge—of losing control, of violence. And what would take them over the edge wasn't always rational. If the Mets lost that night, for example that could be enough. What makes a volcano finally erupt? It just goes. You could see it in their eyes. Read it in their minds.

"The craziest one of them all was Tommy Mendino, their pal. He had been a cellmate of theirs in Attica.

"He was a paroled killer with murky Hispanic bloodlines and a dark, unsmiling face who had already figured in jobs all over New York as everybody's favorite designated hitter. Mendino fell into that category of psychos who were outside of technique. They didn't need judo or karate or the martial arts or any of that nonsense. All they needed was an excuse to turn bonecrusher, to make a bowling ball out of somebody's face; you couldn't bring down rhinos like that with an elephant gun.

"Years back, at the Blarney Stone bar in Manhattan, I had to fight a tough guy just like that. He was another murderer who seemed ready to flip, to become an informant. But our negotiations had broken down over how much a week the police should be sending his sick mother back in Arkansas as his payback for helping them.

"This guy picked me up with one hand—with one hand—along with the barstool I was sitting on. Then he banged me down hard on top of the bar. He happened to have a stomach ulcer at the time and he had been drinking milk for it all night long—milk with scotch. He was bleeding out of his mouth—milk and blood. After I got to know him, he told me that before the ulcer, back when he was feeling better, he could pick up *two* people at once. If this guy liked you, he let you know by butting you in the head.

"I can still see him manhandling me—hands that looked like ham hocks, big gold rings that would fit through a bull's nose, an IQ of room temperature. And the milk and the blood dribbling out of his mouth. Guys like that are torpedoes; once you point them, there's no calling them back.

"And that's what Tony and I were facing now. I was convinced of it. If Sinbad didn't end up getting both of us killed, it wouldn't be their fault.

"Besides Mendino, a couple other hoods worked with the brothers more or less full-time. But Bobby Gagliano and Tommy Mendino were the bad actors.

"If you saw them, and you knew what you were looking for, you knew they had to be a stickup team. They definitely did not appear to be businessmen. They looked like hitters. You could tell by their expressions. They were all in their early to mid-thirties—just the right age, the right everything. People get smart after thirty-five, even hitters. They get a little more wisdom. If you live that long, by then you should have people working for you who can do that. These guys, though, would never be in that position. They were all dead from the neck up, gorillas. They thought they had it all figured out. Violence was the answer to everything.

"And they loved to work over whores; whores almost never fought back. That posture was alien to their line of work. Whores took it lying down—figuratively as well as literally. As soon as a tough guy showed up, they went to their pimp or madam—and there was *always* a pimp, no matter how classy or clean they pretended to be—and the pimp paid off whoever was leaning too hard. The leaners could be cops looking to score an easy note or authentic bad guys. It made absolutely no difference to the leanees. To a whore, a smack in the mouth was a smack in the mouth. And that was how these guys collected their rent, fist first. To a man, they got off on beating up women.

"The guy they reported to—loosely—was Tony

Spots, this three-hundred-pound schlump who ate crates of pasta at a sitting. He knew enough to stay insulated.

"It took us about a month to put names with all the faces. Meanwhile, the gang was still in business. And all the time, Gold was calling me or Tony ten times a day, screaming about his townhouse on Thirty-first Street, the big whorehouse, the Murray Hill joint.

"Sooner or later, we knew that the Gaglianos would hear about it and check it out. For punks like them, New York is really a very small town.

"We agonized through three payments. The Gaglianos kept getting more and more friendly with Tony. They made it clear that they wanted him to join them as their bagman and shake down all the other whorehouses. They liked him—he spoke their language and they could see how bright he was. Whether he liked it or not, he was getting drafted.

"Then, Gold gets me by myself one night. He's acting very strangely. For the very first time, Gold seems like he doesn't trust me.

" 'What's wrong?' I asked him.

" 'They found something in the library that shouldn't have been there.' And he just keeps looking at me; it's my turn to feel uncomfortable.

"Of course, I knew what they had found. In the middle of everything else, with the Gagliano brothers terrorizing everybody on the street, in the Life, they found the bug.

" 'What?' I play dumb.

" 'Don't fuck with me,' Gold said. 'I pay you guys. Now I think I'm being set up, and I have to *pay* for it?' He is glaring at me red hot.

" 'Who set you up? I don't know what you're saying.'

" 'They got the townhouse fucking wired. They found it the other day. We were gonna wallpaper in there and had to move the molding. I guess you expected to get paid pretty good to keep quiet about that.'

"I'm thinking on my feet. Gold is so convinced I'm corrupt that he assumes this is just another level of blackmail, another kind of extortion for me to use against him.

" 'If you really found what you think you found—if you know what it even looks like—it isn't mine.'

" 'The hell it isn't!' He really thinks I'm blackmailing him, scamming him for more money.

" 'Is it still there?' I had to know if they moved it, destroy it.

" 'It's there,' Gold said. 'Nobody goes in that room anymore. The Sicilians were afraid to touch it. They didn't want to tip anybody off. Told me I have to find out what the crap was going on or they were gonna put me under.'

"This is really the problem. Gold is more frightened of the Sicilians than of anybody. And he has a right to be.

"At least the wire was still in place, for whatever good it would do us now. 'Don't touch it. I'll take care of it,' I told him.

" 'No shit—you bet you will.'

"Right there in front of him I made a call; talked to nobody, but pretended I was talking to the office. I asked a few cop questions, then acted like I knew what was up. I hung up and pretended it was all a big secret.

" 'What?' Gold said.

"Now it's my turn to be a bastard. 'You dumb asshole,' I said. 'You come in here and accuse me of running a wire into your whorehouse. And you're supposed to be so smart. You think I'm the only cop in New York? You think every cop is as crooked as me?' I had him now.

" 'You trying to say something?' Gold was physically backing off, walking across the room from me.

"That wire was put in by a new guy from Gambling—I ain't the only Vice cop, you know. I work whores; he works gambling. That wire—and it really is a cop wire—is his and he's straight. Don't even think about reaching him.

" 'You got nowhere to go with him. All you got, you dumb fuck, is me. But I'm a nice guy and I'm gonna square it for you. And it ain't even gonna cost you an extra dollar. But you really owe me now. You tell that to the Sicilians.'

"Gold accepted my lie. Why not? Gold knew all the things he'd done. Plenty of other cops could have known about the casino in the townhouse.

"I saved my ass, but we have now lost that wire for all time. Maybe the townhouse, too. It will only be a matter of time until the Sicilians move on now. Gold will be too hot for anyone to touch. I can see Sinbad dying. It had been a good run, almost a year. That's an eternity in undercover work.

"That very same week, like enough wasn't going on already, the Gaglianos decided to finally visit Thirty-first Street, the Murray Hill townhouse. And the shit, as they say, hit the fan.

"Sure enough, on a Wednesday night, when they usually did their casing of a place, before they would come back and rob it on a Friday, they showed up at Thirty-first Street.

"As fast as we could ascertain, they still did not know that Fifty-first Street was connected to Thirty-first Street. But we couldn't be sure.

"As luck would have it, one of the girls from Fifty-first Street was sent over to Murray Hill—that *same* Wednesday. It was a step up. She was all excited. When the Gaglianos and Tommy M. came in, she recognized them, knew what was about to go down.

"The hooker tells Gold and he calls us. This guy *really* wants protection now. He would now like for us to blow the Gaglianos away—just to make up for the bug they found. I yell back at him that the bug wasn't my fault. But Gold gets ornery again. He handed his telephone to somebody else, to another pimp whose voice I half-recognized. This guy tells me that he has friends in

Brooklyn who will take care of the Gaglianos forever, for a price. Do we want in on the hit? Evidently, they can still use our help.

"Now, my role as a cop on the payroll has just escalated to this discussion about arranging for one or more murders. Never mind the fact that killing the Gaglianos would have been akin to performing a valuable public service. I was still a cop.

"I get him talking and he tells us that all the Manhattan whorehouse owners are about to hire some guns—whoever the hell they are—to protect themselves from our Gaglianos and Tommy Mendino. They are collecting from every house to pool up the money to pay for the contract.

"Next, Al Gold puts out the word that the Murray Hill townhouse isn't going to open on the following Friday.

"That was a mistake. The gang would have to know that something was up if that happened. That would have been bad for Tony because he was supposed to meet them the following week.

"We tell Gold that he *has* to open on Friday, even if they do rob him. It's part of our plan to take care of the cowboys for him.

"All the time, I'm focusing on the Gaglianos like you can't believe. I'm meditating on them. I want to be inside their sick minds. I have to try to take on their identities—outthink them. I'm Mother; that's what I do.

"I can close my eyes and see the brothers and Tommy Mendino, know what they're thinking, feeling:

"We're doing fine with this—this is fun. Getting laid. Shakedowns. This is the Life. What more could we ask for? A steak dinner? This is violent, this is sexual. We go, we case the place. We know that we're coming back to hit it. Even the whores know. You can tell the way they look at us.

"You can't imagine what it's like being there—the thrill of casing the place, the anticipation of coming back

268

and robbing it. This is the race, the excitement, your dick gets hard because the same whore you're going to beat up on Friday night is blowing you right now. That's an explosion of anticipation. That's an orgasm. The foreplay is Wednesday; the orgasm of violence is Friday.

"It's better than a blow-job. We order them around—the whores. Anything we want. Because we've got them scared. It's almost like servitude. It's violent masturbation. You don't participate with them. You're not there to please them or relate to them. Just use them. It's a dog pissing on turf. On the whores. King of the pack. This is the race. The Light. The Vice Marquee.

"We have to put an end to this. But how?

"We didn't want to just surrender our true identities. We might run into the Gagliano crew somewhere down the line. So you don't want to be cops to them. But we have to stop them.

"How can the police department have knowledge of this group and allow them to continue operating? Is Sinbad—no matter how great an undercover operation it is—worth risking the life of every person in New York? They could have killed one of the prostitutes. I always expected that to happen because they thoroughly enjoyed abusing women—sexually and physically. You just couldn't rationalize knowing about this group and not taking them out.

"That was the conclusion that we all came to.

"Tony would meet them on the following Wednesday, as scheduled. Make the payment.

"From a distance, the rest of the team would follow them back to Brooklyn, just as soon as Tony drove away. We'd put them in where they live, put them to sleep. Make sure they didn't hurt anybody along the way.

"We would come back on Friday because we know they're gonna work Friday. Then we would take them out of the house on Friday, stay with them all day. When they hit Murray Hill that night there would be cops waiting inside, masquerading as regular customers. One of them would be on the door and let the Gaglianos in. They allow the stickup to take place.

"Then, at a prearranged signal, the uniforms would come charging in and arrest everybody. Make it look like a legitimate, routine raid on a whorehouse. It will all seem like one big, nasty coincidence.

"If the Gaglianos and Mendino decided to fight back, they would be outgunned ten to one. And we have our cop witnesses inside who will testify that the Gaglianos robbed the place just before the raid. So we won't have to depend on the testimony of a prostitute who might refuse to talk because she's afraid.

"I wasn't going to be there and Tony wasn't going to be there. So, as far as the Gaglianos are concerned, they don't know how the police got there. They're gonna take a collar. But Tony and I won't blow our covers.

"We just had to sweat out Tony Vitaliano's last scheduled meeting with Bobby Gee."

Twenty-six

For cops, *Fear* is a condition of employment. The first day on the job, you walk out on the street knowing that you might be killed.

MOTHER'S MAXIM

2:00 P.M.
HOUSTON STREET

Vitaliano sounded nervous and that could be a problem. Nervous could make him dead. Fast.

McCarthy was listening to the conversation on a remote receiver for a Kel transmitter that was wired to the underside of the dashboard in Tony Vitaliano's flash car. Tony was also recording the deal; there was a tiny Edwards tape recorder stuffed in an empty pack of Camels in his shirt pocket.

But there was something wrong with the way Tony sounded. Just a trace of hesitation. He was coming across as just a little shaky. Actually, more than a little shaky; *very* shaky. And that wasn't like Vitaliano at all.

Vitaliano was sitting in a flash car on Houston Street (he pronounced it *House*-ton, like all real New Yorkers) near the East River Drive and McCarthy was parked a couple of cars in front of him.

The flash car was a biscuit-brown Thunderbird with

wire wheels and a roadster roof—any pimp would be proud to drive it, and that was exactly what Vitaliano was pretending to be. He'd only been there a few moments when one of the bad guys slid into the seat beside him.

As McCarthy knew only too well, the Kel was not the best piece of eavesdropping equipment that money could buy, but it was the best that the NYPD could afford, perpetually strapped as it was to come up with the cash for undercover operations. And the Kel wasn't all that bad. Take away the expected interference from the Manhattan skyline and the Kel could be counted on to do the job.

It was a chilly, early autumn afternoon—one week after McCarthy's seventh wedding anniversary, but he was planning to celebrate it that night. When you were a cop even special dates had to take a backseat to the job. Still, he hoped he could get home a little early.

As he sat in his flash car, nursing a thermos of coffee, listening to Tony the V, he had to settle for being curled up with a shotgun, instead of his wife, Millie.

The big weapon was between his legs—and God, could he think of a few other things that he'd rather have there right about now—doubled-barreled, twelve-gauge, blue steel, as blue as the indigo clouds that were settling in over the murky, calm East River.

All along the sparse riverbank, winter was already leaning hard on the browned-over green spots, drying out the shaggy tufts of wild onion grass, returning the landscape to a mangy no-man's land.

McCarthy didn't talk to his shotgun like some cops did; he wasn't crazy *that* way. He had it there, propped against the steering wheel, just in case. But McCarthy *was* crazy, all right; they all knew that.

Through his rearview mirror, McCarthy could see that Tony still *looked* okay, relaxed and natural. But he kept picking up that little hitch in his voice, and that hitch or whatever the hell it was kept telegraphing a problem.

The shorthand of it was that something was obviously

about to go down—something that the cops couldn't see—and Tony the V was reacting to it. Reacting in that he sounded like he was practically having an accident in his pants.

McCarthy knew what the other cops on the team had to be thinking: *One of Mother's children is in trouble*.

Tony was in a very special kind of jeopardy now, the kind that both of them had willingly accepted. If a cop happened to be walking down the block and a guy came out of a liquor store with a gun in his hand and that cop just happened to find himself there, or if he was in the hallway of an apartment building in Harlem, about to break the door down, and he didn't know what was on the other side, that was incidental, accidental danger. Cops couldn't really bitch about that. It came with the job, with the badge. But this was something they had brought on themselves.

On the other side of the street, in the projects on Houston Street near the FDR Drive, McCarthy had his lookouts hiding in a Puerto Rican guy's apartment and his snipers up on the roof. He had a camera crew up there, too. With a telescopic lens they practically could have produced a documentary of Tony handing over his pay off. The bad guys were under the impression that Tony was just as crooked as they were.

But as the skinny second hand on McCarthy's watch kept ticking past the fat twelve, nothing was happening. Not yet. Tony and the other man were feeling out each other, making simpleminded wiseguy small talk, and there wasn't a thing that he could do, except wait. And worry.

The only thing today that had given McCarthy any cause for concern had been the hot dog guy. He had never seen this particular hot dog guy on this particular block of

Houston Street before. But today of all days, he had been looking right at him—across the street. That was enough. His antennae went straight up like a warrior ant's.

Then there was the guy on the bench.

Outside the projects on Houston Street a white guy was sitting on a bench. He didn't belong there either.

Put those two things together and McCarthy was glad that he'd brought the shotgun.

So now he knew the bad guys had their own backup in the hot dog truck and on the bench; his team could handle that. He had made the bad guys and that was all that counted.

As he continued to listen on the Kel receiver while Tony the V got even more chummy with his wiseguy friend, McCarthy felt the reassuring weight of the twelve-gauge against his knees. A shotgun would get anybody's attention.

Then he glanced around outside again, through his car window, to make sure that his people were where they should be.

Across the street, the hot dog guy was leaning out of his truck now to hand a wrapped bun and soda to some kid. The man on the bench was pretending to read a newspaper. McCarthy just wanted it to be over.

2:10 P.M.

Nothing would go wrong.

Just make the payoff and get it over with.

Sinbad was two minutes away from happening, no more.

Just let the suspects think their extortion plan was working. Nothing fancy. Tony could pull that off in his sleep.

But as he checked the rearview mirror again, McCarthy could make out that Tony was looking sharp, very sharp. More composed now. Maybe that hitch in Tony's voice had only been his own overactive imagination. Maybe.

The two of them—Tony and Bobby, the hood who had moved in the front seat beside him—were still talking.

As the conversation came across on the Kel, it now appeared that these punks wanted Tony to go into business with *them*. Bobby was apparently feeling him out on it.

None of this was in the script that McCarthy had imagined. All at once they were hitting Tony with a set of complications that no one on the team had anticipated.

McCarthy smiled. It seemed like Tony the V had been playing his role *too* well. Now the extortion crew thought he might be better connected than they were.

The words were cryptic, but as McCarthy listened, Bobby kept referring to a "controllership" the crew was about to offer Tony—they wanted Tony to become a kind of bagman for them, not just shelling out protection money for himself, but also collecting from the other whorehouse owners for them.

He immediately saw this as both an opportunity and a danger. They were enticing Tony to go even deeper undercover, but that would really push the chance of Tony's being found out.

Still, there was no good reason to think that the payoff wouldn't go smoothly. No matter what happened, Tony Vitaliano was not going to panic. McCarthy was counting on that.

These guys were slick, give them that; considerably above average; but McCarthy knew that his team was slicker.

This was it. It was coming up fast now.

What should he do? Let Tony play it out or not? Make the payoff and then follow them back to Brooklyn and grab them now?

Once again, he watched through the rearview mirror as Tony appeared to reach into his pocket for the money envelope, but it was taking him an awful long time.

Just then, McCarthy detected an alarming, erratic

movement out of the corner of his eye. It looked as though the rapid succession of events was about to make his mind up for him.

Something was going wrong.

Another man, whom none of the backups had spotted, was squeezing into the front seat beside Tony on the other side—they had him between them now.

Where had this second guy come from?

He could hear the wariness in Tony's voice as it came through on the Kel, as he asked about this third party.

Vitaliano: Who's this?
Bobby: That's my man; let him in.
Vitaliano: What's going on?
Bobby: Don't move till I tell you to.

There was a very brief struggle. McCarthy could see Tony reaching for his own gun; from out of nowhere another gun was suddenly being pushed into the cop's temple, and Tony was being forced to surrender his weapon. Then he could make out—at least he thought he could see this—that they were putting some kind of glasses covered with black tape over Tony's eyes.

Bobby: Don't make me use the gun.
Vitaliano: All right.
Bobby: Put your hands where I can see them.
Vitaliano: Where we going?
Bobby: We're going to see the top man; he wants to see you.

Then there was silence.

They were snatching Tony. God only knew why, but the bad guys were kidnapping Tony, kidnapping a cop.

276

But did they really know that he was a cop?

Then McCarthy heard the words on the Kel receiver that he hoped he would never hear. It was Tony's gravel-pit voice, his cement-syrup delivery.

"No need to pull a gun over this, Bobby . . . no need to pull a gun over this. . . ."

He said it twice.

That was Tony's prearranged abort signal. As soon as the backup team heard that sentence on the Kel, they were supposed to come charging in like the 7th Cavalry and "recover" Vitaliano because it meant that the deal had disintegrated, there was no turning back and Tony thought that he would be killed.

Then he said it again. He was pleading with his back-ups to come in and get him the hell out.

"Bobby, there's no reason to pull your piece on me, we're friends, right?"

McCarthy was halfway out of his seat in the car, ready to blast the shotgun into action when Tony's Thunderbird, driven by the second man who had gotten in beside him, jerked away from the curb on Houston Street, digging ugly black welts into the asphalt as it sped away.

McCarthy looked up at the thickening traffic and felt sick. Sinbad was getting away from him now—hurting like an out-of-control projectile under its own deadly momentum, a runaway, torpedo. Somewhere, somehow, Mother had fucked up.

They were less than a block away from a single-lane entrance to the FDR expressway and that's exactly where the punks who had taken Tony were headed. From there, they could go anywhere in New York, anywhere on the entire East Coast. It connected with every major highway that cut through the city.

McCarthy quickly slid back in his seat behind the

wheel, put the shotgun aside and jumped on his own ignition. He knew that his other backup cars would be doing the same thing.

But just before he had a chance to pull up behind the Thunderbird, a second car that belonged to the extortion crew, a crash car, a beat-up yellow Chevy, raced in front of him, cutting off McCarthy and the backups. The kidnappers had obviously been holding this one in reserve.

As Tony's brown T-bird jetted into the merging traffic on FDR, the Chevy crash car stopped dead on the entrance lane, blocking the cops and everything else behind it.

The two guys in that second car kept looking around for a tail.

All the other backups were waiting, helpless, looking to see what McCarthy was going to try next. But it appeared as though they had outwitted him this time. They couldn't even risk using the police radio because they knew from past experience that the extortion gang Tony had been infiltrating kept police band radios in their cars. All they had to do was pick up one transmission and they would know for dead certain that Tony was an undercover cop.

And Tony would be dead.

After months and months of careful, exhausting preparation, Sinbad was coming apart and Tony was in trouble; one of Mother's children was in trouble.

The yellow Chevy waited, blocking the on-ramp through one full minute, two, until they were sure that the T-bird had vanished into the rush-hour traffic.

They looked on helplessly as first the Thunderbird, then the yellow Chevy eased into separate lanes and merged with all the other FDR commuters, not one of whom was even remotely aware of what had just happened.

Tony Vitaliano was gone. For the first time in the

history of the New York City Police Department, an on-duty undercover cop had been kidnapped. And it was all Bill McCarthy's fault. He was Mother; he was the control; he was the sergeant in charge. Nothing in McCarthy's long career as a cop had prepared him for this.

In his mind's eye all he could see was the empty space beside Tony Vitaliano's wife and little boy—the space where Tony should have stood.

The worst day of Bill McCarthy's life had just begun.

Twenty-seven

When the sirens are going and the lights are on, that's the *Race*. The car is revving and your body's revving; your mind is racing; you're thinking about what you're gonna do and how you're gonna do it when you get there. And it all happens at once.

MOTHER'S MAXIM

2:15 P.M.
HOUSTON STREET

McCarthy was praying that at least one of the five backup cars that had taken off after Tony would be able to bolt ahead of the rest, and cut off the kidnap car at the next expressway exit. That was their best shot. But it wouldn't be easy. It would have to be done inconspicuously— and quickly—because as soon as the kidnappers realized that they were being tailed, one of their first impulses might be to kill Tony right there in the front seat, just for the hell of it, just to eliminate a potential witness. A tail-car would almost certainly tip them off that Tony was a cop.

The most maddening thing of all was that, for a time at least, as long as the interference from traffic and expressway overpasses didn't prevent it, McCarthy could still pick up the conversation that Tony had been secretly taping on the Kel transmitter. And what he heard told him that they were definitely looking for a tail—even though they still seemed to be buying Tony's cover story. As he listened, they were toying with Tony, making vague threats, trying to sound ominous. And, as anyone in his position would, poor Tony was losing it, losing it badly. He was begging to be let out of the car and those bastards were loving every sadistic minute of it.

It was all a strangely unaccustomed role for McCarthy, a passive role. Like most cops, he was a man of movement, of doing, of getting and making things happen. But that was beyond his control now. All he could do was curse and agonize and monitor the situation, as it developed, from a distance. Every other active option had suddenly been superseded as the events snatched decision-making away from him.

Still, the rest of his Vice team was waiting for McCarthy to do something, to try something, to order their next move. Oddly, not one of them had emerged from his hiding place or from behind the wheel of his car—the five pursuit vehicles were already lost in the East River Drive traffic and the rest of them were frozen. Part of it was instinctive cop caution—the kidnappers might have left a lookout of their own behind at the intersection where it had all gone down on Houston Street, just in case. But another part of it was pure shock, a kind of momentary paralysis.

2:20 P.M.
EAST RIVER DRIVE

The five pursuit cars were still enforcing radio silence to avoid being detected by the kidnappers. The only way they could communicate with each other was through visual sightings and that was practically impossible—the afternoon light was already fading and the volume of traffic was a classic New York crush.

The cop who was having the greatest success sticking with the tail was Bernie Bracken, a veteran Vice cop who was as old country as Irish stew. When Bracken became excited—and his heart was practically retching up out of his throat as he weaved through the cars and trucks and station wagons—you could hardly understand what he was saying for the thickness of his County Tyrone brogue. The other cops used to get on the radio and imitate him, hee-hawing like donkeys. Then Bracken would become even more uncontrollable as he got increasingly pissed off and the result was that you could understand him even less. Which was just about where he was now. His favorite comeback was, "I'll kick your fooking arse."

And Bernie Bracken was the only guy McCarthy still had on the trail. He sped along as far as the tollbooth at the Brooklyn Battery tunnel and then had to brake *hard*.

It looked like the whole world was moving in slow motion. Bracken was talking to himself, cursing in a lilting torrent of Gaelic and Brooklynese, "fooking" every car in sight. But he couldn't make the car move any faster.

Tony's Thunderbird was no more than two lengths ahead. One tollbooth lane over. Bracken could make out that he looked okay—except that he seemed to be wearing glasses of some kind, glasses whose lenses were covered by black tape. He sat there stiff, not looking around or from side to side, just like a prisoner.

Bracken kept inching his car up, almost bumping the driver in front of him. He considered jumping out and rushing them, with his own pistol drawn, but that would have really only accomplished one of two things: It would either have gotten Tony killed on the spot or killed on the other side of the bridge, while Bracken stood there, like a chump, as they drove away.

And then, with one abrupt pedal-pull on the ignition, the flash car was gone, through the tollbooth, and Bracken's chance to make any decision had vanished.

Seconds later, Bracken accelerated and didn't even bother to hand the toll taker any money. He left the startled man standing there, threatening to call the cops.

But as soon as Bracken pulled out of the toll plaza, he realized that he had lost sight of the Thunderbird. Traffic had tinned out on the other side and the men holding Tony captive had taken advantage of it. There was a sloping rise in the contour of the road, peaking like a pregnant woman's belly.

The excited Irishman looked from left to right, back and forth. He had to make a quick decision—he could either stay on the highway, continuing up the steep incline, or he could make a right and pull off onto a service road. Going straight would lead to a choice of the Prospect Expressway, or the Belt Parkway.

Bracken almost broke radio silence—he had his hand on the microphone. Then he remembered that this crew had monitored police calls on some of their previous jobs. He decided not to risk it.

Going with his gut, Bernie Bracken wheeled his car straight up the hill. The Prospect Expressway. But his gut was wrong. That's where they lost Vitaliano.

2:25 P.M.
HOUSTON STREET

McCarthy had to get to a telephone to tell somebody what had just happened. There was no page in the NYPD *Patrol Guide*—for what had just transpired, for losing an undercover officer to kidnappers, but he had been a cop long enough to realize that in addition to recovering Tony, there was one more overriding consideration: He had to let the Building One, Police Plaza, know what was going on.

The "building" was One Police Plaza, the imposing fourteen-story brick and concrete citadel in Lower Manhattan that was the hallowed command post for the New York City Police Department.

In McCarthy's world, all energy flowed downward—from the police commissioner's office on the fourteenth floor, under the reinforced steel helicopter landing pad.

The electrical currents that surged forth from that hypercharged, sputtering, and sizzling nerve center then passed through the nearby offices of the NYPD's four-star chief inspector (now the chief of department) the effective boss of the blue army, then circulated outward through the five superchiefs: Detectives, Organized Crime Control, Patrol, Inspectional Services, and Personnel.

From there, the hot charges would be transferred to all seventy-five precincts and five boroughs and thirty thousand assorted cops, quasi cops, cop-fuckers (who differed not at all from star-fuckers), and support minions.

But only the police commissioner could throw the switch that would activate all or part of that complicated circuitry. Cops like McCarthy, mavericks who preferred to free-lance on their own, pursuing private initiatives, were both rare and despised. They actually looked for trouble, and the people who manned the building—desk cops who had not been on the street in decades, paper-pushers in Perry Como sweaters who carried monogrammed coffee mugs from office to office, chatting—had enough problems dealing with all the unsolicited trouble that came walking through the door. A very special ruthlessness was reserved for the troublemakers like McCarthy.

All this was in McCarthy's mind as he drove along Houston Street and searched for a telephone—a telephone that worked. In New York. At dusk. In a lousy neighborhood.

He tried three of them, racing to each other one, frantically, from corner to corner, from broken public telephone to broken public telephone.

The first one had no receiver; the second one had a receiver, but someone had ripped off the earpiece. The third one was intact but he couldn't get a dial tone.

He had to drive all the way through the Lower East Side before he finally realized what he should have done all along.

He spied a pizza parlor across the street; a guy in a dirty white shirt and pants and apron was standing in the window, writing down an order.

McCarthy parked his car up on the pavement, left the ignition running, ran into the store and pulled the telephone out of the hands of the terrified pizza man.

He wasn't trying to make friends at that moment and he just didn't care. "Don't argue with me on this," he barked at the pizza man. "I'm a cop, this is an emergency, and if you say one word you're under arrest."

The pizza man looked at McCarthy, immediately surrendered the telephone, backed away and, as he had been instructed, did not open his mouth. Six or seven customers suddenly got up and left.

McCarthy didn't even know whom he should be talking to at headquarters, in the building, as he dialed an emergency number and babbled what had just happened, pumping, trying to sound calm, coherent, but missing the mark by a mile.

He told them that it had gone bad and that Tony had been kidnapped.

Immediately, the message was passed from a lieutenant to a captain to an inspector, and on to a second inspector, each of whom was stricken by a sense of tremendous personal dread as soon as he heard the bad news. They shared one immediate concern: not for Vitaliano's life, for even as they listened, they were writing him off as a dead man, but for their own careers. Could any of this possibly be blamed on them? Could the simple act of answering the telephone somehow involve them in a loser like this? And everyone who heard it searched desperately for someone else, preferably someone more senior or powerful than they, to dump it on.

They might not have had any idea who Tony was or what Sinbad meant or how high up it went, or what their personal exposure on the damn thing might be; but they did know that this was as bad as it could get. Life and death.

McCarthy had no idea how wild-eyed he looked, how scarily out of control. But as he tried to compose himself, as he handed the telephone back to the pizza man, he could see it in the guy's frightened eyes.

"Thank you," he said in a hollow voice. Then he started to leave.

The pizza man backed away again and just left the telephone receiver dangling by the cord, bouncing off the counter.

Outside, McCarthy pointed his car toward Brooklyn.

McCarthy's first being scared—really scared—had happened during one of his first fights as a cop. Against a woman.

He could remember being on top of the car, struggling with a woman who was trying to stab him. He was down and she was on top, and as he managed to grab at her knife, he deflected the blade. She was turning it, twisting the shiny pearl handle with everything she had. Then, suddenly, the handle just broke off and hit him on the cheek, drawing blood.

And when he saw a few drops of his own blood running down bright red on his blue uniform shirt—*his blood*—McCarthy realized that she might win. *That bitch might win.*

Up until that moment, he didn't believe that a woman could ever kill him, that anybody could kill him.

He stayed scared for the rest of that day and for the next. And McCarthy never forgot that single, enervating moment—that dramatic glimpse of his own mortality. That was the first time he knew what it meant to be a cop. And as soon as it had happened, he told himself that he didn't want to be one.

McCarthy could imagine how scared his friend must be. He'd seen it, felt it, smelled it like the summer sweat that stays with you all day. It was that special kind of cop's fear that would start out when you went to bed at night and still be there when you woke up the next morning, and just because you had lived through it once didn't mean that it would be any less terrifying the next time.

2:35 P.M.
BROOKLYN

Where was Tony now? This was McCarthy's call, his crime.

Reflex had taken him to Brooklyn. But now he needed more, he needed to think.

It was time to take a chance with the radio. Reluctantly, he reached for it.

He broadcasted one order to the five backup cars: "Go to Brooklyn. You gotta pick them up."

The first thing he had to do was establish his frequency on the Kel receiver. That was just in case other people with that frequency, in other parts of Brooklyn—not his people, of course, but other cops, other units—might be able to pick up the conversation that was going on in Tony's car. By that time, he was way out of range.

Almost as soon as the car had crossed the bridge into Brooklyn, McCarthy was intercepted by Larry Hepburn, the Vice captain.

Hepburn was already on the Brooklyn side of the water when McCarthy pulled up. He was in no mood to be slowed down or lectured. All he could think about as the captain approached was the time, a few months before, when Hepburn had accidentally left a tube of toothpaste in his back pocket, sat down on it, never noticed it, and then walked around for the rest of that day with a fragrant peppermint smear all over his ass.

287

"Any word yet?" Hepburn asked. He wasn't formal or threatening and didn't seem about to pull any of the bullshit that most commanders could be expected to invoke at a time like this. McCarthy was relieved. Flash Gordon's crimson, mournful face and square features were set in a concerned frown that had suddenly been drained of its tint, like a color key that had malfunctioned somewhere deep inside. Beyond that, it was impossible to read him, just like always. It was the inscrutability of the gifted. There was already an unlighted pipe in his hand.

"The Building's in on it now," Hepburn said. "They have all the help on the way that they can send."

McCarthy, imagining the mad rush that would now be under way at One Police Plaza to get out from under any responsibility that might filter down over Tony, somehow doubted that. But he kept his mouth shut. For a change.

"This whole thing started back when you took me to that after-hours club," Hepburn said forthrightly, referring to the night, many months before, when McCarthy's team had made the first important connection that would eventually allow them to setup Operation Sinbad. All for Hepburn's benefit. "I feel responsible."

McCarthy hadn't heard admissions like that very often. Especially from a superior officer. Hepburn was a ferocious handball player, a tremendous competitor whom he had admired on the court. He was now seeing that toughness outside the gym for the very first time.

"You don't feel as bad as I do," McCarthy told him. "This is my play; my mistake."

At this point, they were no longer playing detective. McCarthy was no expert on kidnapping. Neither was Hepburn. But at least he was right there with them. Armed.

"I'm going to defer to you on this one," Hepburn said. "Sinbad's been your baby. You make the moves. Do whatever you have to do. I'm going over to the Seven-one precinct, get it set up, lay in some phone lines. It's not that far from Gagliano's house.''

At least Flash knew his way around Brooklyn, McCarthy thought.

''You meet me over there,'' Hepburn said. ''I can imagine where you're headed.''

Twenty-eight

You went out on the street every day and every day
the *Danger* would be there like a whore, waiting,
tempting. But you knew you couldn't get enough of
it, no matter what your brain said. And the crazy
part was, it didn't mean a damn thing.

MOTHER'S MAXIM

2:45 P.M.
FLATBUSH
The Gaglianos lived on a street of dilapidated attached
houses, row houses, in the worst neighborhood in Flatbush, not far from Brighton Beach. Tiny, weed-rotted
gardens in the front, rusted car bodies out back; kids with
bad attitudes on the corners. Their street was canopied
by the kind of old, half-sick Dutch elms that wearily
dipped their leaves right down alongside the curbs.

As soon as McCarthy parked, he realized that he had
gotten there ahead of the cops from Brooklyn South,
Public Morals, who he hoped were on their way. He
knew that Hepburn probably was right—the Building
would have to be turning up the heat on this one by now.
A cop-killing would be bad enough, but sooner or later,
damage control would have to click on to minimize the
embarrassment. New York City, sentimental slob of the
Western World, despite its callous exterior, absolutely

hated to lose a young cop with a pretty wife and a little kid. The NYPD was not unmindful of this fact.

On his way over, McCarthy had noticed an unusually high level of helicopter traffic that seemed to be headed out from Manhattan. They were already flying search patterns for Tony's Thunderbird.

He'd visited the Gaglianos' street before, on a couple nights he'd practically tucked them into bed after he'd followed them home. But he had never been inside, had never made a move against them because the thinking behind Sinbad had called for a cat-and-mouse game of waiting out the Gaglianos and gambling that they would lead to bigger and better rodents. That had never worked out quite the way it was supposed to because the brothers and Tommy Mendino had proven to be far too violent, far too vicious, to be allowed to run loose all over the city. Actually, that had largely been the reasoning behind McCarthy's plan to take them down back on Houston Street.

There was still no sign of the brothers as he crossed the street.

Mama Gagliano was past eighty years old, a snapping turtle of a woman in a floral-print housedress. She looked at least one hundred. Her hair was the color of a soiled mattress and her expression was dominated by two small, plucking eyes. The way she flew across the room at McCarthy he could see how her sons had turned out to be the upstanding citizens and stickup psychos that they were.

She was mad and she had a right to be. McCarthy had gotten into her living room by shouldering the front door with one enormous *crash* and then pounding away until he had splintered the doorjamb. That was police work the old-fashioned way: headfirst.

She only spoke Italian and the only phrases that McCarthy could pick up were the sort of multisyllabic, ripely flowing curses that you most often heard thundering down from the upper decks at Giants games that had gotten out of hand. He had to remind himself to stay as calm as possible and refrain from dropping the old bitch on the spot.

While she was yelling at him, he kept screaming, "Tony, Tony," as he ran through the house. They went on like that for several minutes, he in the lead, she following, trooping from room to room, upstairs and downstairs, cursing each other.

He didn't think for a moment that they had Tony anywhere in the house—or that anybody was there, either, for that matter—but he didn't know what else to do. So he kept it up: "Tony, Tony."

Finally, Mama Gagliano got tired. Slobbering and spitting at him, she retreated upstairs and he just left her alone. That didn't make him feel any better. Scaring eighty-year-old grandmothers half to death wasn't his favorite part of the job. But neither was losing cops.

Her absence gave him a clear shot at the house and he took advantage of it. There would be time to pore over clues later; now all he wanted to do was soak up the feeling of the Gaglianos that permeated the place. Maybe then he would be able to think like they did.

The interior of the house looked a lot more like an animal den than like an air-light in Brooklyn. Not much furniture and an almost empty kitchen.

Apparently, they spent most of their time in the basement—and quite a place it was. They had it set up like a bunker, with boarded-over ground-floor windows and what appeared to be a junkyard for weapons. There were cannibalized parts of rifles and pistols all over the place, firing mechanisms and greasy stocks, dozens of assorted sizes and shapes of guns bows and quivers of steel-tipped arrows and, incongruously, jars and jars of pennies, mayonnaise jars full of pennies. They were great savers, the brothers.

The basement was like their clubhouse. Only instead of baseball cards, they collected weapons. The only thing of any real value that he saw was a list of the whorehouses they had hit for shakedowns and a yellowed copy of *Screw* with the massage parlors and escort services they evidently intended to hit circled in red. Unfortunately, there wasn't anything there that he didn't already know or at least suspect. No indication at all of where they might be holding Tony.

McCarthy knew that the first thing he had to do was put people on the house—and keep the old lady off the telephone. That's when he remembered about her. Abruptly, he stopped what he was doing and ran back upstairs.

Brooklyn South, Public Morals, had never been friends of McCarthy's. They were archrivals. They boosted pinches and manpower from each other. Forget about professional courtesy—even in an emergency, he could not anticipate how they would respond. Maybe he would get lucky and they really would put out for him, or maybe not. It was like rolling the dice. But he did know, to his regret, that at crunch-time, all that "brother officer" crap usually didn't amount to squat. If the occasion of Tony Vitaliano's being snatched represented an opportunity for someone in blue, someone who hated McCarthy, to stick it to him, they would. That was the NYPD.

However, McCarthy did have one high card that wasn't showing that day. By coincidence, he had one of the most dependable cops he had ever met. John Gorman, a member of his Vice team, at Brooklyn South, Public Morals that day, assisting them on an unrelated case. They would be afraid to try any funny business in front of Gorman, who was known to put other cops on their backsides without too much provocation.

Gorman would also be able to tell all the Brooklyn cops

what Tony looked like, because McCarthy was afraid that if there was a shootout Tony would get it first.

He had called Gorman from the Gaglianos' house—Gorman already knew what had happened—and had stayed there until Gorman showed up with a small army of Brooklyn cops. He left them sitting on the place, spread out all around the neighborhood.

There were still three or four more places to check, about ten blocks apart. On the way over, he kept criss-crossing the narrow, dirty streets of Flatbush, searching for Tony's Thunderbird. But the only thing he saw was more helicopters. That had to be the building kicking in. After all that, he decided the best thing he could do would be to head over to the 7-1 and find Larry Hepburn.

Nobody had picked up any transmission from Tony's car, but the wheels were beginning to grind. McCarthy had no way of knowing its full dimension, but a massive recovery plan was already in the works. Hepburn had understated it eloquently when he told him that "the Building's in on it now."

Methodically, with the quasi-military sense of blunt purpose so typical of the New York Police Department, seven thousand cops were being committed to the search for Tony Vitaliano, even as Bill McCarthy was struggling not to give up hope.

With the possible exception of the almost year-long dragnet for the son of Sam serial killer, in which every cop in the city of New York had, at least theoretically and temporarily, been assigned to the case, this was to become the biggest, most intense manhunt ever in New York criminal history. From time to time, the Big Apple press would elevate other glitzy or heartrending cases to a celebrity status, but in terms of a real investment of manpower, equipment, both in the air and on the ground, and especially in terms of departmental focus and concentration, the Vitaliano snatch-and-grab would prove to be the granddaddy. Despite McCarthy's initial skepticism, the NYPD would end up pulling out all the stops and adopting a virtual scorched-earth strategy to retrieve one of their own and to make the people who had grabbed him pay for it.

Those helicopters that kept buzzing Brooklyn were manned by cops with receivers that were homed in on the hardware in Vitaliano's car and on his person. They were trying to pick up any ghost of a reception off his transmitter. Or spot the car. Or both. Many of the cops they sent up in the skies over New York vomited all over themselves, or all over the pilots, because the Perry Como sweaters in the building who were frantically trying to make the best out of a horrid situation had just pulled guys out of sector cars and off the streets. None of them had received as much as five seconds of training to go up in a helicopter and most of those guys were terrified of heights.

But it didn't matter. One Police Plaza was on fire. Even though McCarthy and the other cops in Brooklyn could not see it, the whole building was lighting up. It started slowly, like a serpentine fuse that was just beginning to hiss, then it picked up speed and finally exploded in a cacophony of action and reaction and war-status activity. And the final dark resolution of the ill-fated Operation Sinbad was under way.

Functioning in a parallel dimension, again far removed from the men in the field, from the real cops, an eruption of another nature was also taking place. It was a fire storm of press activity in the city rooms of newspapers, in the soundless studios of isolated radio personalities, and on the stiflingly hot sound stages of New York television. A full-bore media event was in the making.

A COP HAD BEEN KIDNAPPED!
IN NEW YORK.
IN TIME FOR THE SIX O'CLOCK NEWS.

The reporters, at least enough of them, had police band radios too, scanners. Just like the bad guys.

They were conversant enough with police codes and jargon, not to mention being friendly with half the people who worked at One Police Plaza, to know that *something* was up.

Quickly, they had it confirmed. A cop had been kidnapped; but they had no idea who or why or what the circumstances were. The lid on the details was the tightest that any of the reporters had ever encountered. There was something ominous about it all. But by then, even the cops were violating their own broadcast frequencies, talking about it among themselves. Sooner or later, the reporters knew that they would find out. They called around and warned their rewrite desks and assignment editors and news directors to stand by. Something big, something dramatic, was coming their way, rumbling like a runaway coal car.

But what? Where?

If it bleeds it leads—that was the philosophy directing them all.

For their part, the cops weren't worrying anymore about the Gaglianos or anybody else overhearing them. They were beyond all that now.

3:15 P.M.
7-1 PRECINCT, EMPIRE
BOULEVARD, BROOKLYN

The 7-1 precinct was the only secure building that was reasonably close to the Gaglianos' house in Flatbush. The 7-1 was an "A" house, a shit-hole, in the parlance of cops like McCarthy, an action station house where the police arrested real criminals for real crimes almost all the time. There were worse places, to be sure, certainly in Harlem or Bed-Sty, but the 7-1 was bad enough.

McCarthy parked on the pavement outside; all the normal parking places had already been taken. That, in itself, was unusual. It meant there were people inside, presumably doing things. It told McCarthy that Flash Gordon had already accomplished something besides sitting around and wringing his hands.

The borough commander of Brooklyn at that time had a reputation for being a hardcase professional cop. He was big, tall, and mean. McCarthy expected the worst from him. He was the kind of a boss who was so deeply into the macho cop mythology that unless your balls clanged when you walked past him, he looked down on you.

Naturally, he was the first person McCarthy ran into.

The borough commander stopped him halfway up the staircase to the detectives' room upstairs. He practically pinned him against the slime-green wall, chest to chest. McCarthy let out a deep breath.

"Who's in charge of you," he snapped to McCarthy. It had to take something very big, very troublesome, to pull him out from behind his desk and down to a shit-hole like the 7-1. And McCarthy was acutely aware of the fact that he was the sole cause of the borough commander's sudden discomfort.

McCarthy told him Captain Hepburn, who was upstairs, he guessed.

The borough commander, in uniform by choice, bulky as a blue armored personnel carrier, brushed past him. The man's patent leather police shoes were the size of pontoons.

McCarthy followed him up.

He located Flash Gordon, seated at a borrowed desk, his ear plugged into a phone receiver. There was a white fog of pipe and cigar smoke eerily ringing his head like some haunting aura. Flash was smoking both. Ash had collected on the tops of his hands, on his clothes and all around the desk where he leaned his elbows. He never looked up from his business as the borough commander bore down on him. He could have been Sherlock Holmes, not of 221B Baker Street, but of the Bronx.

"Captain, I don't know what you're doing," the borough commander said. "I don't know anything about your case, but you got my desk. You got any thing you need. I'll do whatever you tell me to do."

And then he left. It was the damnedest thing that McCarthy had ever seen.

Flash Gordon had bluffed him.

"What have we got?" the captain asked.

"Gorman's sitting on the house. Nothing there, though. Just guns in the cellar."

Hepburn frowned when he heard that.

There were thirty-seven locations where the six people definitely associated with the gang had been arrested on previous occasions. Most of them were in Brooklyn.

The best plan would have been to send a couple of detectives to every one of the thirty-seven locations. Any address that had ever appeared on a "yellow sheet," an arrest record, should have been covered.

McCarthy started to spill this out to Hepburn. Somebody would have to go get the thirty-seven addresses. And phone numbers.

"I got them." Hepburn cut him off. "The phone numbers, too. And I'm placing calls to the cops we want to cover each spot."

"How the hell did you do that?" McCarthy asked.

Flash did what horses do when they paw the ground nervously. Except he was still seated at his borrowed desk. "Well, see . . . I can do this thing . . . with numbers. Like a trick."

"Do you mean you memorized them all? You don't even have to write them down?" McCarthy was openly in awe.

"Yeah, it's like that. But I don't remember them, exactly. I just . . . ah . . . I *see* them."

"You're talking like seventy, a hundred numbers; thirty-seven locations, Captain."

"Ninety-seven combinations, I think, give or take."

"Ninety-seven . . ." McCarthy slowly repeated.

He stared at the desk in front of Flash. Not so much as a scrap of paper. Instant recall. Like an idiot savant outcomputing a computer. The genius of Larry Hepburn was coming through.

No one in Vice had known this about him. Hepburn was sitting there, in the eye of the Vitaliano nightmare, handling about twelve different things at once. Not missing a beat. Flash was on. Going ninety miles an hour. And the crazy part was, Flash didn't even realize he was doing it.

McCarthy put out his hands in a gesture of backing off. He wasn't about to screw around with a genius at work.

This was going to be another waiting time and he hated that. But the best place for him was right here, where they had slammed together a command post of sorts, where he could get any information they received from any one of the teams that was fanning out all over Brooklyn, tearing it apart, he imagined.

Then, McCarthy took in his first full look at the room and all the activity therein. There were cops everywhere, in and out of uniform, most on the telephones, a few tracing locations and intersections on a big board that was covered by a map of Brooklyn, placing pushpins where they belonged. Nearly everybody was sweating in shoulder holsters and wrinkled ties pulled down from their necks. The whole place stinking of sweat and dyspeptic dispositions. As he glanced from cop to cop, from mask of concentration to mask of concentration, there seemed to be a palpable chemical synthesis taking place, a chain reaction of fused elemental matter as every brain in the room set itself to the business at hand.

Hepburn read him. "Catch your breath," he said.

"Drink some coffee. The first good lead we get you can go out again. There's a time to race around and there's a time to sit." The Captain pushed a steaming mug in his direction. "So sit."

And McCarthy sat and thought about how it had all started, about how the whole damn thing had begun, how his whole police career, how Sinbad, had come to this— to waiting in a smelly, smoke-filled, windowless hellhole of a room in the 7-1 in Brooklyn, wondering if he had somehow managed to get his best friend killed.

As he took the mug of coffee from Hepburn, his muscles relaxed for the first time in hours. He tried lifting the hot liquid to his lips, but as he did so, he spilled two, three, four drops and then an ugly splash of the strong, dark coffee. McCarthy couldn't make his hands stop shaking.

Twenty-nine

Cops have a saying: "Jacks are better for openers," as in blackjacks. *Brutality* doesn't have much meaning for cops. But there are informal rules. You should stop kicking a man once he's no longer in a position to hurt you. But I'm not saying cops always observe that rule.

MOTHER'S MAXIM

4:00 P.M.
7-1 PRECINCT,
EMPIRE BOULEVARD, BROOKLYN

Some of the longest hours of Bill McCarthy's life were spent that afternoon in the makeshift command post on the second floor of the Empire Boulevard police station.

He and Captain Hepburn worked ceaselessly to coordinate the recovery efforts. Someone had to be in a position to direct the efforts of those 7,500 policemen who had been mobilized, plus the helicopters and radio cars and off-duty cops who had joined in on their own.

That task fell to them and they worked at it as they had never before worked at anything in their police careers.

At that point, almost everything was riding on the success of the teams that Hepburn had assigned to search the thirty-seven previous locations where members of the Gagliano-Mendino crew, or their associates, had been arrested.

Every available member of McCarthy's Vice team hit

the streets of Brooklyn, too, backing up the rescuers or searching themselves.

Calls were constantly coming in to both McCarthy and Larry Hepburn—all of them merely reports to update the futility of the mission thus far. None of the Gaglianos had surfaced.

The long afternoon was quickly running into dusk and night-fall. Even the aerial coverage provided by the police helicopters would soon become almost useless.

Time had already run out on the perilous Operation Sinbad. Now it seemed to be running out on Tony Vitaliano as well.

McCarthy and Hepburn were too busy even to talk to each other, fielding calls and questions from anxious cops. But there was nothing to say, anyway.

At one point, Hepburn pushed his chair away from his desk, stuffed the bowl of his pipe full of tobacco and, striking a wooden match against the sole of his shoe, puffed it into life. He looked over at McCarthy and considered reassuring him again that it wasn't his fault—it wasn't anybody's fault—but he decided not to. There would be plenty of time for that later, provided that later did come.

McCarthy attempted to keep his mind clear. At least the task at hand was consuming; it didn't permit much time to dwell on his searing sense of guilt and responsibility.

Messages had come in that Millie had tried several times to call him from home; but McCarthy hadn't taken her calls. He'd just directed one of his men to assure her that he was safe, that no harm had come to him.

He could face admitting to the woman he loved that his inability to get to Tony in time may have already cost him his life. Millie would understand in the wise, forbearing way that she had. That wasn't the problem. Ever facing himself again in the mirror would be the problem.

It appeared that time was passing with a surreal slowness in their command post; actually, the opposite was true. By the time the tightness in McCarthy's own body forced him to get up and stretch and work out the slowly building tension, it was already past five o'clock.

Once he was on his feet, he made up his mind not to sit down again. There was now nothing left for him to do at Empire Boulevard. Somebody else could help the captain work the phones. The rescue teams were in motion, Hepburn had settled into his usual cerebral control.

McCarthy was going back on the street. He knew that no matter what he was not coming in again until he had either found Tony or the Gaglianos. He had to put an end to it that night.

Just out of habit, he had carried his shotgun into the station with him. Very deliberately, McCarthy picked it up.

Hepburn had just taken a call. There was no need to interrupt him. With the big gun swung carefully against his shoulder, McCarthy motioned to his friend that he was leaving. Hepburn half-rose out of his chair, his ear still plugged into the phone receiver.

"Stay there," McCarthy said, waving him off. "I can't wait around here any longer. Later."

But something McCarthy was unaware of was happening. Hepburn put a firm grip on his sergeant's forearm. Flash wasn't letting go.

That stopped McCarthy.

"They just grabbed three of them," Hepburn was barely able to shout out. He couldn't suppress the excitement in his voice; where his cheeks had been ashen, they now washed crimson. "This is John Gorman on the phone. He was getting ready to tell me that the Brooklyn cops spotted them driving around, when they showed up at their house. They must have stopped back to pick something up after you left.

"Gorman was waiting for them. He needs you right away."

McCarthy never even heard that last part. He was already on his way.

"Three of the Gaglianos are in custody. But no sign of Tony or crazy Tommy Mendino, who would have most likely done the job if they decided to kill Tony.

"*Where was Tony now?* That was still our top priority.

"They show up at their house and the cops jump them. John Gorman lays out one guy over the hood of his car and puts a cocked gun right in his ear. And that was how they took down the Gaglianos. That picture made the front page of every newspaper in New York.

"From three Gaglianos, they get five guns. They started questioning them before I arrived on the scene, but learning nothing. Not a word.

"I walked into the house right after that and I saw one of the brothers sitting there on the floor, squirming. Upstairs, I heard their old lady wailing away again. I'd been through that before.

"The first thing I asked was, 'Has he been tossed? Has he been searched.' They said, 'Yeah, outside. He's clean.'

"I said, 'Pull his pants down. Toss him again.'

"He had a gun down there right next to his balls. Even though he had been handcuffed with about a hundred cops looking on, this guy was still armed. They had never searched his balls; they almost never do.

"He'd been squirming around on the floor, trying to get to the gun. It was a derringer. He would have shot a cop right in that house had he gotten the chance. I know he would have.

"Now I have another concern in the back of my mind. There are dozens of Tony's friends there and they are looking for and tasting blood.

"I *know* that as soon as I leave these cops are going to start to beat the crap out of the Gaglianos. They *will* jack them up. That is a given. I'm actually a little surprised that nobody has pounded on them yet. That's probably because, as the immediate supervisor of Sinbad, I outrank everybody at the crime scene, at least for the moment. That's SOP. They must just be waiting for me to leave.

"If they figure Tony's dead—which I know they do—they will just give it to them worse. I'm a cop; I know this. I have seen situations like this all my life. This won't merely be a case of police brutality, this will damn near be assassination.

"And, should that happen, the case against this crew will be thrown out the window somewhere along the line by some bleeding heart judge, and, quite possible, Tony will have died in vain—if he is, in fact, a goner. Deep down, I think he is too.

"I just laid it on the line with those cops. I had to let them know I knew where they were coming from.

"Tony was my friend, this was my fuckup. I was the one who let them kidnap him. Mother was at fault all the way: If anybody was gonna beat the shit out of them, it was gonna be me. I had first call. And I was *not* gonna beat the shit out of them because I was not gonna lose this case. I was not gonna jeopardize it.

"If, at that moment, in that house, I thought that I could have saved Tony's life by beating up one of the Gaglianos, beating him to make him talk, I would have done that. Gladly. But I knew that these punks would just take the beating and still not talk. There would have been no point to it.

"I never beat up people. Never. I never saw police brutality because I wouldn't tolerate it. When three or four cops are locking one guy up and they all take a shot—that's brutality. But that day I would have broken my own rule.

"I screamed at them: 'Don't anybody touch these mother-fuckers. I'll kick *your* ass if you touch them.' I yelled this out to about thirty detectives there. 'This is my case, my partner. If anybody's touching them it's me, and if anybody takes that pleasure away from me, I'll take care of them, too. I'm telling you right now, *don't* touch them.'

"I wasn't going to touch anybody. But I had to make the cops believe that I would.

"Then, once that scene was secure, I talked to each one of the prisoners individually. I took them in a separate room, alone. No other cops.

"I said to each one: 'I know you don't know nothing about this. I know you don't know nothing about kidnapping a cop. I *know* that; but I happen to be that cop's best friend.

" 'I know you don't know nothing, but hypothetically speaking, if you were me, if *your* friend had been snatched, would you worry? If you were just speculating about this, would you worry about your friend?'

"I was letting them understand that whatever they said to me now I could not come back and produce in court. This was man to man.

"Two of them said, 'Bullshit.' Nothing else. Just, 'Bullshit.'

"The third one said, 'No, I wouldn't worry about it.'

"Not one other word. We could have beaten on those guys all night long and it would not have made any difference. Other than the fact that we would have felt a whole lot better.

"What I find out next is that I have a call coming in to their house from Larry Hepburn.

" 'They just located Tony's car,' he said. Then he gave me an address near Neptune Avenue, Brighton Beach.

"I take off, just run right out the door. Leave somebody holding the telephone. I'm on my way.

"But before I can even get there, less than two minutes after I get behind the wheel of my car, I hear an emergency bulletin on the radio—*Tony Vitaliano has been recovered alive.*"

Thirty

**A *Police Car* is a death trap. Whatever year they
bought it, it was the low bid. It's been driven
twenty-four hours a day by people who don't care,
by cops. A police car can kill you.**

MOTHER'S MAXIM

TONY VITALIANO

"We went in cautious that day, September 24th, 1974,
very cautious. We were prepared for it to go either way:
Take them down that afternoon or play it out and let them
go back to Brooklyn.

"The first five minutes went great. Bobby was
friendly, like always. Then we started to talk. I sensed
that something had changed; he was looking at me differently, too.

"The problem was the Murray Hill townhouse on Thirty-first Street. I had never mentioned that place to them,
never indicated that I had a piece of it. But I figured that
they must know more than they were letting on. I came
right out and asked them why they had hit that place the
week before. I made it clear that it was *my* house.

" 'You guys are hanging me, fucking hanging me,'
were my exact words. 'I'm your friend, but now you
done damage to me, not the other guys.'

"I was merely trying to further establish my credibility

307

as a pimp, as a whorehouse owner. They knew all about my interest in Fifty-first Street. I brought up the Murray Hill brothel on Thirty-first Street on purpose. I acted mad.

"Bobby answered: 'Babe, these people are lookin' to help you. Not hurt you.' That was his stock answer.

"He was still insisting that he was just the middleman on the shakedowns. 'If you would have told us the Murray Hill joint was yours, had leveled with us from the get-go, in other words, there would have been no beef. They would have put a red flag on Thirty-first Street, waked up their people to it. They would have gone right over it. But how did they know it was *your* joint? It could have belonged to some nincompoop.'

"I had betrayed whatever relationship I had with them. That was the message he was so intent on giving me.

"Right there I knew I was in deep trouble because I could see instantly that Bobby Gee was lying to me. They had *already* figured out that I had a piece of the Murray Hill townhouse, along with Bill, through Al Gold. They *knew* that going in—before they even robbed the place. I could see that this was really a ruse. They were toying with me, trying to see how much more information they could extract from me.

"If it was information about any additional whorehouses that I had been holding out about, that was one thing. That would have gotten me a beating for sure. But if they were probing to see if I was a cop, then that would be my death sentence. I wasn't sure which it was.

"All this had been a *test* of my loyalty to them and I had failed. I failed because, in their minds, I had been holding out about Murray Hill from the start, about Thirty-first Street.

"Bobby wanted an explanation.

" 'I didn't think you guys could find out about Murray Hill, or hit it,' I told him. 'I was just tryin' to save myself paying protection on the both places.' He did not like that answer.

"Bobby then said, 'This is a powerhouse we work for, Babe. These people can find any-fuckin'-thing out. Ain't nobody gonna stop them. Unless an operation of whores is hooked up with somebody right, they are gonna take that house. You understand what I'm sayin', Tony? They don't care who they got to step on. It's theirs; they want it. They take it. Now, the problem is that we thought you wanted to be a nice fellow about the whole thing, a good fellow—not hold out on nobody. But Tony, you messed up bad about Murray Hill.'

"That was my crime; I was already guilty in their eyes. My sentence would be delivered forthwith.

" 'As far as I am concerned,' Bobby told me, 'you are all right.'

" 'I hope you convey this to your friends,' I said. 'I'm always one to do the right thing, ain't I?'

"Bobby looked hard at me. 'Until now,' he said, very coldly.

"At that point, Bobby Gee grabbed me around my neck with his left arm in a choke hold, and the other guy squeezed in. They reached down to the right side of my waistband and grabbed for my revolver. Then they pointed the gun at me. I didn't resist after that. Bobby said, 'Put your hands where I can see them.'

"I can only imagine what's happening outside. I assume that Bill is now aware of the fact that this has gone badly. But I have no idea what the team's immediate reaction will be.

"Of course, I want them to come in and get me the hell out of there, but I can't afford for them to come in too quickly, because I will definitely get the first bullet. As bad off as I am, I can still feel for Bill. He has to be going through all the fucking tortures of hell out there, what with his heart telling him to go one way and his head telling him to go the other.

"They put these glasses on me—taped with electrical tape. They were cheap five-and-dime sunglasses. I kept saying, 'No need to pull a gun on me'—I must have said it seven times—as the signal to Bill and the other backups to make their play. Quickly.

"But nothing happened after I said it. Then, to myself, I changed it to 'Oh, *shit*!This wasn't supposed to happen.'

"From the time Bobby Gee let the other guy in the car to the time they drove up the ramp onto the river drive, it was no more than a minute, a minute and a half.

"Bill had no chance at all to come in then. I know that Bill has always blamed himself for what happened, but with sixty, ninety seconds, at best, you just have to be realistic. Bill might be Mother, but he isn't Jesus Christ.

"As it was, they even faked me out because I thought they were going to stay off the drive, but at the last minute, they swerved sharply back onto FDR. No way our guys could have followed them with all the traffic we had that afternoon.

"During that trip they kept asking me about other addresses in Manhattan, other places they intended to hit. Just testing to see if I was connected there, too.

"I thought they would kill me then, there's great places to dump a body off the Brooklyn Battery Tunnel. I kept asking them if they were going to kill me. I believed in my heart I was going to be executed.

"Bobby said, 'We're going to see the top man. He wants to see you. Come along nicely, no problems.'

"I'm wired up now, remember. No sign of the backups. I'm blindfolded. And I knew that at some point I was going to be searched. That would be it. I said several Our Fathers and Acts of Contrition.

"Then Bobby said, 'You have a right to be scared, Tony, really you do. You thought you was so sharp.'

" 'I'm so scared I gotta piss,' I told him. That would be the only chance to get rid of the Edwards tape recorder. In a toilet or in the bushes somewhere. I had to risk it.

" 'Hold it in.' And he laughed at me.

" 'I gotta go; I'll go in the car.'

" 'That's the name of the game, Babe. Surprise, surprise, surprise. Thank God, we had that.'

"I know that I started to lose it at that point, lose control altogether, because I was sure that my fellow officers would never be able to recover me now. Not in time. Oh, I knew they would come after me, and I figured there would be a bloody shootout. Bill wouldn't rest until he had taken out whoever had killed me. But by then, what good would it do me?

"I pleaded with them. I asked them to at least get me a drink before they killed me.

" 'Short ride, hold on, Babe' was all that Bobby would say.

"This was a real dilemma. They were prepared to kill me for holding out on them—*not even for being an undercover cop. Let them discover that I was a cop and that would be it, for sure.*

"But almost the second I thought that, it came up.

" 'You have any company back there, Tony? You know, bulls? Cops?' He pointed the gun right at me again. 'Don't you lie to us, Tony.'

" 'Bobby, you think *I'm* a cop? Is that what this is?'

" 'Relax.' But Bobby wasn't relaxed either.

" 'I don't have no way of knowin', Bobby. If cops was back there, they weren't *with* me. Maybe they were after me. That could be it. I'm a badass. Don't kill me now, Bobby.'

" 'We're taking a ride to see the man, that's all.'

"Even with the tape covering the lens, I could still see out of the glasses because they kept slipping down on my nose. A car pulled up next to us and I could see the face of the driver—it was Bobby's brother. This was their crash car.

"My sense of direction never failed, oddly enough. I guess I was just so familiar with the streets in that part of New York that all I needed to do was to *feel* them. For example, they thought that they had really pulled

311

something over on me by driving into Brooklyn, instead of veering off FDR Drive and taking the Prospect Expressway, the Belt Parkway. But with the taped glasses on, I knew where I was at practically all times.

"At another point, much later, we turned left on Neptune and I made out a sign that read *Brighton*. This was another section in Brooklyn. Not that far from Coney Island. It was always cold and wet and windy around there.

"Almost right after that, we pulled up in front of a wood frame house with a large fat man standing outside in a white shirt and pants. I found out later that he was Tony Spots, their main man, their mob connection.

"We went down the block once, made a U-turn and came back to the house. Another guy was there then.

"The big man stopped the car at the curb. Bobby ordered me out. Spots says, 'Jerkoff, take the shades off.'

"They grabbed the glasses off my face and pushed me up the steps. We went in through a kitchen, where a pretty girl was sitting on a stool, playing with something on the oven. She looked kind of surprised to see us, but not so startled that this was something she had never seen before. She just kept quiet and stuck her face in the pot on the stove.

"Spots was obviously in charge. 'Go alongside him, two on a side,' he ordered. Then four of them took me to another room.

"I started begging them about being allowed to go to the bathroom again, screaming that I was going to piss on their floor. The girl must have heard that. She nosed in.

" 'Hold it in,' Bobby told me. 'It's good for you anyway, holding back a piss like that. What you need is control. I do it all the time. It puts muscles on your dick. It'll make you a better fucker—hold that semen way back. It fittens up the muscles, man. Piss, cut it off; piss,

312

cut it off.' Then he turns to the girl and gives her this little tap on her behind. It was one of the crudest gestures I ever saw, like, this-butt-is-my-property. 'Ain't that right, Baby?'

"The girl turned red, but ignored him and said something about nobody better piss on her kitchen floor, because she is not gonna use her mop to mop up no piss. And she sounded just as tough as the Gaglianos.

"I had this flash of my wife's face then, of our little boy. I asked myself: What kind of animals have I fallen in with?

"I said, 'If you guys are gonna kill me, I gotta see a priest, you gotta send me to church. Give me a cigarette, at least.'

"That didn't make a dent.

" 'You search him?' Spots wanted to know.

" 'Yeah, he had a piece on him,' Bobby answered.

"Spots was very surprised I had a gun. 'Why'd you bring a piece with you? You take a piece to the meet, why?'

" 'I always carry,' I said. 'Ask Bobby.'

"He nodded and said to both of us, 'Relax, relax, you guys.'

" 'This is it, Bobby,' I started again. 'The pee. It's comin' now. Sorry.' And I turned to the woman there and gave her the most helpless look that I could manage.

"She started screaming again. 'Get him the hell out of here. Now! You pigs!'

"At least that got them moving. They gave me a shove in the direction of the bathroom. A guy I had never seen before followed me in. I started to lean over the toilet bowl, moaning, like I'm gonna throw up. Then I'm fooling with my fly like I can't get it open. He starts to give me a hard time—but doesn't leave me alone for a second. I was actually trying to gross him out, get him to leave in disgust.

"Then—and I swear this *had* to be the answer to the prayers I had said out in the car—they called him away, back into the room with the rest of them.

"That was all the time I needed. I pulled off the Edwards, looked around real fast to see where I could stash it and all I saw was soap in the bathtub dish. I figured none of these guys are gonna take a bath now, so I just stuck it under the soap.

"As soon as I had stood up away from the tub, and straightened my clothes a little, he came back in and said, 'Strip.'

"That's why they had called him out. Spots wanted me strip-searched. I just beat them to it.

"Tommy Mendino hadn't been around since the snatch. He and I had both gotten out of the car at the same time, but he hadn't come inside the house with me.

"Now, he shows up again. Spots actually deferred to him, asked him if they had been tailed. Did he see any cops?

"Tommy is a stone-cold killer. Just being in the room with him makes it that much more dangerous for me.

"Spots was suspicious because I had no identification of any kind on me and nothing for the car, either. All I had was the gun.

"That was a mistake because all bad guys always carried some phony ID cards just in case the police stopped them for a traffic violation. It was my first nonauthentic bad guy move. Spots had to be suddenly wondering why I'm not even afraid of a routine police search like they are. Particularly since I'm carrying a gun.

"The answer is obvious. But is it obvious to *him*?

" 'The car belongs to one of the whores,' I said. 'She loaned it to me. She's got all the owner's cards and insurance shit.'

"That seemed to make sense to them. Bobby started in again about the other places they intended to hit again. Just like in the car. Were any of them mine? Were they

314

connected to any of the Five Families that I knew of? This was a standard intelligence debriefing. Who else had a piece of Murray Hill?

"Spots, however, was still very disturbed about the car. They called the plate number in to somebody—to see if it was listed as a police undercover vehicle. The guy on the phone turned away and whispered, 'No hit.' The plate was clean.

" 'Search the car again,' Spots ordered. 'Keep it up till you find something.'

"I figure I've just bought myself—and the backup teams out there, Bill—some time. The car would take a while for them to go over thoroughly. I wasn't too concerned about that either. I should have been.

"We sat at a wooden table and started to go over whorehouse addresses in a black book they had taken from one of their robberies. I had no idea what they were showing me, none. The addresses were not known vice locations. They figured I had to know, though. I was in the business too. I guessed that maybe these were the apartments of individual hookers who just serviced a handful of clients on their own. That's what I told them. I guess it was the wrong thing.

"All of a sudden, Bobby snapped out. 'NO BULL-SHIT NOW!' he yelled.

"I was humiliating him in front of Spots. I was either giving them wrong answers to questions they already knew the answers to—and assumed I *had* to know, too— or I was just sounding stupid.

"Bobby cuffed me in the head with the flat of his gun. God, did that hurt. It made me momentarily deaf on the left side and sent this sharp pain through the back of my skull. I saw stars and planets and a rainbow. He drew a lot of blood and I nearly passed out.

"Then I made up a story that the book belonged to a madam who had been holding out on me, too. I was just trying to hide my other places from them again. They looked at one another like that could be plausible. A good lie they would accept, not the truth.

"Tommy Mendino came in from the living room then and pointed his gun at my head, cocked: 'TALK!'

"The lids of my eyes were caked with blood and I could just about make out his face. I saw these two black eyes with absolutely nothing alive behind them.

"Spots calmed him down, and Bobby, too. But they acted afraid of him, which made me very afraid.

"Then Spots started to play with me. He pulled out two hundred dollars, slammed it on the countertop and said, 'How much is your life worth to you? How much?'

"Mendino pointed his gun at me again and said, 'Call Al Gold. That cunt is his partner. See if Gold pays the ransom.'

"Then, *I* got it. This *was* a real kidnapping. Up to that point, they had no idea that I was a cop. I had been worrying about that for nothing. They did believe, truly, that I was some fringe Mafia guy like them and that *somebody* would pay to get me back.

"Meantime, people are coming and going. They never stay put. The woman, who I think was Bobby's girlfriend, walked around like nothing unusual was going on, like there were just a bunch of Bobby's friends there watching a ballgame. It was weird, let me tell you.

"They whacked me a couple more times for no particular reason; just being tough guys, showing me they were in control.

"The whole side of my face had blown up by then and my one eye was completely closed. By that point, I guess I presented no threat to anyone, I was so banged up. They all started to loosen up a little. It was still tense, but not like before.

"They put a fifth of scotch in front of me and we all started to drink. I drank the most. This went on for better than a half hour. I was getting drunk, fast. But at least I was alive.

"Two of the brothers came back in from the car after they finished the search. No problem there, I thought. I was wrong.

"They shoved a piece of paper in front of Spots, smiled, and said, 'This is all we found. Under the mat in the front seat.'

"I'm thinking: *Mat? What mat? What paper? What could they have possibly found?*

"Spots looked the paper over and then pushed it right into my teeth. I stared at it through my one eye that still worked.

"It was an official 'Property of NYPD' motor pool inspection slip.

"Somebody had left it—a 'tire card'—under the floor mat in the front seat. A 'tire card' is a police department form which identifies the tires on the car as belonging to the New York City Police Department.

"Some asshole at the Puzzle Palace must have made them go through the unmarked flash cars like they did with ordinary police blue-and-whites, just to check to see if we had ripped off the good tires and put bad ones back on. It was the kind of all-too-typical bureaucratic bullshit that could get undercovers killed.

"The tire card was right there—like putting a fucking NYPD decal on the door of my T-bird.

"I had just been using the flash car that day to pull up and pay them off and go away. We weren't expecting a full-blown search.

"It got real quiet then. The girl left. Everybody in the house checked his gun. I reached for another drink and they slapped it away, across the room. I got punched again.

"Mendino put his gun up to my head. 'I'm going to kill you, cop,' he said calmly.

"Bobby went nuts. Totally nuts. Total disbelief. He

317

lunged at me, got one hand around my throat, and started to choke me, but Spots pulled him off.

"He sent them out to the car to look some more. It was quiet for a few minutes. I was sitting there, thinking about my son, my wife, my mother; I was going over my whole life, preparing myself to die.

"When the two Gaglianos came back for the third time, they had found some wires in the ceiling of the T-bird and a lot of other electronic paraphernalia under the dashboard that really was obvious to the experienced eye. My car had been equipped like one huge listening post and now they knew it.

"Then it was like, 'Well, yeah, I *am* a cop. But I'm taking money from these whorehouses and I am a *crooked* cop and I shake down people. I'm just like you guys. We can work this out.'

"I had to admit everything, the whole story. I knew that if they called Al Gold, he would have confirmed that I was working with Bill McCarthy and that we were rogue cops on his pad.

"Spots listened and concentrated. 'We were looking to make some money from you,' he said. 'But if you're a cop, that's no good. You got no money.'

" 'Al Gold will still pay,' I said.

"Spots just made a face like I was being ridiculous. But I thought they half-bought that explanation and half didn't buy it. They were weighing the next move.

"They didn't know what to do with me. Bobby Gee kept talking about Frank Serpico, whom I knew, of course. Way before he was even famous. They were afraid that I had to be another Serpico. They were paranoid that I might be undercover instead of corrupt. If they only knew.

"They produced a tape recorded from somewhere in the house and made me repeat the rogue cop story again.

" 'That's for my lawyers,' Spots said. 'That's for entrapment. If they try to hit us with that.'

"Twenty more minutes went by and they broke up into small groups. Every so often, Tommy or Bobby would bang my head again. I couldn't see much at all by that point because the blood had clotted over my hair and eyes. I don't even remember what they were talking about. I imagine I had become semiconscious. I do recall that even sitting down and in pain, I had this strange sensation of floating. Something inside was attempting to very gently, but firmly, detach me from my predicament. Today, after what I've read and learned, I look back on that as something approximating what they call a near-death experience. Whatever it was, I came to feel a deep sense of resignation and tranquillity.

"The thing I feared most was being left alone with Mendino. I knew by his eyes what he wanted to do.

"Of course, that's exactly what happened. Everybody walked out of the room except me and Tommy. I made my mind up that I would get it then. I tried to make my peace with God.

"A telephone call had been made, and it seemed like all they were waiting for was a call back. Maybe they needed to clear the decision to kill me with somebody higher up. I was trying to make sense of it.

"Then the telephone rang. I never saw who answered it.

"Finally, Spots came back into the room where I was. He walked over, yanked up my head by the hair and said, 'So you're really a cop.'

"I think he must have called somebody in the police department to check on me and whoever it was—to this day we have no idea—gave me up; the whole thing. After that call Spots knew all about Operation Sinbad. They had penetrated our top level of security.

"Spots just wanted to make sure that I knew that he knew and then he turned his back on me.

"Before he left, I heard him instructing Bobby that they had to make sure they left separately—except for

Tommy and Bobby. Spots told those two, 'You wait here and take care of the cop.'

"That was it—my death sentence.

"I was positive that as soon as Spots left the house, it would all be over. He would have never let anything happen to me while he was there, because he didn't want to take the heat. On their own, though, they could do what they wanted. And Tommy and Bobby wanted to kill me.

"In about a minute, they pulled me to my feet again and they dragged me across the floor, to the door.

"What I found out much, much later, was that the Edwards in the bathroom soap dish *had never stopped recording*. Any time they went in there to talk out of earshot of me, their conversation was recorded. They never did think to check the bathroom or look in that soap dish.

"The very last thing the Edwards ever picked up was Tony Spots's voice, loud and clear, saying: '*Kill the cop, but make sure nobody finds him.*'

"Then the front door opened. The cold air brought me to a little bit and Bobby started to push me down their steps.

"Tommy Mendino's voice sounded far away as he said, 'You're going for another ride.'

"My head was down. I didn't want to look at them. I was concentrating on my mental image of my wife. This would be my last ride."

Thirty-one

No one ever recovers from being a *Victim*. They are
sad, pathetic, rattled, ruined. They will never be
the same again. Including cops.

MOTHER'S MAXIM

7:00 P.M.
ONE POLICE PLAZA, TWELFTH FLOOR
TONY VITALIANO:

"As soon as I felt that cold, wet air on my face, just as
they're shoving me down the steps, BOOM! the Brooklyn
Homicide cops hit them like a wave. More cops than I had
ever seen in my life. Cops everywhere. Guns, shotguns,
rifles, riot gear; mounted police galloping down the street
in a cavalry charge formation. I could hear the helicopters
closing in, descending and landing. The wind from their
rotor blades almost blew me over. I felt just like I was in
a war.

"Then somebody was lifting me up. I had hands and
arms under me all the way around. I was being carried
like a baby.

"Tommy and Bobby disappeared under this mountain
of bodies, tackling them, laying them out. I thought that
everybody had been killed right there. Bobby went for
his gun. I knew that. Tommy, too. But it was all over.

"It was finished. I was still alive. I shouldn't have been. I should have been killed a dozen times, even back in the car, in the beginning.

"All I was aware of at that second was that, somehow, Mother had made them recover me."

BILL McCARTHY:

"Vitaliano had been rescued, semiconscious, but alive. Bobby Gagliano and Tommy Mendino were captured while dragging him out of Bobby's girlfriend's house. They were taking him to the place where the undercover cop was to be executed.

"They could not go for their guns quickly enough and Brooklyn Homicide was all over them.

"*Tony*'s in shock. He's less than three miles away. He's unconscious—and he's drunk. *Drunk?* That's what I'm hearing. But he's okay. They're checking him over at Coney Island Hospital. A real pit.

"I wanted to go to the hospital to see Tony; I wanted that more than anything, but I couldn't go. There were other responsibilities—all mine—and I still had at least one person to apprehend.

"I figured that the one major player connected to the Gaglianos was this Tony Spots, so he had to have the answers.

"At the hospital, Tony had mentioned his name, too, to the Brooklyn Homicide detectives. They called me immediately with that information. We have five of the six people involved in the kidnapping in custody. Tony Spots is number six. We have to get him.

"Somebody had been sent to Tony's house to be with his wife and little son. The police chaplain was there, too. The Building was doing all the right stuff by that point, but I wanted to be there too. Instead, I had to report to the Building myself. Get this squared away.

"Tony Spots wasn't a big mob guy. He was just a mob guy. A Gambino soldier. He was just a very greedy

322

earner. The sort of person the Gaglianos would gravitate to.

"He's the big fish. He's the catch. He ties us into the official Mafia on this case. But how do we get him? We don't know. He's hiding. He's gone. He's like the wind.

"We know there are twenty gambling places, mostly old neighborhood social clubs, that are linked to Spots.

"Those were the places where we sent out shotguns teams. Six teams of six detectives, with six sergeants, all wearing flakjackets, heavy bullet-proof vests, and armed with shotguns, *empty* shotguns.

"I made up the list of places to visit. All six teams had to go into each club racking up the shotguns, screaming. 'We want Spots! If Spots don't surrender, your place is going to be destroyed!' And every place got six visits— all from different cops.

"I contrived that hysterical, angry police response. I wanted them to believe that the cops were out of control over this.

"The word went out that night that there would be no peace in Brooklyn until Spots was surrendered to us.

"As soon as they would enter a place—by that I mean break down the door; we figured we had this one won and we were feeling pretty good—they started racking up the shotguns.

"That is a sound that you never forget once you hear it. You look at those two barrels and figure they will blow you through a wall.

"The cops only had one thing to say: Give up Tony Spots.

"At location after location in Brooklyn, it was the same. It was like the cops had gone mad. *That's* what we wanted them to believe.

"There was a sergeant, a black, Puerto Rican guy, very black, very close friend of mine. His name was Paul Enrique, now retired. Paul was only about five-nine, 135 pounds. But he had this old bullet-proof vest; it must have weighed 80 pounds. It went all the way down to his knees. When he wore it he looked like a knight in armor—the Black Knight.

"I remember saying to Hepburn that night, 'Can you imagine seeing this guy going in the door of an Italian social club in Brooklyn, racking up the shotguns?'

"Paul Enrique was my hard-charger that night. Paul took on Brooklyn all by himself. Can you imagine sitting in a social club, playing poker? You feel perfectly safe because you know you're the Mafia, nobody can touch you. But all of a sudden, the door comes crashing down and these gladiators break in with shotguns, and there's Paul Enrique like the Black Knight, yelling at you in Spanish.

"If you tried to do something like that today, the cops wouldn't even know how to do it. You had experienced cops then. Good cops. The kids today—they just don't know.

"They don't know how to control without actual violence. But there was *no* violence that night; just the *threat* of total destruction. That was real police work.

"And we also had license that night. No one was going to entertain a civilian complaint against us. Just the cops against Brooklyn. May the best man win.

"I couldn't leave headquarters. This night is going on forever. The police commissioner is there; the district attorney is there; four or five assistant district attorneys are there writing warrants.

"A few hours before, none of these people were even available. They didn't even want to know what was happening. But now it's safe. This is a win.

"Every boss in New York City wanted a piece of me. Some of them were prepared to ream me out; others had decided that this had been a heroic rescue and they wanted in on the happy ending.

"All that would have to wait. I had better things to do.

"I now have all sorts of obligations to inform the police

department. I am getting calls from ten thousand people. There are now all kinds of chiefs wanting to talk to me as the immediate supervisor. Plus, people in the public information division have to have something to tell the press. They all want an interview.

"They tell me that the governor is on the phone. He can smell how well this is turning out.

"The police commissioner wants to know about the case and the mayor and, of course, the first deputy commissioner wants to know—Sinbad started in his office with my undercover assignment—and they're all asking me.

"At this point there is an information hysteria. It's a combination of natural curiosity and of people in authority who need information to communicate to other people. This is the Puzzle Palace taking over.

"In the meantime, I get a surprise call from Tony Spots's lawyer.

"I said to him, 'You better get your client to surrender, because if he goes out on the street he might get killed because there's a whole army of angry cops out there. You better have him surrender right away; every hour it's getting worse.'

"The lawyer, he doesn't know anything. Naturally. This is part of the game. He says, 'I don't know where my client is. I don't know if I can find him. I don't know what his problem is. He didn't do anything.' And I'm guessing that as he's saying this, Spots is probably right next to him.

"I pushed it. 'Yo, be a friend,' I told him. 'Have him surrender. We want him. Alive. He's considered armed and dangerous. There could be a confrontation. He could get killed. By accident. Protect your client from getting "accidented." '

"The next call from the lawyer came in at two o'clock in the morning. 'You can come out and pick him up,' was all that he said.

"Spots had surrendered himself to the police in Nassau County. He didn't have the guts to surrender to the New York City Police Department.

"It was only then that I started to come down a little.

"I just wanted to be with Millie. I still hadn't apologized to her for missing our belated, once-postponed anniversary dinner. Tony's kidnapping had gotten in our way.

"I was really ashamed of myself for not having called her sooner. Now she would be seeing it all on television, instead of hearing it from me.

"Still, I was celebrating—celebrating in my mind and heart. Tony was back. I knew he was in shock, and the whole side of his head was swollen. And I'm just beginning to find out how badly he'd been beaten during all those hours of his captivity, but he *was* alive.

"But once again, I would have to make Millie wait. It was important for me to get to the hospital. I owed that much to Tony.

"Coney Island Hospital was like a slaughterhouse in those days—old, blood-splattered hallways, depressing. It was awful to see him in there. And he looked bad. Like he was *very* lucky to be alive.

"I still can't recall all of it—I know I got there, probably, by then, it was the next day. I was just numb. I couldn't even talk to him. We just hugged each other.

"Then I said, 'You bum, all you had to do was wait. *I* was the one who had to get you back.'

"He was hurt, in pain, but he smiled, pushed himself up a little on his shoulder and said, 'Never again, Mother, not even for you.'

"I think I might have cried after that."

326

Thirty-two

Most of the *Lawyers* that cops deal with hang out in the lobby of the criminal courts building. Polyester suits and gravy stains on their ties. They steal your money and then plead you. They have about as much social conscience as a strain of AIDS virus. Lawyers are ghouls who make their money off your grief.

MOTHER'S MAXIM

Sinbad's impact on Bill McCarthy was profound. Nothing would ever be the same again. Nearly losing Tony Vitaliano had frightened the entire team.

Before, there was a sense of invulnerability about them. They went out, did their jobs, and believed that nothing tragic could ever happen. They existed in a world of shocking unreality of reckless risks and rash impetuosity. But Sinbad had proven just how fragile that precarious code of manhood could be. Their new feelings of mortality united Mother's team with an eerie sense of just how close to the precipice they had ventured.

Sinbad had made him reevaluate the whole concept of undercover work. Accordingly, McCarthy began to rewrite the department's operational procedures; often, he was spelling them out—at least as far as undercovers went—for the very first time.

Other units in the NYPD soon picked up on his concern. From his restlessness emerged a well-considered policy and protocol for covert action. It was adopted piecemeal at first, then department-wide.

Despite his unorthodox methods, McCarthy was developing an unlikely reputation as "command material." In the beginning, that was no more than amusing to him; later, however, it became an opportunity that he would have to come to terms with.

In the protracted criminal trial that followed Vitaliano's abduction, the defense attempted to portray Mother's shaken team as out-of-control, kamikaze cops—police mavericks who were every bit as dangerous as the felons they pursued.

As the sergeant in charge, Mother took most of the heat.

"I was cross-examined for nine hours by five defense attorneys. Vitaliano was on the stand for almost six days. The first thing they tried to nail me on was our reluctance, throughout the case, to return to the pool hall on Saint John's Place to make all the subsequent payoffs. Why had I insisted on meeting the Gaglianos in Manhattan?

"It was hard to see the point they were getting at. This seemed so totally unrelated to the kidnapping.

"But as soon as I realized that there were four black jurors, I caught on. They were trying to backhandedly portray me as a crazy, racist cop.

"They said I wouldn't go back to that part of Brooklyn to make the subsequent payoffs because I didn't like black people and I refused to travel to a black neighborhood in Brooklyn, if I could help it.

" 'Isn't it true that you don't like black people?'

"They asked that question a hundred different ways. I could see by the faces of the four black jurors that a seed of doubt about my character was definitely taking root.

"This was absurd, considering the other issues at stake in Sinbad, but these defense lawyers didn't care.

"I was a racist. That was their defense. Nobody black was even remotely connected to the case. I was still a racist.

"During that cross-examination, my daily activity reports—DARs—also came up.

"Now, I was supposed to be a corrupt cop throughout Sinbad. I had all my expenses in order. As part of my undercover role I was drinking half a bottle of scotch every night. I was supposed to be a crook. A bad guy. I gotta be doing something wrong. You can't go in those after-hours clubs and pimp bars singing *Kyrie, Eleison.*

"You have to be a mover, so I'm smoking and I'm drinking. Gambling. I was making dirty money. I had to buy, buy, buy. Drinks all around. Every night. So on my DAR, I had expenses of forty and fifty dollars for drinks. 'Food and drink for cover,' it was called. The defense had full disclosure of my DARs.

"One of the lawyers tried to make use of his interpretation of the 'Food and drink for cover' by asking me, *'Do you still have you drinking problem, Sergeant?'*

" 'I wasn't aware that I had one,' I said.

"He throws up nine months of activity reports and says that I spent all this money on drinks, so I had to be an alcoholic. The DARs are his proof. So now he's trying to tell the jury I'm a drunk as well as a racist. And we haven't even gotten to the kidnapping yet.

"I remember thinking to myself: This son of a bitch, I should have gotten my family in here. My wife is Puerto Rican, one-third black, actually. My kids have to get the sickle-cell anemia test. My kids are part black. Puerto Ricans are descended from black blood and Indian blood. One of Millie's aunts is called 'Negrita,' which means 'little black lady.' Millie's grandfather *was* a black man. There's black blood in every drop of blood in my children's veins.

"Now, I'm sitting there mindful of all this, wishing that I could somehow communicate it all to the jury, and he's trying to crucify me. But you have to answer the questions.

"His bias is that I am an Irish-Catholic-pig-racist-head-breaker-cop. Billy Lace Curtain.

"I resented what they were trying to do. I hated them for that. But there wasn't a thing I could do about it.

"All the defense lawyers were mob lawyers and these were some of their favorite tactics. One of them was a partner of the guy who had just successfully defended the BLA, the Black Liberation Army. And he was excellent.

"Mob lawyers are always on; they're never off. They're always looking to suck up to you; they'll bullshit you; they're flagwavers; they're patriots; they're anything that works; they're always trying to buy you lunch; always sweet-talking you and then, once your defenses are down, they will lunge right for the jugular vein.

"They'd shoot your first-born; they'd kill your kids. And they don't realize they're trapped. When they become a mob lawyer, they're a mob lawyer for life. You ain't allowed out. You can't decide that you're no longer gonna retain this client. *He* retains *you*. You're in. And you're in for life.

"They're just part of the mob; no different from criminals. They're the mouthpiece and they hide behind reasonable doubt.

"Their whole drill is to create a smoke screen, like they were attempting to do in Sinbad. If it's apparent that their clients are guilty, then brand the cop, the accuser, as a racist. Confuse the issue. Better yet, obscure it altogether.

"All they need to do is create that reasonable doubt in the mind of a jury. Or fear. Either way, they get paid and they don't especially care. Whatever they have to do, they do it.

"This rejection of conventional moral choices allows

them to live very well, make a lot of money. A few of them are actually star-struck by Mafia types. They like to get down and wear the pinkie rings on their own little fingers. In that way, they are identical to the star-fucker whores who like to hang out with the big Mafia types. You can see them in any high-class bar in Manhattan.

"A mob lawyer is manicured—white, clear nail polish on his nails. Razor haircut. Reeks of cologne. A hint of gold—maybe a neck chain, a wrist chain, a Rolex watch, and thin, thin shoes, expensive leather.

"Most of the prosecutors we had on our side were young, inexperienced, didn't know a thing. They were either afraid of the competition or overly impressed with themselves; some of them were very idealistic but as soon as they'd get smart, and get their ticket punched for their two or three years of public service, they'd get out and become defense attorneys too.

"There were all kinds of meetings throughout this entire case. I can't say that I saw our side, the prosecutors, at their best. They didn't like cops, either. Probably didn't believe us.

"Aside from the racist innuendoes, one of the big problems that the prosecution had was that there were about 250 tape-recorded conversations that had been made during Sinbad. All of that was part of the case. Just a mountain of work.

"They had real difficulty mastering all that evidence.

"At one point during the trial, one of the defense lawyers asked me, *'Sergeant, when you were with these prostitutes, when you were being corrupted and taking money from these prostitutes; when you were drinking, when you had your alcoholic problem; how much money did you get paid, Sergeant?'*

" 'I don't know,' I told him.

" *'You mean to tell me that you were in charge of the case and you don't know how many bribes, how much money you received from those whores? Those pimps?'*

"I said, 'No, I have no idea.'

" 'Sergeant, you tell me you were in charge and you don't even know how many times you were bribed by those whores?'

" 'No.'

" 'Why, Sergeant?'

"I said, 'Counselor, my obligation to truth is to remember as vividly and as accurately as I can until such time as I have made a competent police report. Then I allow the report to remember for me, so, if you would like, I can do the statistical search of my accurate police reports, and provide you the number of incidents and the actual amounts, if you'd like.

" 'All I have to refer to are my accurate police reports. I have no obligation to remember after I have accurately documented the event.'

"He laughed in my face, then turned to the jury and tried to get them laughing at me, too.

"It went on like that for the whole day that I was on the stand. And these guys were pissed. They were outraged. All they wanted to do was run rings by me.

"Then they brought up the fact that during one day of Sinbad, one day during the course of a case that had gone on for parts of two years, I had not been to work. I had either been off sick or on another undercover assignment.

"A call had come in for me that day, and Tony had taken it. Tony wrote up a report on it. He followed procedure to the letter. It was very important information. Very, very important information.

"But I wasn't there to countersign Tony's report of the call. It just happened. An oversight.

"The lieutenant who was there had signed the report in my place. So, in this entire case there was that one piece of paper that I hadn't signed personally.

"The defense spent the entire day, during cross-examination, trying to trap me with this thing. Why didn't I sign the paper? Why? Why wasn't I on top of the case?

Was I some lazy, half-drunk sergeant who hated black people, who never reported to work, and who failed to countersign the papers he was supposed to sign?

"It was fun, though. I loved it. I loved being cross-examined. I loved dueling with the best.

"I guess I convinced them after all. We got our convictions."

As a result of Operation Sinbad, six people connected with the stickup and extortion crew that kidnapped Tony Vitaliano were sentenced to prison terms ranging from seven and a half to fifteen years.

Additionally, sixteen people were either arrested or indicted on an array of Vice charges that developed from the investigation centered on the Murray Hill townhouse.

The amount of raw intelligence that Sinbad provided was staggering. Much of it was used by investigators and prosecutors who would later score a number of spectacularly successful victories against all five New York crime Families in the years to come. Also extremely significant were the leads that grew out of Sinbad's early warnings concerning the existence of the Sicilian Mafia on American soil. That harrowing story of international drug smuggling and assorted other crimes would not be resolved until the prolonged series of investigations and trials known collectively as the Pizza Connection case.

However, not everything connected with Sinbad lent itself to such satisfying resolution. No corrupt cops were arrested. Several, however, were transferred or forced to accept early retirements.

Bill McCarthy remained convinced that the electronic "bug" that was so mysteriously detected at the Murray Hill townhouse was the result of a leak. But he was never able to pinpoint the fellow cop who had sold him out.

McCarthy left the Pimp Squad, Public Morals, the Organized Crime Control Bureau, on December 12,

1976. That was a sad day. It marked the end of Mother's Pimp Team.

Years later, he would return as a lieutenant to command Vice. But of course, it would never be the same.

After the Knapp Commission, to encourage the police to avoid corruption, and to reward good arrests in the bribery area, the NYPD created the Integrity Review Board.

"When a guy made a big bribery arrest—Sinbad was the textbook example—he would be sent before the Integrity Review Board to be promoted to detective or transferred to a more desirable assignment.

"I was 'rewarded' by being transferred to the Detective Bureau. I didn't particularly want to go to the Detective Bureau. It was a coveted assignment, but I was already 'permanent cadre' in the OCCB, the Organized Crime Control Bureau. That was actually a better job—the old five-borough concept. The real reward would have been letting me the hell alone.

"For me, it was take your reward or else. Mainly, their secret agenda was to rotate me *out* of Vice because they didn't want you to stay there too long or you really would get too friendly with the bad guys.

"Then, a guy could go ten years without the gold shield, the detective's badge. He might make hundreds of collars, do all the overtime, work on his own time, perform brilliantly as a plainclothes cop, but when he was evaluated, if he wanted to stay in Vice, he had to be in the top quarter even to be considered for permanent cadre or for the gold shield.

"Today, with equal opportunity, and racial and promotional quotas, if you're breathing and you have two years in an investigative assignment, you usually get the shield whether you deserve it or not.

"That, more than any other single thing, has probably

destroyed the professional caliber—and certainly the morale—of the NYPD.

"Going to the Detective Bureau meant catching cases. Everything that came in. You caught it. You got all the paperwork, all the missing persons, robberies, commercial robberies, assaults, homicides; it was really a lot of clerical work. There was tremendous pressure to maintain a high clearance rate.

"It had been much better to work at the Organized Crime Control Bureau. That was like a ticket to have fun. But the Detective Bureau was my reward and I had to accept it.

"What was Tony's reward? They promoted him to sergeant—after calling him out of his hospital bed to take the civil service exam—and allowed him to stay as a boss in the OCCB.

"Tony was really messed up from the experience of the kidnapping, from being pistol-whipped so savagely. He developed a twitch in his face, which was the physical scar, but he was even more battered by the psychological after effects.

"Before, Tony had been a happy-go-lucky kind of a good guy type detective. He joked about everything. Yet it changed him so much—it changed all of us so much—that seven or eight years after the incident, Tony still couldn't talk about it. Before, he was always cheery, upbeat, talking fast.

"After Sinbad, his nerves were shot. That's the only way I can put it.

"Years later, after they came to appreciate the significance of a hostage incident like this, they interviewed Tony, tried to get a sense of what it was like to be held captive under such life-threatening circumstances.

"Eventually, Tony's experience—his insights—helped the NYPD put together one of the finest 'hostage negotiation' units in the world. But it had been a tough way to go about getting on-the-job training.

"Back when it happened they just told him to take a couple sick days and didn't even rotate him out of routine duty. No counseling, no follow-up, no nothing. I was worried. I was afraid that he might go out on the street and try to shoot somebody, just as a result of poststress syndrome. He had gone through hell. They were aware of that postcombat as a result of soldiers coming home from Vietnam, but I guess they figured it didn't count with cops.

"They only replaced you if you dropped. Nobody had any concern or sentimentality. But now, sixteen years later, they give long talks about police stress management. None of that existed then. They wouldn't have cared, anyway. There was a different notion of what made a good cop then, it was a different time, a much wilder time.

"If you weren't useful to them, you were gone. They'd get somebody else. That's all. The command structure of the NYPD just kept rolling along. Individual cops like me and Tony would always come and go; the Building was forever."

Thirty-three

You can arrest all the pimps, seize all the drugs, close down all the gambling, scare all the johns, drive all the pornography underground and chase away all the hookers and when you're all finished, the *Life* will still be there, just the same as before. All the cops do is keep score.

MOTHER'S MAXIM

In every way, Operation Sinbad had changed Bill McCarthy's life. Initially, the personal sacrifice seemed unbearable. There were times when he had to question whether the job, especially Vice, was worth it. Had he been dedicated or merely foolish?

His always-neglected off-duty life came in for a sober reevaluation. Millie and the children were growing further and further away from him. No matter how hard he tried to leave Vice, to leave the Life behind him when he went home to Sloatsburg, he never quite managed to do it.

Even when he was at home, he wasn't always *there*. Bleak moods and a deepening sense of desperation left him withdrawn. In his mind, he kept playing out Sinbad again and again. He could see what was happening to himself and his family. At the very least, McCarthy needed some radical change from Vice, from the stress and surreality of staying undercover too long.

There was a genuine crisis at home, too. His father,

an invalid by then, had moved in with them and the family was running out of living space as well as patience. McCarthy's once excusable neglect of the home-front in favor of a single-minded devotion to his career was putting the whole family in jeopardy.

Something had to give. He would have to find a larger house, and one probably much further away from the city to be able to afford it. That would mean an even longer commute and that many more hours stolen from Millie and the children.

During his years in Vice, McCarthy had earned his master's degree at John Jay and was already embarking on the long road toward a doctorate. That would require a tremendous investment of his time too.

McCarthy had always moonlighted—driving a cab, teaching pickup courses at John Jay, anything to supplement what the City of New York paid its warriors. Now, the prospect of establishing a second career, not just part-time work, took on some urgency.

Medicine had always fascinated him, so he had begun a course of study that would get him a nurse's degree—psychiatric care—and later, he hoped, a well-paying position in hospital administration. That would be a radical departure from police work, but he was becoming alarmed, almost despondent, about all that he had already sacrificed.

Despite its seductive pull on an ambitious cop, there was a limit to how long anyone could survive in the Life. Eventually, even Bill McCarthy had to accept that.

"I could only survive running undercovers for so long. It was dangerous work; I knew that I was spending too much time away from my family and I was already serving my second tour in the Life. I could not expect to stay hot—or lucky—forever.

"I had almost convinced myself that either a fantastic

338

opportunity would have to open up within the department, where I would have total administrative control and the semblance of a normal schedule, or I would take my master's degree and my nurse's certification and put in for an early pension.

"I was directionless, but if leaving the police force was what it would take to keep my marriage going and let me begin acting like a father again, then I was willing to put in my papers.

"I was just coming off three years in the Puzzle Palace as the commanding officer of the Public Morals Headquarters Unit. This was 1984.

"I'd been through the Son of Sam murders with the Bronx Detective Homicide Task Force, I'd pulled desk duty in the 2-0 precinct, and Sinbad had been over for almost ten years, but I was still living it every day.

"I was just about to start a new undercover role with a trucking company in the garment center. I had made the preliminary contacts with a millionaire designer we had our eye on.

"For the first time I was beginning to ask myself if I really *wanted* to go underground again. Unless your response to that is instantly affirmative, more reflex than reasoning, then you shouldn't do it.

"I never wanted to become one of those cops who needed the department *more* than it needed him. I was probably lying to myself about that, but I had to hold on to something. That something had always been Millie and the children, even during the worst undercover days.

"Now, I was determined to make a decision based on what was best for them instead of what I wanted.

"Very few of the people who worked with me ever understood the police department or their place in it. I did. I had very, very few romantic notions. My run in Vice had come to an end. It came down to either getting out of the Life while I still could or allowing it to consume me. I just wouldn't do that to the people I loved.

"Cops make a big show about *Family*. But it's almost never sincere. You trot out the wife and kids when it's convenient or politic to do so. Cops are basically selfish. I always hated that about myself.

"But it was sad, though, just like the end of the world. I really didn't know if I could face not being a cop."

Afterword

You never have to worry about a *Big Bomb*. The big ones you never even feel. It's the *Little Bombs* you worry about. They will take an arm or a leg or an eye, but leave the rest of you.

MOTHER'S MAXIM

NYPD BOMB SQUAD HEADQUARTERS
10TH AND BLEECKER STREETS
GREENWICH VILLAGE
APRIL 1984

The chief of detectives had only been in his new job for three weeks when he buzzed in Bill McCarthy. His office in the Puzzle Palace had that unpacked look; as though the occupant were still a little uneasy about hanging up the pictures of his wife and kiddies. But the new chief had a decision to make, about the Bomb Squad and about Bill McCarthy.

"Why do you even want the Bomb Squad?" he asked as McCarthy sat down.

"Six months ago, I didn't want it," McCarthy admitted. And he told him what his career in Vice had meant, what Sinbad had meant.

Then the chief of detectives repeated his question. "Why do you want the Bomb Squad *now*?"

"*You* come highly recommended," McCarthy said. A classic Motherism.

"What? Are you some wiseass Vice cop?"

They both knew that McCarthy was.

"Listen," McCarthy told him, "the word about you is that you're a good boss. Do you think I'd be here for an interview, after everything I've been through in this department, if your reputation wasn't way up there? They're still very happy with me where I am. I can stay in Vice till it kills me."

"Which it will," the chief said. "Probably sooner than later." Then he laughed. "But wait a minute, who's interviewing who here?"

"Look, Chief, if you want someone to say black is white, you got the wrong guy. If you want somebody to be a hero, you got the wrong guy. If you want a mule, I'm a good mule. All I will say in my behalf is this: If I had worked for you before, you'd want me to work for you again."

The chief of detectives gave McCarthy a glassy fish-eye. Every boss at One Police Plaza seemed to be issued that particular look along with his room assignment. "Jesus Christ, you're spunky."

Nobody had called Bill McCarthy "spunky" in twenty years. That expression took him all the way back to the playgrounds at Rockaway, back to the endless summers of basketball.

"Chief, this is what you get, no more, no less."

He had McCarthy's folder open on the desk in front of him. He was rated the number one lieutenant in the Organized Crime Control Bureau. He had earned that rank every year for the last thirteen years, wherever he had served.

"I think that will be enough," the chief of detectives said after long moments of reflection.

"Enough what? You want me to leave?" McCarthy was a little puzzled.

"No, I want you to stay," the chief said. "I think we might still need you for a long, long time."

On April 24, 1984, Bill McCarthy was assigned to the Bomb Squad, New York City Police Department, as the commanding officer.

McCarthy had gotten his wish. One last meaningful opportunity had opened up inside the NYPD. The hours would be more regular, the paranoia of undercover work could be left behind forever and, most important, McCarthy would be able to remain a policeman just a little while longer.

"The first time I had been approached about becoming the commander of the Bomb Squad was by the chief of the Arson Explosion Division. I said no.

"I was still decompressing from Vice at that point. And I did need a change—my marriage and my entire family needed a change. But I refused even to consider a transfer to a unit as radically different from what I had known as the Bomb Squad. I think I was still trying to prove something to myself after Sinbad.

"But considering who was asking me, it was a difficult offer to turn down. The person telling me to take the job was Kenneth Gussman, now *Inspector* Gussman. If I had an older, better friend, I never met him.

"The second time he asked me—the position as Bomb Squad Commander was still vacant—Gussman pressed me on it.

" 'I'll go for the interview,' I finally said.

"This was high-level NYPD politics; there was no kidding myself about that. The Bomb Squad was one of the premier assignments in the entire city. I was a little scared. Was I just going to be camouflage as part of the selection process? Had the stiff with the political juice already been preselected? Or was this a legitimate shot? In other words, had the deal already been cut by the long knives at the Puzzle Palace?

"Gussman didn't hold back. 'I don't believe that any person has been selected yet,' he said. 'This one is too important; this one is life and death on one of those bomb sites.'

" 'Nobody's sending me out for cigarettes, you mean?'

"He remembered our special lifelong code. 'No cigarettes,' Gussman said.

"I knew that the Bomb Squad was isolated from the rest of the police department. It didn't care about the rest of the world. It was an inbred, notoriously dangerous place to work. They were still using the same manual from the World's Fair days, back in the 1960s. The most technologically complex unit in the NYPD would have to be dragged into the twentieth, into a world of terrorism and mass murder.

"It was a private fiefdom. Even the police commissioner and the mayor backed off from the Bomb Squad Commander. In the trenches, when a hot package was being gingerly handled, his word was better than God's. No NYPD boss exercised as much personal power, as much raw command prerogative. In action, the Bomb Squad Commander's orders were *never* countermanded. There was just too much danger, too much at stake.

"The Bomb Squad Commander didn't just sit down with other cops, he went to power meetings called by every federal agency, by the mayor, by the governor, by the White House; every foreign embassy in New York needed him for security; every bomb cop in the world took his cue from New York.

"As much as I had loved Vice, this was looking pretty damn promising. I was already angling to achieve a distinction in the department known as 'a lieutenant with the money,' a detective commander—still a lieutenant— who earned captain's pay or better, while enjoying considerably more authority than the normal captain. That's

344

an anomaly, but in the NYPD anything is possible, even an archaic but cherished tradition like lieutenant-with-the-money. As the boss of the Bomb Squad, I would have a clear shot at it. Eventually, even that did come, too, in 1986, after I had been at the Bomb Squad for two years.

"Depending on your personality and your tolerance for pressure, the Bomb Squad could either be Siberia or paradise. I was crazy enough to buy the paradise angle.

"Something as simple as Fourth of July fireworks was a paramount—if bizarre—part of the job. That was also part of my indoctrination. Fireworks were and are, of course, illegal. That's because they are so unstable and so extremely dangerous in the hands of anybody but experts. Civilians hardly ever get blown up by bombs, but they lose hands and eyes to fireworks every summer.

"There's a huge black market in New York, especially in Chinatown, for underground fireworks. Cops are among the worst abusers. They figure they are immune to getting in trouble for supplying all their friends in the neighborhood with fireworks—after all, the guy is a cop.

"The Bomb Squad does—or should—police this black market. Only one problem. Traditionally, the Bomb Squad was the best place to boost contraband fireworks—and I'm not talking about Joe Patrolman, I'm talking about calls from Gracie Mansion, from the mayor's office, or even from the state capitol in Albany, telling the Bomb Squad Commander where he should *deliver* the fireworks. It was usually to so-and-so's annual picnic or Fourth of July party.

"Were these people in for some surprises. If I had refused to buy cigarettes for Kenny Gussman way back when, I was sure as hell going to refuse to act as delivery boy for the politicians.

"I knew going in that traditions like that—illegal as they might be—would die hard. But, die they would.

"My mind was made up. Fireworks was the perfect

target of opportunity for me. If I could fight and win this pure insider's battle, as the new kid on the block, testing my will and reputation for maniacal integrity against all the major players in the city, then I was sure that I would also win the life-and-death decisions later on—the ones that would affect the safety of every man in the Bomb Squad.

"I went in looking for a fight. Hoping for one. And whenever it came, I knew I would survive it, because I had survived the Life."

For the next three years and four months, until he retired as a lieutenant-with-the-money, detective commander, New York City Police Bomb Squad, Bill McCarthy would divide his time between the Bomb Squad headquarters at Tenth and Bleecker and the bomb disposal range—City Island at Rodman's Neck.

On that barren, windswept peninsula, bordered on three sides by some of the coldest water in the North Atlantic, with the police pistol range in the foreground and Pelham Parkway climbing on steel girders in the distance, the men and women of the NYPD Bomb Squad go about their perilous ritual of deactivating, disposing, and investigating bombs or explosive devices of any description.

The moment you drive through the gate and begin passing the Quonset huts, the kennels for the explosives-sniffing police dogs, the classroom buildings and the nine firing ranges on the left, a parking lot on the right, you realize that you have entered a very separate existence.

For incoming bombs, hauled at maddeningly slow speed on fat, armored wagons that look like parade floats save for the distinctive NYPD decals, the destination is always the sand bunkers. There, the actual nerve-wracking technical work of taking a bomb apart, piece by piece, fuse by fuse, mechanism by mechanism, is carried out. It is a grim ceremony, a thorny rite of passage for every cop who has ever worked on the Bomb Squad.

Occasionally, cops die here. They firmly believe that the devices they have brought back to the range can be rendered safe enough to dismantle—and they are wrong. One of McCarthy's predecessors was seriously injured under just such circumstances, his face literally blown off.

Some of the most memorable, tension-charged explosives incidents in the history of New York City would occur during McCarthy's Bomb Squad tour.

"For as long as I can remember, the Bomb Squad headquarters has been located on Tenth Street, between Bleecker and Hudson. That's the Village. Millie lived right around the corner on Charles Street when I first met her.

"It's one of the truly magical neighborhoods in New York. On a buttery spring day, With the late breeze picking up and the old trees beginning to turn green, you can stroll along that block and forget that Manhattan Vice ever existed.

"My first day on the job there, my state of mind reflected those feelings. Of course, there were questioning looks, doubtful glances, the old bomb vets grumbling. But I was used to that. In Vice, back on Centre Street, the same thing had happened and I had been able to overcome it. I was confident—I was more than confident, I was like a kid on Christmas morning. I knew I was going to *love* running a proud outfit like this where tradition was more important than anywhere else in the NYPD.

"I was at my new desk for exactly fifteen minutes when they put my first call through. I thought it was Millie. I hoped it would be Millie. It wasn't.

" 'Good morning, Lieutenant,' the strange voice said. 'This is Detective Richard Pastorella.'

347

"Richie Pastorella had been a bomb expert—until one blew up in his face. Now he was blind, partially deaf, and he had lost the use of one hand. And he was suing the police department for millions.

"I was the new boss and Richie was still such a great cop that he felt it was his duty to let me know the score. Just in case the Puzzle Palace had given me a snow job, he intended to set me straight about the level of risk, the competence—or lack thereof—of my people, and the appalling neglect of any and all safety procedures that had built up over time.

"Richie was preparing me for the worst.

"I thanked him for it. Ever since we had nearly lost Tony Vitaliano, I had become Vice's fanatical, pain-in-the-butt Mother about caution, protection for undercovers, and contingency planning. Compared to the imminent threat of death in the Bomb Squad—every day, on every call—Vice had been almost tame.

"Richie wanted me to remember him, wanted me to be aware of what had happened to him because of the existence of a sloppy, unprofessional disregard for the safety of the brave men and women who had to go out there and take the damn things apart.

"He just wanted to make sure that I wasn't some One Police Plaza medal-maggot parade cop, the kind of cop who would be willing to deliver fireworks to all the politicians. That was something else he warned me about.

"But I wasn't that kind of cop and never had been. Not in Vice, not in the Bomb Squad.

"I promised Richie Pastorella during that first phone call that I would prove myself to him.

"Then he said, 'Mother'—which was the very first time that any cop connected with the Bomb Squad had called me that; I didn't even know for sure if they knew about the name—'Mother, that's just what I wanted to hear. Coming from you, I would not have expected anything less.'

"All at once, this strange new office, these skeptical people, this overwhelming challenge—it all felt like home to me. Thanks to Richie Pastorella."

Bill McCarthy would finally retire from the NYPD on July 1, 1987. One of his last and most memorable official duties while with the Bomb Squad squad was to to provide all bomb and explosives security for the Statue of Liberty celebration during the summer of 1986. Among the people he was protecting then was the President of the United States.

"I felt like I was exiting at the right time. In a blaze of glory, so to speak. I couldn't help but contrast that triumphant departure with one of my first-ever bomb runs.

"It happened at Saint Patrick's Cathedral, at Christmastime.

"An explosive device had been left on the main altar. The call came in and was relayed to me on the street.

"That night the city, glowing and twinkling with Christmas lights and traffic and all the maddening, irresistible energy of New York, had never looked better to me.

"I think I felt like every other cop I've known who was willing to be honest with himself—I felt like the city *belonged* to me. I was a New York *cop*, it was the best thing a man could ever be.

"I had beaten the slow-moving Bomb wagon there by several minutes. A nervous young priest greeted me on the pavement. The Traffic Division already had barricades set up; the pavements had been cleared. It was just me and the priest.

"We walked up the main aisle together. He was shaking, but I felt this eerie calm.

349

"Halfway up there, just far enough for him to show me where the device was hidden, I sent him back. But he hesitated, felt that he had to stick with me. Maybe he was preparing to administer the last rites. I'll never know.

"As soon as he was gone, I just stopped dead and *listened*. The stillness was haunting; the arch of the ceiling seemed to vault as high up as the stars outside.

"I was alone with God and the bomb.

"Then I saw him. The bomber.

"He was just an ordinary-looking guy, except for one thing. He was holding the detonator button down on the switch, a deadman's switch. If he moved his finger, we both would die. Instantly.

"I got as far as the altar rail and realized that I could not catch my breath. I could not keep pace with my own heartbeats.

"The bomber stood there like an altar boy—waiting for the sacraments.

"I thought that I could actually hear the bomb *ticking*.

"I looked at the face of every statue in that church, at every plaster feature, every painted eye. I knew they were looking back at me wondering what I was going to do.

"All I could hear was the *ticking*.

"I was *Mother*; what would I do?

"Then, I thought of my own mother again. How she had prayed so hard for me to become a priest and how I had disappointed her so deeply. I wanted to tell her that at least I had made it to the main altar at Saint Pat's, at least I had made it that far.

"Then, this feeling of tranquillity came over me and I actually relaxed. I looked up at that guy, at that bomber, and knew—*knew*—that everything was going to be fine. He wasn't going to press that button and he wasn't going to kill us.

" 'Don't move,' I told him, calmly, almost gently. 'I'm coming up there and we're walking out of here together. You, me, and the thing in your hand.'

350

"Then I began to slowly walk toward him. I had my hands out in front of me so that he could see that I wasn't going to hurt him.

"And if I happened to be wrong this time, if my bluff finally failed me, at least I *was* on the main altar at Saint Pat's. Doing my job. Being a New York cop.

"This had to be an express bus to heaven. The Big Guy had to be up there waiting for me."